THE DEMON
CONSPIRACY

R .　L .　GEMMILL

Cottingham-McMasters Publishing House

"For you, Mom…FINALLY! I hope they have bookstores where you are."

WARNING!

The American Security Administration has determined that THE DEMON CONSPIRACY book series can cause nightmares and unexplainable feelings of being watched. The conspiratorial thinking and utter terror within these pages may be hazardous to your psychological health. READ WITH CAUTION.

Marcus Conn
Deputy Director
American Security Administration

AUTHOR'S NOTE

This novel is meant to be a fun and exciting read. Much of the general research in *THE DEMON CONSPIRACY SERIES* I did myself, but a lot of the scientific and conspiracy information was originally collected by Stephanie Matzgannis, a former student of mine and good friend, who has an uncanny knack at finding strange facts and uncovering the science-related weird. Thank you, Stephanie!

I would also like to thank award-winning author, Mark Spencer, for his editing expertise and constructive comments. Fiction readers should check out his books, they are excellent! Any author who needs professional editing should visit Mark's website at: **http://authormarkspencer. com/Writing_Services.html**.

Also, a huge thanks to Laima Klavina for her original design and art work on the book cover, as well as the website design and Demon-of-the-Month demons. Every time I look at the cover I'm mesmerized because there is so much going on. Laima's art is also worth checking out at: **www. amunalaima.com**

CONTENTS

The Demon Conspiracy Series continues with Book #2:
The Doomsday Shroud

Chapter 1

THE ACCIDENT

KELLY

The car windows were smashed. Pieces of glass were everywhere.

My tummy hurt real bad, but I was stuck. I couldn't get out. I wanted Mommy.

I tried to unsnap the seatbelt, but it wouldn't open. I pushed the button hard as I could. The seatbelt made my tummy hurt and I wanted to get out. I pulled hard on the belt. I was stuck. I needed somebody to help me. Mommy?

Where was Mommy? I couldn't see her but in my mind I could tell she was hurt.

"Mommy?" It sounded like there was cotton in my mouth. I couldn't talk right.

Something smelled like gas in Daddy's lawnmower. I looked up, which was sideways because we were all sideways. Daddy was hanging sideways too. His face had blood all over it. I closed my eyes. I hated blood. I started to cry. I didn't want Daddy to die. But he had blood on his face. Lots of blood! I couldn't hear him.

I pushed on the seatbelt button again. It wouldn't let go. I cried harder.

"Poor...Daddy. I love you, Daddy." I kicked and wiggled. It hurt my tummy even worse, so I stopped.

Travis was in his car seat in front of me. He was blurry because my eyes were full of tears. Then I heard him sucking on his thumb. He was still asleep. And alive.

I wiped my eyes on my sleeve. I sniffled and hiccupped. "Help me!"

JON

Ten-year-old Jon Bishop woke up in a blur. His forehead ached and burned. He felt like he'd been baptized with a hammer. Where was he? Why did his stomach feel like somebody had tried to peel the skin off with a weed eater?

Jon blinked. He rolled his head and sort of looked up. He saw Kelly hanging above him, arms and legs dangling.

"Jon...h-h-help...me!"

"Kelly? What happened? Were we in a wreck?"

"No, we...w-w-were in a accident. Help m-me...Jon." She began to sob. "M-m-my seatbelt is stuck! And my tummy...hu-hu-hurts real bad. I can't get...out and Mommy doesn't hear me any more!"

Jon's mind cleared somewhat. Things became familiar. They were in the family minivan, but the van lay on its side with the windshield smashed out. The driver's side door was crushed inward and pressed against his father. Mr. Bishop was utterly motionless, still held in place by the seatbelt. His right arm hung limp, like the deflated front airbag beside him. Blood drained from a gash in the side of his head.

Jon had never seen so much blood. A coppery taste rose in the back of his throat. He couldn't hold back the sudden spew of vomit that sprayed over the back of the van.

Jon couldn't see his mom in the other seat. What had happened? Where were they? He worked hard to remember.

They'd been driving on winding back roads in the middle of nowhere when all at once everything had vanished. Jon sat up on full alert. The highway, the trees, even the stars disappeared. One minute it was all there, a second later—*gone!* Jon looked right, then left, then up. *Nothing.* Was it fog? A moment later he caught the smell of rotting plant matter.

"That stinks!" he said, pinching his nostrils. "What is it, dad?"

"A fire in the Dismal Swamp," said his father in the driver's seat, pointing to the right. "About sixty miles that way. Been burning for weeks." He slowed the car to a safer speed, but speed had nothing to do with visibility.

"How can you see where you're going?"

"I can't, but there's no shoulder to pull off to. If we stop, or slow down too much, and somebody comes up behind us...well, it's better if we keep moving."

Jon got the message. He kept a nervous eye out the rear window. The only thing he could see was the reddish glow of their taillights reflected in the noxious gray smoke. A split second later the air cleared. Jon blinked, startled. He watched the wall of smoke shrink away behind them.

"There," said Mr. Bishop. "Much better."

"Thank, God," said Mrs. Bishop, riding shotgun. "I don't know how you drove through that."

"Me either," admitted her husband.

Mrs. Bishop let out a long sigh of relief, like she'd been holding her breath the whole time. The road was clear now, but Jon knew she was too much of a worrier to relax.

On the other hand, his dad didn't seem rattled at all. If he'd been even a *little* afraid he didn't show it. How'd he do that? How'd he stay so calm? Jon made a mental note to himself: *look brave no matter what.* Dad could pull it off, why couldn't he? After all, everyone said they were practically clones. They had the same sandy blond hair, intense blue eyes and easygoing manner. Mr. Bishop often joked that someday one of them would have to grow a mustache so people could tell them apart. It made sense. If dad could do something, Jon could too—with a little practice.

"Are we there yet?" Kelly Bishop popped up in the captain's seat behind their father, still half asleep. Kelly was a miniature version of Mrs. Bishop with the same warm, brown eyes and matching curly hair. She was six now and would finish the first grade in another month, but she could already read on a fifth-grade level. That kid read just about anything. Jon didn't see the point. He didn't care about books unless they had something to do with karate, swords, or computers.

"Kelly, honey," said Mrs. Bishop. "Why don't you go back to sleep? It'll be hours before we get home."

Jon laughed softly. Suggesting something like that to Kelly was a bad idea, if that's what you really wanted her to do. Kelly hated to go to sleep at night almost as much as she despised getting up in the mornings. Right away she perked up a little and tried to rub the sleep from her eyes. "I don't want to miss anything."

"All you're going to miss is a whole lot of nothing," said her dad, winking at her in the rear view mirror. Jon got a kick out of that. Kelly tried to wink back, but she couldn't shut just one eye, so she blinked them both. As usual it made them laugh. Minutes later Kelly closed her eyes and nodded off again.

"Travis has the right idea," said Mr. Bishop. "He's been asleep since we left."

Three-year-old Travis Bishop sat in his car seat with his curly blond head tilted to one side. Travis had dad's blue eyes and mom's smile, but other than that he hardly looked like part of the family.

"That kid could sleep through an earthquake," said Jon, laughing. He slouched in the seat and stretched his long legs into the space beside Travis. There was a cardboard box on the seat beside him that contained two trophies. Jon took up the trophies and studied them in the dim light. The first trophy had a small karate figure on top that was forever frozen in the middle of a big kick. The second showed a samurai sword surrounded by some leafy patterns. Jon put them back in the box while he dwelled on the single word engraved at the bottom of each trophy. *Champion.* Oh, yeah.

He'd competed in two events, kumite, or fighting, and weapons—both in his age group. But as he watched other kids in the tournament he realized he could have beaten most of them, even kids that were years older than him. The strange thing was he didn't just *think* he could've beaten them, he *knew* it. Maybe next time Sensei would let him move up. That'd be sweet, he loved tough competition.

Jon got the feeling he was being watched and looked up. His mom was studying him with her mouth kind of scrunched over to one side, like she was biting the inside of her jaw. She usually had that look when she was thinking.

"What?" he said.

"I wish your grandparents were alive," said Mrs. Bishop with a sad smile. "They'd be so proud of you!"

Jon grinned and hung his head modestly. This was the most awesome day ever! He was absolutely sure nothing could ruin it for him. *Nothing.*

All at once everything outside vanished again. Mr. Bishop quickly switched to the bright headlights, but it was like bouncing a spotlight off a mirror right back into their eyes.

"That didn't work," he said, dimming the lights. He returned to a lower speed. "I'm sure there's an intersection around here some place. Wish I could see."

He'd barely spoken the words when a bright, yellow glow appeared in front of them. Mr. Bishop hit the brakes. They skidded to a complete stop just as the light changed to red. Travis never stirred, but Kelly woke up immediately.

"Good call, dad." Jon gripped his seat with white knuckles. That was *close.* Scanning the area he could just make out dim lights and ghostly outlines of a few old buildings around the intersection. It looked like a small town. There were maybe a half dozen houses, a gas station, and some kind of store. People lived there, but the smoke made the whole place seem deserted.

"Are we there yet?" asked Kelly groggily.

"We're at Boyd's Crossroads," said their dad, looking right and left.

"I don't remember this," said Mrs. Bishop. "Do you *really* know where we are?"

"Never been lost in my life. The smoke makes it look different, that's all." Mr. Bishop pointed ahead. "See? There's the sign for I-95. It's four miles to the interstate."

"Does that mean there won't be any more smoke?" asked Jon.

"It'll be four lanes and a safer drive either way."

"What time is it?" said Kelly.

"Why?" asked their dad jokingly. "Do you have an important meeting tonight?"

"Oh, Daddy, I was just wondering." She rolled her eyes and giggled.

Mr. Bishop checked his watch. "Ten after ten."

It wasn't unusual for Mr. Bishop to tell them what time it was, since he wore a watch and they didn't. Even Travis asked about it, now and then, as he rapidly learned to talk. But this was the one time of day that Jon would never forget as long as he lived.

The light turned green. Mr. Bishop eased the minivan forward. Smoke covered them like a shroud as they passed through the intersection. Jon wondered how his dad could even tell where the road was. Suddenly, a bright flash tore aside the darkness. Jon saw it coming. Headlights! A truck!

At that moment he recalled the time. *Ten after ten.* It would be the last thing his father ever said. Then everything went black.

———

Jon understood now. They *had* been in a wreck. His stomach hurt because the seatbelt had saved his life, but right now it was putting a major squeeze on him. He caught a pungent smell in the air. *Gasoline.* Something was smoldering too and it smelled foul. The car could catch fire at any moment. They needed help fast. *Somebody* had to do *something*!

But nobody else was there. He was the only one who could do anything at all.

All at once Kelly cried out. "M-m-mommy! Daddy! Help me!"

Jon released the buckle on his seatbelt and dropped to the passenger side window, which was now on the street. Slowly, he stood on wobbly legs and got his bearings. Kelly thrashed above him. She cried and kicked wildly. The toe of her shoe poked his forehead, nearly jabbing him in the eye.

"Kelly, stop! I've got you!"

She calmed enough for him to unlock her seatbelt and catch her. He reached overhead and manually opened the sliding door. "Are you okay?"

Kelly trembled with relief. She wiped her eyes with the back of her hand. "I...I think so."

"Good. Get out. I'll lift Travis up to you. Take him over to the sidewalk, okay?"

Kelly climbed out the side door, which was now on top.

"Here," said Jon from below. "Don't drop him." He lifted Travis up through the door. Kelly took the little boy and set him beside her on the van. Jon frowned. His little brother was utterly still, arms and legs dangling listlessly. "Is he all right? Is he...you know...alive?"

"He's still asleep."

"He really *can* sleep through anything! Can you see what happened to us?" Jon looked up and watched his sister scan the area.

"We were in a accident." With a six-year-old's vocabulary she went on to describe the scene around them. The bottom of the van was jammed against a telephone pole. Smoke rose from somewhere inside the engine compartment and fluids leaked all over the street. About thirty feet away a huge dump truck rested with its front partially smashed in. Steam rose from its engine, but she didn't see anyone inside the truck.

"Go," said Jon solemnly. He climbed through the door and poked his head into the night air. From there he kept a cautious eye on Kelly as she did her best to climb down the luggage rack to the street without losing her hold on Travis. She made it and carried her brother to a safe spot. Satisfied, Jon dropped back into the van. Two down, two more to go.

He stepped over and around the captain's seats until he got to his mother. Mrs. Bishop lay curled up on the passenger door, still in her seatbelt. He released the seatbelt and bent to pick her up. Jon was strong and his mother was tiny, so he thought he could handle her weight. But her limpness made her heavy. It was everything he could do just to move her.

Luckily, the windshield was completely gone, broken and scattered all over the street. He climbed through the opening and carefully took his mother by her arms. With all his strength he dragged her out of the vehicle.

Kelly put Travis on a patch of damp ground and ran back to help. Broken glass crunched under their shoes as they dragged Mrs. Bishop to where Travis was curled up sucking his thumb.

"Jon, you're bleeding!" Kelly touched the edge of his forehead. A two-inch wound bled freely down the side of his face.

It explained why his head hurt. He turned away from her. "Don't. I gotta get dad." He was about to go back to the van when he noticed Kelly staring oddly at their mother. Jon looked down. Something about her neck didn't look right. It had an unnatural bend to it, as if snapped to one side.

All at once flames rose from inside the engine. They both jumped back.

"Jon!"

Jon froze at the sight. He couldn't believe this was happening. He wanted to act, but his feet wouldn't move. The van could explode any second and all he could do was watch.

Jon! Hurry!

The words were shouted inside his head. He recognized Kelly's voice, but somehow her mouth hadn't moved when she said it. The urgency in her eyes made him jump. He raced to the van.

"Dad! Dad, wake up!"

Fire spread over the van like a hot flood. The front license plate read *Bishop 5*, but the letters curled and turned black in the intense heat. In the flickering light Jon saw his father more clearly than before. His head and face were bloodier than he'd realized. Jon fought off a wave of terrible thoughts that his dad might already be dead. *No! Not dead! He has to be saved!*

Jon tried to crawl through the windshield. Scorching flames shot up and blocked the way. Fire was everywhere. How could he possibly save his father? He went toward the windshield opening again. The heat was intense. Flames licked at his face. He drew back in near panic. All at once he began to cry. He couldn't help it.

"DAD!" he screamed. "DAD! WAKE UP!" Jon had never felt so helpless. Frustration gave way to desperation.

"DADDY! PLEASE, WAKE UP!"

His father never moved. But the fire responded with the roar of a hungry beast. Desperation gave way to madness.

Ignoring the danger, Jon broke through the wall of fire and got inside the minivan. Flames licked at him from every angle. It didn't matter any more. He'd rather die with his dad than live without trying to help him.

Hot smoke filled the van. Jon tried to recall what he'd been taught about fire safety at school. But those lessons had only covered being in a burning house. This was completely different. The toxic smells of melting plastic and burning fuels were suffocating. It didn't seem to matter whether he stood tall or kept low. Either way he inhaled scalding, poisonous gases. He groped around and found his dad.

Beside him Mr. Bishop hung from his seatbelt, unconscious—or worse. His face and head were a bloody mess.

"DAD!"

Jon tried to undo the seatbelt. The buckle was hot. It burned his fingers just to touch it. A strip of molten plastic dripped off the door and landed across his left forearm. It seared the flesh instantly.

Jon screamed in agony. But he never stopped fighting the seatbelt release. He pressed the release button with all his strength. It was locked tight.

"I can't get it open!"

"Jon! Get out of there!" Kelly had moved closer to the fire.

"I'm not leaving him! Get away!"

Jon fought furiously with the seatbelt. His fingers burned every time he touched the hot buckle. He pulled and punched and even chewed on the belt. Nothing could open it. Any second now the van was going to blow up. If it did, he would die with his father.

Fine! Then I'll die, too!

NO! cried Kelly inside his head. *You can't!*

Jon looked up, stunned. It sounded like she was in his mind again.

"I can't get it open!" He coughed, desperate for clean air. Tears poured out of his eyes. He needed to get away from the fire—but not without Dad.

Suddenly, Jon got the feeling he wasn't alone. He looked back.

An older man in blue jeans and white running shoes also risked the flames. He stooped over the dashboard and reached out his hand. Resting in his palm was a Swiss Army knife, the longest blade pulled out.

"Here, kid!" cried the man. "You'd better hurry!"

Jon took the knife and quickly sawed through the seatbelt. His father landed hard on top of him. Luckily, the man caught some of the load. Together they dragged and tugged Mr. Bishop out of the van. By now several other people had arrived to help. Moments later the van exploded in a ball of fire.

"I called the police and the rescue squad," said an old woman who stood beside the man with the pocketknife. "An ambulance is on the way."

Jon coughed uncontrollably in long, deep heaves. The man patted him on the back to help loosen the nastiness in his lungs. His face, arms and hands were burned and bloody. The old woman started slapping his right leg just above the ankle.

"Your pants are on fire!" She quickly put it out.

"Kid, that's the bravest damn thing I've ever seen in my life," said the man with the knife. "Or the stupidest. But I understand why you did it." The man looked at the Swiss Army knife and shook his head. "It's so strange. I didn't own a pocketknife until a half hour ago. Some guy I didn't know came up to me and put it in my hand. He told me it was a good knife and might come in handy some time."

Jon barely heard him. He looked down. Kelly sat between their mom and little brother. She leaned close to her mother's face and whispered to her.

"Mommy! Wake up, Mommy! Are you okay? Can you hear me?"

Their mother opened her eyes ever so slightly. She half smiled at her daughter. Then her fading gaze settled on Jon as she let out a long, last breath and lay still. Kelly jerked and cried out like she'd been electrocuted. She grabbed her own head with both hands and began to sob.

"I love you, *too*, Mommy! Oh, Mommy, please don't leave us!" Kelly looked up at Jon. "She said goodbye. She said she loves us all. It hurts my head *so* bad!"

Jon stared at his mother in total shock and disbelief. "No! She's not dead! I saved her! They're just hurt!"

"No...." Kelly wailed in spastic throbs. "They're...dead!"

Kelly flopped across her mother's body and pressed her face into her breast. Jon looked down at his mom, then at his dad. Dad hadn't stirred the entire time they moved him and he clearly wasn't breathing now. It finally struck him like a bolt of lightning. Kelly was right. Their mommy and daddy really were dead. Jon collapsed from the shock. The man caught him and set him on the ground.

The old woman checked Mrs. Bishop's pulse. After a while she bit her lip and went to Mr. Bishop. She shook her head sadly. "Little girl's right. I don't know how she knew, but she's right."

All at once Travis sat up, thumb in mouth, looking dazed. He smiled groggily at the woman. Then he curled up in the crook of his dead mother's arm and went back to sleep.

Chapter 2

THE BULLY—SEVEN YEARS LATER

KELLY

I hate Kelly Bishop. I just wanna kick her face in.

The random thought snapped me out of a deep sleep. I wiped drool off my cheek and pulled a strand of curly brown hair from my mouth. I looked up, totally confused. Where was I? What day was it? What's this puddle of saliva doing on my desk?

Then it hit me. Monday morning, first hour, math class. Oh yeah, talk about your major letdown. As usual I'd dozed off listening to the teacher, Ms. Zach, drone on forever about the value of x or y or some other dumb letter. Ms. Zach was old, gray and still single after like a hundred years. That woman could put the Energizer Bunny to sleep. I rolled my eyes (something I'm really good at) and was about to plop my head back on the desk, but the *hate* thought was a definite wake up call. Why would somebody think like that? I mean we're talking about Kelly Bishop here. That's me!

I'd been an eighth grader at Franklin Middle School in Chantilly, Virginia, for a whole month, so there were plenty of kids I didn't know yet. But for someone to hate me already, well, that didn't seem fair. I was sure if they knew me they'd realize I wasn't the kind of person people hated. Maybe they were thinking about some other Kelly and got the last name wrong.

If I could just find out who it was I'd talk to them, maybe even be friends. Of course to do that I'd have to tune in to their thoughts. I decided to start with three of the more popular and pretty girls in the next row.

Brandy Barnette: *Anthony's so cute. I wish he'd go out with me.*

Heather Hoskins: *If Anthony looks at me I'll die! How come he won't look at me?*

Ann Bockman. *Should I invite Anthony to my pool party? He'd probably say no.*

Okay, the only person those girls cared about was Anthony Mall, the tallest and cutest boy in the eighth grade. Since Anthony was in such big demand I got curious about which girl *he* might like. I peeked into his thoughts from across the room.

I bet I failed that science quiz. I'm gonna play pro football some day. I really like cheese pizza.

I fought off a major chuckle. I shouldn't have been surprised though, after all he *was* a boy. I wiped the drool off the desk with a tissue and spent the rest of the period trying to track down the *thinker* who despised me. Minutes before the bell I still had no idea who it was.

I first knew could I read minds when my younger brother, Travis, was just a toddler. Whenever he got upset I could enter his thoughts like a light breeze and sing him to sleep, or just speak to him inside his head. He talked back to me that way, too, but he's not telepathic. As far as I knew, I could read the thoughts of just about anybody, except crazy people and my older brother Jon. Crazy people were on a different wavelength so I couldn't tune into them. And Jon, well, I could read his thoughts just fine until he sensed something was going on, then he'd completely block me out. Travis and I kept my ability a secret. Jon must have known, too, since he blocked me all the time, but we never talked about it.

Travis wasn't telepathic but he had a special skill, too. He could feel emotion in other people like it was his own. Usually it was a good thing, but it took him a few years to get it under control. There was this time when he was seven and we were standing on a sidewalk waiting to cross the street. A whole line of cars went by with headlights on. It was a funeral.

13

All the sadness of the people in that funeral procession literally knocked Travis to the ground. He started bawling uncontrollably and couldn't stop until the cars were way down the road. I just stood there, all embarrassed, and looked at him like he was crazy. Good thing I could read his mind and figure out what the problem was.

My brothers and I had been orphans ever since the accident. I shivered every time I thought about it. A judge made us live in separate state homes or with different foster families for seven years, which kind of sucked. The foster families I stayed with were nice enough and I made plenty of friends at the children's home. But I hardly ever got to see Jon or Travis, usually only at Christmas or on our birthdays. It was the loneliest time of my life until last month when Angie and Chris McCormick took in all three of us. They're two of the nicest people I've ever known.

The school bell rang and I gathered my things. I pulled on my backpack and followed the rest of the class out the door. Along the way somebody shoved me into the doorjamb. I lost my balance and nearly tasted floor wax. Without looking back I figured it must have been my fault.

"Sorry," I said. But abruptly I sensed something was terribly wrong. I turned.

Donnivee Fox glared back at me with fierce green eyes and a sneer on her face that would have scared a pit-bull. I didn't have to scan her thoughts to know she wanted to start a fight right there.

"What're *you* lookin' at?" Donnivee clenched her fists.

"Nothing," I said, trying to walk away from her. Though we were nearly the same height, Donnivee was heavier than I was and probably stronger, too. She'd been in fights before and whether she'd won or not didn't matter. I didn't want to fight her. *Ever.*

"That's bull crap!" Donnivee pushed me into the wall. Students gathered around us to watch. I realized I might have to fight just to stay alive. That would get me a black eye, maybe a broken nose and a three-day suspension. What would Angie say about that?

Suddenly, a smallish, pale girl dressed entirely in black stepped between us. I'd seen the girl before in science class, but we'd never spoken to each other. The girl stood before Donnivee with a tilted head and bulging eyes. Her lower jaw hung slack. She looked positively *psycho*. Was she going to start drooling next? I don't read emotions like Travis, but it was clear as crystal that Donnivee was afraid of that girl.

Luckily, Mrs. Cecere, my last-hour teacher, happened to walk by.

"Donnivee Fox!" said Mrs. Cecere sternly. "Go to your next class. *Now!*"

Donnivee never looked at the teacher. She tried to glare at me, but her gaze kept darting over to the girl in black. "Yes, Mrs. Cecere." She shot me one of those I'll-get-you-later looks, then stomped down the hall.

"Are you okay, Kelly?" asked Mrs. Cecere.

The fear must have shown in my eyes or maybe she saw my hands shaking. It's kind of hard to explain, but whenever I almost get the crap beat of me I get pretty scared. I can't lock away my fear the way Jon does.

"I'm fine." Thank God my voice was steadier than the rest of me.

"If you have a problem with her you'll let me know, right?"

"Yes, ma'am."

The girl in black looked normal again and winked at me. She went down the hall as if nothing had happened. I thought about winking back, but I couldn't close just one eye. I don't wink, I blink. It's kind of embarrassing, like having dust in both eyes.

I shook badly well into my next class and my stomach felt like it was tied up in squishy knots. From that day on I tried to keep mentally tuned in to Donnivee whenever she was within range.

———

When I got to life science class at the end of the day Mrs. Cecere had moved the girl in black to the vacant seat beside me. The classroom didn't have desks, just these black tables with shiny tops where you could cut up crayfish or frogs or other gross stuff and the juice wouldn't soak into the furniture. Each table seated two people and since I was the last person to join an already even-numbered class I had sat alone.   But not any more. The girl in black introduced herself.

"I'm Melissa," she said, grinning with perfect, ultra white teeth. "Melissa Godwin. Since we sit at the same table now I figure we should get to know each other."

"Kelly Bishop," I said. "Thanks for helping me."

"No problem. You're the one Donnivee hates so much."

"Why does Donnivee hate me?"

"Because you're way prettier than her."

"No, I'm not. She's got that gorgeous blonde hair."

"She's cute for a *thug*. But most boys are afraid of her. That's because she's beaten most of them up."

"She beats up boys?"

"Or girls. Sooner or later Donnivee hates you. And when she hates you, she beats you up. Your last name is Bishop, huh? That's a good name for a chess player. It's not as good as King or Queen or even McQueen. But it's still pretty good." As she spoke Melissa reached into her backpack and took out a brochure. She passed the brochure to my side of the table. I read the heading out loud.

"The Halloween Classic Open Chess Tournament? Why'd you give me this?"

"If you're really good at chess you'll want to play in that tournament. There's scholarships and prize money and stuff. Even if you're not sure how good you are, you should still find out."

I lightly explored Melissa's thoughts, but she suddenly looked me right in the eye. "What?"

I stopped the scan and backed off. Had she detected me inside her mind? "How'd you know I play chess?"

"Easy. I'm gonna be a detective. And if you need a body guard I'm your girl."

I sized her up from head to foot. Melissa was possibly the skinniest girl in our class. "Why is Donnivee afraid of you?"

"She thinks I'm crazy and *nobody* messes with a crazy person. If I'm around you all the time, Manson Stanfield won't bother you either."

"Who's Manson Stanfield?"

"Donnivee's only friend. Manson isn't tough, but she likes to watch fights, so she hangs out with Donnivee 'cause sooner or later Donnivee will get in a fight with somebody. But not with you, if I'm around. I'm your only hope."

I wasn't sure if this girl was serious, kidding, or just plain weird. But I liked her just the same. I played along. "Okay, you're hired."

"You're safer already."

Mrs. Cecere started class then and we didn't get another chance to talk until after the bell rang. But when science class was over, I decided that I'd stumbled onto my newest best friend. I really liked this strange girl. We traded phone numbers and planned to go to the mall together that Sunday.

"I don't have a cell phone," I said. "I live with foster parents. I don't think they can afford to get us cell phones."

"That would be rather pricey, three phones, for you and your brothers."

I looked at Melissa sideways. "Seriously, how do you know so much about me?"

"Maybe I'm not really going to be a detective. Maybe I'm a stalker."

———

I'd hate living with neat freaks. I've never had a lot of clothes and stuff, but I like to keep what I do have in its proper place on the floor. I've had dressers and bins and closets, but never used them. It probably seems odd, but hey, it's my system.

The first time I saw where Chris and Angie McCormick lived I figured they *had* to be neat freaks, and that could mean trouble. Their house was an ordinary two-story with a double-car garage. But they kept it in flawless, apple-pie order. The lawn and shrubs were trimmed like a golf course and the country-style front porch was so clean you could eat off the decking. Not that I would, of course. I prefer plates. Generally speaking, the place was so perfect I never saw a single cobweb in the house. When I showed up the very first time I just knew they'd yell at me for walking on the lawn, or dropping crumbs, or even sitting in the rocking chair on the front porch. I could almost hear them.

Stay off the grass! Pick up your crumbs! Don't rock, you'll scratch the decking!

Fortunately, Chris and Angie weren't like that at all. They were neat, but not OCD. To prove it, all anyone had to do was look in their basement. It was jammed with boxes, old furniture and other junk all stacked from floor to ceiling. We couldn't even find space to play down there. I guess everybody needs at least one junky looking room. Of course, after I moved in they had two.

I think somebody ought to do a case study on Angie and Chris about opposites attracting. They're both forty-one, but Angie seemed way younger and looked it, too. Maybe if Chris had more hair and lost a little weight it wouldn't have been so obvious. Yet as different as they were, I knew their love for each other was true. They sort of reminded me of my real parents. I could tell they were in love.

Chris taught English at Chantilly High School, the same school where Jon had started his junior year. Chris was your typical guy—average height, build, paunch and receding hairline. He wanted everyone to think he was laid back and easy-going, but I knew he was a worrier. That man worried about everything from the economy to whether he should become a vegetarian to the possibility of UFOs existing. He even had a deep down fear of becoming a zombie, which might be why he'd lost so much of his hair. But there wasn't a cruel bone in his body and he got along with kids. I liked him a lot.

And Angie? Well, Angie was special. She was *so* pretty with her slim body and short cut, auburn hair. Her large, dark eyes could stare a sarcastic hole right through somebody when she was annoyed with them. She did it often with Chris, but I figure he probably liked the attention. It took a lot to get that woman bothered; she had a sort of philosophy of calm. In her own words, "Why worry? Action beats fear almost every time." I liked that.

Angie worked out a lot too. She did yoga, lifted weights and walked for miles and miles, but nobody ever walked with her. Anyone who did would have to run to keep up. She was a fitness freak.

Since living with them I'd even heard the A-word pop into their thoughts every so often. *Adoption.* The McCormicks hadn't spoken to each other about it yet, but the possibility was on both their minds. I tried not to think about it. I didn't want to get my hopes up for nothing.

Like I said, the McCormicks kept a neat place, but unfortunately the house next door to them was a real dump. It was vacant, and no wonder with a sagging front porch, broken windows, and a desperate need for paint. Both houses were settled side by side in a quiet cul-de-sac with the next nearest place over a mile away. Talk about privacy! There wasn't even traffic noise. Everything around them was just trees, *lots* of trees.

When I got off the school bus that day I took my usual detour up the driveway between Chris' Mustang and Angie's minivan. I cut across the yard and dragged my fingertips over the bark of the huge oak tree out front. Call me weird, but I just love touching tree bark. It feels so, I don't know, rough? I dashed into the house.

I tracked down Angie in the family room. She was looking out the sliding glass door by the deck. "Hey Angie!"

"Hi, Kelly. How was school?"

"Good. I have a new friend. Her name's Melissa and she's real good at math and she's way cool and she saved my life today and we wanna go to the mall this weekend."

"I hope you didn't tell her Saturday. The cave trip should take up most of the day."

"No way. I'm not missing the cave trip for *anything.* Oh, and she gave me this." I dug the chess tournament brochure out of my backpack and passed it to Angie. She looked it over.

"Do you want to do this?"

"I want to see if I'm any good, you know?"

"Chris thinks you are. I mean, you beat him pretty bad every time you play and he was on the chess team in high school. Let's see, it's on Halloween weekend, two weeks away. Okay, I'll enter you."

"Thanks, Angie! What're you looking at?"

Angie pointed out back. "I'm watching Jon practice with his swords. He's *really* good. I wish we could afford to get him into a class, or something. You wouldn't happen to know the name of his old instructor, would you?"

I looked out the door. Jon had no idea we were spying on him and it was probably a good thing, too. The fifteen-inch knives he twirled— one in each hand—were razor sharp. As he stabbed and sliced the air his moves were fluid, graceful and incredibly dangerous looking. The mastery he showed with the long knives took my breath away.

"The only weapons instructor he ever had was Mr. Riker. When our parents died we moved around and Jon stayed with the Rikers for like three years. Mr. Riker was in the army. He was a black belt in karate and taught self-defense to soldiers. Jon was already pretty good at karate, but Mr. Riker taught him all kinds of new stuff, especially with weapons."

"Where's Mr. Riker now?"

"Dead. He got blown up." Angie got quiet so I finished the story. "Afghanistan. Mrs. Riker really liked Jon, but after her husband died she fell apart and sent Jon back to the children's home. Since then he hasn't had a weapons teacher, or a karate teacher either. He pretty much learns everything now from the internet."

I watched Jon practice as we talked. As usual he wore school clothes— tan slacks and a snug fitting blue T-shirt that just showed the muscles in his arms. He stood nearly six feet tall now, with strands of dirty-blond hair dropping in and out of his eyes while he worked. I noticed his sword case was open on the steps. His other three weapons—a Marine Corps officer's sword, a Roman gladius and a Scottish Claymore—glistened in the sun on a blanket spread across the deck.

Jon finished, stepped back and bowed toward the woods behind the house. Then he twirled the fighting knives and slid them both into a pair of sheaths strapped under his shirt at the base of his neck. The move was slick and controlled.

I was impressed. "Whoa! He's *way* better. Last time I saw him do that move he almost cut his finger off. It bled so much!"

Angie pulled me away from the door. "Don't let him hear you say that. Come on, I cut up some fruit for a snack. You can tell me all about Melissa."

"Melissa's so cool. She's kinda weird, but I can tell we're going to be great friends. She always wears black, you know."

As we entered the kitchen Chris McCormick came up the stairs from the basement, covered with cobwebs and dust bunnies. He looked like he'd been crawling under beds or something. He carried a baseball bat and a long steel pipe, one in each hand. "Angie, I don't know what to do with these. I found them under the stairs."

"Take them back where you found them," said Angie. "That's what you can do with them."

Chris nodded. "Uh, right. So how was school, Miss Kelly?"

"Fine. What're you doing, Chris?"

"Cleaning the basement. Well, I'm trying; it's such a huge job I don't know where to begin. I want to make a room down there and rent it to a college student so we can take in some extra cash, you know?"

"Get Travis to help. He's really good at keeping inventory and organizing stuff."

"Oh yeah? I'll talk to him when he gets home from school."

"Want a snack while you're working?" asked Angie.

"You bet." Chris took a plate of cut up apples and headed back downstairs.

About then the patio door opened and Jon came into the kitchen. He set his sword case on the floor, wiped his forehead on his sleeve and grinned at me. "What's up, Kel?"

"You're all sweaty and gross is what's up," I said. He *was*, too. I was afraid he'd try to hug me and get me all slimy. Jon had been hugging Travis and me a lot since we'd moved in with the McCormicks. He'd really missed us and I knew he felt responsible for taking care of us. "Hey, you've gotten really good with those knife thingys. We were watching you."

"Thanks." Jon blushed. His eyes became intense. "They're Elvish fighting knives, like Legolas carried in the *Lord of the Rings* movies."

"You have amazing skill with them, Jon." Angie passed him a plate of apple slices, neatly cut and skinned.

"I've got a long way to go with the knives, but at least I'm not bleeding this time." He grinned at me. "The Claymore, that's my best weapon. But if I'm gonna be a stunt man in movies I've got to be good with lots of weapons."

"A stunt man?" Angie nodded like she thought it was a good idea. "That'd be really cool. Are you working tonight?"

Jon glanced at the clock on the kitchen stove. "Gotta be there in an hour. I better get cleaned up. Can I eat this upstairs?"

"Bring the plate back down before you leave."

"Thanks!" Jon hurried out of the kitchen with his sword case and the fruit. On the way up the stairs he yelled, "Trav's home!"

As soon as he said it I heard a school bus drive away. It's funny how I never noticed that bus unless it was leaving. A moment later Travis came in the front door. As usual he stopped in the foyer and switched on the crystal chandelier. Travis had a thing about chandeliers and even the small ones amazed him no matter how many times he looked them over. He switched the light off, dropped his new backpack by the stairs and ran into the kitchen.

"Fruit!" he cried. "That's what I'm talkin' about!" He dug into the apple slices like he hadn't eaten all week. One thing about Travis, he could eat and eat and never get fat.

Why do you eat so much? I asked inside his head.

Cuz I'm hungry! thought Travis back to me. I smiled. Travis almost always kept it simple.

Travis' white-blond hair stuck up wilder than usual. That kid had some crazy hair, for sure. He was pale, too. Except for his deep blue eyes he almost looked albino. Travis smiled while he ate, which made me feel pretty good inside. When he was younger he rarely smiled around us because he was too worried about the next time we'd be separated. But since we'd moved in with Angie and Chris, he smiled more and worried less. He had a great smile, too. He usually won people over the first time they met him. Everybody liked Travis.

"Your turn to mark the calendar," I said.

Travis' eyes got big as he munched on an apple slice. "Yeah!" He turned to the fridge and grabbed the black Sharpie that hung by a string on the door. He found today's date and drew a big X through it. He must have scanned the rest of the month because he pointed to Halloween and looked back at me.

"You're in a chess tournament? For real?"

I shrugged like it was no big deal. Chess was cool, of course. But right now for me, it was all about the cave.

"You guys aren't *too* excited about the cave trip, are you?" asked Angie.

"I can't wait," I said. "Jon's excited, too, but he doesn't show it. How many caves has Chris been in?"

"Chris doesn't do caves. He's more of a putt-putt golf kinda guy." Angie paused to think. "I mean, the only cave he's ever been in that I know of was Luray Caverns, but that's got walkways and lights. This will be his first real cave exploration."

"Is he gonna lead us?" asked Travis.

"Lord, no. A good friend of ours at the high school, Anton Edwards, will be leading. He knows all about caves, especially this one. Anton is Jon's English teacher."

"Cool," said Travis. "Does the cave have a name?"

"Yes, Pandora's Cave."

"Pandora's Cave," I repeated. "I like it."

Somebody had written *Crystal Creek Park caving trip* on the calendar for this coming Saturday. Travis made his usual count down.

"Two more days 'til we crawl through cave slime. Yeah! That's what I'm talkin' about!"

Chapter 3
THE HAUNTING OF PANDORA'S CAVE

NED

People were a pain in the butt. That's what Ned Taylor thought and he had good reason. It was people who tore up the campground and left trash all over the picnic areas that *somebody* would need to clean up. It was people who'd sneak into Pandora's Cave at night to party and write graffiti all over the walls that *somebody* would have to remove. And it was people who'd drink too much and get into fights that *somebody* would have to break up. Guess who that *somebody* was?

Yep, in Ned's mind people were a royal pain. But without them he wouldn't have a job.

Ned had been a seasonal ranger in Crystal Creek Park since he'd graduated from high school three years ago. The tiny park was located about twenty miles south of Front Royal, Virginia, and backed up to the northeast boundary of the Shenandoah National Park. Ned had Googled Crystal Creek Park more than once, but nothing ever showed up.

A rich old widow named Pandora Wilby still owned the park property, though she had already deeded the land to the National Park Service. On her death the NPS would absorb the additional four hundred acres of forest and low mountains into the Shenandoah National Park. Until then Mrs. Wilby's shrewd attorney made sure the park service was solely responsible for maintenance and operation of land they didn't even own yet.

Ned Taylor worked as a park ranger three seasons a year. The salary wasn't much, but it was enough to keep him in a small apartment, own a used car and go to college. Working the graveyard shift never interfered with class schedules while he went after an accounting degree. And now that it was mid-October people hardly mattered. The campground was closed and the only reason anybody even came to the park was to hike or go on a picnic. As long as Ned worked eleven to seven he wouldn't have to deal with people again until next summer.

His cousin, Eric Wooden, had gotten him the ranger job. Eric was three years older and had been working in the park system for nearly seven years. He loved the work, but he also loved confrontations. With Eric the more problems people caused the better he liked his job. Eric should have been a cop.

Ned parked his Jeep in front of the one-story log rancher that served as the ranger station. Lights glowed from inside the building and right away he heard the deep barking of Ripper the wonder dog in the pen around back. Ripper was Eric's dog, a black Lab-German Shepherd mix that was the park's unofficial mascot. Eric had originally gotten Ripper to keep him company on the lonely evening shifts, but now all the rangers preferred to have the dog around. Ned sure did, especially in the middle of the night when he finished studying and all the shows on TV were infomercials or reruns. Ripper was friendly, but he looked dangerous and answered only to the rangers. Campers and hikers had a healthy fear of the dog, which helped the rangers keep order.

"Hey, Ripper!" called Ned as he got out of the Jeep. "How you doin' boy?"

Ripper whined and jumped excitedly. Eric and Ned had set up Ripper with a fenced-in dog run, a first-class house and plenty of dog biscuits.

"You wanna cookie? I got a cookie!"

Ripper licked his mouth and barked again.

Ned was a bit stocky, standing about five-eight, with medium length burnt-orange hair. He liked the outdoors and enjoyed quail hunting and fishing. He'd given up hunting larger animals ever since he'd shot and killed a seven-point buck four years ago. Man, that whole scene had given him nightmares. He'd never forget looking into the deep brown eyes of that dying animal and seeing the life fizzle right out of it. His hunting friends laughed at him and said he had Bambi syndrome. Ned didn't know about that. He just figured he'd stick with quail.

Ned zipped up his jacket against the chilly October breeze, then checked his pockets. Plenty of dog biscuits. Satisfied, he tossed his backpack over one shoulder and stopped by the pen to give Ripper some love and a couple of biscuits. Then he went inside the station.

The head ranger, who normally worked the day shift, was a serious looking, dark eyed woman named Melinda Laarz. Laarz was in her forties, with a friendly personality and a definite take-charge attitude, especially during emergencies. Laarz was a full time, year round ranger—a lifer, and that was okay with Ned. Somebody had to do it. One reason he stuck with being a park ranger was because he *wasn't* in charge. Being a supervisor would make it seem too much like a *real* job. The only real job he wanted was to be an accountant.

"What's up, Melinda?"

"Hey, Ned," she said, marking on the work calendar. "Are you awake?"

He yawned and nodded. "How about you? You just pulled a double."

"I'll live. I hope Eric's hot date is worth it. He's the one pulling a double tomorrow."

Ned laughed. "Eric's never had any trouble finding girls, so this one must be extra special. She's that Russian girl who goes caving around here. Is there coffee?"

"That pot's fresh. Russian girl? You mean Anya? She's a pretty one, all right. I didn't realize they knew each other."

"He met her at the summer camp."

Laarz dismissed the topic with a shrug. "Keep an eye on the spotlights, okay? They went off twice last night and I don't know why. If they go off again pop the breaker switch pronto. Are you going to stay awake?"

"I got a test tomorrow. I'll be awake."

"Good enough. I need a beer and some shrimp fried rice. See ya later."

"G'night, Melinda." When Laarz left, Ned got out his books and poured a cup of coffee. Then he got to work studying.

Nearly three hours later Ned got up and made a big, joint-popping stretch. He felt pretty good about the test and decided to watch TV for a while.

Five hours to go, he thought, searching for the TV remote. *Not so bad.*

About then Ripper started barking like crazy. Ned flinched. The dog never barked like that unless someone, or *something* was close by. Ned swallowed hard and took up his flashlight.

Please don't be a skunk, he thought as he went out the door.

All the spotlights around the station were off, including the ones in front of the cave. Ned gripped the long-handled flashlight securely, like a short club. If somebody was messing around with the breaker box he might have to bash some heads in. He touched the cell phone in his pants pocket to make sure it was there. Sometimes even rangers needed to call 911.

Ned moved through the shrubs on the south side of the station until he came to the breaker box under the window. He removed the heavy padlock and opened the panel. Nothing looked out of the ordinary. He flipped several switches off and back on again. Everything outside stayed dark.

"Dammit."

All the while Ripper continued to bark. Ned shined the flashlight on the dog. Ripper's full attention was on Pandora's Cave, about thirty yards away. Ned aimed the beam of light at the cave entrance and finally saw what the dog saw. He was so startled he jumped to his feet.

A man stood alone near the cave entrance, staring back at him. He was tall, at least six feet and wore a dark, three-piece business suit with highly polished black leather shoes. His fingers were interlaced in front of him in an undertaker's pose.

"Can I help you, sir?" Ned glanced over his shoulder at the parking lot. His Jeep was the only vehicle there. How'd this clown even get here?

Ned noticed some kind of metallic looking object on the ground beside the man. It was shaped like a chrome fire hydrant and stood about hip high. What the hell was that supposed to be? He shined the light in the man's face and approached him warily.

Ned stopped about ten feet away from the stranger, but kept the light trained in the guy's eyes. From that distance, Ned could see him clearly. "Sir?"

The guy looked so out of place it was ridiculous. He was dark and distinguished with a neatly trimmed beard and a touch of gray at his temples. He was probably about forty years old and looked like a model in *Gentleman's Quarterly*. He smiled back at Ned, as if amused. But he never spoke. Then he slowly dropped one hand to his side, allowing his fingertips to touch the device beside him.

Ned saw the movement and hesitated. He reached for his sidearm. He frowned. Rangers didn't carry guns, one of the dumber rules of the job. His personal handgun and hunting rifle were in the Jeep.

"Sir? Do you understand me?" Ned tried to appear less nervous than he really was, but this guy was spooking him out. Ripper was going nuts. "What's that thing beside you?"

The man smiled at him again and shook his head. Then, without a sound, both he and the device disappeared.

Ned staggered back, stunned. Ripper barked even louder.

"Damn!" He shined the flashlight in every direction. Unless a UFO had taken the guy, there was only one place he could have gone. Into the cave. But how?

Ned swallowed hard and marched toward the entrance. Abruptly, he thought better of it and ran to the dog's pen instead. He opened the gate and turned Ripper loose. The fierce-looking dog took off straight toward the cave. Ned followed at a cautious jog, watching their backs.

As they reached the entrance, a host of colorful glowing eyes appeared within the cave's pitch darkness. Ripper skidded to a halt. He settled into a low, ominous growl. Ned froze beside the dog. The eyes in the cave glared at them hatefully, glowing like dim flashlights. Some were red, some blue, some even bright yellow, but clearly none were human. A snickering sound erupted from the darkness. Someone—or *something*—was laughing at him.

Ned's legs shook. His heart pounded. Against his better judgment, he aimed his flashlight at some of the eyes. Something moved. A flash of blue! No, green! No, yellow! Whoever—or whatever—they were turned and ran. Ripper yelped. The huge dog took off toward the office. Ned shuddered. One of those things in the cave must have been at least ten feet tall. A cold, stiff breeze blew across his neck. He inched away from the cave.

Were they wild animals? Or were they something else, something... unnatural?

Abruptly, the floodlights popped back on. Ned jumped in surprise, half blinded. He saw Ripper standing on two legs, pawing at the door to the station.

Thanks a lot, Ripper. The thought was sarcastic but Ned totally understood why the dog had run. He listened carefully. The area was utterly silent. Ned swallowed hard. He'd never experienced anything like that before. He had a frightening thought.

Dogs were supposed to be sensitive to the presence of ghosts, and Ripper had certainly seemed overly sensitive to whatever was in that cave. A lonely chill raced through Ned's entire body. With a shiver, he glanced back at the dark entrance.

Pandora's Cave had never been haunted before. So why now? He decided it didn't matter. He ran back to the ranger station and let both himself and the dog inside. Then he locked all the doors and windows. Ned wasn't going to have any problem staying awake now. Hell, he might never sleep again!

Chapter 4
THE EARTHQUAKE

KELLY

I was half asleep and it was still dark when we drove into Crystal Creek Park in Anton Edwards's eight-seat SUV. In my opinion, getting out of bed in the middle of the night is not a good time to do *anything*. I guess Anton thought differently. He *liked* to go caving early and since he was the only one who knew what he was doing, the rest of us went on his schedule.

Anton Edwards was head of the English department at Chantilly High School and worked with Chris. He was a ruggedly handsome black man with graying hair and intense, dark eyes. He had on a loose fitting long-sleeved tan shirt, worn blue jeans and jogging shoes. I could tell he was an athlete because of his strong looking hands and it really surprised me to find out he was forty-two. He sure didn't look that old. In my mind anybody over forty was over the hill, though Anton might be an exception.

Another man I'd never met before, Dr. Mark Parrish, had also come with us. He was Jon's chemistry teacher and was even older than Anton Edwards, like in his fifties. He was ancient! Parrish wore thick, horn-rimmed glasses and had a gray mustache that looked like a stiff scrub brush. He was *so* big, just over 6'4", and though he wasn't exactly fat, he took up a lot of space just the same. The three men were obviously good friends because they spent most of the trip cracking jokes at each other.

Jon nudged me when we parked. "You awake? Let's go."

I gathered my old pink *Barbie* backpack and trudged along with the others to a one-story, log building with a sign out front that read, *Ranger Station*. I really wanted to see the cave but being there so early was not the best way to spend Saturday morning. Saturday afternoon would have been just fine.

"I can't believe you brought your old *Barbie* pack," said Travis. "It's fallin' apart."

"Well I'm sure not taking my *new* one into a cave," I said defensively. "You're going to mess up your new backpack."

Travis shrugged as Chris knocked on the door to the ranger station. A dog barked from inside. Chris jumped back, a look of terror on his face. A lady ranger came out to greet us with a big smile and a steaming cup of coffee. A huge, black-and-tan dog came out, too, and started sniffing everybody. The dog looked scary, but it seemed friendly enough.

"Welcome to Crystal Creek Park," said the woman. "I'm Melinda Laarz, Head Ranger here. And this is Ripper the wonder dog. He belongs to one of the rangers, but we keep him around for company. You won't bite, will you, Ripper?" She patted the dog and sipped her coffee. Ripper wagged his bushy tail in a friendly way.

Chris was uneasy around the dog, but Jon knelt beside it and rubbed it behind the ears. Right away the tail wagged harder. When Travis and I petted him, Ripper didn't complain at all, he just licked our hands and got dog slime all over us. Yuck! Good thing I liked dogs.

"I'm pleased to meet you," continued Laarz. "If anyone needs help waking up I've got a fresh pot of coffee inside, so help yourself. Anton tells me he's taking you on a tour of Pandora's Cave?"

"Yeah!" said Travis excitedly. Jon and Chris nodded.

"You're going to love it in there."

"Are there any blind cave crickets or bats?" I asked. "We learned about them at school."

"No bats in this cave. Not yet, anyway. But you're right about the cave crickets. And there are blindfish, too, in the lake." She called to Anton, who was busy getting equipment out of his car. "There's no rain in the forecast till next week, so don't worry about flashfloods. I'll look for you guys no later than one or two. Are you taking them to the Cathedral room?"

"Absolutely," said Anton. "It's the best thing in the cave."

"He's not kidding," said Laarz. "It's *fabulous!*"

I briefly scanned the lady ranger's mind. Laarz had a genuine love for the park and seemed excited for us. I also got thoughts about the woman from Travis. He liked her right off, which was usually a good sign.

Jon moved closer to Laarz and lowered his voice so only those nearby could hear what he said. "Mr. Edwards is my English teacher at school. Just between you and me, does he really know anything about caves?"

Laarz nodded vigorously, whispering back to him. "Oh, yes! Anton's been exploring caves since before you were born. He knows all the caves around here, and especially this one. He works for the Park Service in the summers as a cave guide. Believe me, he's an expert."

Jon nodded his approval as Anton called everyone over to the SUV and began handing out the gear. He gave out waterproof flashlights, extra batteries, hardhats with headlamps mounted on the front, kneepads, candles, matches and a other necessary equipment. He also gave a coil of nylon rope to Parrish, who stuffed it into his pack.

"How much rope is it?" asked Parrish.

"About seventy-five feet," said Anton. "I doubt we'll need it, but I never go into a cave without rope. Now let me show you guys how the headlamps work." For the next few minutes Anton explained what all the equipment was for and how to use it. When he was done, he warned us about the upcoming journey.

"Whenever you go into a cave, or anywhere else in the park for that matter, you always pack out everything you bring in. I mean *everything.* You take out all your trash, all your equipment, even your fingerprints if you can find them. Also, it's going to be wet when we get near the Cathedral room, so get used to the idea."

"How wet?" I asked. I was mostly awake, but I wasn't in the mood for an early morning swim.

"We have to crawl through a shallow stream."

"*Crawl* through a stream?" I shot a distressed look at Travis, who was smiling. OMG! He couldn't wait to crawl through water! What a moron.

Anton led us to the opening of Pandora's Cave, where a ragged brown sign with white letters marked the entrance. Off to one side a larger sign offered a brief description of what to expect and how to treat the ecology. It also warned people about going in without an experienced guide.

By now the sun was just rising above the foothills in the east. The area was much brighter than before. Jon surprised me when he took a digital camcorder from his backpack. The entire unit was no bigger than some cell phones I'd seen, but it looked like something a professional would use. He tested the battery and the LED lamp.

"Where'd you get that?" I asked. "It's nice."

"It's Brandon's. He wants me to make a sort of documentary of the trip. He thinks we can use some of the cave footage in one of our films."

"Why don't you just use your cell phone?" asked Dr. Parrish. "That thing looks expensive."

Jon wasn't sure how to answer without hurting Chris' feelings. "Uh, Brandon wants decent sound, and all, too. Not just good video."

Chris was embarrassed. "Angie and I have talked about getting the kids cell phones, but even the family plans are pricey. They do need something, though."

Anton changed the subject. "You're going to make films? That's interesting, Jon, really. You and Brandon make a good team."

Jon agreed, as he turned on the camcorder and aimed it at himself. "This is the great expedition into Pandora's Cave led by super cave explorer, Mr. Edwards. Also on the journey are the brilliant Dr. Parrish, the amazing Chris McCormick, and, of course, all the fantastic Bishops!" He turned the camera briefly on everyone, and we waved back shyly. "Just act natural while I'm taping, okay?"

All at once Anton and Parrish went from acting natural to walking and groaning like zombies. Jon paused the camcorder. "Never mind."

Everybody laughed except Chris. "Please don't do that."

"Sorry, Chris, I forgot." Anton spoke as if he knew something about Chris that I should know too. I was about to inspect his thoughts and find out why Chris didn't like zombie jokes, when Jon approached me.

"Take this." Jon handed the camcorder to me and explained how to use it. "Try to keep the picture steady, okay? Remember, what you see in the viewfinder is exactly what you're recording."

I was taken aback. Was he kidding? That thing cost a lot of money. "What if I drop it?"

"Don't."

"What do you want me to do with it?"

"Get me some cutaway shots."

"What's a cutaway shot?"

"You know, like a cat in a window, or a bug crawling on the ground. You see them all the time in movies to show what an actor is looking at, or to show continuity. They cutaway for a quick look at a plant, or something."

"I can tape anything I want?"

"Knock yourself out."

I searched the area around the cave entrance for a bug or a cat or a cool looking plant. Nothing. Just for practice I got a close up of Ripper the wonder dog. Ripper tried to lick the lens.

As we were about to go into the cave, a yellow, original style VW Beetle raced into the parking lot and skidded to a halt beside Anton's car. Maria Sanchez, Jon's girlfriend, got out of the Beetle and ran to Jon. Maria had thick dark hair and big, beautiful brown eyes that made Jon want to hold her whenever she looked at him. I knew that because I was inside his head again. It was *so* romantic being around them. He quickly blocked me out.

She wrapped her arms around his neck and they kissed without shame in front of everybody. She gave me a quick girly hug and even rubbed Travis' white hair, which messed it up a little more than it already was. It seems funny to me how people rub his hair like that. Is it because he's got curly Troll hair? I mean what's the big deal? Does it bring good luck to rub it?

As usual Travis blushed just being near her and I knew exactly what he was thinking. Maria was drop-dead gorgeous and genuinely kind all rolled into one.

"Want some gum?" Maria produced a pack of gum from a pocket in her very tight blue jeans and passed it around. Of course Travis took a piece, he always did. He's got a thing for gum like he does for food. I took one, too, to be polite. Travis whispered to me.

"She's pretty *and* she gives us gum! No wonder Jon likes her so much!"

"No wonder." I rolled my eyes at him. Not a major roll, but enough to calm him down.

Travis popped the gum in his mouth and wandered off toward the cave. I, on the other hand, hit the record button and kept the lens pointed at Jon and Maria. This was good stuff and I didn't want to miss a second.

"I can't believe you came here!" said Jon happily. "It's so early!"

"I wanted to wish you good luck," said Maria, kissing him again. "So good luck! And be careful, okay?"

I moved around them, taking in every romantic shot with the camcorder. I even zoomed in on their interlaced fingers. I'd call that a cutaway shot.

"That's good. Now don't move your hands. Okay, I got it." This directing stuff was kind of cool. Maybe I should look into it.

"Get out of here," said Jon, grabbing for the camcorder. I dashed out of his reach but came back to finish the scene.

"I wish you could come with us," said Jon. "Mr. Edwards makes it sound like a life changing experience."

"Don't change too much, okay? I like you the way you are."

"Do you want to go with us, Maria?" said Anton, stepping over to greet her. I changed the camera angle to include Anton in the shot. "I've got some extra equipment."

"No, no, no, Mr. Edwards!" said Maria quickly. "Thanks, but I don't like dirty old caves. Call me when you get back."

"Absolutely." Jon kissed her again and they pulled apart. Maria waved and got back in her car. When she was gone Jon caught up with the rest of us and got a big applause. He blushed, but grinned from ear to ear as he took back the camcorder.

"When a girl gets up this early and drives forty minutes for a kiss, it's serious. Nothing beats true love." Anton said it matter-of-factly, but Chris and Parrish both nodded like they totally understood and approved. "Are we ready to hit the underworld? Let's go, team!"

———

The cave opening was half the size of a normal doorway and made of smooth, gray rock. A path of loose dirt led into the cave, where a jagged, curved ceiling gave it a yawning, toothy look.

Anton stopped at the edge of the darkness. "Follow me." The way he said it was kind of eerie and when he stepped into the cave he was completely swallowed up by gloom. I couldn't see him at all and it had a spooky feel about it. Chris took a deep breath and went after him. Then Jon and I went in, followed by Travis and Dr. Parrish.

Something about walking into pitch-blackness made my stomach flutter, and not a little flutter either. But as we entered I found out it wasn't quite as dark as it seemed from outside in the morning light. We passed through a sort of twilight zone where the walls were lined with pale, ragged plants and spider webs. Farther in it was like entering a dark movie theatre after using the restroom. I couldn't see a thing. Apparently Parrish couldn't see either. He bumped into Travis.

"Sorry, Travis," said Parrish. "I'm walking blind."

Anton turned on his headlamp revealing steep, rock walls on both sides. Parrish stood up straighter when he saw the high ceiling.

"Stay close to me," said Anton, who turned and went ahead, leaving us all in total darkness. He laughed and called back. "You can switch on your headlamps."

Well, duh! I'd forgotten all about it. Luckily, I wasn't the only one. The others murmured with relief and turned on their headlamps. Now

I could see the smooth rock path we'd been descending, which led into a narrow tunnel. So that's what the place looked like.

"The cave is named for Pandora Wilby, a local heiress," said Anton, giving us a little history lesson along the way. "When she dies the property will belong to the National Park Service. This cave is completely natural. No electricity, signs, or handrails. But don't worry, I brought spotlights to show off the impressive stuff. Now pay attention, everybody." Anton bent down and drew a tiny arrow with a piece of white chalk near the floor. "I know my way around this cave, but if for some reason one of you needs to get out without my guidance, just follow the arrows. I'll rub off the chalk when we leave."

When the group moved again, I saw Travis glance back, which of course made me look, too. The cave entrance was out of sight. Travis was really good at finding his way around, and I don't think he'd ever been lost. He must have gotten that trait from our real dad, who never got lost either. Even now I had to fight off tears whenever I thought about the accident. But this wasn't the place to get sidetracked. I clamped my jaw tight and focused on the cave.

Like I said Travis had never gotten lost, though keeping track of where we were in a cave was different. With all the turns, rises, passageways and drops, it was hard for Travis to get his bearings. To make matters worse there were pitch-black side tunnels, which seemed to drop into nothingness. Personally, I've never been a big fan of nothingness—especially the dark kind. I did *not* want to get lost in this place, but I noticed Anton was careful to make a tiny chalk mark at every intersection.

"Where do all the other tunnels go?" asked Travis.

"Some just end," said Anton. "A few go down to an underground river. And one leads to a side exit. You could lose your way in here very easily."

"So there's another way out," said Jon. "Is it hard to find?"

"Not if you know where to look. The other way's actually shorter than this one, but it's boring. If there was an emergency, though, I'd bring a rescue team in that way. Cuts time and distance in half."

Anton led us through narrow passages and small holes where we had to crawl. Travis kept making weird sound effects whenever we had to do something other than walk.

"Bierrrrol. Bierrrrol. Gudda-gudda-gudda." The echoes of his battle noises, if that's what they were, sounded distorted and alien.

"What's that supposed to be?" asked Parrish.

"I dunno," said Travis. "I'm just havin' fun. Blecka-blecka-bierrrrol."

That was an understatement because I knew Travis was having the time of his life. The only thing he wasn't sure about was his headlamp. Every so often it flickered like it might go out, but Anton always got it to work again.

We hardly needed our headlamps since the camcorder had its own bright light. Jon was recording practically every step we took. He went ahead of the group and got shots of everyone crawling through a shallow stream beneath a low ceiling. This was the stream Anton had promised, and the water was cold. Travis loved it. I didn't. Parrish wasn't too crazy about it either when his glasses got wet. He came out of the stream and gave them to Travis.

"Travis? Can you wipe these off? I can't see a thing without them."

"Sure," said Travis. He wiped them clean on a dry part of his shirt and gave them back. Parrish put them on again and blinked.

"Much better. Thanks."

A half hour into the journey we stopped at a dead end where a narrow path rose steeply to the ceiling. Anton took a rope from his pack that had series of knots tied in it.

Parrish winked at us. "So, Anton, is this the exciting part you were telling us about? The blank wall, I mean."

Anton just smiled. "Mark, you should do standup comedy. You're a real card."

"Yeah," said Chris. "He's a card all right. He ought to be dealt with."

Chris' joke was so bad everyone just stared at him. He looked from person to person hoping for support. All at once we burst out laughing, the noise echoing eerily around us. Anton clapped him on the shoulder. "Chris, I beg you. Stay away from anything related to humor. Please?"

"Yeah, Chris," I said. "Please?"

"It's funny!" Chris argued good-naturedly. "You probably didn't even get it."

"Oh, we got it. Along with a case of heartburn." Anton pulled hard on the rope to tighten the knots. Satisfied, he set it down.

Parrish looked up. "So, Anton, *is* there a way around this wall?"

"Not around—through." Anton carefully crawled up the incline until he reached the top. He looped one end of the knotted rope around a rock column, then shined his light on a hole about the size of a truck tire. "This takes us down to the Cathedral room. You can use the rope to climb up, but coming back is a breeze. I didn't name it the Sliding Board Rock for nothing."

Travis looked at me. "Cool!"

Parrish groaned. "That hole's small. I hope we don't have to leave in a hurry."

Anton disappeared over the wall and called for Chris to follow next. Chris wasn't very athletic and he didn't climb so well, but he used the rope to slide, pull and kick his way to the top. Eventually we all got up the slope and through the hole, even Dr. Parrish. Luckily, the hole was bigger than it looked from below. I'd gotten a little chilly after crawling through the water, but the climb was a fun challenge and it warmed me up nicely. I noticed the warmer I was the dryer my clothes got.

We passed through a dark tunnel to arrive at a broad underground lake. A natural walkway, like a ledge, curved off to the left, skirting the edge of the lake until it disappeared under the water.

"Have a seat, everyone," said Anton, as he shined his headlamp at some amazing rock formations on the wall just below us. Some of the rocks were as thin and delicate as toothpicks.

"Cool," said Travis. "Those look like flowers!"

"They're amazing!" said Chris.

"They're beautiful," I added. "How'd they get there?"

Anton pointed. "See that water dripping on the flowers? There's a trace amount of limestone in every drop, and when it splashes, some limestone settles on the rock. After thousands of years, the limestone builds up and takes on its own unique shape. The design is made by the splash or drip pattern. Now I want everybody to scoot over next to the column on the right and kill your lights. I'm going to show you one of the most amazing natural rock formations you'll ever see."

Anton removed some Frisbee-sized spotlights from his pack while our group moved to the edge of a shallow dip in the rock that was between us and the lake. We switched off the lights and waited. Anton scurried around setting up the spotlights and then got close to everyone and turned off his headlamp.

"Are you ready?" he asked. "Ladies and gentlemen, I give you the Cathedral room!" He flipped a switch. Four blinding spotlights flashed on. I gasped. I'd never seen anything like it.

The Cathedral room was much larger than it had looked in the dimmer light of the headlamps. Before us rose a series of shiny yellow, almost gold, columns that went from floor to ceiling, like the pipes of a church organ. Incredibly, the pipes were longer on the left side, but became progressively shorter to the right. Travis counted nineteen of them, some at least ten meters tall. Anton pointed at the base of the natural "pipes".

"Take a look down there," he said. He aimed one of the spotlights at the foot of the pipes under the water, where a flat-topped, limestone formation rested. It had a white stripe across one edge.

"That kinda looks like organ keys!" said Travis.

"Incredible!" said Chris. He looked up and pointed. Again, we were amazed.

In addition to the organ, multicolored spiral columns rose in clusters all through the room. Mixed among the columns was a virtual forest of stalactites and stalagmites all around the lake, their images mirrored in the glassy water. It was nearly impossible to tell which ones were real and which were reflections.

"Wow!"

40

"It's beautiful!"

Anton Edwards leaned back on his elbows and crossed his long legs in front of him. I knew exactly how he felt. Anton loved teaching and it didn't always have to be English.

"Dr. Vu from my department would love this place," said Parrish. "He's a geologist, you know."

"Incredible," Chris said again. "I'm so glad I came."

"Me, too," said Travis. "Thanks, Dad." Travis spoke without thinking and it came from his heart. At the same time, he hugged Chris. Chris absolutely beamed.

I knew the dad thing wouldn't go over well with Jon and sure enough Jon gave Travis a discreet little poke in the arm. He mouthed the words, *He's not our father!* Travis glared at our brother. He had just broken Jon's cardinal rule: *Never call foster parents mom or dad.*

Well, tough. Let's face it, we all wanted parents and in Travis' mind Chris and Angie were perfect. He socked Jon in the leg and moved closer to Chris. Jon was shocked. His frustration skyrocketed. It was obvious Travis felt it, but he didn't care.

You hurt Jon's feelings, I thought to Travis. *He doesn't want us to forget mom and dad.*

I can't help it. I don't even know what they looked like.

You've seen them. You've got the picture hanging on your wall.

They don't seem real to me.

I studied him thoughtfully, then scooted closer to Jon. As Travis looked on I kept my voice low.

"Travis didn't know mom and dad as long as we did. He doesn't have all the great memories we do."

Jon looked at me, his eyes moist. "I've told him everything about them I can remember. What else can I do?"

"Telling isn't the same as being there. He needs a dad."

Jon scowled. He got up and went into the tunnel alone. Dr. Parrish must have noticed, because he followed Jon. A moment later, Anton rose and went after them both.

"I'll talk to him," said Anton, touching me on the shoulder.

I got worried that Chris might have heard what we said, but when I tuned in to his thoughts, Chris was still excited about the unusual beauty in the cave. He may not have noticed Jon's irritation.

I know how you feel, Travis, I thought to him. *It's good to have family again, even if it isn't really our own.*

They might be our own. They really love us, jus' like we're their own kids.

I nodded and hugged him. *You're right.*

Travis relaxed. Things might finally work out. And this cave was super cool!

But my pleasant thoughts changed abruptly when the ground began to shake. Travis groped at the floor, but it was flat. There was nothing to hold on to. Instead, he grabbed two of the backpacks. The shaking got worse. I tried to stand up but the ground moved too much. It knocked me to my knees.

"What...is...it?" said Travis, shouting over the dull roar that filled the cavern. "Kelly...ghost fingers!" He dragged the backpacks over to me and wrapped his arms around one of my legs. Chris rolled over. He hugged us both hard.

"I think it's an earthquake!" shouted Chris.

"Whutta we do?" said Travis.

"Hold on! And pray!"

A moment later the floor dropped out from under us. We fell fast. The spotlights went out. A heavy darkness and a deafening roar closed in. I did the only thing I could, considering the situation. I screamed.

JON

A terrible rumbling filled the air. The floor of the cave shook violently. Jon struggled to hold the camera steady but the view became blurry and dark. Something kept making him go off frame. Gazing through the viewfinder he saw Kelly stumble. A moment later the ledge broke. Kelly, Travis and Chris all dropped out of sight.

Jon looked up from the camera. What? Oh, hell! An earthquake! They were underground during an earthquake. He turned off the camcorder and tucked it under his arm. What should he do? He started after Kelly and Travis, but the ledge was gone.

All at once part of the ceiling landed on his hardhat and knocked him to the ground. Chunks of rock showered over him like a thundering downpour. Jon rolled to his hands and knees and curled up in a tight ball. He kept the camcorder safely hidden under his body. Since the accident took away his parents, Jon had secretly wanted to die in a blaze of glory, in the heat of battle. But not like this. Not buried alive.

Chapter 5

TRAPPED

KELLY

The thundering roar seemed endless. If I screamed, I didn't hear it. The hollow drop straight down made my stomach flip over. We were going to die, I knew it.

We hit bottom suddenly. The jolt knocked the wind out of me. My head snapped back on impact, smacking into rock. My flashlight went out. Water and pieces of limestone showered over me like heavy sleet, pricking the skin on my face. I rolled quickly to my belly and covered my head with both hands. I waited in terror for the rest of the ceiling to come crushing down.

After what seemed like forever, the earth stood still. Rivulets of water, rock fragments and loose powder drifted down, but eventually tapered off. The cave was quiet again. I lay flat on my face spotted with a dust-like residue. I wanted to look around, but was afraid to move. What if my movement made the rocks shift again? What if it caused another earth-quake? Not far away Travis moaned. That's all it took.

I bolted upright. I found my flashlight in the rubble, but when I turned it on nothing happened. Then I realized I didn't need it. The cave was dim, though it should have total dead blackness. So how come I could still see? I noticed a strange reddish glow that clearly had something to do with it. Travis raised his head and coughed.

"Are you okay?" I asked.

He sat up, dazed. "Uh...I guess...knocked the wind out of me." He pointed at a crumpled heap a few meters off. "Is that Chris?"

I looked. Chris had been holding us when we dropped. If that was Chris, how did he get so far away? I crawled toward the heap and found another flashlight. The crystal was cracked and the light flickered, but it still put out a dim, yellow beam. I shined the light on the heap.

"Chris? Can you hear me? Chris?" Chris didn't move or make a sound.

I studied his head and didn't see any blood, though a large lump had formed on his forehead. I gently probed his mind, but there weren't any organized thoughts. As usual, an unconscious person showed only white noise, like snow on an old TV when the programming ended. He was out cold, but I sensed his head injury was relatively minor. He looked unharmed and asleep—until I saw the bend in his right leg just above the ankle.

"Oh my God, his leg is broken!" I gagged and turned away. I put my other hand over my mouth in case I threw up. "I can't look. What are we going to do?"

"We need Mr. Edwards." Travis stood up cautiously. He picked up something shiny from the rock floor. "Dr. Parrish's glasses. They're smashed. Ya think he's dead? Where's Jon?" His voice became urgent. He couldn't hide the fear he felt for our brother.

I came over and put my arm around him. "Jon and Dr. Parrish went back in the tunnel. So did Mr. Edwards. You stay with Chris, I'll go look for them."

Travis caught my arm as I turned. "Kelly, I can do a splint on his leg. I learned how at Cub Scouts with Mrs. O'Brien."

"I don't know, Travis. It looks pretty bad. Have you ever done it?"

"We practiced. I put a splint on Josh O'Brien's leg and he put one on mine. Mrs. O'Brien is a nurse. She said my splint was the best."

I shook my head. "You went to the cub scouts for one month. Let's find Mr. Edwards." I scanned the rock wall overhead and pointed straight up. "Look! The organ pipes! And there's the tunnel! That's where we were before the quake. We must have dropped a good fifty feet!"

"How'd we drop fifty feet?" asked Travis, confused. "Wouldn't that kill us? What about all the rock flowers? And the lake? And the organ keyboard? Where's everything?"

"Gone. The cave we're in now must have been *under* the cave we *used* to be in, only this cave is way bigger. It was under the lake, too. Maybe Mr. Edwards knew about it. Maybe he was going to show it to us, but we just hadn't gotten there, yet."

Travis shook his head sadly. "All the flowers are gone forever."

I considered the loss, then looked to the top of the wall. "I'm going up."

"Better be careful. How're we gonna to get Chris up there?"

"If I can find Mr. Edwards or Jon, or Dr. Parrish, we'll figure it out."

I searched for hand and footholds in the dim light, but the walls were dripping wet. They'd held lake water until a few minutes ago. I started to climb, but the rock wall was too slick. I lost my grip and had to jump down.

"This isn't good. We have to get help for Chris as soon as possible. But we're trapped down here, too!" I sat beside Chris and buried my face in my hands. What should we do?

"I'll look for a splint," said Travis. "At Josh's we used pieces of flat wood or magazines. But I don't see nothing like that here."

While Travis scoured the ledge searching for some kind of splint material, I fought the urge to cry. We were in big trouble. What if the quake had closed off the entire cave? What if nobody ever came after us?

A voice from above broke my troubled silence. "Hey."

I looked up. Jon peered down at us from the tunnel where the edge of the lake used to be. At that distance his eyes were black orbs in the reddish glow.

"Jon!" I cried. "Are you okay?"

"Yeah. You guys?"

Travis nodded. "But Chris has a broken leg. It's bad. He got knocked out, too."

"Travis says he knows how to put on a splint," I reported.

"Yeah?" Jon sounded surprised. "Good, cuz I don't. Is Dr. Parrish down there? Or Mr. Edwards?"

"They're not here. They followed you into the tunnel. Didn't you see them?"

"No. I was recording. My light got smashed, it's pitch dark in the tunnel. Good thing for that red light or we'd be blind. I'll see if I can find them."

"Be careful!"

"The red light," I said. "I wonder where it's coming from?" I noticed a drop-off, like a ledge, where the light was strongest, so I crawled to the open side and peered over the edge. When I saw what had happened to the cave and where we were I could hardly believe it.

We hadn't fallen to the bottom of a deeper cave like I'd thought. If we'd fallen all the way to the bottom, we'd be dead. No, the entire ledge that we'd been standing on at the time of the quake had slid down and gotten stuck on a rock shelf that jutted out high above an enormous open cavern. The cavern itself must have been at least five or six football-fields long. Thousands of stalactites of varying lengths hung from the ceiling. On the floor below, a wide, flat rock butted up against one of the walls, almost like a stage. It even had a larger open area in front of it where an audience could gather. But, of course, it had no curtains or seats. The floor of the open area was soaking wet.

"I can see rocks and stuff down there that came from our cave," I said. "There's water everywhere, it's a mess. I guess sometimes nature makes a mess in order to get things cleaned up better, you know? Like a forest fire or a flood."

"I guess." Travis crawled up beside me. "See that big, roundish rock? That's makin' it all red. It sorta glows. It looks smooth, too, like the walls."

Jon returned to the ledge above us and called down. "The main tunnel caved in. I'm not going in without a light. I found Dr. Parrish's backpack with the rope. I'm coming down."

"No!" I was afraid the sound of my voice might cause another quake. "We won't be able to get back up!"

"Sure we will. Watch out."

I waited anxiously while Jon tied his end of the rope to something I couldn't see. Then he threw the other end below. I caught it and pulled on it several times. I even swung on it to test its strength. "It's good."

A moment later Jon scampered down the rope and joined us. When Travis went back to Chris, he found something under a pile of rubble.

"My hat!" He dug it out and tested the headlamp. It still worked, but it flickered again. He spotted something else. "Mr. Edward's backpack." He pulled it from the debris and dumped everything out. "A first aid kit! Water! And batteries!" He held up a pack of batteries and passed them to me. I replaced the batteries in my flashlight and right away the yellow beam turned bright white again.

In the first aid kit Travis took out seven rolls of tape. "This backpack has a metal frame."

I was confused. "It's aluminum. So?"

"So I need a splint."

I watched our little brother separate the nylon pack from the metal frame and toss the pack aside. He held up the frame. "This'll work. We've got plenty of tape."

"You sure about this splint?" said Jon.

"We can't move him without it."

"I don't think we're gonna move him as it is." Jon looked up the steep ledge. "He weighs more than we do. If it's just us, it might be impossible getting him up there. One of us should go for help."

"Not yet," I said, trying to take charge of my squeamishness. If I didn't get over my fears in a hurry I'd be utterly useless to everyone. Right now we all needed to be alert and ready to help. "Let's get this splint on before he wakes up. What do we need, Travis?"

"Something kinda soft to wrap around his leg. Jon, can you break the frame so we can splint his leg on both sides?"

"Let me see it." Jon took the frame and started twisting it. He fought with it for a while, until finally, it broke into several pieces. "How's this?"

"That'll work great!"

Meanwhile, I went through the available backpacks and brought out some extra clothes. Jon took my flashlight and shined it on Chris' broken leg as he videotaped it.

"Why are you doing that?" I asked.

"Because it's gross. Brandon would want to use it in a movie."

When Jon was done taping I passed his backpack to him and he carefully placed Brandon's camcorder inside it. I held up some clothes. "Travis, will these work?"

Travis nodded. "Yeah. Lift his leg, Jon, but be *real* careful."

Jon gently raised Chris' leg, doing his best to keep it immobile. Even so, Chris moaned softly. I stood to one side biting my lip while I watched. I was scared and grossed out. *You're amazing, Travis! Just amazing! I'm sorry I can't help you much.*

Travis looked up and smiled to let me know it was all right. He began groping around the point of the break, touching the leg itself and concentrating. As sickening as it was, I watched every move he made.

"Jon, pull his leg," said Travis. "I'll show you. Kelly, you have to hold his shoulders so he won't move."

"You going to set the bone?" asked Jon.

"Yeah. When I touch it I can feel how things need to go." Travis spoke like it was no big deal.

I wasn't so sure. "You can't set a break without X-rays."

"I can. Hold him tight. Pull, Jon. Straight away from his body."

I exchanged a disturbed glance with Jon and dug in my heels against a rough edge in the stone. I gripped Chris by the shoulders and held him fast. At the other end Jon had the ankle.

"He might yell," said Travis. "I would." Travis closed his eyes and repeatedly traced his fingertips over the broken area of Chris' leg. Then he instructed Jon on how to pull, turn, or twist the lower leg. "Ready? Pull."

Jon tugged, gently at first, but soon he was straining. Chris moaned loudly several times, but remained unconscious. I scrunched up my face. It was gross, but I couldn't look away. All at once the leg was straight again.

"It's set. Now the splint."

I helped wrap some of the clothes snugly around Chris' leg. I even tore off the tape needed to keep it all in place. Travis lined up two pieces of the broken pack frame with the injured leg and wrapped more tape around it.

While he worked I entered Chris' mind again and caught flashes of his returning thoughts. He seemed okay. Chris would wake up soon.

I got the camcorder from Jon's pack and recorded the rest of the first aid treatment on Chris. It took nearly a half hour to get the splint done right. When we were finished, Travis tested it. The leg was secure. Jon carefully lowered the leg back to the rock floor.

"That looks great," I said, studying the repair work. I took some more video shots of the splinted leg. "How could you do that?"

"I dunno." Travis shrugged. "I just could."

"I'll never make fun of the Cub Scouts again," said Jon.

"Listen, guys," I said. "We've either got to find Dr. Parrish and Mr. Edwards, or go get help ourselves. And we'd better save the lights before they burn out. Just use one at a time. The spare batteries won't last forever. Jon, you should go for help."

"I can't find my way out of this place. Do you know the way, Trav?"

"I think so," said Travis. "We can follow the little arrows."

"You and Kelly go, it'll be safer that way. I'll stay with Chris. You can take both flashlights, too, since we've got that red light down there. What's causing that?"

"It looks like some kind of big rock is glowing," I said. "The cave we're in now is humongous!"

"I want to see." Jon crept to the edge of the rock shelf.

"Be careful!" said Travis nervously. "We're on top of a ledge. If it breaks we're dead!"

I watched, holding my breath. "Have you guys ever heard of aftershocks?"

Travis shook his head. "What's that?"

"It's like extra tremors that come after an earthquake. If we have a few of those, it could really shake this place up."

Travis gulped. "We gotta get out of here."

Suddenly, Jon turned back, looking almost terrified. He pointed down, struggling to find the words. He kept his voice low.

"We're not alone."

Chapter 6

THE SALESMAN

KELLY

Travis and I crawled beside Jon as he pointed at the cavern floor. At first I didn't understand why Jon's voice sounded so shaky. Something had him rattled, but what? Then I noticed the floor was moving. Only it wasn't the floor. In the audience area in front of the stage were hundreds—no, *thousands*—of creatures. They gathered in growing numbers like it was some kind of town meeting. As I studied them I got goose bumps. Those things were the stuff of nightmares.

The creatures definitely weren't human, but they weren't exactly animals, either. Most of them had one head, two arms and two legs like people. But there were plenty with extra limbs and extra heads. A few of them even had tentacles, claws, or long feelers, like a lobster or a cockroach. Their skin was scaly, slimy, or covered with spines, and some looked hairy. Most of them appeared to be man-sized and their most striking characteristic was color. Each showed colors ranging from deep red, to gray, to green, to dark blue. A few were gold, and some were multi-colored, but usually not in any recognizable pattern.

I passed the camcorder to Jon. After he checked it over, he gave it to Travis.

"We've only got an hour left on the battery," he whispered. "And I don't know where the other battery is. Get everything you can."

"Get what?" asked Travis. "What do you want me to do?"

"Record what's down there. Maybe we can sell the video to TV news stations. You don't usually see something like this in a cave."

"Something like what?" I asked. He offered a slight shrug for an answer.

Travis blinked in understanding. "What're *you* gonna do?"

"I'm gonna watch."

Travis steadied the camcorder against the rock and began taping the mysterious scene below. The viewfinder was small and the three of us huddled close together in order to see it.

"Zoom in," said Jon. "It's that button."

Travis pressed the zoom button. The picture in the viewfinder greatly enlarged, but now he had to work to keep it from shaking. He eventually brought the creatures on the cavern floor into focus.

"What are they?" said Jon in a low, quivering voice. His eyes were wide with doubt. It was one of the few times I'd ever known him to be truly afraid.

"Whatever they are," I said. "I don't think it would be good for us if they knew we were here."

Jon nodded. "You got that right. Keep it at a whisper."

Behind us, Chris moaned loudly. We looked back in horror. He moaned again, even louder. I quickly crawled beside him. Travis continued recording the amazing scene below.

"Chris," I said in a low voice. "How do you feel?"

Chris blinked his eyes open. "Everything's all red. Am I in Hell?"

I glanced over my shoulder and patted him gently on the arm. "You might be. And your leg is broken. Travis put a splint on it."

"That would explain the fiery pain. *Travis* did the splint? You kids amaze me. How is everyone?"

"Jon, Travis and I are fine. But we haven't found Mr. Edwards or Dr. Parrish."

"You've got to find them. Anton knows the way out."

"We'll find them. Just be quiet, okay? Something's down there. Something dangerous."

"What are you talking about?"

"Just be still."

A collective roar went up from the creatures below, as if they were cheering about something. Chris grabbed my arm, terrified. I touched my index finger to my lips.

"Shhh. Not a word. We're right over here." I crawled back beside Jon and watched.

A giant beast, scarlet colored with wide, great wings, stomped across the stage. Its footsteps echoed through the cavern like the booming of a bass drum. The beast fanned its wings and folded them behind its back, sort of like a butterfly at rest. But this was no butterfly.

Demons! I thought to Travis. Travis nodded. The camcorder shook. He used both hands to steady it.

Jon looked up suddenly. "Did you hear that? Somebody said demons!"

I shushed him. "What else could they be?"

"That big one must be the boss!" said Travis. "He's huge!"

The Boss Demon stood well over twenty feet tall with long, powerful arms and hands the size of tractor tires. One massive hand carried a long wooden staff as thick as a telephone pole, the top end sharpened to a ghastly point. The beast stood on two enormously muscled, deep-red legs with long ebony claws in place of toes. Its belly was covered in grayish scales. Its massive, ugly head had one long, horn growing out of the center.

I fought to keep my shaking to a minimum.

The Boss stopped in the middle of the stage. He looked out across the screaming, cheering hoard and raised the staff, which he pounded on the stone floor three times. *Boom! Boom! Boom!* The creatures before the stage grew quiet. The Boss spoke.

"Affkd gkdnki!! Gityyhlls asinfoihen!!" His voice was powerful, like the diesel engine on a tractor-trailer truck, but *much* deeper. And he wasn't speaking any language I'd ever heard. In fact, the words were so garbled that it hardly sounded like language at all. But it must have made sense because every time the Boss paused, the other creatures cheered. Then the Boss waved a hand as if presenting something on the right side of the stage. It seemed like an introduction.

Travis sent a mental message to me. *What are they thinking?*

I don't know, we're too far away. Either that or I can't read them.

Next came the greatest shock of all. A man—a human!—walked out on the stage. He was tall with dark hair, wearing a dark blue suit with a red necktie, and really handsome, like a movie star. The Man carried a white clipboard in one hand and a strange-looking object, like a silver fire hydrant, in the other. He stopped in the middle of the stage beside the Demon Boss. He set the silver thing down, turned and faced the grisly audience.

The demons in the audience glared at him, like deer staring at the headlights of a car. I wasn't sure if they were surprised to see a human among them, or if they just didn't know what he was. Next, they traded disbelieving looks. Some shook their heads. Others scowled. They waved their long claws in the air or shook angry, scaly fists at the Man.

A six-legged demon with two ugly, spine-covered heads climbed on-stage. It rushed toward the man with claws and teeth bared. The other demons cheered it on.

He's going to be sacrificed! I cried inside Travis' head. I didn't want to see the poor guy be torn to shreds by the monsters, but I'm human, and when there's going to be blood, humans just watch. I stayed out of his head, too. No need to get caught up in the middle of somebody's gory death.

Remarkably, the man watched the charging beast with nerves of cold steel. He never flinched. It was going to be a bloody massacre. I mean, what were the options?

Quick as a snake the Demon Boss swung the heavy staff. It cracked the charging beast in one of its skulls. The beast fell off to the side, away from the Man. Then the Boss kicked it offstage like a soccer ball, out into the audience. It crashed into several other creatures and lay on the floor, rubbing its head with one of its feet.

The Boss pounded the staff on the floor three more times. *Boom! Boom! Boom!* "Knnsylk!!" The place went completely quiet.

"Knnsylk," I repeated. "That must mean shut up." Jon shook his head at me. He knew I had a fascination with languages, though the only one I'd ever taken was intro French last year in the seventh grade.

The man stepped forward to the edge of the stage. From his coat pocket he withdrew a small device, which could have been a tiny microphone. He attached the device to his coat lapel and smiled with perfect, white teeth. He cleared his throat and jerked his head from right to left, cracking his neck. When he spoke, his voice echoed throughout the cavern in a proper British accent.

"I know you can all understand me, so to make it easier for me to understand you, I want you to eat the sugar cube you were given when you came in. Each cube has inside it an XB7 universal translating chip. Now don't wreck it by chewing it. Let the cube melt in your mouth. It's quite tasty."

The demons on the floor growled and yelled. But the Boss raised one hand high above his head. Between two thick red fingers he held a tiny, white sugar cube. The place grew silent again. A moment later, all the creatures on the floor raised up their own sugar cubes. Travis panned the camera to take in every creature in the underground room. The Boss dropped the cube into his mouth and waited. He made a face and nodded agreeably. The floor demons looked at each other, then reluctantly followed their leader's example. Except for slurping sounds made as the sugar cubes melted in their mouths, the room was silent. The demons all nodded to each other approvingly. Travis licked his lips and looked back at me.

We haven't ate since breakfast! he thought to me.

Eaten, I returned. Apparently the foster families he'd stayed with hadn't thought good grammar was important. I tried to correct him when he needed it most, but not too often.

"Give it another ten seconds," said the Man, checking his wristwatch as he counted silently. "There. Now speak."

"What do yer want us ta say?" shouted a Gray Demon with nine eyes.

"Yeah, what's the big deal?" called a Blue Demon with two horns in its head and an extra arm.

Travis and I looked at each other in total shock.

"Are you picking up sound?" asked Jon. Travis nodded. "Good. Don't miss *any* of this, Trav. This is good stuff." Jon shook his head. "I hate to say it, kids, but I think we're in deep doodoo."

The demons were still upset about the way their fellow had been treated by the Boss. Apparently, it wasn't in good taste to help a human.

"Why'd you defend 'im, Boss?" cried a Multi-colored Demon with long tusks and seven horns in its head. "We should be cookin' that one! He looks tasty enough!" That got some laughs, but most of the other demons were still mad.

A Green Demon up front pointed one of its tentacles at the Man and got personal. "Yer a human! Why shouldn't I rip out yer heart and eat it in front of ya? What's to stop me?"

"I say slap 'im in irons!" cried a husky, Blue Demon with three noses. "We need more slaves! After all, who's gonna brush my teeth?" The Blue Demon grinned horribly. Its enormous mouth was full of sharp, yellow teeth. "I say get 'im!"

"Yeah! Get 'im!"

Maybe demons had really short memories. Or maybe they just didn't get it. They *still* wanted to attack the man. I guess demons were like some people. They didn't learn something unless they learned it the hard way.

After much prodding and shouting, the Green Demon gathered its nerve. It climbed onto the stage and raced toward the man, tentacles flapping. The Boss scowled and raised the staff again. But this time the man signaled to the Boss to stand down. The Boss lowered his staff and leaned on it, apparently content to enjoy the show.

Unruffled, the man watched the attacker. When the Green Demon was a few feet away, the man finally did something. He raised one finger and pointed at the demon. The charging demon froze in mid-stride. I couldn't believe it. It was like watching some kind of stop action in a movie!

The Green Demon struggled vainly against whatever invisible force the man wielded. But the only thing it could move was its head. It looked at its comrades in the audience, helpless and rather embarrassed.

Travis mind-spoke to me. *What's goin' on?*

I have no idea.

The man dropped his nice-guy attitude. He threw the clipboard hard on the floor. It landed with an echoing *SPLACK*, which got their complete attention. Then he marched to the front edge of the stage and looked down on the demon hoard just below him. He'd clearly had enough.

"Go ahead, all of you. Attack me! See if I care. Rest assured, just like this fellow here, not one of you will even touch me! But if that happens, I will take away from you the most exciting bargain of the millennia!" I could feel the power of his voice reverberating throughout the cavern. The demons held onto their anger. The man looked them over. He frowned. "Forget it! You don't deserve this offer! Good day!"

He turned and marched off the stage, leaving the silver fire hydrant.

Suddenly, the Green Demon was able to move again. It looked around, feeling foolish. Then it leaped back into the audience.

The Boss got very upset. "You fools! Listen to him or I'll lop off your foul heads and put them in my soup!" The Boss hurried after the man, returning a moment later. He beckoned the man to come out and try again. If it hadn't been so terrifying, I might have laughed. That giant demon acted like a humble servant to the much smaller human. The Boss made a threatening gesture at the audience, then stepped aside.

"Listen to him!"

The man stood before the horrific mob, confident and now in control. "I'm here with a serious business proposition and I will *not* be disrespected again. I represent a business group called The Concern and I'm going to offer you something you haven't had for a very long time."

Jon shook his head. "That guy acts like a salesman!"

Travis wasn't worried about job descriptions. He was more concerned about the danger. "Jon, we gotta to get outta here! They're gonna to see us, an' you know what they'll do to us."

"You're right," said Jon. "Keep taping, don't miss a second. Come on, Kelly, let's see what we can do about Chris." We crawled back to Chris, while Travis taped. We were only a few feet away, but I didn't like leaving Travis alone on that ledge.

Jon looked over the splint and nodded. "It's a good splint, Chris. Do you think you can climb if we help you?"

"No," said Chris. "I've never climbed before. My head is busting and the pain in my leg is really bad. I'm afraid I'll yell, or something."

"That wouldn't be good with those things down there," I said.

"What are those things?" he asked. "I don't understand what's going on?"

"Neither do we, Chris. It looks like some guy is trying to sell them something."

"A guy? Who's he trying to sell to at the bottom of a cave? What's he selling?"

Jon looked at me gravely. "I don't know, but Travis is taping it all. We'll figure it out later. What do you weigh, Chris? One-sixty?"

"One-seventy-five. Are you thinking of pulling me up with the rope?"

"I doubt I'm strong enough, even with Kelly's help. I weigh ten pounds less than you. If we had a pulley we could get you up, but then we'd need a lot more rope."

"Find Mark," said Chris. "He could pull me up by himself. The man's a bull."

"That's just it. We don't know where he is."

At first I was curious about what Jon had planned for Chris. But the Salesman became louder and more animated. I crawled back beside Travis who was still taping.

"You are Demon Nation! You are mighty! But when was the last time you stayed on the surface in your own bodies? A thousand years ago? Ten thousand years?"

The Green Demon called out. "Ever since the frickin' sun popped up! Forever!"

Other demons agreed. "Yeah, forever!"

"Yes," said the Salesman. "The sun. Your dire enemies, the humans, stay on the surface while you remain trapped down here in these caves.

And it's all because of the sun. The sun is your nemesis. If you take my offer and do everything you're supposed to, in a very short time the surface will be yours. And humans will live in the caves!"

The applause was deafening. But the Green Demon wasn't completely sold.

"What's the timetable on this, eh? Another thousand years? Maybe two thousand? 'Ow do we know it's worth our effort?"

I heard a low growl and even without looking I knew it was the Boss. The Salesman spoke.

"A good question, your Lordship. You have a smart, young demon there."

The Green Demon stood up taller. It stuck out its chest proudly. Some of the other demons patted it on the back. The Salesman was winning them over.

"I'm here to make it happen with a timetable you can live with. For thirteen of you, it will happen very soon. And if those thirteen do their jobs on schedule, your Demon Nation will rule the surface in less than sixty moons."

A low murmur spread through the ranks. Sixty moons. Barely five more years!

"But what about the sun?" called out a Gray Demon. "We can't live on the surface with that hangin' over our heads."

The Salesman smiled. He paused dramatically. "My friends, listen to my promise. The surface will be yours again, dark and filthy, just the way you like it. If humans survive at all, they will be entirely underground."

The cheering was explosive, it made my ears throb. I looked up, expecting the heavy sound to bring the ceiling down on all of us. The creatures shouted in unison, "Demon Nation! Demon Nation! Demon Nation!"

Through it all Travis kept recording. This was incredible. That man—a human!—was offering evil demons a chance to overthrow mankind! I decided the tape had to be shown to the police as soon as possible.

"Kelly," Chris whispered as loud as he dared. "Are they terrorists?"

"They're monsters, Chris! I'm not kidding, either. They're monsters, like demons. All except for that salesman guy. He looks like us."

"Maybe he can help us get out?"

"I don't think he's on our side."

A forceful, loud noise erupted from our left, like a huge sheet of canvas flapping in a stiff wind. I looked. Two great winged demons flew down from the ceiling not far away. They descended toward the stage area carrying something between them. Whatever they carried must have been alive because it put up quite a struggle. Travis followed the flying demons with the camcorder. They dropped their burden on the stage near the Boss. It was a man. One demon bowed and presented it to its leader.

"We found it up top, your Lordship. It must have been trapped in the quake."

Travis gasped when he finally saw the man's face through the viewfinder.

"They got Mr. Edwards!" he said.

Jon and I raced to his side.

"Who has Anton?" said Chris. "Who?"

We turned and shushed him. Travis adjusted the camcorder so the three of us could better see what was going on.

Anton stood up slowly, looking at the Salesman in wonder. He was about to speak when he apparently realized something quite large was beside him. He spun quickly. His gaze traveled slowly from the Boss' huge clawed feet, upward to his massive head. The Boss grinned at him. Anton gawked in terror. He shook his head in disbelief.

"No!" he said, just loud enough for us to hear. "It can't be."

"Oh, but it *can*," said the Boss. The great demon leaned over toward Anton, as if to share a secret. Then he shouted, "BOO!"

Anton scrambled close to the Salesman. He looked from the Salesman to the Boss, confused and in shock. He heard mocking laughter from offstage. He turned again, very slowly, terrified at what he might see. When he faced the hordes of demons, he dropped to his knees.

"I must be dreaming."

"Your absolute worst nightmare," said the Salesman.

Anton pleaded with the Salesman. "Help, me, sir! Please, in the name of God!"

The instant he said God demons from the audience erupted in angry growls and threats. They started throwing rocks at him. Two larger ones near the front got in each other's way trying to climb onto the stage. They wanted to get to Anton, but they got into a fistfight instead. The Salesman was amused and clearly saw an opportunity to close the deal.

"I wouldn't use that word in here if I were you. And I certainly am *not* going to help you. These are my business associates and your timely arrival has made it possible to move on to the first step of our agreement."

With that, we watched the winged demons fly back up to their perch in the ceiling. They were completely out of sight.

They've got us outflanked, I thought to Travis. *But I don't think they can see us.*

Jon drew back from the monitor with a determined look in his eyes. "You two are getting out of here, *now*. Put everything in two backpacks. Haul it all with you. We don't want those things to know we were even here. I'll stay with Chris. Trav leads, he can find his way no matter where he is. Be careful. The cave-in changed the tunnel."

Chris looked up at us. "You guys go. You too, Jon. If you can send back help, do it, but don't worry about me. Just get out of here now!"

Jon shook his head. "I'm not leaving you behind."

"You have to!"

While they argued, Travis kept taping, but I knew he listened more to the discussion behind him than what was going on below. Jon was right. We had to get out of there as soon as possible, or we'd be the next ones down on that stage beside Anton Edwards. I wanted to see if Anton was still alive, but I hesitated. What if there were parts of Anton all over the stage area? Well, he hadn't screamed yet. I bit my lip and looked over the ledge. Anton was still there, but he stood like a statue, glaring at the demons in the crowd like he wasn't afraid of them anymore. The Salesman continued.

"Now, your Lordship, allow me to give you one more gift." The Salesman held out his empty hands, both palms up. A second later a long knife in a jeweled scabbard appeared in them. It was a magnificent weapon. The Salesman passed it over to the Boss. "It will destroy anything it is used against. You will need it in the fight to reclaim the surface."

The Boss gripped the hilt of the knife, withdrawing the short blade. He looked at the Salesman, puzzled.

"Am I supposed to reclaim the surface with a fancy little knife?"

"It's adjustable," said the Salesman. He touched one of the jewels on the side of the hilt. The blade became longer from within itself, like a telescope. In seconds it was a very long sword. *Very* long. The Salesman winked at the Boss. "The length of the blade automatically matches up to your height and great strength. It will cut through anything, like slicing hot butter."

The Boss grinned horribly and pushed the jewel again. The blade shortened to dagger length.

"A real piece of work," said the Boss, placing the dagger back into the scabbard. "Yes! We'll be ready to fight. But before we seal the agreement, answer me one question, human. Why are you doing this to your own kind? What do *you* get out of it?"

The Salesman adjusted his necktie and interlaced his fingers in front of him. His voice was somber, almost dreamy. "I get exactly what I want from this agreement. A magnificent retirement bonus, corporate stock options and a ten-percent commission based on long term profits. Besides, I know a winning team when I see one!"

Both the Salesman and the Boss spit on their palms and shook hands. The agreement was sealed.

Chapter 7
FLYING DEMONS

KELLY

We watched Jon scamper up the rope like a spider. When he got to the top, he called back down in a loud whisper. "Come on, I've got you."

I nodded, but knelt beside Chris first. "I'm so sorry we have to leave you, but Jon will take care of you. We'll get help as fast as we can."

"I know you will," said Chris. "I wish Jon would go with you. I want you kids to be safe."

"I love you." Sometimes when your life is in danger your feelings become clear. I really wanted Chris to be our next father, the permanent kind, so I gave him a big hug. Chris lit up, surprised. His eyes got a bit teary as he swelled with happiness. Travis smiled. The love Chris felt for each of us was genuine, just like Angie. I knew Travis had never experienced that before, except when he was too young to remember. Chris hugged me back and patted my shoulder.

"I love you, too, girl. Now get going."

Travis turned off the camcorder and dropped it into Jon's pack. He went over to Chris. "We'll be back. An' we'll bring the whole army with us."

"That'll be *great*, Travis. Just please be careful." I felt bad for Chris. If his leg hadn't gotten broken he'd be leaving now, too. So would Jon.

I tied a sturdy loop in the end of the rope. I tested it, then told Travis to go up first. "Jon might need your help pulling me up. I don't think I can climb the rope the way he did. Hurry!"

Travis put on his hardhat, making extra sure the headlamp was turned off so he wouldn't attract any unwanted attention from the local inhabitants. He tightened the strap snugly under his chin and shook his head. The hardhat must have felt good, so he spit on his hands and started up the rope. Near the top Jon grabbed his shirt and lifted him onto the new ledge.

Travis glanced below. Chris and I must have looked small and dark.

We were lucky, he thought to me from way up there.

I scanned the ceiling searching for any demons that might be lurking in the higher shadows. It looked clear. Jon waved to me. I nodded and looked back at Chris. He bit his lip and spoke encouragingly. "You can do it, Kelly!"

To my surprise it took me less than a minute to reach the top. Jon and Travis both helped me up.

"Sorry I was an ass," said Jon, rubbing Travis' hair. "I get how you feel about Chris and Angie. Call them mom and dad, if you want."

"It's not like you could stop me," said Travis boldly. "I'd kick your butt."

Jon grinned big. "That's why I changed my mind. I didn't want to get hurt."

We laughed, then hugged each other.

"The camcorder's in your pack," Travis told Jon. "There's still ten minutes on the battery."

"Thanks, Trav. Both of you hurry, but be super careful. Parts of the tunnel might not look the same. Where's your flashlight, Kelly?"

"Here." I pulled the light out of my jacket pocket and shined it at the tunnel. Large rocks and loose gravel partially blocked the way, but the window to the sliding board rock was still open. "I have extra batteries, too."

"I'll go down and tie your backpacks to the rope. If for some reason the rescue team doesn't find us, the camcorder is in my backpack under the rocks where Trav found his hardhat."

"Don't say that, Jon!" Travis was almost in tears. "You'd better be here!"

Jon smiled bravely. "No problem, little brother. Just make sure whoever comes after us is well-armed, okay? Remember, Trav, you da man!"

"That's what I'm talking about!" said Travis, sounding more positive than I knew he felt.

I hugged Jon again, very hard. "If those things find you...I can't think about it. How can you protect yourself and Chris? You don't have any swords here."

Jon reached behind his neck and whipped out the two Elvish blades. He twirled them once and carefully slid them back into the sheaths under his shirt. "I almost always have a sword."

I couldn't believe it. "You brought swords into a *cave*? You're obsessive! Why would you do that?"

"In case I needed them." He dropped the rope back down the wall and started over the edge. "I'll send up your packs."

"You'd better be careful," Travis told him.

"You, too." Jon dropped out of sight. Travis turned on his headlamp and studied the tunnel. It was a mess of crumbled stone.

"Can you get us out?" I asked, not feeling very sure of myself.

He nodded slightly. "Sure. We'll be outta here in no time."

JON

Back on the ledge with Chris, Jon got his own backpack and took out the camcorder. He found a black trash bag in his pack and wrapped the camcorder inside it for protection. Then he slid the camcorder into a side pocket on Kelly's Barbie pack and zipped it shut. He tied her pack and Travis' pack to the rope.

"Good idea, sending the camcorder," said Chris. "Nobody will believe there are monsters down here without proof."

"That's what I figured." Jon yanked on the rope and signaled for Kelly to pull it up. The backpacks rose slowly up the wall.

"Jon, I want you to know how sorry I am." Chris hung his head. "I never meant for any of this to happen. Caving was supposed to be fun, you know?"

Jon bent down beside the older man and put a hand on his shoulder. "It's not like you planned an earthquake, Chris. We'll be okay. Travis will find his way and send help soon."

KELLY

At the mouth of the tunnel I untied the packs and tossed the rope back down. We put on our backpacks and started into the tunnel.

"Maybe we should try to get Chris up here before we go," said Travis. "The three of us might be able to pull him."

"Don't you think Jon would have tried it already? The best thing we can do is get help fast."

Suddenly, I heard the flapping sound again. We turned. One of the flying demons swooped down and landed on the ledge. Its hideous orange eyes lit up hungrily when it saw us. Travis looked at me and I knew why. I was frozen in fear. My mouth and eyes were wide open but I couldn't move. Dammit! Why'd I have to be such a wimp? The demon flashed a big, toothy grin and rushed at us.

"Go!" Travis pushed me ahead of him. "Hurry!"

I blinked, then came alive. Turning on the flashlight, I hopped over a broken stalagmite and took off running. I headed for a narrow gap where the ceiling had collapsed against the wall. Travis was a step behind me. The space looked tight. Could we even fit through it?

I glanced back. The demon was right there! "RUN!"

The demon lunged forward, claws wide. It caught Travis' backpack and jerked him off his feet. He landed hard on the stone floor with the wind knocked out of him. The creature dragged him back toward the tunnel opening.

Travis gasped for air. At the same time he groped about for something—anything. His hand caught a loose rock. He tossed it blindly over his head at the demon. The rock bounced harmlessly off one of its wings. The demon laughed and dragged him further. Travis looked ahead. The ledge was only a few meters away. Then his shoulder struck something solid. The broken stalagmite! He grabbed it and held on with all his strength.

"Let go of the pack!" I cried.

"No! It's new!"

I scooped up a rock and threw it at the demon. I threw it *hard*. It struck the demon over the eye, cutting its slimy, blue skin. A rivulet of black blood trickled down.

The demon shook its head angrily. I covered my mouth in surprise.

"I'll rip off his legs for that!" said the demon fiercely. It pulled Travis even harder. Travis' hands were slipping.

"It's just a backpack, you moron! Let it go!"

The demon spit on its hands and re-gripped the pack. "Yer comin' with *me*!" It shifted its full weight and gave a mighty pull.

At that instant Travis let go of the stalagmite and raised his arms straight over his head. The backpack slipped away without resistance. The demon was taken by surprise. It back-peddled off balance and slammed into a wall near the ledge. It collapsed there dazed.

Travis got up in a panic. He looked back. The demon's down time was short. It tossed the backpack aside and charged again. We raced for the window to the sliding board rock and I dove straight through it. Travis must have done the same thing. He was so close he crashed into me on the level side of the gap. We tumbled together in a tangled heap of arms and legs. My flashlight struck the wall and went dim. Travis looked up. The demon was coming fast. We were trapped!

The demon started into the gap. Half way through its great, leathery wings became jammed against the walls. It stopped cold. It growled and shook its ugly head, still trying to get to us. Travis looked around for another rock to throw at it. I caught his sleeve and pulled him along. Then my flashlight went out. I shook it and tapped it against the wall. It was completely dead.

"Turn on your light!" I said. "Get us out of here!"

Travis felt around for the switch. The headlamp finally came on, flickering. The demon was gone.

"Come on!" Travis took the lead. He slid down the sliding board rock, landing at the bottom of the slide. I slid down a moment later.

"I couldn't read its mind!" I said, catching the knotted rope that was still there. "I tried, but I just didn't get anything."

"Maybe there's nothin' to get," said Travis. "Or maybe it's better if you don't know what a demon's thinking. Whutta we do with the rope?"

"Leave it. The rescuers can use it."

"Come on. The stream's this way." The thought of crawling through the water again didn't thrill me, but we had to get out. If we didn't get a rescue team back in there soon enough, Jon and Chris could be lost forever. Time was against us.

Several turns and rises later we heard the trickling of water. Then Travis' headlamp went out. When he smacked the hardhat it came back on, but kept flickering and got very dim.

Originally, we had crawled through the stream because it was the only way to get past the rock arch. But the earthquake had caused the arch to collapse. Now all we had to do was climb over a short wall instead. It was way better than getting wet again.

"That's what I'm talkin' about!" said Travis.

In another tunnel we came to a familiar sharp turn. Travis knew exactly where we were. "We'll be out in twenty minutes!" He'd barely said the words when his headlamp went out again. This time it stayed out.

"We can still make it," he said, inching forward. "I remember the way." Travis crept along very slowly. Sure, he knew the way, but at this pace, we'd never get a rescue team in time.

"Wait!" I said. "We've got matches and candles!" I threw off my backpack and fumbled around in the dark. I opened a plastic bag and groped about inside it. Then I lit a match. The tiny light flared up and seemed to illuminate that whole part of the cave. I lit two candles and gave one to Travis. There's a lot of beauty in the world, but I can say without a doubt that nothing is quite as gorgeous as a candle's glow when you've been standing in a dark cave for several long minutes.

"Mr. Edwards had us prepared, even if we didn't know it," I said. "I never thought a candle could be so bright."

"Yeah," said Travis. "It's kinda hard to see, though, light's in my eyes." We experimented, trying to find the best way to hold a candle and walk.

"Hold it high. That works."

We traveled the next ten minutes in silence. Since Travis knew the way out, our biggest concern seemed to be keeping the melting wax out of our face. Some of it ran over our bare hands. It burned a little, but it wasn't that bad. As we rounded a long turn, a strong breeze blew past us. The candles fluttered and went out. Once again we were in total darkness.

"Hold on," I said, reaching into my pocket. I lit another match. I was about to re-light my candle, when I looked up. Just then something moved behind Travis. A large, cold hand clamped over his mouth. Another breeze blew out the match. We were caught in the dark.

Chapter 8
CAPTURE

JON

Jon heard the flapping and looked up just as the flying demon entered the tunnel. The other demon dropped from the ceiling and glided off in a wide arc around the cavern, scanning the area for more humans. Jon crawled over to Chris.

Chris had seen them, too. His eyes were wide with fear. "You guys weren't kidding about monsters! One of them went after the kids! What can we do?"

Chris had always seemed a little high-strung and there was no need to upset him. Jon kept calm, but he never took his gaze off the ledge above them. "The wings on that thing are huge. It can't go far into the tunnel. As long as Kelly and Trav see it in time, they'll get away."

"But it knows they're there! It'll call the others."

"They're all in the bottom of the cavern. Without some serious short-cuts, they'll never catch up to them."

Even as Jon spoke, dust and rock chips rained over them. They covered their heads and looked up. The winged demon was perched at the edge of the tunnel, searching the cavern.

Jon whispered, "Don't move." He gripped the hilts of his knives, but left them in the sheaths under his shirt.

The demon jumped. It dove straight at them. Then it glided away, following the same flight path the other one had taken. Jon and Chris both let out a sigh of relief.

"Do you think it saw them?" said Chris.

"It was empty-handed. I'm hoping it didn't see *us*."

They sat silently for a while, listening for more demons flying about. The area appeared clear. Chris spoke.

"I'm not trying to replace your father, you know. Even if you let me, I wouldn't allow it. Nothing is more special than your parents and you need to remember them your whole life."

Jon was embarrassed. He liked Chris. He didn't want to hurt him. "Sorry. I keep forgetting Trav hardly knew our parents. He hasn't got all the memories I do, no matter how many stories I tell him. I overreacted. It's not personal."

"I don't have a problem with that," said Chris. "I just want us to be friends."

"Friends? Let's get something straight, Chris. You and Angie are the best thing that's happened to us since mom and dad died. I don't *ever* want to lose it. Kelly and Trav feel even stronger. We're way more than friends."

Chris' eyes got a little bleary. "Thank you. I hope we can make it work."

"We already have."

Chris grabbed Jon by the scar on his forearm. "Jon, I really want you to go before it's too late. Don't worry about me. Just please tell Angie I love her."

Jon chuckled. "I'm not going anywhere unless it's to get you up that wall."

"No, Jon, listen to me. Kelly and Travis need you. It's crazy for you to stay here with me. If those things come back…."

"If those things come back we'll kick their butts right off the ledge."

Chris looked incredibly relieved. "I'm glad you're here." He glanced up. "Anton!" Jon turned. Sure enough, Anton was up there looking down at them. He waved.

"You got away!" said Jon in a whisper. "Yes!"

"I got rescue equipment!" said Anton in a harsh whisper. "But I can't bring it in by myself. Can you help?"

Jon looked to Chris for the answer. Chris nodded fervently.

"Yes! Yes! Go, Jon! I'll be fine."

Jon's gaze went back to Anton. "I wonder how he got away?" He shook it off. "We'll be right back. Do you want one of my knives?"

Chris shook his head. "I'd probably cut off my own arm. Go!"

Jon climbed the rope in a hurry. He met Anton at the top of the cliff and shook hands vigorously. "It's great to see you!" he said. "We thought those things were gonna kill you!"

"So did I when they started arguing about who would eat my legs. A couple of them got into a fight, so I ran and they never even noticed. Come on, it's this way. We need to hurry. I have much work to do. I must work hard and fast."

"We'll both work. Lead the way!"

Anton led them past a bend in the tunnel. Jon spotted one of the chalk marks near the floor. He caught Anton by the arm.

"Isn't that the way out?" He pointed in the other direction.

"I know a shortcut," said Anton.

"Oh, yeah, you said that on the way in. Go ahead."

Anton led them downward on a slick, irregular path. He glanced over his shoulder and nodded confidently at Jon.

"This way is much shorter," he said. "Much shorter. It will take us right where we want to go."

CHRIS

Chris lay on the broken ledge and tried to ignore the throbbing in his leg and head. He had far more pressing issues to worry about than a little pain. Okay, it was a *lot* of pain. But his greatest problem, as he saw it, was staying out of sight until Jon and Anton got back. If those flying demons found him first…well, there wouldn't be enough of him left to put on a stretcher. He got an idea.

Wincing in agony, he dragged himself close to the cave wall. Along the way he gathered all the loose rocks he could carry or push ahead of him. Then he piled the rocks in a line beside him from his head to his feet. When he was done, he nestled in between the line of rocks and the wall. There. Now he was hidden, except from above. He nodded approvingly and checked his watch.

"Ten after ten," he muttered to himself.

Chris tried to feel brave, but it didn't seem to be working. He was sweating more than usual and his hands shook. His breathing was labored and he kept thinking he heard scratching sounds from below the ledge. He sat up fearfully and looked around. Either the noises stopped or his imagination was working overtime.

This was ridiculous. Nobody could climb up that way.

He thought about nine-year-old Travis putting the splint on his leg. It's a good thing he'd been unconscious. He probably would have screamed like a baby. Those kids were really amazing. Each one had some incredible talent, or skill. They were great kids and after only a few weeks his love for them had grown. And that's what it was, he suddenly realized. Love. He'd hardly known them for any time at all. He hoped they got out okay.

He thought about Angie and became sad. He realized he might never see her again. "I love you, Angie," he muttered softly. "Whatever happens to me, I'll always love you."

He gazed up the steep wall beside him. How in the world were they going to get him up there? Were they going to carry him all the way out of the cave? That would be so hard. He felt guilty just thinking about it.

If he ever got out of this place he'd have quite a story to tell in school. But who'd believe all the demon stuff? Then he remembered. The kids videotaped it. He nodded, satisfied. Somebody might believe him after all. And that videotape could be worth plenty of money! Maybe it could pay for Jon's college tuition in a few years.

A tall shadow rose on the wall beside him. At first Chris thought it might be Jon, but the shadow wasn't being cast from above. It came from behind him on the ledge. His heart nearly stopped beating. Another shadow appeared. And another. Chris' blood ran cold in his veins. He swallowed hard. How could anyone—or anything—climb up that way? Please be Jon or Anton! He turned slowly.

Through a tiny gap between some of the rocks in his hiding place, he saw three horrid looking demons standing a few feet away. They stared up the cliff with more hate than he could imagine in his worst nightmare. A gold demon with seven eyes let out a low, sinister chuckle.

"They went that way," it said, blinking all of its eyes. "The Boss says we need twelve more. At this rate we'll meet our quota by the end of the week!"

Six more demons reached the ledge, but none of them saw Chris. They climbed up the wall toward the tunnel. Chris watched them, amazed. They were as skilled and nimble as houseflies. Then he realized where they were going. His mouth became dry, like sandpaper. The demons were going after Kelly and Travis.

No! The kids had to be kept safe, no matter what happened to him. At that moment Chris did the bravest thing he'd ever done in his life. Though Kelly and Travis were most likely too far away to hear, he yelled as loud as he could.

"RUN, KELLY! RUN, TRAVIS! DON'T COME BACK! RUN FOR YOUR LIVES!"

The demons jumped back and gawked at him. They couldn't believe a human had been right in their grasp and they hadn't even noticed him. The Gold demon dropped down from the wall. It clamped a slimy hand over Chris' mouth. Chris struggled against the powerful grip. A shorter Green Demon came up and cracked him over the head with a long club. For Chris, it was lights out.

Chapter 9
BATTLE TO THE DEATH

JON

Anton led the way on a narrow path that spiraled downward along the cavern wall. Jon followed, but he kept a wary eye on the floor below. Each step took them closer to the stage area where the demons had met. If any demons were in the area, he didn't see them, but an uneasy feeling in his gut told him they were still around. So where was Anton's shortcut to the outside? Where was his rescue equipment?

Jon periodically glanced up at the ledge to check on Chris. But this far down he couldn't see much. Anton picked up the pace, practically jogging down the path. Jon reluctantly stayed with him, step for step. Every so often he touched one of the knives under his shirt for reassurance.

"RUN, KELLY! RUN, TRAVIS! DON'T COME BACK! RUN FOR YOUR LIVES!"

The words echoed through the cavern loud enough for every demon in town to hear. Jon stopped in his tracks. He looked up at the ledge again.

Anton turned, his eyes gleaming. "What's wrong?"

"Chris is in trouble!" Jon started running back up the path.

"I heard. There's nothing you can do. Not a thing."

Something about the tone in Anton's voice made Jon hesitate. He stopped running. That didn't sound like the Anton Edwards he'd known *before* the quake.

Anton gestured for him to follow. "It'll be easier if you come voluntarily."

"*What'll* be easier?"

Anton smiled. "Your execution, of course."

Jon's eyes narrowed. "Forget that." He sprinted up the path. Suddenly, the dark places in front of him came to life. Four large demons stepped out of shadows that had clearly been too small to conceal them. Each demon was a different color and type. But they all had something in common—long claws and sharp teeth!

Jon slid to a halt. He looked back. Four more demons appeared behind him. It was a trap. Had Anton been compromised? No, it must have been something else.

Jon turned. "You're not Mr. Edwards."

Anton grinned. "It doesn't really matter now, does it?" He started laughing.

Jon remained unruffled. The look in his eyes was cold and deadly. "*Nothing* matters now."

Anton stopped laughing. "He's all yours, boys!" The demons surged forward, slowly at first. Then they came in a rush.

Jon stood utterly motionless until the first demon reached for his throat with six-inch claws. Before the demon could react he whipped out the elvish knives and sliced off the creature's hand. The hand dropped to the floor. Black blood spurted from the stump. The demon—a big Blue one—cried out in agony. A Red demon next to it snatched up the hand and gulped it down. Jon winced at the grotesque sight. But he wasted no time worrying about it. His knives flashed silver. He hacked up the Red and left it bleeding on the floor. Then he went after the others. Black blood splashed about the cave. In seconds Jon had literally carved them all up. Dead and wounded demons lay all around him.

Jon's eyes were wild and alert. He breathed heavily as he wiped the blood from the sword on his pants. It left ugly, black stripes in the material. He started after the creature pretending to be Anton. Demon Anton shook his head and retreated down the path. Jon let him go. He had to find Chris, so he turned to go the other way. What he next saw stopped him cold.

The path ahead was blocked by dozens of horrid demons of all sizes, shapes and colors. They flowed in from dark side tunnels like streams of massive ants. Jon shook his head and spat. There was no way he'd get through them all. He looked behind him. Down the path it was even worse. An endless sea of monsters raced his way.

"This could have been easy for you!" cried Anton from a safe distance. The monsters rushed by him, closing in on Jon. "Now it's gonna hurt so *bad*!"

Jon thought quickly. Chris had given up his life for Kelly and Travis. That took some serious guts. Maybe Jon could buy them some time. He twirled the long knives adroitly. His eyes flashed coldhearted rage. He spoke in a low, icy voice.

"That depends on who's inflicting the pain."

Jon yelled maniacally as he charged straight into the horde.

Chapter 10

ESCAPE

KELLY

The demon that held Travis was big and strong. Travis pulled on the hand that covered his mouth, but it wouldn't budge.

"Shhh," it said softly. "Keep it down. The place might cave in."

I knew that voice. Travis recognized it too and quit struggling. The "creature" let him go. I lit another match.

"Dr. Parrish!" We both ignored the man's warning to keep quiet. We jumped into his arms and hugged him fiercely. I mean I hardly knew the guy, but I was so glad to see him, well there just weren't any words for it. Having an adult with us made everything seem more hopeful.

Parrish was obviously relieved too because he hugged us right back. I dropped the match and the cave went black again. I couldn't believe it. Parrish was alive!

"How'dja get here?" asked Travis, as Parrish set us down. "Do you have a flashlight?"

"Lost it in the quake," said Parrish. "So I crawled here."

"You crawled all this way in total darkness?" I struck another match. "That's almost impossible."

"Almost," he admitted. "But I lost my glasses, so it didn't matter if I had a light. I can barely see you now."

"I found your glasses," said Travis, watching my match burn down. "But they were smashed. Kelly, the match."

I looked at the flame. It nearly touched my fingers. I quickly lit my candle and dropped the match, but not before it burned me.

"Ow!" I sucked on my stinging fingertip.

Parrish shushed me again. He looked up nervously, as if he thought something was crawling on the ceiling. Travis lit his candle from mine and cupped his hand around it as a windshield. "No loud noises, *please*," Parrish said softly.

"You're right," said Travis. "We don't want the demons to hear us. You've seen 'em too?"

"I don't know about any demons, but the noise could cause another cave-in. That's why I covered your mouth, Travis. In case you yelled when you saw me."

"Why do you think it'll cause a cave-in?" I asked.

"Because right after the quake when I called out to find you guys, half the ceiling fell on my head! It was not a pleasant experience."

"Good point." I raised the candle for a better look at Parrish's face. He had streaks of blood running down both sides of his head and neck. Most of it had dried, but it still looked bad enough.

"You're hurt!" cried Travis, disregarding the warning to be quiet. "You got blood all over ya!"

"With *my* face it might be an improvement. Really kids, it's not as bad as it looks. Just a few small cuts."

"You wouldn't say that if you could see it." I frowned. "But we left the first aid kit with Jon and Chris. Otherwise, Travis could fix you right up."

Travis disagreed. "I never learned nothing about cuts."

"You never learned *anything* about cuts," I corrected. "I guess it's a good thing Chris only broke his leg."

"Chris broke his leg?" said Parrish. "What about Jon and Anton?"

"Jon's fine," said Travis. "But Mr. Edwards got grabbed by demons. I think they ate him."

Parrish raised his head. "Do what?"

"Travis!" I couldn't believe he said such a thing. "You don't know that!"

"What else would they do with 'im?"

"What are you kids talking about?"

I sent Travis a mental message. *Parrish is confused. He doesn't believe about the demons.* I changed the subject.

"Do you want a candle? I've got a bunch in my pack."

"No, thanks, Kelly," said Parrish. "Can't see anyway. I left my spare glasses at home. I knew I should have brought them. What do you mean by demons? Do you mean like wild animals? Are there bears in here?"

"Not animals," said Travis. "Demons!" I flashed him a warning, but he clearly had to tell somebody. "Thousands of 'em! They had a big meeting and the salesman told 'em they were gonna conquer people and make *us* live in caves!"

"The salesman? What?"

"At first the demons wanted to eat him, too, but the big red demon stopped 'em!"

"He was the Boss," I said, chiming in. "He was huge! Look, we don't have time to talk about it now. We've got to get help for Jon and Chris. We'll tell you everything when we get outside. Let's go, Travis."

Travis pulled Parrish's arm. "Grab my shoulder. I know the way."

We went forward against a steady breeze that rushed through the cave. Travis carried the candle with one hand, and shielded it from the wind with the other. Parrish followed, keeping a grip on his shoulder. He walked stooped over and tried not to trip on anybody's feet.

I could tell we were close to the opening. The path was familiar and the air smelled fresher.

Travis led us into the narrow tunnel. "I thought you were a demon when you grabbed me."

"That's what everybody says," joked Parrish.

Suddenly, an intense feeling of jagged pain shot through me. It felt like I'd been electrocuted. I dropped to my knees, shuddering.

"Oh, my God!"

"What's wrong, Kelly?" asked Parrish. "Did I step on your foot?"

I could hardly speak. Tears welled up in my eyes. "No...much worse... Jon... Chris...."

Then I flashed a terrible, burning message into Travis' head.

RUN, KELLY! RUN, TRAVIS! DON'T COME BACK! RUN FOR YOUR LIVES!

It startled Travis so badly he staggered against the wall. Parrish caught him by the shirt before he fell.

"What's going on?" Parrish looked from Travis to me, confused and concerned. "Are you two sick?"

I began to sob. It wasn't the best time for it, but I couldn't help it. "Demons got Chris! Jon fought 'em, but they got him, too!"

Travis' grief overwhelmed him. It was all he could do just to nod.

Suddenly, all my grief changed to terror. "They're coming after *us*!"

Travis felt the back of his neck tingle, which usually meant danger was near. "Ghost fingers!"

Once again Parrish was confused. "What?" But he didn't have time to find out what ghost fingers meant. Travis tried to run, but he only moved as fast as Parrish would let him. With every step I could feel the demons closing in. I cried so hard I was nearly as blind as Parrish. I dropped my candle and grabbed Parrish by the shirttail. I stumbled after him, terribly wounded by the deep pain in my heart.

I knew Travis felt every bit of it. Jon was gone. Chris was gone. There was nothing that could be done for them now.

The creatures were gaining on us. I heard the clicking of their claws on the cold stone floor. There were *lots* of them, getting closer with every step. I moved as fast as I could but the cave was pitch-black. I was blind as a post and apparently those things could see in the dark! I glanced back, choked with fear.

They're right behind us! The terror in my thoughts made it clear. Travis ran.

"Slow down!" said Parrish. "I can't run in here!"

Travis didn't give him a choice. The back of his neck must have been icy cold by now. The demons were close.

"Light!" he said excitedly. "The exit!" He picked up the pace.

"Travis, take it easy," said Parrish. "I don't want to hit my head again."

"High ceiling!" Travis tossed the candle aside. "We're here!"

I pushed Parrish from behind. "GO!"

The cave opened up a little. I rubbed my eyes on my forearms and saw gray outlines of rock formations. A few scraggly plants grew in the corners. A low snakelike voice hissed from behind us.

"Pretty girl. Waits for us, pretty girl...."

The blood in my veins turned to ice. The creature was so close I could almost feel its hot breath on the back of my neck. And it was talking to *me*! I pushed Parrish harder to make him hurry.

"Pretty girl!"

"Who's that?" said Parrish. "Who's there?"

"JUST RUN!"

I glanced over my shoulder. A host of evil glowing eyes appeared in the darkness beyond. Red, yellow, blue, green...so *many* eyes. They came at me fast.

Darkness became twilight. Freedom was only a few steps away. But the groping horrors were close. I could almost feel their nightmare of clutching hands pulling me back into darkness.

"Pretty girl!"

I stumbled. Then Parrish stumbled, which made Travis stumble.

The cave opened up a little. I rounded the last turn and saw a shaft of sunlight on the farthest wall.

I began to have doubts. What if they came after us out of the cave? What if sunlight didn't really bother them? How could we fight them?

All at once a clammy hand caught my ankle. I tripped and landed hard on my face. One of the creatures came beside me. I could see its squat gray form in the dim light.

"Help me!"

Parrish stopped. He squinted mightily. "Kelly? Where are you?"

"Here! Help!"

The thing gripped my leg like a vise. It dragged me back into the cave. I dug my fingernails into the smooth rock floor, but it didn't help. I kicked and fought like a wildcat. No! I didn't want to be eaten alive! Why did I ever come into this stupid cave?

Parrish groped for me like a blind man. He kept missing my outstretched hands. I cried out again.

"Help!"

"Oh, hell!" Parrish squinted really hard to see. He dove blindly toward the sound of my screams.

DR. LEBARR

Dr. Clara LeBarr put the last of the picnic food into the wicker basket and wiped the jelly stripe off her youngest daughter's cheek. They had come to Crystal Creek Park for a family picnic and things had gone rather well. As an emergency-room doctor and single parent she didn't often spend all the time she should with her girls. Taking the day off and coming to the park had been just what they needed.

"You really like PBJs, don't you, Katie?" said Clara to the little girl.

"I love 'em, mommy," said Katie. "I could eat 'em all day."

"You probably could," said her older sister sarcastically, taking up the basket for her mother. "You're such a little oink."

"Am not!"

"Are to!"

Clara cut them off. "Girls, stop it! We just had a great picnic and I will *not* listen to any bickering. Mandy, stop calling your sister a pig. If I hear it again, you'll be grounded for a week."

"I didn't call her a pig. I said she was an oink."

"You know exactly what I mean."

They got to the parking lot and set the basket and blanket on top of her white Mercedes sedan. Clara took out the keys from her purse. All at once she heard a scream. Her blood turned cold, but she looked up alertly.

"What was that, mommy?" said Katie. The little girl fearfully gripped the pocket on her mother's blue jeans.

"Somebody screamed," said Mandy. "It was in the cave."

"Mandy, take your sister to the ranger station and tell them what we heard. But do not, I repeat, do *not* come out until I come to get you, okay?"

"Okay," said Mandy. "Come on, Katie. Hurry."

Clara watched until the kids got safely inside the station before rushing over to the cave. She heard voices echoing inside.

"Dr. Parrish!" It sounded like a young child, a boy? She stopped in front of the cave entrance and listened. She heard sounds of a struggle. Then footsteps. Lots of footsteps on the run.

A second later three people burst into the sunlight. A very big man, a young girl, maybe Mandy's age, and a younger boy with white blond hair. The man and the girl ran until they collapsed by the Pandora's Cave sign. The girl sobbed uncontrollably. The man held her in his arms.

"Dr. Parrish, come on! Run!" The boy was frantic. He pulled on the big man's arm, absolutely terrified. "We're too close! They'll get us!"

But the man—Dr. Parrish—shook his head. "Travis, can't you see Kelly's upset? Something grabbed her! It pulled her into the cave! I couldn't see it!"

The girl named Kelly didn't try to speak. She just cried and cried in his arms.

The boy, Travis, was really scared. "They're still there! I can feel 'em!" He watched the cave warily. He scooped up a rock and faced the cave entrance. That was when Clara noticed the blood on Parrish's head. She ran over to them.

"I'm a doctor!" she said, kneeling beside Parrish. "What happened?"

"We were in the cave!" said Travis excitedly. "We got caught in an earthquake! An' there's demons!" He pointed at the cave.

"Travis, you don't know there were demons," said Parrish. "It was probably some wild animals."

"Stay away!" yelled Travis at the cave. He tried to act fierce, but Clara noticed his whole body shook with fear. "Stay in your hole!"

Clara looked up. Something moved in the blackness, she was sure of it. She narrowed her eyes. The boy was right, something was there. Something alive. Travis hurled the rock into the cave. Whack!

At once a dozen evil, hungry eyes appeared from inside the darkness. A voice cried out. But it clearly wasn't human. "Ow! You little maggot!"

Clara gasped. "Oh, my God!"

"What the devil was that?" said Parrish.

"Not a wild animal," said Clara. "Unless it's the talking kind."

Travis pulled on Parrish's arm again. "We gotta get out of here!"

The creatures in the cave spoke. "We gots yer brother! An yer father, too! We're gonnsa rips out their soul and eats their flesh!"

"You let 'em go!" cried Kelly through her tears. Parrish released her. He sat up, obviously stunned at what he was hearing.

"You'll never see them again!" said a second, higher-pitched voice.

Kelly stood up, sobbing. She shook her fist in useless defiance. "No! Let them go, or I'll get you! I swear it!"

"No!" said another demon in a deep, gravelly voice. "*We'll* get *you*! We know where you live, Kelly and Travis. We'll grab you in the dark, when the night comes. The dark belongs to *usss*!"

Chapter 11

RESCUE

KELLY

After we left the cave it took a long time for us to stop crying. Travis was embarrassed to cry in front of people, and if Jon or Chris had been there, I know he would have stopped. Of course, if they'd been there he wouldn't have had any reason to cry to begin with. He didn't know for sure what had happened to either of them. But he knew that I had somehow seen what they saw when the demons attacked and I'd delivered an upsetting glimpse for Travis to see. His understanding of what happened wasn't clear, but he realized, with good reason, that our brother and Chris were most likely dead.

Of course they were dead. How could anyone fight off so many demons? Chris wasn't a fighter to begin with and he couldn't run with a broken leg, so the demons probably just grabbed him and took him away. Or maybe they ate him right there on the ledge. I shuddered all over and caught myself before the images got any worse. So much terror and pain. Poor Chris.

"Jon hacked a lot of them to pieces before he went down," I said. "A *lot* of them. But there were *way* too many demons." What I'd seen made me both proud and sad. I was proud of Jon's fearlessness in battle, but I felt sad because we'd never see our big brother again.

I wasn't sobbing any more, but I hadn't completely stopped crying. My eyes were puffy and red, and I kind of hiccupped sporadically. Every so often random tears rolled down my face, then I'd wipe my eyes and try to regroup my emotions again. Travis struggled to stay clear of my feelings, but it was next to impossible. He was just as upset as I was, and he couldn't help but sense every bit of my suffering.

We sat close to each other on a bench in front of the ranger station. Ripper the wonder dog kept his head on my lap to let us both rub his soft ears. We were upset, but something about rubbing the dog's ears had a calming effect. I glanced over my shoulder through the window. Dr. LeBar was still treating Parrish. Apparently, he'd been correct about his injuries being minor. Dr. LeBar told us that facial and head wounds often looked worse than they were because they tended to bleed a lot, even when they were tiny.

The office door opened. Parrish came out with the blood cleaned up and several small bandages on his head. He groped his way almost blindly to the bench and took a seat beside Travis. "Ranger Laarz called in a search-and-rescue party. They'll be going into the cave within the hour."

"Are they soldiers?" asked Travis. "They'd better have *lots* of guns."

"I don't know. But I'm sure they'll find Jon and Chris. And Anton, too."

"They gotta have guns!" cried Travis. "You know what's in there!"

Parrish looked at him, frowning. I could tell he was worried and didn't know what to say to a couple of scared kids. If only he hadn't broken his glasses.

The door opened again. Ranger Laarz and another ranger named Eric Wooden came out of the office. Wooden was twenty-four and looked very fit with his broad shoulders and muscular build. He had dark eyes and dark hair, and large, rough looking hands. I thought if anybody could handle a demon, maybe he could.

Laarz carried a shotgun and a box of shells. She transferred all the shells from the box to her jacket pockets and left the empty box on the windowsill. Wooden had a rifle slung over his shoulder and a handgun in a holster on his belt. Dr. LeBar was with them.

"I don't know what they were, Melinda," said the doctor. "I only know what I saw and heard. I already told you what they said."

"Yes," said Laarz. "But demons? Come on now. Isn't it more likely just somebody playing a joke? If I go in there shooting, two things can happen. One, I kill a harmless prankster by mistake. Or two, a bullet ricochets off the stone and hits me, or someone in my party. Guns and caves don't mix."

"There's a third thing you need to worry about," said Parrish. "The earthquake affected the infrastructure of the cave. If you fire a gun in there, the ceiling might come down on your head. All I did was yell and it happened. You said the quake registered a three point six on the Richter scale?"

"That's what the U.S. Geological Service told us," said Laarz. "But it felt worse than that to me."

"You should have been *inside* the cave!" Parrish's eyes got wide. "The noise was intense. I've never been so scared." Travis and I both nodded in agreement.

"I just hope there aren't any aftershocks until we get back out." Laarz looked at us again. Her tone became more serious. "Kids, the only reason we're taking these weapons is because you're so upset about us going into the cave. Don't expect us to go in there shooting up the place, okay? We'll do our best to find your friends, I promise."

"Are any army guys going?" asked Travis.

"Not specifically, no. Why?"

"Because when the demons attack, you're gonna run out of bullets. You need *way* more ammo than that!"

Wooden chuckled and Laarz rubbed Travis' hair. They both smiled at him, but it made Travis madder. I was pretty angry too. What was wrong with them? Did they think we were joking?

"You don't believe us, but they *were* demons! I got a good, close look at one of them. It grabbed my leg!" I showed them the side of my pantleg. The blue jeans were shredded from the knee down to the ankle.

"Yeah," said Travis. "One of them grabbed me, too! It took my new backpack!"

"Why would a demon want your backpack?" asked Wooden sarcastically. "He need it for demon school?"

"Cuz I was still wearing it!" Travis didn't hold back the anger in his voice.

Laarz looked to Parrish for some rational support, but he only nodded.

"*Something* grabbed her," he said. "And then it dragged her back into the cave. I heard them, too, but I couldn't see anything. Still can't. Damn glasses."

"I saw eyes," said Dr. LeBar. "Lots of different colored eyes that were much too large to be human. I'm not saying they were demons, but these kids were traumatized by something strange and horrible. I've always been anti-gun, but in this case I think the weapons are a wise precaution."

"Guns are dangerous and heavy," said Laarz, closing the topic. "I just hope we can afford to bring along some rescue equipment, too. Let's get packed, Eric." They went to a nearby car and opened the trunk. I could still hear them talking.

"I called Anya and Karen to guide us," said Laarz. "Next to Anton, they know this cave better than anyone."

"Works for me," said Wooden. "When's Ned supposed to get here?"

"He's on his way. He'll be exhausted after working all night."

Laarz and Wooden loaded up two backpacks and hauled them near the entrance to the cave. Soon the quiet little park became center stage for a massive rescue effort. A few reporters tried to find out what the commotion was all about, but Laarz dealt with them quickly and made them leave.

"I called Angie," said Parrish. He stood up and opened the door to the ranger station. "And Yvette, too. They should be here soon. Hey, Travis, how do I get to the men's room?"

Travis looked in the window and pointed. "Take a right, go straight. End of the hall."

"Thanks, buddy." Travis watched the big man grope his way down the hall until he found the correct door and went in. A few minutes later a red Ford pickup drove up and parked next to Anton's SUV. Two pretty college-age girls got out and began gearing up for the rescue. They pulled on some coveralls and kneepads and hauled their equipment to the entrance of the cave.

We were upset about Jon, Chris and Anton Edwards, but we were also scared for ourselves. The demons knew our names and said they'd come after us when it got dark. We hoped Ranger Laarz and her crew could rescue everybody really fast, because we didn't want to be anywhere near this place after the sun went down.

"How'd the demons get our names?" said Travis. I looked at him with fearful eyes.

"When Chris tried to warn us. Or maybe they could read *my* mind, but I couldn't read theirs." I sniffed and wiped my eyes. "I don't want those people to go in the cave. If they do, terrible things will happen to them. But if they don't and Jon is somehow still alive...I don't know."

"Do you think he's still alive?" asked Travis hopefully.

"When mom and dad, died this terrible flash of pain and emotion sort of exploded inside my head. It hurt really bad when it happened. But I haven't felt anything like that from Jon, so I keep thinking there's a chance he might be okay. I don't know about Chris or Mr. Edwards."

More rescuers came to the park and gathered stretchers, numerous backpacks, and lots of rope. An ambulance pulled in and parked. An East Indian man and a woman got out to unload a special backpack full of first aid equipment. Laarz called them all over by the cave. She was ready to go in.

"How come Ranger Laarz doesn't believe we saw demons?" asked Travis. "Does she think we're lying?"

"She just doesn't believe in them. But Dr. LaBar does. She's very upset. She knows what they are, but she doesn't want to admit it to any adults. She's afraid they'll think she's crazy."

"That means they think *we're* crazy. What about Dr. Parrish? What's he think?"

"He needs more evidence. He's a scientist, you know."

"When the rescuers see the demons, they'll believe then, won't they?"

"Oh, yeah, they'll believe. But if they see demons, it won't matter. If that happens, the rescuers won't be coming back either."

———

"Earthquakes east of the Mississippi are more prevalent than you'd think," said Ranger Laarz to the rescue team gathered at the entrance to Pandora's Cave. "From what I've seen on the news there hasn't been any damage to bridges, buildings, or other structures in the area. It only registered a 3.6 on the Richter."

I could tell some of the rescuers were worried about going underground after an earthquake and Ranger Laarz was trying to ease their fear. I shook my head. If that's all they had to worry about I'd go back in myself.

I assumed the warm sunlight blasting the cave entrance would fry any demon that might stick its head out of the shadows. And the park was busy—almost crowded—with police officers, firefighters, EMTs and other rescue personnel. The area was secure, and yet I still shivered every time I glanced at the cave. The demons had made their intentions clear and I couldn't get their threat out of my head: *We'll grab you in the dark, when the night comes. The dark belongs to usss!*

It wasn't dark yet, just midafternoon, but night would come like it always did. We clearly had no business being so close to the cave, but we really needed to know what the rescue team was planning. And we weren't leaving the park until Jon was found.

Ranger Laarz scanned the faces of her co-rescuers with a steel-edged look in her eyes. She was a take-charge kind of person and had clearly decided that her first order of business was to settle their nerves as quickly as possible.

"Where was the epicenter?" asked an older black man with massive shoulders and a deep, bass voice. This guy looked bigger than Dr. Parrish. Could he even fit through some of the narrow places inside the cave?

"Right here in the park," said Laarz. "Or more accurately, about a quarter mile into the cave. "Look, we're all a little nervous about going into a cave after what happened, but there are three men trapped in there who need our help, and one of them has a broken leg. Most of us have extensive search and rescue experience and I'm sure we've all faced worse dangers than this. So let's get our heads on straight and get these guys out of there before their flashlights die. Does anyone have a problem with caves? If you do, you'd better let me know *now*." Laarz paused dramatically, leaning on the shotgun like a cane. But the tone of her voice dared anyone in the group to back out.

Some of them shrugged and shook their heads, but nobody stepped down. Laarz went on.

"Good. I know a few of you, but not everyone. I think it would be a good idea if we learned everybody's names and what we do, starting with me. I'm Melinda Laarz, the head ranger here at Crystal Creek Park. I've been in this cave a few times, but I don't claim to be an expert caver. That's why I called some of you to help us. Eric?" She looked at Wooden, who pretended to be serious.

"Eric Wooden, second in command of this park. That's second...out of three."

Everyone laughed. He lightened up and offered a winning smile that helped keep the tension down. "I'm just another ranger here, but I've always wanted to explore the cave, so I guess this is my big chance."

The athletic looking girl beside him sent a smile his way. She had blonde, shoulder-length hair and the face of a mischievous angel. She spoke next. "Anya Sapunenko. I'll be guiding some of you into the entrance on the other side of that big rock wall. It's the shortest way in." She spoke with a Russian accent, but her English was very good. Her equally athletic and cute girlfriend spoke next.

"I'm Karen Otero and I'll lead the rest of you through this entrance. The reason we're using both entrances is in case one of them is impassable because of the quake. Anya and I have been in this cave a million times and we know every path." Laarz and Wooden nodded in agreement.

"The kids say the quake made some changes," said Laarz. "Kelly, didn't you say the arch collapsed?"

"Yes," I replied. "But that's good, because you don't have to crawl through water any more. And there's a giant hole in front of the organ pipes where the lake used to be."

Anya and Karen looked at each other, confused.

"Used to be?" said Anya. "But that area was solid rock. Where did the lake go?"

"The entire floor and the lake dropped into a cavern below. You can still see all the pipes, but the organ keys and the flowers are gone."

"The new ledge is in a really *big* cave," said Travis. "It's huge!"

"Cool," said Anya.

"New territory," said Karen, brushing her medium-length brown hair out of her eyes. The girls tapped fists with each other. Their confidence seemed to lighten the fears of some of the other rescuers.

Karen nodded to the police officer next to her. It was his turn to speak. The officer was much older than the girls, maybe in his sixties, with a rather large potbelly bulging under his uniform. He carried a pistol on his belt and kept a cardboard box full of radio equipment. Travis told me he counted the bullets in his belt. Still not enough ammo.

"Ah'm Sheriff Andy Ford," he said in a thick country twang. "Ah'm in charge of communications. Ah'll be setting up about a hundred feet, or so, inside the entrance. The radios don't work as well *inside* a cave, so we'll position a person with a radio at any point where the signals start to fade. You'll relay all messages to me." He looked at the woman beside him. "Beth Ann?"

"Beth Ann Foster, EMT." I recognized Foster as the other EMT who had arrived in the ambulance with the east Indian guy. She spoke softly and trembled when she said her own name. Why would she force herself to go into the cave when she was so obviously terrified of it? I listened to her thoughts and found she wasn't afraid of the cave at all. She was afraid to speak in front of other people. Her shyness made her seem less attractive, even plain, but she had potential good looks. Foster immediately glanced at her partner to take the group's attention away from her.

"Malik Parikh, EMT," said the lean dark-skinned man, who had spiked, black hair and wore wire-rimmed glasses. "I assure you, we're both stronger than we look." He said it as a joke and flexed his thin arm muscles. The group laughed. Malik was probably born in the United States, or he'd lived here most of his life because he had absolutely no accent. Where Foster made the effort to stay out of the spotlight, Malik clearly loved it. "Is everyone here certified in first aid?" The others all nodded. "Good, that'll make our job a lot easier."

Next, the black man spoke for both himself and the smaller man beside him. "I'm Sigmund Holzmayer, but most people call me Siggy. And this is Van Nguyen, just call him Van. We're firefighters with Loudoun County and we've been on several cave rescues together. Van's from Vietnam, but his English is decent and he really knows his stuff. Plus, he's small enough to squeeze into some of those tight spots where the rest of us aren't gonna fit."

The last guy was tall, thin and completely bald. I couldn't tell if he shaved his head or not, but it looked like he did. He had small earrings in both ears and tattoos on his arms. He nodded to everyone.

"Marcus Conn, volunteer firefighter, Ashland. I happened to be in the area when I heard about your trouble. This will be my first time in a cave."

Laarz took charge again. "Thank you all. If we're still here by this evening, a backup team will spell us. If you have trouble with names, just ask, we're all professionals and should know procedure. When Sheriff Ford gives you a headset, check the batteries and make sure it works on both channels. Anya's route on the other side of the mountain is significantly shorter than this one, so if that tunnel isn't blocked, her group should arrive at the Cathedral room first. I want Eric, Siggy and Beth Ann to go with her. Karen will take the rest of us through this entrance. Like I said, we're looking for three men, Chris McCormick, Jon Bishop, and Anton Edwards. McCormick is the kids' foster father and has a broken leg. I understand the children splinted it for him."

"Travis put on the splint," I said proudly. Everyone nodded their approval and Siggy rubbed Travis on top of his head. There it was again, the hair rub, and from a total stranger.

"Nice work, Travis," said Malik, winking. Travis blushed.

"Maybe we take him, too?" said Van. "He fit in even smaller space than me."

Everyone laughed, but Travis shook his head. "No way! I'm not going back in. There's--"

Laarz quickly cut him off. "Some of you know Anton Edwards. He's been on numerous cave rescues across the region. When the kids came out about an hour ago, his exact whereabouts were unknown, but the Bishop boy and Mr. McCormick were last seen on the broken ledge. It's about a fifty-foot downward climb to reach them, but Kelly told us a rope should still be there. Any questions? Okay, folks, gear up."

Ranger Laarz clearly didn't want Travis to mention anything about the demons, which wasn't fair at all to the other people going in. I was going to have to do something about that.

The rescuers gathered their equipment and strapped on packs. All of them wore hardhats with headlamps and carried extra flashlights. Travis looked at me, but I was concentrating on Laarz. Whether the head ranger wanted to or not, she was going to say something about the *real* danger in the cave. Laarz blinked funny and turned back to the others.

"Okay, one more thing. This is going to sound weird, but I'd better warn you before we go in. There might be some kind of animals in there."

"Animals? What, like bats?" asked Otero. "We've never seen bats in there."

"Are these animals dangerous? Is that why you're hauling the heavy artillery?" Siggy nodded at the shotgun. "I wanted to ask, but *you* were the one holding the gun."

"Are we going to be in danger?" asked Malik. "Are they rabid?"

Before Laarz could open her mouth, Travis blurted it out. "There's demons! Lots of demons!" The others looked at him incredulously, except for Van Nguyen, who seemed suddenly nervous.

"Demons? What's he talking about?"

"Should we *all* be armed?"

"I gotta handgun in my car."

"Is he serious?"

Laarz glared at Travis. "Nobody saw anything except the kids. Dr. Parrish was with them, but he'd lost his glasses and couldn't see much at all. I'm guessing the quake may have opened a new passage into the cave and possibly some wild animals fell in."

"They weren't animals!" cried Travis. "They were demons an' they talked! They said they're gonna get Kelly and me *tonight*!"

Stop it, Travis! I said inside his head. *They don't believe you*!

He looked at me angrily. *How can they be so dumb?*

I took over. "My other brother, Jon, brought a camcorder. It should be in a backpack on the new ledge under some rocks. We recorded some of what happened, so if you can find it, it'll show what we saw."

"We'll look for it," promised Laarz, relieved to be off the demon subject. "And we'll do our best to find your loved ones. Let's go, everybody."

A third park ranger drove up in a Jeep and parked in front of the station. He got out and hurried over to the cave, tucking in his shirt on the run. He was kind of short, about the same height as Laarz, but stocky, too. He seemed a bit disoriented.

"Hey, Melinda," said the new ranger, almost out of breath. His uniform was wrinkled and his copper hair disheveled. "Sorry I'm late. Accident on the beltway."

"There's *always* an accident on the beltway," said Laarz with a smile. "I hated to call you back in so soon, Ned. Did you get any sleep?"

"I'm fine."

"Eric and I are going in. I'm leaving you in charge of the afternoon shift. Depending on how long it takes, you could be here a while. Are you okay with that?" Ned nodded, Laarz went on. "I want you to coordinate things out here and stay close to the radio. Ned, this is Sheriff Ford. He'll give you a radio and you'll be our link to the outside world. Get some paper and take notes on pretty much anything significant you hear. The

State Police will keep the press out and help you with security. Just run the park and stay in touch with us, okay?"

"Yeah, no problem. I'll be fine. Good luck."

Travis walked away from the group with his hands stuffed in his pockets. He was *so* mad. He looked down at the ground and noticed a mound of red ants. The ants kind of reminded him of the demons, so he kicked them and messed up their mound. The ants ran everywhere. I joined him.

"Sorry, Travis," I said. "But some of them thought you were crazy. I mean *really* crazy."

"I figgered. I could feel it. They don't have enough ammo or guns. They're all gonna die! Then another rescue team will go after them and they'll die! *Somebody's* got to do *something*!"

I checked my watch. "It's nearly three o'clock. The only thing I want to do is get Chris, Jon and Mr. Edwards out of that cave...and leave this place before dark."

———

Six hours later the park's floodlights were on and the original rescuers were still underground. Travis stayed inside the ranger station and watched the flurry of activity from the front window. He'd grown more and more worried for everyone who was still in the cave, fearing they'd all been taken or killed by demons. And now that it was dark, we might be next.

I went from the front window to the door to the rear window, checking the shadows around the building and fighting off tears. I hadn't said or thought anything to Travis since the sun went down, but he clearly sensed my fear. Up to now I'd only been worried for Jon, Chris and Anton Edwards. But with the onset of darkness I feared for my own life, and Travis' too. Ripper the wonder dog followed me wherever I went and stayed just within ear-scratching range.

Dr. Parrish sat on a desktop, flipping channels on the small TV with the remote control. He went from one news channel to the next, hoping to pick up information about what was happening in the park. He still couldn't see much, so he leaned close to the speakers on the TV and listened with the sound turned low.

Outside I counted five additional work lights powered by gasoline generators. The space between the cave and the ranger station was well lit with numerous fire trucks, squad cars, and other rescue vehicles crowding the parking lot. Rescue personnel moved all about the place and police kept curious onlookers and reporters away. None of that mattered to me. The additional lights made the area seem somewhat safer, and so did the presence of all the rescuers. But I knew, deep down, if the demons wanted to get us, all they had to do was come. Their sheer numbers would be enough to get by those people outside.

Angie had shown up an hour before dusk, and we'd been so glad to see her we wrapped our arms around her and held on tight. She had embraced us both, but became confused when we tried to explain about the demons and how it wasn't going to be safe at night any more. I sent Travis an unexpected thought.

Don't talk about what really happened! Angie's losin' it!

But she's always calm.

Not this time.

Travis tuned in to Angie's emotions and nodded back at me. *You're right!*

Yvette Edwards had arrived some time later. Yvette was a tiny woman, slim and pretty. She had a friendly smile, bouncy hair and dark eyes that were tired with worry. She showed amazing strength and self-control, even when Angie fell to pieces and cried into her shoulder. But Yvette couldn't completely hide her true feelings. Travis felt her fear and I knew her worries. Her emotions hung by a thread. Both women had stayed close to Ned Taylor at the cave's entrance for over an hour, but now they headed back to the ranger station.

When they came in Angie's eyes were swollen and red. Her hands trembled like she was cold.

"Anything in the news?" asked Angie, stifling another cry.

"No," said Parrish. "It's like nothing is happening."

"They're keeping it quiet, aren't they?" Angie went to the coffee machine and got another cup. She made a wounded sound as she took up the coffee pot.

"How many cups of coffee is that for you?" asked Yvette. She looked at Travis, who held up seven fingers. I don't know why, but he'd kept track for some reason. "Maybe you should hold off on the caffeine, girl."

"I can't. I'm just so scared." Her hands trembled badly as she poured the coffee. She spilled a little on the table and got flustered. When she tried to wipe it up with a napkin, she knocked over a bowl of sweetener packets. Then she stood there shaking her head and getting ready to cry some more. Yvette rushed to her.

"Go sit." Yvette set the bowl upright. "I'll get this." She put the packets back in the bowl and grabbed a handful of paper napkins. Angie looked at her thankfully and sat in one of the office chairs while she sipped the coffee in silence.

Travis looked at me. "Do you wanna go hang out with the ranger?"

I shook my head. "No. Why? Do you?"

"I just wanna see what's happening."

Dr. Parrish overheard us and handed the remote to Angie. "I'll go with you, Travis. I need to stretch my legs. But you'll have to lead me."

Chapter 12

MUCH WORK TO DO

TRAVIS

Travis felt safer with Parrish, especially now that his head was bandaged. It was Parrish who had rescued Kelly from the demon that had grabbed her by the leg. The big man hadn't been able to see a thing at the time, but he'd dived after her anyway, and luckily caught her hand. He'd jerked her right out of the demon's grip.

Travis and Parrish stepped out into the clear, cool night and went over to Ned Taylor. Ned picked up the radio and clicked on a switch.

"Base to Relay One. Do you read?"

Sheriff Ford's static-filled voice responded. "Relay One. I read you, Base."

"Have you heard from Relay Two?"

"I've not heard from anybody in twenty minutes."

"Sheriff, we've got ten people out here equipped and ready to go in. Maybe you should tell Melinda and the others to come out for a dinner break." For a few moments all they heard was more static. Then the Sheriff called back.

"Good idea, Base. Relay Two's out of range. I'll go check on him. I may be out of touch for a few minutes."

Ned put away the radio and got up. "Man, I'm tired. I'm working a triple shift right now. But if I know Melinda Laarz, she won't come out unless she finds the people she went looking for. She's kind of hardheaded about stuff like that, which I guess is what makes her a good boss. I think maybe--"

Ned was interrupted by a blast of static on the radio. He adjusted a knob and listened. More static. He called out.

"This is Base. I'm not reading you. Come again?"

The Sheriff's voice was barely perceptible because of a static burst. He sounded out of breath. "This is Relay...can't hear you...something's after...can't find others...oh my God!"

At the cave entrance everyone froze and listened. *Pow! Pow! Pow!* Some firemen rushed toward the cave.

"Were those gunshots?" Parrish looked from Ned to the cave.

Ned signaled for him to be quiet. Everyone's full attention was directed toward the cave entrance. Two Virginia State Troopers moved closer to the gaping dark entry. The troopers were concerned, and Travis could tell from their feelings that, yes, it *had* been gunfire. So why was anybody shooting inside a cave? Travis knew why. Demons were coming. He tensed and glanced back to the ranger station.

Ned kept trying to contact the Sheriff again. "Base to Relay One. Sheriff? Are you there?" Nothing but more static. Ned grabbed a flashlight and looked at Parrish. "He can't be very far in, I better go after him. Take the radio for me." He gave the radio to Parrish and rushed into the cave. A lady firefighter took up an axe and ran in after him. The state troopers stood ready, hands on their sidearms.

Everyone got quiet. Travis stared wide-eyed into the cave. At any moment he expected demons to appear. He was ready to run for his life.

"The demons got 'em." He said it to Parrish in a low voice. Parrish glanced down at him. The concern in his eyes suggested it could be possible.

Travis saw a flashlight beam from inside the cave. A voice echoed. Ned and the lady firefighter burst into the night air.

"They're back!" cried Ned. "The team is back!"

Dr. Parrish and Travis stepped ahead of the troopers. Travis crossed his fingers and held his breath. For the first time in his life he wanted to be wrong. He wanted to be absolutely wrong about demons even existing. And he wanted to be wrong about what might have happened to Jon and Chris.

A murmur rose from the crowd. Ned Taylor looked into the cave. He smiled and started clapping his hands. Everyone else applauded, too, as the first person came out.

Eric Wooden emerged from the cave empty handed. His clothes and face were filthy and his pants had a tear in one knee. As soon as the bright lights hit him in the face, he ducked and covered his eyes. But slowly he looked up and blinked. Ned Taylor went up to him and shook his hand.

"Welcome back, cousin," said Ned. "How'd it go in there?"

Before Wooden could answer, police, EMTs and firefighters swarmed over him with a barrage of questions.

"Did you find the missing men?"

"Were they injured?"

"Are they alive?"

"Did everyone make it back?"

Wooden raised his hands to speak. Everybody got quiet. "I'm Eric Wooden, and I'm fine. But you'll have to excuse me because I have much work to do. I must work hard and fast." He smiled and marched straight to the ranger station.

"What did that mean?" asked Parrish. People around him shrugged or scratched their heads. But Eric's cryptic response was momentarily dismissed as the two EMTs came out of the cave. They were covered with grime and sweat and had no equipment. The lady EMT stepped bravely up to the crowd and spoke in a loud clear voice.

"I'm Beth Ann Foster and I'm just fine. But I need to go now. I have much work to do. I must work hard and fast." She smiled and waved to everybody, apparently cured of her shyness in front of a crowd. Some people applauded her, but Travis knew they had no idea why they were doing it.

Malik Parikh was beside her. When Travis had first seen him, he was funny and outgoing. Now he was different.

"I'm Malik Parikh. I'm fine, too. But I have much work to do. I must work hard and fast." They both followed Wooden to the ranger station. The people in the crowd let them go, but Travis blurted out the one question that was on everybody's mind.

"Did they rescue anybody or not?"

A moment later Sheriff Ford and Anya came out. They ducked and covered their eyes like the others when the light hit them. Were they afraid of the light? Or was it just a shock after being in the cave for so long?

"'ello, everybody, I am Sheriff Andy Ford. I 'ad a bit of a fright in there when I saw th' others. But I am fine. An' I got much work to do. I must work hard and fast."

Travis noticed something distinctly different about the way he spoke. At first he couldn't place it. Then it struck him. The man no longer had a country accent! What was that all about? Sheriff Ford looked down at Anya, who stood beside him.

"I Anya Sapunenko. I fine. I got much work to do. I work hard and fast." They marched through the onlookers toward the ranger station. Anya's Russian accent had changed completely and her English was much worse than before.

A man in a suit stepped in front of them, blocking their way. "Sheriff Ford, we heard gunshots. Did you fire your weapon? What were you shooting at?"

Ford paused and shook his head. "I do not know what you heard but it was not me." Sheriff Ford and Anya passed by the man in the suit without saying another word.

The man in the suit looked at a nearby cop. "I don't get it. What's all this talk about work? Do they have a mess of paperwork to fill out, or something?"

"Maybe it's some kind of joke?" suggested a female officer. "It almost sounds like a patented FBI response. Unimaginative and boring." She and the man in the suit chuckled.

Yvette came up with Kelly and Angie. Angie put one hand on Travis' shoulder and one on Kelly's. Her hand trembled but Travis didn't say anything. He listened to her emotions, but backed off immediately. She was a mass of confusion and pain inside.

Kelly was also upset and Travis sensed it. "What's wrong?"

Kelly gave him the you-don't-want-to-know look, but told him anyway. "Those rescuers came into the ranger station, but they didn't say anything to us. They just stared at us like we were supposed to leave. So we did. It was creepy."

"*Very* creepy," said Yvette. "That's a cold bunch, if you ask me."

Angie looked warily back at the station. "I wanted to know if they found Chris, was he okay, you know? But the young ranger just opened the door and pointed the way out. The others all said they had to work, or something. What's going on? This is so strange."

And getting stranger by the minute, thought Travis, even without demons being involved. He listened as police and rescue personnel spoke in undertones about what was going on. They didn't understand it either, and they were clueless what to do about it.

Travis and Kelly stood close to Parrish. Yvette stayed shoulder-to-shoulder with Angie and chewed on her index knuckle. The next five people who emerged from the cave all ducked and covered their eyes until they became adjusted to the brightness. Then they moved on. But nobody carried any equipment, not even a flashlight.

"Where's the stretchers and stuff?" asked Travis. "Did they just leave it all in the cave? Where's Jon and Chris?"

"And Anton," added Yvette.

Kelly was an emotional time bomb waiting to explode. But so were Angie and Yvette. If the people they cared about didn't show up soon, they were going to lose it. Travis might lose it, too. He was pretty excited about seeing Jon, but where was he? He had to be coming. He just had to be. The rescuers wouldn't have left him behind.

"I'm Sigmund Holzmayer. I'm a firefighter from Loudon County. I'm fine. But I have a lot of work to do and I must work hard and fast."

"I'm Karen Otero and I have much work to do. I must work hard and fast."

"Marcus Conn. I'm from Ashland and I'm fine. But I have much work to do. I must work hard and fast."

"Van Nguyen. I am fine. But I have much work to do. I work hard and fast."

"I'm Melinda Laarz. Thanks for being here. But I can't talk to you now. I have much work to do. I must work hard and fast."

Angie's powerful emotions were contagious. Travis could hardly stand beside her without feeling a strong need to sit down and cry. She became more and more anxious searching the rescuers' faces as they passed by her and marched toward the ranger station. Yvette was starting to lose her cool.

"Where's Chris?" Angie asked Laarz as she passed. Laarz ignored her. "Why didn't you bring Chris out?"

"Anton?" called Yvette. "Where's my Anton?"

"There's somebody else coming!" a voice called.

Travis held his breath. He didn't like to admit it, but secretly he hoped it was Jon. He knew it was selfish, but Jon was his brother and he really wanted to see him again. When Anton Edwards stepped into the light, he was happy for Yvette. But he was also really disappointed.

KELLY

Anton got past the light and smiled like the others. Then he said his piece.

"Thank you for helping me. Really, I'm fine. I'm Anton Edwards. I've got much work to do. I must work hard and fast."

Yvette ran to him and wrapped her arms around his neck. He smiled again as she kissed him.

"Baby, where's Chris? And Jon?" she asked. But Anton just smiled and walked off toward the ranger station like the others. Yvette clung to him, but looked back at Angie. "I'll find out where they are." She went away with her husband.

I couldn't believe it. Travis looked at me, his jaw slack, Angie collapsed to her knees. Parrish knelt on one leg beside her.

"Something's not right here," said Parrish. "They've *got* to be okay."

Murmurs arose within the crowd.

"How come they left the people behind that they went in to rescue?"

Somebody cried out. "Here comes another one!"

I looked up hopefully, but what I saw next wasn't even possible. Chris walked out of the cave as if he'd never been injured, and he wasn't wearing the splint Travis had made for him. He didn't even show a slight limp as he stopped before the crowd.

"Are you Chris McCormick?" said one of the troopers.

"Yes, I'm Chris McCormick and I'm fine. But I have much work to do. I must work hard and fast."

"We heard you had a broken leg!"

Chris ignored the comment just as he ignored Angie. He would have walked right by her, but she caught his arm and turned him around. She hugged him hard.

"Oh, darling, I was so worried! Are you all right? What about your leg?"

I also ran to him but stopped short of giving him a hug. "Where's Jon? And what happened to your leg? It was broken!"

Chris gazed down at us. When he spoke, his voice was cold. "It was only a sprain. I'm fine now because the rescuers fixed it. Excuse me, I need to meet with my new friends." He pushed us away and marched to the station. We gawked at each other, startled almost to tears.

"His leg was broken! It was bent like this!" I tried to demonstrate the angle with my arm. "We got a picture of it. It's on Jon's cam...." I stopped. "We don't have the camcorder. Where's Jon?"

I looked at the ranger station where all the people from the cave had gone. Chris stood among the group of rescuers like he belonged with them, which was very weird. The only guy there he even knew was Anton. I tried to scan Chris' mind from outside, but I was too upset to concentrate. Through the window I watched them gather in a tight circle, almost like a football huddle. I hung my head, moving slowly toward the cave. Travis came up behind me and took my hand. My eyes burned.

"Jon should be here," I said.

Travis could only nod slightly. He choked back the urge to cry.

Something moved in the shadows of the cave. I heard footsteps. My blood ran cold. Was it demons? Travis glanced over his shoulder and tapped me on the arm. We were the only ones left by the cave. If it was a demon we were in deep trouble.

A moment later, Jon walked out into the bright light. He ducked and covered his eyes, just as the others had done. He seemed completely disoriented.

"Jon!" We ran to him and hugged him hard. I'd never felt so happy in my life...until I looked into our brother's eyes. Something wasn't right about him, but I couldn't tell what.

Travis must have noticed it too. *Ghost fingers!* he thought to me. I saw Jon glare down at him with cold hatred, as if Travis had personally caused all the troubles in his life. Travis released him and backed away.

"I am Jon Bishop," he said in a crisp, British accent. "I am fine. But I have much work to do. I must work hard and fast." He pushed me aside and went to the ranger station to join the others. Travis and I stood behind bewildered and hurt.

"What's he mad at *me* for?" asked Travis.

"Maybe he's mad because it took us so long to send help?"

"Well, he's the one who made us go! I don't get it."

"Me either. He acted like he didn't even know us. Chris, too!"

We suddenly looked at each other, thinking exactly the same crazy thing. *Did Jon just speak with a British accent?* We took off to the ranger station at a sprint, determined to hear our brother talk some more.

———

When it was finally time to leave Pandora's Cave, Travis was still concerned about why Jon was angry at him. I mean, Jon and I were close, but Travis and Jon are real pals. I suggested that since Jon had been trapped in a cave full of demons for over seven hours, he was probably exhausted. Jon was always grumpy when he got tired and he had to be totally wiped out by now. I told Travis to leave him alone until he'd eaten something and gotten a good night's sleep.

Of course, being tired didn't explain Jon's new accent. When we were younger, Jon had sometimes tried to use a British accent when he practiced with his swords, like he was pretending to be a knight, or something. But the accent was horrendous and we laughed at him so much he never spoke it again until tonight. Tonight, though, he sounded more British than an Englishman!

On the way to the van Angie asked Chris if he wanted to drive home. Chris looked at her as if he had no idea what she was talking about. We heard Yvette say the same thing to Anton.

"Anton, if you don't drive your car home it's going to be in the park all night. Why don't you want to drive, honey?"

"I can't drive," said Anton. "I'm…too tired."

"Well, I don't know what we're going to do. We can't leave it here."

A nearby policeman offered his assistance. "Ma'am, would you like me to drive his car to your house? I could follow you home."

Yvette quickly nodded. "Thank you, officer. Thank you very much. Anton *must* be exhausted if he wants me to drive him some place. He says I drive too slow."

Chris looked at Angie and smiled a big, goofy smile. "I'm too tired to drive, too! You drive."

Angie smiled sweetly back at him. "Okay, honey. Get in."

The whole way home Chris acted like a little kid, getting excited about nearly everything he saw. He clapped his hands and pointed at traffic lights and cars and brightly lit stores. He even yelled once when he saw a woman walking a dog. It was like he'd never seen any of it before. If that wasn't weird enough, Angie laughed and laughed at every odd thing he did or said. She must have thought he was playing. Either that, or she figured he was just really glad to be alive.

When I scanned Chris' mind I got nothing, which came as a complete surprise. I tried again, but either he blocked me the way Jon did, or something was different with his brain. I wasn't sure what to think about it, but I had to wonder if he had a head injury or some other problem. Of course, even with head injuries I usually got TV snow or broken thoughts. It got me thinking about what might have happened to them after we got out of the cave.

Unlike Chris, Jon stared straight ahead like a statue. He seemed to have absolutely no interest in anything, especially us. I leaned my head on his shoulder and tried to hug him, but he totally ignored me. Maybe he was thinking about Maria, I don't know. I tried to check his thoughts, but he blocked me right off.

Angie was so grateful to have everything back like it was that she never noticed how different things were. I couldn't figure her out. She talked endlessly to Chris and smiled at him a lot. Sometimes she'd squeeze his hand and pull him close to her so she could kiss him. She nearly wrecked the car twice doing that.

"Honey," she said. "I'm so glad you're okay. It was brave to take the kids caving, but from now on let's stick with bowling, or putt-putt golf, okay?"

Chris grinned at her like an idiot. She looked in the rearview mirror and smiled again, this time at Jon. "Jon, you're quiet tonight. I guess it was a pretty long time to spend in a cave, wasn't it?"

"Yes," Jon responded coldly, still using the British accent. "Three thousand years is a long time."

Travis blinked at me in disbelief. *That's gotta be the dumbest thing he's ever said!* I quickly agreed. *Jon wouldn't say somethin' like that.*

Travis had a point. I'd never heard of anyone acting different just because he went into a cave. And I didn't believe demons could make themselves look exactly like a specific human, so I had to assume Jon and the others might be possessed.

Travis was about to ask Jon what he meant, when a sudden wave of anger and nervousness washed over him. I saw Travis shudder like he'd just bitten into a lemon. A moment later he realized the prickly feelings had all come from Jon. He looked at me, alarmed.

He's tired, I thought back to him. *He needs rest.* Travis wanted to believe me. I wanted to believe me too, so I didn't say anything about demonic possession. Not yet. I wanted to be sure before I told anybody else. Neither of us spoke to Jon again for the rest of the ride home.

Chapter 13
MEMORY LOSS

Maria stood by her car at the house when we drove up, still wearing her waitress clothes. She ran to Jon when we got out of the van and hugged him hard around the neck. Jon stood passively and didn't hug her back. When she kissed him, he didn't kiss her back.

"Jon, are you okay? What happened?"

Jon shot her an ominous glare, then redirected his gaze at the front porch. "I am fine. I must work hard. I have much work to do."

Maria released him and stepped back, bewildered. "Are you mad at me? I only just found out what happened a few minutes ago. Dr. Parrish called my dad and told him about the earthquake. I didn't notice it, but some of my friends did. Jon? Can you hear me? Jon?"

Jon pushed by her and went into the house. I got close to Maria and lowered my voice.

"He's been really weird like that since he came out." I wanted to say something about my demonic possession theory, but I didn't have any proof yet. Even if I did she probably wouldn't believe me.

"He acted like he didn't know me." Maria was taking this hard, like the rest of us. Her eyes got moist and she wiped them with the back of her hand.

"He did the same thing to us," I explained. "He gets grumpy when he's really tired."

112

"I've seen him grumpy. He still knew who I was. Does he also pick up a British accent when he's tired?"

"I don't know where that came from."

"Kelly, what do I do?"

Angie answered her question. "Go home, Maria. I'll call you tomorrow. Thank you so much for coming by, we'll make sure Jon knows you were here."

Maria nodded and gave me a lingering, questioning look. All I could do was shrug and shake my head. She left in a hurry.

When Angie and I got inside, Jon was looking around the house like he had no idea where he was. He asked Travis a very strange question.

"Where do I sleep?"

"In your bed," said Travis. "Where do you think you sleep?"

"Show me."

"Show you what? Your bed?"

"Yes."

"I'll do it if you tell me who taught you how to speak with a real British accent."

"What do you mean?"

"Your accent. You've been practicin', or somethin'. It never sounded this good."

Jon's tone became severe. "Show me my bed."

TRAVIS

Travis decided it might be better to find out about the accent *after* Jon had gotten some sleep. He led his brother upstairs to their bedroom and jumped into the top bunk.

"That's yours," said Travis, pointing to the lower bunk. "I sleep on top cuz I'm the coolest." Ordinarily when Travis said something like that, Jon would have a snap response about how *he* was the coolest and Travis was just lucky to share his universe. Then they'd both laugh and maybe wrestle a little. But this time Jon ignored him.

"Can I have those swords?" asked Jon. "And the computer?"

"You're kiddin', right? All that stuff's already yours, the computer, too. But everything on the other wall is mine, so don't mess with it." For the first time Travis realized how bare his wall was. There was only one poster he'd gotten from an Army recruiter and a calendar he made at school.

"They belong to me?" Jon immediately took the swords off the wall and laid them on the floor. Next he turned off and unplugged the computer, monitor and printer. He looked at Travis, emotionless. "I need a large box."

"There's boxes in the basement. Why are you takin' everything down? How come you unplugged your computer? It's the only computer in the house!"

Jon looked up thoughtfully. "I'm selling everything. I need money."

Travis' mouth dropped wide open. Was Jon insane? Lost in the cave, or not, this was pure madness! "You can't sell your swords! How can I do my homework without a computer? Why do you need more money? You have a job! You get paid every week!"

"I need to buy magic kits. I will become the greatest magician in the world."

"You get lost in a cave and now you're a magician? I don't get it. What kind of magic? Are you gonna to pull a rabbit out of a hat?"

Jon glared at him so intensely Travis got a little scared. He'd never seen his older brother act like this, and that look in his eyes was almost threatening. Jon scanned the room and spied a baseball cap hanging on his chair. Travis had never seen him wear the cap, but sometimes Jon tossed it in the air to himself while he did his homework.

"Yes. I can do a rabbit out of a hat," he said. He held up the ball cap with one hand hidden under it. "Watch."

KELLY

About then I walked in to say good night and to see if Jon had gotten any friendlier. I nearly tripped over his sword collection that was piled on the floor in front of the computer. "What's going on? Why'd you take down your swords?"

Jon shushed me. "I need quiet. What kind of rabbit do you want?"

I didn't even know what they were talking about, but it was still an easy question. Travis' best friend, Mathew Dunlop, once had a big white rabbit named Fang, which had died of kidney disease. I figured Travis would want a rabbit just like that.

"A white one," said Travis. Ha! Do I know my little brother or what?

Jon glanced at me, then looked Travis right in the eye. Suddenly, he took a small white rabbit out from under the hat and set it on the bed. After I picked up my jaw off the floor, Travis scooped up the rabbit and hugged it. OMG! How in the world did Jon do that? Where'd he get the rabbit?

"He's soft," said Travis with a smile. "An' nice." The rabbit wiggled its pink nose and let us pet it.

"Jon!" I said excitedly. "That was awesome! Where'd you learn that?"

"His name is Fang II," said Travis, who was not as concerned with how Jon had done the trick as he was with having a new pet. "Matthew'll like that. Hey, can you do it again with an X-Box?"

Jon was clearly pleased with himself. He almost smiled. "You must leave. I need to practice."

"When are you gonna do some more tricks?" asked Travis.

"I do not do tricks. I do magic. *Real* magic. Now get out of my room."

Travis gawked at Jon. "Your room? It's *my* room, too! You can't kick me out!"

"Yes, I can." Jon took the blankets and pillow from Travis' bunk and tossed them into the hallway. Then he physically shoved both of us out of the room. "I need to practice magic. I must be alone. Go some place else."

The door closed almost in Travis' face, leaving him stunned and silent. I knocked hard on the door. "Open the door, Jon Bishop! You can't do this!"

Nothing happened. I knocked again and we listened. Whatever magic he was doing must have been very quiet. Travis gathered his blankets, pillow and Fang II, and went down the hall.

I got mad. "Nobody treats my little brother like that! Not even my *big* brother! I'm telling Angie!"

Travis turned and shook his head. "Don't tell her. Not yet."

"Why not? He can't toss you out of your own room!"

"It's okay, Kelly. Jon's actin' kinda weird, you know? I'm not sure I want to sleep in the same room with him for a while."

"But where are you going to sleep?"

"Behind the couch. Till Jon starts actin' like Jon again."

"That's silly."

"No, it's not. He can have the room. I wanna be safe." Travis hung his head for a moment, then lowered his voice. "Do you think maybe he might not be Jon?"

The question baffled me until I got a mental picture of what Travis meant. The whole concept made my gut churn from both fear and confusion.

"You think he might be a demon? But how? I mean, he looks and sounds like Jon to me. Well, except for the accent."

"What if he's possessed?"

I moved close to Travis and whispered in his ear. "I was thinking the same thing! How can we be sure?"

"I dunno. Until we figure it out I'll leave him alone."

TRAVIS

Travis camped out behind the couch in the living room. He figured nobody would notice him there, and if Jon really was possessed by a demon it was as good a hiding place as any. Sure, sooner or later Angie or Chris would make him go back into his own bed, but first they'd have to find him. He got a cardboard box from the basement and put the rabbit in it, along with a bowl of water. Then he put Fang II's box at one end of the couch to help hide his blankets.

"You need some food, Fang," he said to the rabbit, which wiggled its nose at him. "I'll be right back."

Travis headed for the kitchen to get some lettuce for the rabbit, when he heard Angie talking. He stopped in the hall and listened.

"Chris, we've always had a basement. But you can't work in there, it's a mess."

"I must work there. I must work hard and fast."

"When are you coming to bed?"

"I have much to do. Take me to the basement."

"Chris, you know very well where the damn basement is. Oh, forget it. Follow me." Angie reluctantly led the way. Travis decided to follow them at a discreet distance.

"Why are you talking like this?" She opened the basement door. "You sound like you're from another country. And why the basement? What about the garage?"

"Not the garage. I need a place to work undisturbed."

Angie flipped on the light and led Chris downstairs. Travis took a seat on the top step and peeked at them below the basement ceiling as he listened. Right away Chris started moving things around.

"What kind of work are you talking about? I don't understand. Chris, don't clean the basement now! It's nearly eleven o'clock. You have to go to work tomorrow!"

"I must work now. I must work hard and fast."

"You have school in the morning. Did you forget about your job?"

Travis watched as Angie tugged on Chris, trying to get him to go back upstairs. She even kissed him hard on the mouth and wiggled close to him, holding him tight.

"Honey, don't you want to go to bed now?" she asked. Her voice was soft and sultry. She whispered something into his ear. He looked at her curiously for a moment, then pushed her aside.

"I must work hard and fast."

"What happened to you in that cave? Why won't you listen to me?"

"I don't have time to listen. I have much work to do. I must work hard and fast."

"Can you hear yourself? You sound like a frickin' robot! What are you going to do down here, anyway? This place is too cluttered to work in."

"I'll clean it. And then I'll work. I must work...."

"Yeah, I know, hard and fast. What are you going to work on? What's more important than me?"

"My idea is more important than anything," said Chris. "I'll make a product that will be popular around the world. Everybody will want it. But I need ingredients."

Angie shook her head and ran to the stairs. Travis scrambled out of the basement before she saw him and waited in the kitchen like he was just coming in. When Angie came upstairs, she was crying. Travis didn't like to see her sad like that, so he hugged her, really big. She hugged him back so hard he thought she'd squeeze him to death.

"Travis, you're so sweet. What's wrong with him? Why is he acting like that?"

Travis didn't know what to say, until he recalled something from Mrs. O'Brien's first aid course. "Maybe he's in shock. Maybe he needs to keep busy until he gets over it."

Angie released him and paced about the kitchen. She wiped her eyes and quit crying. "Oh, I'm such a fool! You're right, Travis! He *is* in shock! He's always been fragile, and that whole cave thing must have really upset him. What should I do?"

Travis shrugged. "Ask him what he wants?"

Angie stared at him for a few moments as if she'd been frozen in time. She pointed a finger at him. "You are one smart young man!" Grabbing a pencil and some paper, she hurried back downstairs. This time Travis went with her.

"I'm going to help you," said Angie. "Let's make a list. What do you want?"

For the first time since he'd come out of the cave, Chris smiled at Angie like he meant it. The effect it had on her was immediate. She looked relieved and happy again, all in an instant. She smiled and melted into his arms. He even hugged her back.

"Pear juice," he said. "I need pear juice."

Angie looked straight at Travis. "Have you had a chance to go through the pantry? Do we have any pear juice?"

Travis shook his head. "No pear juice."

Travis had always taken an interest in inventory, especially food, and he'd kept an accurate mental list of whatever was in stock in any house where he lived. It started for him at the Children's Home during a three-day ice storm. Nobody could get to or from the Home for nearly two weeks, causing food supplies to rapidly dwindle. Travis liked to eat, so he'd quickly put together a rationing schedule that included everyone in the facility. It was so well done that the counselors were going to put it to use, but as soon as everything was in place, the National Guard showed up with supplies.

Most people who found out about his odd skill often took it for granted. Rather than look around to find what was available, they'd usually ask him first. Travis didn't mind because it made him feel kind of important.

"That's okay," said Angie. "I'll go to the store. What else do you need?"

Chris got excited. "I like you helping me! I need lots of paper and something to write with." He called out a list that included everything from different fruit juices to test tubes and beakers, to graduated cylinders. He also included a hot plate, some eyedroppers, a metric scale, and lots of pots. Angie wrote fast and eventually got it all down. When the list was complete, Chris went to work cleaning up the basement.

"I need space to work. I must work hard and fast."

"I'll go to the grocery store right now. But where am I going to get test tubes and beakers? What's a graduated cylinder?"

"Ask Dr. Parrish," said Travis. "He teaches chemistry, I bet he's got test tubes."

She rubbed his curly white hair. "Good thinking, young man. We'll get the rest of the stuff tomorrow. This has been such a crazy day. You'd better get to bed."

She collected her purse and jacket and rushed out to the car. A moment later Jon walked by Travis and stopped in the kitchen. Somehow he didn't seem angry this time.

"Where's the basement?" he asked.

Travis pointed and Jon went down the stairs. There was a loud crashing sound. Then Jon returned with a large, now empty cardboard box. He took the box upstairs. Travis watched him go by, totally bewildered.

KELLY

I hate earliness. And Monday morning came way too early, as usual. I was so tired I could hardly get out of bed for school. Travis was the only one who tried to wake me, but after three attempts with no sign of success he gave up. Suddenly, ten minutes later I shot out of bed on my own, as if some inner sense of duty told me I had to hurry. Inner sense of duty? I never had that before. Go figure.

I dressed quickly and rushed to the kitchen where Angie had five steaming bowls of oatmeal on the table ready to eat. Travis was just finishing his breakfast, but the other bowls were untouched, including Angie's. Travis gave me the psychic scoop.

Angie's still upset. I think she's been crying all night again.

Right away I noticed the puffiness around Angie's eyes that had been there for the last two days. After a brief mind scan I realized that, yes, Angie *had* been crying much of the night. The poor woman couldn't deal with the very weird way Chris had acted since he'd come out of the cave. I wanted to cry, too, but more because of Jon than Chris. Our brother's personality change seemed like it might be permanent, which really upset me. I wanted Jon the way he used to be, complete with his swords, karate, lousy English accent and sometimes stubbornness. I wasn't sure I liked this new, possibly possessed Jon. I certainly didn't trust him.

"Morning, Angie," I said, hugging her around the neck. "You seem sad."

Angie frowned and nodded. "I'm tired, mostly. Chris didn't come to bed again. He spent another whole night cleaning up the basement so he can make his *product*, whatever that is. I don't understand what's happened to him, Kelly. He goes into a cave for one day and comes out a completely different man." She looked around the table. "Speaking of different men, where's Jon? He's usually the second one up."

"I'll go see. It'll be great to wake *him* up for a change."

"I'll go, too," said Travis, putting his empty bowl in the sink.

I guided Travis out of the kitchen and up the stairs, where we both knocked on Jon's door really hard. He didn't answer right away, so Travis banged again.

"Jon? You up? We gotta go to school."

Jon opened the door with the same bland expression he'd had on his face for three days. He looked wide-awake, but his hair was a mess and he still wore the same clothes he'd had on in the cave. He needed some deodorant too, he smelled like dirty socks. He glared at me challengingly. "Don't bother me. I'm practicing magic."

I quickly went into his mind to see what was going on in there before he blocked me, but Jon must have anticipated it. He blocked me out before I could get even a peek at his thoughts.

"You have to take us to school," I reminded him.

"I can't go to school. I have much work to do. I must work...."

"Hard and fast," I interrupted. "But you've got to work hard and fast in school, too, you know. If you don't go to school, all they'll let you do is flip burgers, or something. You can forget doing magic if you don't go to school."

Jon considered this. "They won't let me do magic unless I go to school?"

"Nope."

"Then I will go to school. When does school end?"

"High school lets out at three o'clock, like always. Why would you ask that?"

"I will be down in a minute."

I got my books together and set my new backpack by the front door next to Travis' old one. Travis came in and studied both packs for a moment.

"You were right. I shoulda taken my *old* pack to the cave like you did. I can't believe I lost the new one."

"You can always borrow my Barbie pack from under my bed. Of course, it's still got cave dirt all over it." I grinned at him just to rub it in a little.

Travis shook his head. "Gross! I'm not takin' a *girl's* backpack to school!"

"In that case you'll have to use a shopping bag when your straps break." I didn't need to read his mind to know he was considering the idea as a backup plan. I looked upstairs. "Jon! Come on! We have to go!"

When Jon finally came downstairs he still had on the dirty caving clothes and his hair looked like a bird's nest. He carried no books or backpack and walked through the kitchen without even a glance at breakfast.

"Eat, Jon," said Angie. "You'll be starved by lunch. Where's your backpack?"

Jon shrugged. "Must have left it in the cave."

"He did," I said. "I think your brain was inside it."

Jon grabbed his own head and felt around. "No, I am certain my brain is right here." I exchanged uneasy glances with Travis and Angie. Was he kidding? I scanned his mind, but as usual, couldn't pick up on any thoughts. If only he couldn't block me so effectively.

"I'll get you a new pack today, Jon," said Angie.

"I need a new one, too," said Travis, holding up the old pack. "Sorry, I lost my new one in the earthquake. I couldn't help it."

"I wondered why you had that old thing," said Angie. "I'll get you a new one, too. Are you ready to go?"

"We're ready," I said. "But, Jon, you've got to change your clothes. You can't go to school looking like that. And put on some deodorant, you stink."

"I agree," said Angie. "Toss the clothes in the hamper, Jon."

Jon looked down at his filthy clothes and then at us. "What is a hamper?"

"What's a…?" Angie pointed to the ceiling. "The hamper is where we put dirty clothes. Our hamper is the upstairs hall closet. Now make it quick, or you'll all be late for school. And brush your hair."

Without protest Jon went upstairs. Travis looked at us nervously.

"I'd better go with him," he said, following Jon up the stairs. "In case he's forgotten what a hair brush is."

When they returned, Jon's hair was neatly brushed and he wore shorts and a T-shirt. He smelled better, too. Hooray! He actually looked more like my normal teenage brother again. I nearly forgot about his possible demonic possession. We said goodbye to Angie and headed out the door.

I waited with Travis by the Mustang, but Jon made no effort to get his keys out. He just stood there, clueless.

"Unlock the car," said Travis, trying the handle.

"Hurry, we're going to be late." I gave Jon a look, but he seemed puzzled.

"What?" He blinked at us.

"You're driving us."

Jon's eyes showed confusion, then fear as he figured out what I was talking about. "I don't want to drive. I forgot how to drive."

"You forgot how to drive?" I couldn't believe it. "What kind of moron forgets how to drive a car? How does that even happen?"

"I don't know, I just forgot."

We looked at him for a while, expecting him to grin and produce the keys. But he seemed genuinely lost. If Jon were truly possessed by a demon, it must have been a dumb one. I shook my head and stomped back into the house.

"You have to take us to school, Angie. Jon forgot how to drive!"

"He forgot…oh, lord, he must be in shock, too! Let me get the keys."

Angie came out and everyone piled into her minivan. "I guess this means I'll be picking all of you up. Jon, I want you to stay after school with Dr. Parrish today. I'll get Kelly and Travis first, and you last. Mark has some things that Chris needs, so this driving arrangement might work out for the best, at least for today."

"Cool," I said. "I get to see Jon's classes."

"I forgot all my classes," said Jon. "Where do I go when I get to school?"

"You forgot your classes?" I was exasperated. "You must have hit your head in the cave after we left."

"Yeah," said Travis. "Maybe that's why you're actin' so weird."

Jon thought about it. "Yes," he said. "I hit my head after you left."

Angie started up the minivan and looked first at Travis in the rear view mirror, then at Jon. She smiled hesitantly. "Jon, honey, don't you think we should go to the doctor this morning, instead of school?"

Jon nearly panicked at the question. He looked my way. "No. They won't let me do magic unless I go to school."

"Okay. So about that head injury. Would you happen to know if Chris also hit his head in the cave?"

———

Traffic was congested on the way to school and Angie grew weary of stopping and going every inch of the way. I know because I was in and out of her mind a lot during the drive. Still very sad, Angie leaned her head on the driver's side window as she waited for the cars in front of us to move again. She thought about Chris and how he'd filled her life with tenderness and love. And how, with the addition of the children (namely us), she had finally achieved the one goal in life she coveted above all else. With the help of her willing husband, Angie now had a family of her own. That made me feel really good inside. I even heard her think the A-word again.

Chris had never been a particularly brave man and he wasn't driven by financial success. He was a schoolteacher, which most likely meant they'd never be rich. But for Angie, their relationship was much more than that.

For her it was strongly personal. Chris had something inside him that no other man had ever displayed to her. He had the subtle ability to emotionally move her, heart and soul, and she loved him deeply. Angie had been proud and happy with her simple life—until Pandora's Cave ruined everything.

Sooner or later she had to face the truth. Something had happened to change her man, and it wasn't just the cave. Chris no longer acted like Chris, not in the slightest. Angie tried to see some of the old personality traits in him, but after only two days she knew there weren't any left. Where he had once been her best friend and lover, now he was more like a boarder in her basement who didn't pay rent, never slept, and grouched at her whenever she went down to see him. He still looked like Chris, but his voice was different and his personality was, well...disturbed. She didn't want to admit what she really felt was wrong with him, but it finally came out in her thoughts. Chris might be insane. She forced the idea out of her mind, but I knew it would come back to haunt her.

Angie sat up again and glanced in the mirror. Travis and I had taken the captain's seats, but Jon had chosen to sit alone in the back of the van. She studied Jon for a moment and realized that he wasn't the same person any more, either. What could have happened in that cave to make two well-adjusted people become so strangely different? Had they really been struck in the head as Jon suggested? Or was it something more sinister? Angie sadly shook her head. She had no answers for her own questions. Neither did I.

Traffic began to move along at a regular pace again. Angie looked up and saw an old man standing over a recycling box on the side of the road sifting through the trash. He had white hair, a tan, leathery face, and wore glasses with clear frames that seemed to add to his age. Beside him was a red, three-wheeled bicycle with a large basket mounted on the front and two more baskets on the back. In the front basket was a black trash bag filled to the top with aluminum cans.

Angie smiled. "Hey, kids, it's Doug One. I haven't seen him for years. Wave to him."

Angie gave the man a friendly honk as she rode by. He looked up and waved, but the distraction nearly sent him stumbling over his bicycle into a ditch. Somehow Doug One caught himself and went back to rummaging through the trash.

"Who's Doug One?" I asked, leaving Angie's mind and offering a half-hearted wave to the old man.

"Why's he pickin' up trash?" asked Travis.

"Doug One doesn't pick up trash," said Angie. "Doug Four picks up trash. Doug One only picks up aluminum cans."

"Doug Four?" That got me. "How many Dougs are there?"

"Seven," said Angie. "They each pick up something different. And they give out chewing gum to kids."

"Gum? They must be pretty cool," said Travis. "Are they really all named Doug?"

"I think so," said Angie. "I remember my grandfather said they used to ride bikes around picking up stuff in the area when he was a little kid. He said they all lived in the same house, and their neighbors called it the House of Seven Dougs. It's like they've *always* been old. I don't know much else about them."

ANGIE

After dropping off Kelly and Travis at their respective schools, Angie drove Jon to the high school and went with him to the main office. She explained to the principal, Mr. Dillon, about the caving incident and about Jon's possible head injury. Dillon was a short man, barely taller than Angie. But she discovered that what he lacked in stature, he made up for with a take-charge attitude and a loud voice.

"I understand," said Dillon agreeably. "Dr. Parrish told us all about it. Has Jon seen a doctor?"

"I'm taking him to one today, but he insisted on coming to school. Except for his memory he seems perfectly fine. I guess he needs to be around his friends."

"He should stay out of caves from now on, too, if you want my opinion. They all should. Anton Edwards called in sick today, and so did Chris, though they both waited until this morning to contact us. Please remind Chris the next time he needs a sub to call our secretary the night before. And if he can't get here himself, he can email the lesson plans to us."

"Chris called in? I'm surprised he remembered. He's acting very strangely, Mr. Dillon. So is Jon, for that matter."

"What do you mean?"

"Jon speaks with an British accent now. And he seems to have some minor memory loss. He forgot how to drive, which is why I had to bring him today. And he's forgotten what classes he takes. But Chris...." Her voice trailed off sadly. "I think he's in shock. He started working on some project in the basement. Nothing else seems to matter and I don't think he's slept at all."

Dillon studied her. "I'm sorry to hear that about Chris. I hope his condition doesn't last long, we need him. As for Jon, if his injury isn't too severe, I suspect he'll probably remember things once he gets back into his schedule. I'll assign a student to show him where his classes are each day until he's reoriented. Let me know if there's anything we can do for him."

BRANDON

Brandon Cole considered Jon Bishop to be his closest friend, so he wasn't surprised when Mr. Dillon chose him to guide Jon around the school. Ordinarily, it would have been cool, since he and Jon hung out anyway. But Jon didn't even recognize him, not at all. In fact, he didn't seem to know anybody, including the love of his life, Maria Sanchez! Brandon knew a little about amnesia, but this was the first time he'd ever experienced it. And the British accent, man! That was strange! With what Brandon knew about memory loss, picking up foreign accents didn't seem to fit.

By lunch Maria had gotten pretty frustrated with Jon, but Brandon convinced her to stop by Dr. Parrish's room before chemistry class and talk with him again. He was sure Maria was the key to Jon's memory. Maria was one of the hottest girls in school and no boy could spend time with her and not have his memory jogged. When Maria met them by the door to Parrish's room, Brandon stepped aside to let them talk.

"Jon, do you want to come over to my place after school?" asked Maria, taking his hand. "I think we need to get reacquainted."

"I can't. I have much work to do...."

"Stop it!" Maria cut him off. "You said that ten times at lunch! And stop that stupid accent, you don't talk like that! I want my old Jon back. Two days ago you said you loved me more than anything. Ever since the cave you don't even remember my name."

"Your name is Maria."

"Not bad, only three tries. Look, call me tonight...if you still want to. I've got to go to class." She hurried off and left Jon standing at the doorway. He looked blankly at Brandon, who nudged him into the room and directed him to their lab table in the back.

Brandon traded troubled looks with Dr. Parrish as they passed by his desk. Parrish had on a new pair of glasses and some bandages on his head. Brandon was relieved when Parrish didn't ask about Jon's memory loss. He was tired of explaining it to everyone, especially when he really didn't know anything. Brandon patted Jon on the shoulder and held up the chemistry textbook.

"This is chemistry, Jon. Here's the book."

Jon nodded. "I saw one like it in my locker. What do I do with it?"

"You bring it to class. Or take it home to study if we have homework, or a test."

Parrish found a spare notebook in the prep room and gave it to Jon, then proceeded to give notes for the chapter. Jon took notes like everyone else, but he seemed distracted. When the school day was over, word had gotten around that Jon was much different than he used to be. Brandon gave up trying to defend him. Instead he told everyone Jon had gotten a head injury and left it at that. The last bell finally rang and everyone left.

"Where's your car?" asked Brandon, loading up his backpack.

"My car?" said Jon.

"Your Mustang, man. Did you drive today?"

"No. Angie brought me. I forgot how to drive."

"You forgot?" Brandon scratched his head. "Do you need a ride home?"

"Angie told me to wait here with Dr. Parrish."

"Okay, that's cool. So do you want to get together tonight? We could go by Maria's and try to help you remember who she is. She's pretty pissed at you, man, but don't worry, she loves you. She'll come around when you get it back together. Right now, though, you're freaking her out. You're freaking us all out."

"I don't have time to get it back together. I have much work to do...."

"Yeah, yeah, I know, you're in a hurry. Look, man, I gotta go. Don't forget to study for the history test tomorrow."

"Test? Study?"

Brandon looked at his friend, disbelieving. If this was how Alzheimer's patients were, then he had a whole new respect for their caregivers. "If you don't study you won't keep up your grades. Do you know what grades are?"

"Grades?" Jon nodded slightly. "Yes, I know what grades are now. What kind of grades do I get?"

"I don't know, you just started school here last month. But you got a C on a homework assignment in chemistry. And in history you got a couple A's. That's probably your best subject. You should try to get at least a B in everything."

"Okay, I will get Bs. Then I can work hard and fast." Jon walked away from Brandon without another word. Brandon felt bad for Jon. That boy was all messed up.

Chapter 14

MAGIC

KELLY

We got a surprise when Angie picked us up from school that afternoon. She'd spent a good part of her day at a store picking out cell phones for the three of us. Travis got a bright yellow phone that was hardly bigger than a credit card. I got a pink one. Jon's was red.

I couldn't believe it. All my friends had phones and I always felt dumb when one of them asked for my cell number. It was kind of hard to explain that I lived with foster parents who really didn't have the money for something like that. Well not any more! I hugged Angie around the neck and thanked her big time.

"You're certainly welcome," she said. "I think it's important that each of you has a way to call home."

Travis gawked at his phone. "Where do I put it?"

"Put it in your backpack," said Angie.

"Or your pocket." I demonstrated by stuffing my phone into my blue jeans pocket.

"But I dunno anybody's number."

"You will," said Angie. "Why don't you get Mathew's number tomorrow in school? You're going to spend the night with him next weekend, right?"

Travis nodded. "Yeah! Thanks, Angie!"

130

"You're certainly welcome."

"Angie?" I asked. "Are you sure we can afford these? You know how Chris worries about money all the time."

"Chris worries about everything, at least he used to. I went to the basement this morning to ask him about the phones before I ever went to the store. You know what he did? He grunted at me, like I was aggravating him, or something. I took his grunt as a yes and got the phones anyway."

"Can I call Melissa?" I asked eagerly.

"It's your phone," said Angie. "But try not to use too many minutes."

By the time we got to the high school the buses were long gone and most of the students had cleared out. A guidance counselor gave us directions to Dr. Parrish's room, where we found Parrish at his desk working at the computer. He got up and smiled when he saw us.

"Hey, kids. Hey, Angie. Jon said you were coming. What can I do for you?"

"I was hoping you might have some things we could borrow for a while," said Angie. "Chris needs them for his project and I didn't know where else to get them. Here's his list." She gave the list to Parrish.

Parrish scanned the list and nodded. "I've got everything but the groceries. And there's no rush to return it, just bring it all in by June. Here, let me get it for you." Parrish went off and found a box, which he began to load up with test tubes and beakers. Travis and I followed him.

That's when Travis noticed Jon in the back of the room, sitting alone at a table. He nudged me and pointed. Jon either didn't see us, or he didn't care that we were there. He sat utterly motionless with one hand in front of him, palm up. He stared at his hand as if he were in deep concentration. I didn't know what he was trying to do, but I was impressed that anybody could be completely still for so long.

Suddenly, a light green tennis ball appeared in his hand. He hadn't moved a muscle, so there was no slight-of-hand trickery. It just appeared.

"Wow!" said Travis. "Do it again!"

"Is that a real ball?" I asked.

Jon bounced the ball on the floor to show it was real. He placed it back in his hand the same way.

"Watch," he said softly. He stared at the ball hard.

I only had a vague idea what was coming next, so I counted off the seconds in my head. As soon as I hit three, the ball vanished. I blinked. That was no ordinary trick. Once again Jon had never moved at all. Maybe he *was* going to be the greatest magician in the world. Could a head injury cause such a huge change in someone? Maybe he wasn't possessed. Maybe he'd just gotten his brain wires crossed.

I looked back and saw Parrish gawking at Jon as if his whole way of scientific thinking had just been crushed. The big man gave us a look of troubled amazement, then wrapped more glassware in newspapers and loaded them in the box. I changed the subject away from magic and tennis balls.

"So, Dr. Parrish, you said you're a microbiologist. What exactly do you study?"

"I've developed a faster method of classifying or identifying spores of all kinds."

"What's a spore?" asked Travis, giving up on Jon. He sat on the counter and dangled his legs.

"It's kind of like a seed, usually much smaller. Lots of organisms use spores as a way to reproduce, like some plants, most fungi, and even bacteria." He put several beakers and a graduated cylinder into the box. "Angie, I've got an electronic scale that Chris might want instead of what he's got listed here. Would that be okay?"

Angie answered. "It's okay with me. I don't even know what he's using it for."

Parrish nodded and set the electronic scale in the box. "Kelly, how'd you like me to teach you a few things about chess before your big tournament?"

"Really? That'd be cool!"

"Yeah!" said Travis. "Can I watch?"

Angie shook her head. "I can't stick around while you guys play chess. I want to get this stuff to Chris right away so he can get this product thing out of his system. If he doesn't do it soon I might go crazy. You can play chess another time."

"Angie, you can go if you want," said Parrish. "I'll bring them home. Besides, I need to stop by the old place and make a list of materials I'll need. I've decided it's time to finish the house."

"Really?" said Angie. "That's great, Mark! I know Chris will be excited to hear we'll be neighbors after all."

"Well, I'm not sure I want to live there. It's a lot of house for one person. I'll probably just sell it."

Angie's excitement faded. "That's too bad. Chris and I were hoping you'd move in. But it's good you're going to finish it."

"What house?" asked Travis. "Is it big?"

"The house next door to you," said Parrish.

"Yuck! That place is a mess!"

"You own that?" I was surprised by that bit of information.

Parrish laughed. "Yes and yes. It's not so bad on the inside, though I haven't worked on it for a couple years. But I'm psyched now. I'm getting restarted bright and early a week from Saturday."

"You'll miss the chess tournament," I said, half hoping he might come and support me.

"That's true," he acknowledged without any hint that he wanted to go. I was a little disappointed until I scanned his thoughts. Though he'd saved me from the demons in the cave, he still wasn't comfortable hanging out with kids he hardly knew. "Maybe I can help you. Angie, how about if I bring Kelly and Travis home right after I teach her a few things about the game." He winked at me and reached into a cabinet to get a chessboard and a box full of chess pieces. He placed them on the table and I set up the pieces.

I tried to wink back, but of course, I blinked instead. "Sounds like a challenge," I said with a grin.

"Are you sure, Mark?" Angie looked at Parrish, who nodded. "Thanks, so much. And thanks for this stuff. Let's go, Jon."

Jon got excited. "We're going home? Good! I can practice magic!"

"That's all you've been doing since school ended," said Parrish. "How do you make that ball disappear, anyway?"

Jon smiled devilishly. "I can't tell you. It's magic." Angie gave Jon the box of materials to carry and took out the red cell phone as they left the room. I heard them talking in the hall.

"I got you a cell phone, Jon," she said. "Do you like the color?"

"I like the color," said Jon. "What is a cell phone?"

Angie stopped in her tracks and gawked at him. "I can't believe a teenager doesn't know what a cell phone is. You must have hit your head pretty hard. Speaking of, I got you two doctors appointments tomorrow. You've got a physical in the morning so you'll have to fast tonight. And you'll see a psychiatrist later. Maybe they can help you get some of your memory back. You'll have to miss school." They went on down the hall.

Travis climbed onto a stool to get a good view of the chess match as we sat down to play.

"You go first," I said.

"Thanks," said Parrish, moving one of the pawns.

I moved my knight to see how he'd react, and sat back in my chair. I watched Parrish carefully while he thought about his next move. After he made it, I smiled slightly.

What do you think? asked Travis inside my mind. *Can you beat him?*

My response didn't surprise him. *This'll be a quickie.*

ANGIE

The next day Angie took Jon to the doctor for a complete physical examination. Apparently his vitals were all humanly normal, which was a good sign. The doctor even took X-rays of his head, but she found nothing to explain why he had lost so much memory and why he now spoke with a

British accent. She thoroughly searched his scalp, almost like she was picking for lice, and didn't find a single bump or scratch. She finally declared that the stress and fear of being trapped in the cave could have been a contributing factor. Jon was still young, and though he seemed tough on the outside the prolonged worry may have been a little more than he could handle.

She also said the amnesia and the possible personality disorder should be looked at by a mental health professional.

"We're seeing Dr. Sanderlyn at one," said Angie.

The doctor nodded enthusiastically. "Dr. Sanderlyn is the best! You'll like him." She sent Jon off with a note to stay out of school for the rest of the week.

When Angie got him back home, Jon rushed upstairs, wild-eyed. "Now I can practice magic!"

"Hold on, Jon!" she said, aggravated by his newfound obsession. "The doctor said you should rest in bed and that's exactly what you're going to do. Don't even think about practicing magic until you've rested."

"How long do I have to rest?"

"At least until I get back. I need to run some errands. Remember we're seeing the psychiatrist at one."

Jon nodded obediently and went straight to bed. Angie was surprised and a little suspicious. What? No argument about going to bed in the middle of the day? She decided to check up on him before she left, but once again she was impressed. He appeared to be fast asleep. The doctor was right. He *did* need rest.

Chapter 15
SATAN'S SIDEKICKS

TRAVIS

By five o'clock that afternoon Travis Bishop was going crazy. Not crazy like Denny Martinez at the children's home. Nobody was *that* crazy. Denny and Travis had been roommates at the home and Denny would wake up in the middle of the night screaming about monsters that were hiding in dark corners or in the closet. They'd turn on the lights and he'd still see them in the shadows, though nobody else saw anything. It scared Travis to think about it. No, Denny was *insane* crazy. In fact, he'd been placed in a crazy house two years ago, a hospital called Sunnyside Mental Health Clinic. Sunnyside was Denny's home now.

Jon had been to Sunnyside, too, earlier that afternoon. Angie had taken him to see Dr. Sanderlyn, who spoke with Jon for an hour before determining that nothing was wrong with him. Even so, they set up a second appointment for the week after Thanksgiving.

No, Travis wasn't *Sunnyside* crazy, not at all. He was *bored* crazy. He wanted to play with some friends, but they all lived too far away to walk to their houses, which meant Angie would have to take him. His best friend in the whole world was Mathew Dunlop, but he hardly ever got to play with Mathew. He decided to let Angie know how he felt. He sat beside her in a rocking chair on the front porch.

"Angie, I'm going crazy."

She looked at him and rubbed his hair. "You'd better not be. We've got enough crazy people in this house."

"But Dr. Sanderlyn said Jon wasn't crazy."

"Dr. Sanderlyn doesn't know as much about Jon as I do. Everybody who knew Jon before the cave trip has noticed changes in the way he acts. I tried to explain it to Sanderlyn, but he didn't get it. Honestly, I think he was psychoanalyzing me instead of Jon."

"What's sykoanzulizing?"

"Psy-cho-an-alyzing. It's just doctor talk. They like big words. It basically means they study your mind." She took in the view in front of the house and sighed contentedly. Travis liked the feelings she was having, all warm and fluid. She went on. "I love fall. Look at all the different colors in the leaves. You know, it's so nice outside, I think we'll eat on the deck tonight. We won't get many more days like this before winter. Do you and Kelly like hamburgers and hotdogs?"

"Yes!" cried Travis emphatically. "With cheese?"

"Absolutely. I'll call you when dinner is ready.

Hours later Travis heard his stomach growl, so he wandered out on the deck where he found Angie cooking burgers and dogs on the charcoal grill. She had already set up dinnerware on the picnic table and the smell of all that food made Travis' mouth water. He was starved as usual. He leaned against Angie.

"Angie, I'm bored."

"Not crazy any more? That's good. Are you bored or just hungry?" Angie flipped a row of burgers, one after the other. Flames shot up as juice from the patties spewed over hot coals. The grill was situated next to the outside wall of the house, allowing the smoke to be drawn up and away from where they were standing.

"Both. There's nothin' to do."

"Why don't you find Kelly? I'm sure you guys can come up with something to keep you busy. You could play a game."

Travis swiped a pickle from the relish tray and popped it in his mouth. It crunched all sweet and juicy. "Maybe."

He moped through the house and up the stairs into Kelly's room, but she was talking on the phone with her new friend, Melissa.

"Go find Jon," said Kelly, waving him off.

Travis left disappointed. He could usually count on Kelly to come up with something fun to do. He stopped in the hall. The door to his room was closed, so he tried to open it, but it was locked. Jon was most likely inside practicing magic, which was mostly the only thing he did any more. He didn't bother to knock, Jon had gotten too weird lately, kind of scary, too.

Travis hung his head and went back downstairs. He thought about watching TV, but nothing was on. He went out on the front porch and sat in one of the five rocking chairs Angie had bought so they could all rock together. As he rocked back and forth he imagined the thrill of going on an adventure, but that only reminded him how bored he still was. He wanted *real* excitement and he wanted it *now!*

That's when he heard the distant rumbling of powerful engines. At first they were far away and the noise only made him curious. But they got closer and became louder and louder. Whatever made the noise was definitely coming this way. Travis sat up, alarmed. The noise was so loud it was getting scary.

Angie came out on the porch and stood at the top of the stairs. Surprisingly, Chris also showed up, looking very nervous, Travis could feel it. Chris had gotten so protective of the secrecy of his product in the basement that the family rarely saw him any more. He'd gotten mean, too. Angie was cautiously calm, so Travis moved closer to her.

"What is that noise?" asked Chris, his eyes darting fearfully from Angie to the road. Travis could barely hear him.

"I think we're going to have a visitor," shouted Angie. "I almost forgot."

"Forgot what?" Travis practically screamed as he covered his ears. This was louder than the stupid fire alarm at school!

A moment later, Jon and Kelly joined them. Jon stood off by himself levitating the tennis ball. Kelly went to the end of the driveway and looked up the road. She ran back.

She yelled excitedly. "Bikers! Like fifty of 'em!"

She'd no sooner said it, when a long line of motorcycles rolled down the street into the cul-de-sac. The noise was deafening and powerful. Travis swallowed hard.

Angie turned to her husband. "I can't believe she came."

"Who?" asked Chris. "They better stay out of the basement."

Angie shook her head at his narrow train of thought. "I finally get to meet her."

Dozens of bikers made the loop around the cul-de-sac, then found places to park in the road, the driveway, and all over the yard of the vacant house next door. Luckily, most of the bikers eventually put their powerful machines into a sputtering idle. Even so, one of them gunned an engine now and then. The sudden, earsplitting blasts made Travis jump halfway out of his skin.

Travis shivered and grabbed the back of his neck. *Ghost fingers*! In his mind bikers were dangerous. These bikers didn't act threatening, but their mirror shades, Nazi looking helmets and dark leather jackets were disturbing.

One of the riders, a husky woman with broad shoulders, parked her bike in the driveway behind the minivan and turned off the motor. She stepped off the bike, removed her helmet, and adjusted a rag tied over her head as she strutted toward the house. She wore a black leather jacket and faded blue jeans.

A huge, bearded man on the lead bike called out to her. "Later, Matilda!"

The woman turned and waved. "See ya, Jake! You blokes take care!"

Travis saw a picture of an evil-looking devil on the back of her jacket with the words *Satan's Sidekicks* printed underneath. A second later the bike noise blasted the air again as the powerful machines roared back up the street. Travis kept his hands over his ears until the last one was gone and it was quiet again. For a while the silence seemed to make his ears ring.

It's a good thing there aren't any neighbors, thought Kelly to Travis. *They're so loud!* Right now Travis didn't care about neighbors. He was too worried about this stranger named Matilda. Who was she? Why was she here? He decided maybe being bored wasn't so bad after all.

The woman turned and faced them again. "G'day, Angie," she said in a thick, Australian accent. "It's been a while."

"A lifetime," said Angie coldly. "So you made it."

"Looks like it."

"You're early. We didn't expect to see you for another month. This is my husband, Chris McCormick."

Matilda offered to shake his hand, but Chris stood there stupidly. Angie nudged him. "Shake hands."

Chris reached out and took Matilda's hand. She squeezed hard. He tried to pull away, but she wouldn't let go. It wasn't until he grimaced in pain that she released him. Chris rubbed his throbbing hand. "That hurt. You stay out of my basement. You stay away from my product!" He turned and retreated into the house. Matilda was baffled by his response, but she felt good that he was weaker than her.

Travis sensed the woman was trying to conceal a deep sense of hurt, but mostly from herself. As hard-nosed as she seemed on the outside, he could tell she had delicate feelings. She might have been fooling everyone else, but she wasn't fooling him.

Matilda's gaze went from face to face as if sizing them up for a fight. She settled on Travis, who was practically glued to Angie's side. Angie was utterly calm, he could feel it. But this biker lady had him shaking.

"Hello, li'l mate," she said warmly. "How's it going?"

That was weird. She seemed friendly. Travis nodded slightly.

"It's okay, Travis," said Angie. "Everyone, I'd like you to meet Matilda Price. My birth mother."

KELLY

"I'm not looking to stay long," said Matilda, sounding humble and embarrassed. "I'm hoping to reconnect with you, that's all."

"I'm not looking for you to stay long either." Angie was curt, cold as ice. "And I wouldn't call it *re*connecting, Matilda, since we've never connected to begin with."

I looked at Travis, who shrugged. I couldn't tell if Angie liked her mom or not, but it sure didn't seem like it. The two women were alone in the living room, while the rest of us had gone some place else to give them privacy. Chris had escaped to the basement, and I do mean escaped. He'd only just met Angie's mother, but he was pretty upset about that handshake.

Travis and I were in the den pretending to watch TV, but we were really spying on Matilda Price. Jon sat in a rocking chair on the front porch throwing the tennis ball into the yard and making it come back to him without moving a muscle. I think he couldn't have cared less about Matilda.

"I want to show you I've changed, Angie. I came to listen to whatever you want to say to me. I deserve yer worst. I've never been a mother to you."

"No, you haven't. It's only the third time you've ever seen me, if you count being born. Do you remember when you came to my high-school graduation? At first I didn't want you anywhere near me. But then I thought, she's my mother, I need to meet her. Before long I got brave and thought we were going to finally meet that day. But we never even talked. You took off on that damn motorcycle without saying hello *or* goodbye!"

"I couldn't. I didn't want to go, but I couldn't face you either." Neither of them spoke for several moments, which I guess you'd call an awkward silence. Heck, I felt awkward and I wasn't even involved.

"Why are you here? Why shouldn't I just tell you to leave right now?" Angie meant it like an ultimatum.

"You'd be right to tell me to leave. But hear me out first, please. I can't explain it, but I got feelings, you know? Like you might need my help."

"I...*we* don't need your help. I've been just fine for forty-one years, and I'll be fine for the next forty-one—*without* you."

"Angie, I was a dipstick parent and never pretended to be otherwise. But I'm through with that. I want to be as good a parent to you as I can with the time we have left. I'll do whatever it takes."

"It's too late. In my heart you'll never be my mother. *Never.*"

"I understand that, really I do. But you're the only living rellie I've got. I just hope we can be friends."

"Friends don't get on their motorcycle at a whim and just leave." Angie sounded bitter, but I knew she was afraid. I mean, who'd want to waste her time getting to know someone who might just run off again and stay gone for decades?

"I won't do it again. I *have* changed, you'll see that for yourself. I'm no bludger, I'll get a job right off and start by paying for my room and board for whatever time you'll let me stay here. That is, if you have any room. I didn't know you had kids."

"How could you know *anything* about me? Unlike you, I can't physically have children of my own. Also unlike you, I've always *wanted* them. Chris and I see them as precious gifts, not inconveniences. We wanted children any way we could get them. We're foster parents, Matilda."

"Foster parents? That's noble. So what about these kids? Are they any trouble?"

"Trouble?" Angie's tone instantly went from angry jilted daughter to loving mom. "They're *wonderful.* We're so lucky. They've only been with us a couple months, but I already feel a connection, like they belong."

Travis and I exchanged happy looks. It's always great to hear when someone likes you, especially someone you care about.

"That's great." Matilda sounded sincere. "You have so much love to give to them. I can tell, even if I don't know you. You see, Angie? What we just did, that's all I'm hoping for by being here."

"What did we do?"

"We had a moment together, you know? You talked about the kids and how much you care for them. All this time I assumed they were your own children. Don't you understand? That's the kind of girl talk I'm hoping for. I'm so sorry I wasn't there for you at any time in your life. Krikey, I'm really sorry I left you at graduation, that was a stupid mistake. And I know it sounds selfish, but I'm sorry for me, too. I've only gotten to know you for twenty minutes and already realize I've lost a lifetime by not staying around." Matilda sniffled.

She's crying? I thought to Travis.

She's pretty upset, he replied back.

Wonder if she's ever done that before?

"Chris and I share in *all* big decisions," said Angie. "If you stay here, well that's a big one all right. It's as much his choice as it is mine."

"I understand. I'll go outside while you talk to Chris. I have a tendency to intimidate people."

"Really?" Angie's voice dripped with sarcasm, but she must have been smiling because both women chuckled as they started for the foyer. I caught a flash of confusion from Matilda when she saw that Jon had been sitting within hearing distance.

Matilda stepped out on the porch and glared at him. "Get an earful?"

"What?" said Jon, clueless. Travis snickered, so I covered his mouth.

I peeked out the window and saw Matilda shoot Jon a challenging glance. She stepped down to the sidewalk. A moment later Angie came outside and marched right up to her. Jon threw the ball almost to the mailbox by the street. It came to a complete stop, then began to roll back to him. It rolled past the big oak tree, bouncing over its roots, and then *up* the steps and into his hand. I was amazed. Travis tugged on my arm to make sure I'd seen it. For the first time Matilda noticed what he was doing. Jon shot a cocky glance to the older woman and went inside.

"Does he always do that?" Matilda scratched her head.

Angie ignored her. "Chris doesn't care if you move in as long as you don't go in the basement. He's gotten kind of weird. On the other hand, *I'm* not so sure if you should, even if you do pay room and board. You've been such a *lousy* mother."

I cringed. It wasn't so much the word, it was *how* she said it. She sounded almost nasty. Was she testing her mother?

"Yes," said Matilda, not reacting like I thought she would. "I want us to be friends, if we can. I want to get to know your husband and your kids, too. I want to be part of your life, at least for as long as you'll let me."

Angie went on. "We don't know anything about you except that you rode up with a motorcycle gang called *Satan's Sidekicks*. I suppose you can be nice when you're not crushing the hands of people you meet for the first time. You could have hurt Chris, squeezing it like that! And I wonder what kind of influence you'll be on the kids, because I assure you, the kids will continue to live here whether you stay or not. Frankly, I don't see you fitting in."

Matilda hung her head and I kind of felt sorry for her. I had a feeling Angie was going to tell her to hit the road. She went on.

"The five of us, well, we're a little late getting together, but we're a family. Matilda, as long as your influence on the children remains positive, then the family includes you, too. And if you don't mind sleeping on the floor, you can have the small bedroom at the top of the stairs. We'll bring up an old mattress from the basement."

Matilda smiled and nodded politely.

Boy was I shocked. I didn't expect Angie to say anything close to that.

"Travis?" said Angie. "Kelly? Kids, you've already met Matilda. Well, she's going to live with us for a while. One more thing, Matilda. Don't you dare bring any guns into this house. I am staunchly against firearms. Do you understand?"

"I understand," repeated Matilda with a slight nod. "Lots of folks don't want guns around." She lowered her voice so only I could hear her. "Until they need 'em."

I smiled, but didn't say anything. I nearly raised my hand to tell on her, but that would have been stupid. To my surprise Travis did raise his hand. I winced. I didn't want him to say what I'd just been thinking.

Matilda seemed bewildered. "Is that for me?"

"Yes," said Travis nervously. "I have a question."

"Oh. Well, go ahead, li'l mate. Fire away."

Travis lowered his head shyly, then looked up. "Whutta we call you?"

I let out a breath of relief when he didn't mention guns.

"What do you call me? You mean, like Angie and Chris call me Matilda?"

Travis nodded. Matilda thought about it for a while then smiled again. This time the smile was warmer and made her look pretty, like Angie.

"Well, li'l mate, here's what I think. I'm hoping you three and Angie and Chris will all be together for a very long time. That would make me sort of like your grandmother, wouldn't it? So why don't you call me Granny?"

"Granny?" Angie's eyes nearly popped out of her head.

"We've got a grandmother," I said calmly. "Wait till Jon hears."

"We never had a grandmother before," said Travis. "Not a live one, anyway."

I smiled and nodded but I wasn't sure how I felt about this unusual woman. Something else got my attention. "What's burning?"

Angie looked up with a start. "Omigosh! The burgers!" Suddenly, she charged back into the house. We started to go with her, but we didn't want to leave Matilda—Granny—stuck outside alone.

"So much for supper," I said.

Travis smiled. "Granny, I hope you like pickles."

Chapter 16

THE FIGHT

KELLY

Giant flames from the grill shot up in the air, licking at the vinyl siding on the back of the house. Angie freaked when she saw it, but reacted like a pro. Crouching, she moved the grill away from the house to the center of the deck. Then she carefully scraped the ruined burgers and hotdogs onto a large plate. When the juicy meat was off the grill, the fire died down a bit.

Granny helped by grabbing a box of baking soda from the fridge and sprinkling it all over the coals. It was mostly dead in seconds.

The burnt siding looked and smelled as bad as the burgers. The heat had melted and charred an area eight feet above the grill, warping the vinyl, and giving it a curdled texture. Angie hung her head.

"I wonder how much that will cost?" She was so frustrated I gave her a big hug. Travis joined us. Granny looked on without comment.

"I'm sorry about supper," said Angie. "Chris is the one who usually cooks on the grill. Would anyone like to go with me to Tony's Pizza?"

"Why not send Jon or Chris?" asked Granny. "Though it's not my business."

"They forgot how to drive," said Travis.

"Forgot how to drive?" Granny half shrugged. "How does that work?"

"We've had some, uh, issues to deal with," said Angie. "Kelly, can you make a list of what everyone wants? Travis, I'll need you to help carry the drinks, okay?"

"Okay!" said Travis. "Kelly, I want a turkey sub!"

"Figured that." I found a sheet of paper in a kitchen drawer and jotted it down. "Can I have a pepperoni pizza?"

"You can have whatever you want," said Angie. "Let's get a large, we'll split it. Matilda, what would you like?"

Matilda "Granny" Price had two requests. "A roast beef sub would do me fine, Angie. Thanks. Would you mind if I joined you on this trek? I'd like to pick up some job applications."

"Not a problem. Let's go, guys. I'll get Jon."

When Angie left the room Granny looked at me confused. "Forgot how to drive? I mean, Chris must have been driving for what? Twenty years? Kelly, what's going on?"

"It's complicated," I said. "One of those long stories."

"Can't wait to hear it." She called out to the other room. "Angie? Would you mind giving me five minutes to freshen up a bit? I don't want to make a bad first impression with any potential employers."

"Hurry." Angie was so upset over burning both dinner and the house that Granny's delay nearly set her off. I heard her think, *If you hadn't shown up I might not have burned anything. At the very least I wouldn't be waiting for you now!* I quickly got out of her head.

I followed Angie into the den where Jon sat on a bar stool, staring out the front window. She tapped him on the shoulder to get his attention.

"Jon, Tony called yesterday. He asked me to remind you about your paycheck. He also wanted to know when you were coming back to work. He hired Brandon to fill in while you're out."

"I know Brandon," said Jon in his British accent and deadpan expression. "I met him at school."

"He's your best friend, or he was. You really need to go with us and talk to Tony."

"I will talk to Tony. You must introduce me."

"Introduce?" Frustrated, Angie gave up any attempt to spark his memory. She tried a different strategy. "Maria's working tonight, so if you want to take some time and visit with her we can eat at the restaurant."

"I know Maria. It took me three tries to learn her name." Jon spoke like a robot with half a brain.

Twenty minutes later Granny had showered and changed into a newer looking pair of blue jeans and a white blouse. Her hair was fixed nice, too. I was impressed. Without the do-rag she looked a lot like Angie. But waiting twenty minutes was nearly too much. Angie was beyond irritable.

"Can we go now?"

"Sorry," said Granny. "Yes, certainly."

We hurried to the van before Angie blew her top. Granny looked back at the house. "Did anyone get Chris' order?"

"Chris doesn't eat any more," said Angie. "Or he doesn't appear to, though he hasn't lost any weight. And don't ask why because we don't know what's going on either."

———

I walked into Tony's Pizza with Angie, Jon, Travis, and our new grandmother, too. I'll admit it felt weird calling this total stranger "Granny," but that came easier for me than calling her Matilda. Angie was a little ticked off about it, but like Travis said, we had a grandparent. We should just enjoy her while we could.

Maria waited on a table by the window. She waved when she saw us and hurried over to hug Jon, who was totally unresponsive to her. She hugged Angie and me, too, before rubbing Travis' hair again. Maybe the hair rub was a ritual, or something, because she did it every time she saw him. She also offered him another piece of gum, which he took, of course. That kid just loves gum.

"Maria," I said. "This is our foster grandmother. You can call her Granny Price."

"Glad to meet you, Ms. Price." Maria smiled pleasantly at Granny. Granny nodded politely, though I think she felt a little out of place.

A balding Hispanic man behind the counter got Maria's attention and pointed to a table. Maria nodded. "I gotta work. Brandon's in the kitchen. It's good to meet you." She went off to her customers.

"She's spunk," said Granny. "Looks like a model and seems nice, too."

"Nicest person I know," I said. I looked at Jon, wondering why he didn't react in some way to the girl he wanted to marry. "Jon said her parents are nice, too. Her dad's a good boss. That's back when Jon remembered things."

"Were Jon and Chris in an accident?" asked Granny.

"You could say that." Angie gave their order to Tony, who took it all down and thanked her. He nodded to Jon.

"Sure you don't wanna work tonight, Jon?" he asked. "We're busy as hell."

"I must work hard and fast. I will be the greatest magician in the world." Jon stepped away from the counter and instantly became distracted by a nickel-sized spot on the floor.

Angie introduced Matilda to Jon's boss, Tony Sanchez, who was Maria's dad. She told him Matilda was looking for a job.

"I can get you an application," said Tony. "But I just hired Brandon. I don't really need more help now, unless Jon isn't coming back. Has he given you any idea what his plans are?"

Angie looked at Jon, who still studied the spot on the floor. "I wish I could help you with that, but Jon is having...problems." She and Tony nodded in agreement. He lowered his voice. "He's really bad, isn't he? Maria said he wasn't the same. Has he seen a doctor?"

"Yes," whispered Angie. "Physically he's fine. The psychiatrist we took him to didn't note anything, but we're scheduled to see him again."

I listened to them, but I watched Jon because something was happening on the floor. The spot, probably made of grease, began to lift away from the surface. It drifted up to Jon's hand where he caught it midair and held it tightly in his fist. He gave me a sly, sidelong glance and opened his hand. The spot was gone. I looked at Granny and Angie and even Tony, but they hadn't noticed the trick at all. Travis missed it too. Jon winked at me and became distracted again. I tried to wink back, but as usual, I only blinked.

"I saw a help-wanted sign in the window next door," said Granny. "Do you know if the job's still open?"

"At Mike's? Yeah, it's open, but Mike's kind of particular who works for him."

"Thanks, mate. I'll be back." Granny adjusted her hair and left the restaurant.

Tony looked at Angie. "Is she serious? Mike's looking for a bouncer. Hey, Jon, your paycheck's in my office. Let me know when you're coming back okay?"

Jon gave Tony the deer-in-the-headlights look. "What is your office?"

Tony looked at me. "Kelly, you know the way, don't you?" I nodded. "You can all go back, Brandon's there. Maybe you can give him some pointers on washing dishes."

"Kelly, I'll be in the car," said Angie, taking out her cell phone. "I need to call Yvette." Angie and Tony nodded at each other and she left through the front door. I tapped Jon on the arm.

"This way."

In the kitchen we talked with Jon's best friend, Brandon Cole. Brandon was a lanky black kid who was about an inch taller than Jon. Where Jon used to have quiet ambitions of being a stuntman and a movie producer, Brandon wanted to write and direct. He had loaned Jon his expensive camcorder to record our caving trip, but unfortunately, it was still in the cave some place.

As usual Brandon whistled when he saw me. "Kelly, you get hotter every day. I can't believe you're just thirteen. Look me up in five years, I'll put you in a movie."

"Are you really going to make movies?" I asked.

"You bet. Jon and I are gonna take over Hollywood. But right now I gotta take out the trash. First things first, you know."

Brandon hauled two overloaded trash cans out the back door. I took Jon to the tiny office space and pointed. "Your paycheck's in here."

Jon stared at the office, utterly confused. "Where? What does it look like?"

I went into the office and found an envelope with Jon's name on it taped to the wall. The check was inside. I took it off the wall and gave it to Jon.

"What is this?" he asked.

"Your paycheck," I said. "You sign your name on the back and take it to the bank where they give you money."

Jon lit up. "Money? I can use money. I need to buy more magic supplies!" He stuffed the envelope into his back pocket.

I wanted to talk to Brandon or Maria again about Jon, so the three of us took a seat on a wooden bench near the rear entrance of the kitchen and waited. Jon had only been back to school for one day and I was curious how it had gone. When Maria hugged him a few minutes ago, he didn't flinch, and that wasn't right. He used to get all flushed just talking about her.

Brandon never came back. That dumpster must have been a mile away.

———

For Travis, life was good. It could be better, especially as far as Jon and Chris were concerned, but for right now Travis was happy. As we sat in the kitchen I listened to his thoughts while he went over the recent changes in his life. The three of us were together again. *Nothing* could beat that. And we had a foster family who liked us, maybe even loved us, though it was still too early to tell. Angie and Chris were two of the nicest people we'd ever known, and they were *our* people. Admittedly, Chris had changed a lot since Pandora's Cave, Jon too. Maybe they were demonically possessed, or maybe they were having one of those extreme reactions to stress, but at least they were with us.

Travis was excited about having a foster grandmother, too, though she was a strange woman. And he had gum. And one of Tony's hot turkey subs was on the way. Tony always toasted his sandwiches, which made the cheese all gooey. Travis' mouth watered.

I got out of his mind and leaned back on the bench. Travis was definitely happier than he used to be. Good, that's what I wanted. He looked up and smiled when Maria entered the kitchen.

"Did you guys see Brandon?" she asked.

"He took out the trash." I pointed.

"Thanks." Maria disappeared out the back door.

A second later Travis gagged on the gum. He coughed hard and blew the gum across the floor. I jumped off the bench in surprise.

"You okay?"

Travis shook his head. His expression was pure terror. "Maria!"

I grabbed Travis by the hand. "Come on!" When we got outside I was shocked. Brandon was trapped between the dumpster and the building. Three other boys threw punches at him while he struggled to fight them off. Maria stood off to the side yelling at the boys.

"Stop it! Leave him alone!"

"Grab him!" said the biggest guy, who stood half a head taller than Brandon. "Hold him, Robbie! Get his arm, Spider!"

The boys named Robbie and Spider out flanked Brandon. They each caught one of his arms. All at once Brandon couldn't punch back.

The big kid swung at him. He caught Brandon in the side of the head. *Smack!*

Brandon shook off the punch. He stomped on the foot of the boy named Spider, the boy on his left. Spider cried out in pain, but he didn't let go.

The big kid grinned at Maria. "You can stop this, Maria! Right now!" His eyes flashed.

He's hateful! cried Travis in my head. *He likes hurtin' people!*

I'd already gathered that much. But what did he mean when he said Maria could *stop it*? Stop what? Stop them beating up Brandon?

Maria looked helpless. She was about to say something, but Brandon cut her off. "No, Maria! Not a word!"

"Brandon! I have to!"

"Do it! Do it! Do it!" The kid named Robbie chanted while he held Brandon's other arm. Robbie was tall and skinny with big ears and too many zits. I could tell Robbie enjoyed pain, too. As long as it was someone *else's* pain.

Maria charged at the big kid. "Stop it, Kurt!" She punched him hard in the back. The big kid, Kurt, turned and pushed her backwards. She stumbled and fell into me. I caught her and held her up.

"Just say the magic words and I'll stop. You *know* what I want. Hold 'im still, Spider! I'll finish him off!"

Jon! Get out back! They're beating up Brandon! When I sent the mental message to Jon, Travis heard it, loud and clear. The problem was Jon must have blocked me out. He never responded. I ran back inside.

"Where ya going?" asked Travis in a panic.

"Getting Jon!"

Jon was still sitting on the bench where we'd left him. He glanced up at me in surprise when I grabbed his arm and pulled him outside. He came with me, apparently sensing my urgency.

"You've got to help Brandon!" I told him.

Jon stopped when he saw Maria. He took in the brutal scene as if he didn't quite understand what was going on. Kurt focused on him at once.

"Well, if it isn't Golden Boy. This is the wimp you're dating, Maria? Instead of *me*? You gotta be kidding."

Kurt went up to Jon, face to face. He seemed to tower over him. He was a *big* guy! Jon stood passively, like he had no idea Kurt wanted to pound him. I tried to warn him inside his head, but he continued to block me out. Maria looked at me desperately. I quickly read her thoughts. *Does Jon remember how to fight?*

I shrugged helplessly. We were about to find out.

Kurt shoved Jon backwards. Jon didn't fall, but he stumbled and caught his balance.

"You don't seem so tough to me." Kurt grinned at Maria. "I think I'd rather beat the hell out of this one."

Kurt swung hard, a knockout punch straight into Jon's left jaw. The blow caught Jon completely by surprise. He blinked a few times and cleared his vision. All at once his eyes narrowed, he bared his teeth, like a wild animal cornered by hunters.

"Ooh, he's gonna bite me." Kurt swung again, straight for Jon's nose. Now I'm not certain exactly what happened at that moment, but something did, something nobody expected. Kurt's big knuckles struck Jon squarely in the face. But Jon's head never moved and Kurt reacted like he'd just punched a brick wall. The bigger boy nearly collapsed in pain.

"Aaaah! You ass, you broke my hand!" Kurt gripped his broken hand with his good one, rocking up and down in pain. Jon watched him impassively, then tilted his head slightly as if he was trying to understand something. He raised both hands, palms out. A terrific force blew out of his hands, or at least that's how it seemed. I felt the wind from it, and Kurt felt the full power. Kurt was lifted from his feet and tossed like a rag doll a good twenty feet away. He slammed into some cardboard liquor boxes piled behind the business next door.

Kurt got up, his eyes burning in fury. "Robbie, get 'im! Spider, you got Brandon!"

When Robbie ran for Jon, Spider's eyes grew large with fear. I scanned his mind and found out he wanted nothing to do with Brandon on his own. Brandon tore loose on him. He began punching Spider everywhere like a whirlwind. His fists pounded him in the face, head, arms, chest, belly...pretty much everywhere he could reach. Spider was getting his butt kicked good!

Robbie came in from Jon's blindside. He threw a haymaker punch, head-high. Jon leaned away from the punch and caught Robbie's arm. He pulled down the wrist and landed a solid elbow to Zit boy's unprotected face. Robbie's head snapped back as he fell over.

A moment later Kurt and Robbie were back on their feet, ready to finish the fight. Travis ran to help Jon, but I grabbed his arm. "No, Travis! You're too little."

"It's not fair!" Travis wanted to beat those guys up *bad*! So did I, but I'm not so brave. I was already shaking worse than one of those paint-mixing machines.

The fighters squared off. Jon's expression was icy cold, fearless. He never moved a muscle, he just stood and watched Kurt. He paid no attention at all to Robbie.

Kurt didn't back away, but he was clearly unnerved.

"Are you okay, Brandon?" called Maria. Brandon actually had to make himself stop beating up Spider, who lay moaning at his feet, bloodied and bruised.

Brandon nodded. He wiped blood from his nose on his sleeve. "Let's take these chumps, Jon!"

Kurt laughed. "Maria, when you're ready for a *real* man...." Kurt pointed to himself.

"I got a *real* man, Kurt. And he's not a jerk like you! Go to hell!"

"When I'm done with your boy here, I'll come after you next. Only we ain't gonna fight. We gonna love."

Maria spit in Kurt's general direction. "Drop dead, pig!"

Kurt glared at her. "You forget who I am? You want me to tell my daddy about how you won't go out with me?"

"What's he talking about?" asked Travis.

"Nothing," said Maria. "He's a piece o' crap."

"Piece o' crap?" Kurt shook his head. "I'm wastin' my time here. I'm goin' home." He turned as if to walk away. Suddenly, he spun back around. He threw a rocket punch straight at Jon's stomach.

Jon never flinched, but somehow a bolt of lightning exploded out of his belly. The lightning slapped Kurt with so much force he went flying into the brick wall. Kurt struck the wall hard and collapsed like a wet rag. His face was scraped. Blood spewed from his nose, which was now bent in the wrong direction.

Jon had always had an amazing sense of impending danger. It was one of his special skills. I was telepathic and Travis read emotions. But in a fight Jon had some kind of built-in advanced-warning system. He sensed what his opponents would do a split second before they ever did it. He once told me it was like getting a phone call ahead of time to warn him.

But I'd never seen him shoot lightning bolts out of his body before!

Brandon saw it too. He had started after Kurt until he saw the lightning. Now he froze in place. "What the hell?"

Robbie quickly raised his hands and backed away from Jon. "I'm outta here."

Somehow Kurt rolled over and staggered to his feet. A heavy stream of blood poured down his face and over his light blue tee shirt. He touched the broken area of his nose gingerly.

"You broke my nose, too, asshole! This ain't over, Bishop! It ain't over, I'm tellin' ya!" Kurt was burning up with hate and anger, but he was also afraid and he wobbled on his feet. The fear made Travis smile. Kurt was mostly talk unless he had the advantage.

Kurt's gaze shifted. He smiled slowly. I looked. The kid named Robbie crept up behind Jon. Robbie took a steel pipe from under his jacket. He raised the pipe to smash Jon in the skull.

Travis started to cry out. "J—...!"

Robbie swung hard. Jon turned slightly when he heard Travis start to yell. It probably saved his life. The pipe slammed into his shoulder instead of his head. Jon spun about and raised his palms toward Robbie, who drew back for a second try. The pipe came down fast.

From nowhere a hand reached in and caught Robbie by the wrist. He tried to continue the swing but he couldn't move his arm.

"Come on, Robbie!" cried Kurt. "Pound 'im!"

Robbie looked. Granny Price gripped him tightly. Robbie tried to jerk free, but he may as well have been caught in a vise. He yelled at her. "Leggo, old woman!"

"Who you callin' *old*?" Granny squeezed.

Robbie cried out. He dropped to his knees. "You're breaking my arm!"

Granny released his arm and took the pipe away from him. I was stunned. So was everyone else. Taking the pipe from Robbie was extremely cool, but what happened next was legendary.

Granny gripped both ends of the pipe and started to push. In no time the steel pipe folded in two. She tossed it aside and glared at Robbie. He gawked at her, openmouthed. We all did.

"I despise cowards," she said to him. "You three'd best get out of my sight."

Robbie jumped to his feet and took off running. Kurt followed, with Spider hobbling after him.

Maria took napkins from her apron for Brandon to wipe the blood off his face. "Are you all right?" she asked.

"Heck, yeah," said Brandon. "I get a bloody nose every time the weather changes." He picked up the folded pipe and tried to straighten it. He couldn't. "How'd you do that?"

Granny Price chuckled. "I eat my Wheaties."

Travis got very excited. Wheaties was his favorite cereal. "Wheaties does that?" We all laughed and Granny rubbed his head. She'd been kidding, of course, which made Travis feel dumb.

"Come on, li'l mate," she said, putting a hand on his shoulder. "Let's get Brandon some ice for his face."

As we entered the restaurant, Granny whispered advice to everyone.

"Kids, don't say anything to Chris and Angie about the fight, okay?"

I readily agreed, but Jon seemed to ignore her as he watched Robbie and Kurt, who had stopped running. They glared at him from a safe distance. Kurt was pointing at us, making empty threats.

Travis couldn't believe it. "We can't tell? Why not? Jon and Brandon won! And, Granny, you're like super woman!"

"Just don't mention it until I get to know 'em better," said Granny. "Chris seems a bit distracted, I need to figure him out. And we wouldn't Angie getting the wrong idea about Jon, okay?"

Everyone but Jon glared at him and Travis felt the pressure. "Okay. But I want to be the one to tell 'em when we can!"

"Cross my heart," said Granny. "But only when the time comes." She gripped Jon by the bicep and squeezed his arm. "Nice moves, Jon Bishop. You too, Brandon. I'm glad I got back in time to see the action."

"Thank you," said Jon, keeping a wary eye on Kurt. "I used magic on them."

"Magic, you say?" Granny laughed. "Whatever magic you used made 'em bleed like stuck pigs."

"Yeah, Jon," said Brandon. "We make a pretty good team, don't we?"

"You make a *great* team, Brandon." Maria said it proudly as she clapped her friends on the shoulders.

They were excited about the fight, but I needed more information. "Who was that guy? Why'd he go after you, Brandon? How come he knows Jon?"

"Kurt Lazarus. His rich daddy owns at least a dozen strip malls in northern Virginia, including this one. Kurt's a pig. He told me his father would raise the rent on the restaurant if I didn't date him. He was gonna keep beating up Brandon unless I said I'd go out with him. He must have checked up on Jon when he found out I had a boyfriend."

Granny let out a low growl. "Maria, have you told your father about this?"

"No way. If Daddy knew, he'd probably beat up Kurt and end up in jail. Please don't say anything about what happened."

Even as she spoke, her father appeared in the doorway. I gulped. Tony Sanchez's eyes burned. "Please don't say anything about what?"

Maria was the only one who spoke. "I'll tell you in your office." She hung her head and went off. Tony looked at Jon. "Get Brandon a new shirt out of the storeroom. And get him a bag of ice. Brandon, you can stay out of sight in the back and wash dishes for the rest of the night. I don't want my customers thinking I beat up my employees."

Tony walked off. Jon murmured, "Storeroom?"

The others went inside, but Jon stopped and went back out again. I followed him, mostly to call for help in case Kurt was dumb enough to return and try something. Kurt and Robbie were still there, about three businesses over, standing near a dumpster.

"When you least expect it, Bishop!" cried Kurt. "We're gonna take you down hard!"

"Yeah!" added Robbie. "*Real* hard!"

Jon glanced back at me, then raised one hand like he had when he was learning to make the tennis ball disappear. He lowered his head and took in a deep breath.

Suddenly, both Kurt and Robbie went flying up into the air. They sprawled and thrashed at nothing until they dropped into the dumpster with a solid thump. The heavy lid slammed shut.

"Magic," said Jon, winking at me again. He brushed by me and entered the kitchen. I looked back at the dumpster. I heard Robbie talking from inside.

"That ain't natural, man! You can kick his ass on your own, I ain't goin' anywhere near Jon Bishop again."

———

On the drive home Travis was still talking about Kurt Lazarus. "Brandon said Kurt's nineteen and drives a Corvette. He gets into fights a lot and he's been in juvie for selling drugs and stealing. What's juvie?"

"Juvenile detention," said Angie. "Prison for kids."

"I don't get it. Why's he do that? His dad's rich."

"Some people are born bad," said Granny Price soberly.

"Who are we talking about?" asked Angie. "Who's been in juvie?"

"This guy Brandon knows," I said quickly, remembering that we'd agreed not to mention the fight. "A real loser."

"Yeah," parroted Travis. "A real loser. Hey, Granny, I almost forgot. How'd your job interview go?"

"It turns out Mike, the boss, wanted a bouncer for the place. And the only way to get the job was to beat him at arm-wrestling."

I laughed. "Mike's a beast! His arms are bigger than my body. He can't do that."

"He can and he did."

"How'd you do?" asked Travis.

"Let's just say you're lookin' at the new bouncer for Mike's Pub." Granny grinned big. "What'd you expect?"

Chapter 17

FANG II

TRAVIS

Travis had gotten used to riding the bus to school and he'd gotten so he liked it just fine. He preferred riding with Jon in the Mustang, but since Jon was most likely possessed by a demon who didn't know how to drive, Travis was content to hang out with his friends, Addie Stamen and Tony Valdez. On the way home he hardly noticed it when the bus dropped off some kids about a mile from where he lived. He was too busy telling Addie and Tony about how Jon had made the tennis ball appear and disappear.

"He held out his hand and bam! It was gone!"

"Did it really go bam?" asked a small third grader in another seat.

Travis was irritated. He wasn't even talking to that kid. "It didn't make noise. It was just gone!"

"He probably put it up his sleeve."

"He didn't put it anywhere! I told you he didn't move, you moron!" Travis didn't have much patience with third graders. They were just too young to understand.

"My mom made us do zombie escape drills last night," said Tony.

"What's a zombie escape drill?" asked Travis, not even sure what a zombie was.

"My mom drives her car really slow and me and my sisters practice getting in and out on the run. It's kind of scary at first, but we're really good at it now."

"Your mom thinks zombies are real?" asked Addie.

Tony nodded. 'Yeah. She's kind of weird sometimes. She told me she's seen real zombies and thinks they're going to be a problem some day. She wants us to be ready, ya know?"

Travis nodded like he did, but he really didn't. What the heck was a zombie? He decided not to ask about it now.

The bus stopped in the cul-de-sac. The door opened and everyone waited.

"Hey, Travis," said Addie. "Here's your stop."

Tony laughed. "Didja forget where you lived?"

When Travis realized they were in front of his house, he laughed too. "I kinda forgot I was going home. See you guys!" He got off the bus and ran inside.

After a brief study of the chandelier with the lights both on and off, he went all over the house looking for Angie, but she wasn't there. In fact, the only person he could find was Chris in the basement.

"Don't come down here any more! No one can know my secret recipe!"

"I don't care about your *stupid* recipe!" Travis had never mouthed off at Chris before. But now Chris was working on his top-secret product and nothing else mattered to him. He didn't seem to care what Travis said as long as he stayed out of the basement when he said it. Travis decided to check on his new rabbit, Fang II. But the rabbit's box behind the couch was empty.

"Fang?" Travis didn't know how the rabbit had gotten out of the box, and he realized locating it could be a real problem, especially if it was hiding. Did Angie get a cage for it? Did she put Fang II back in his bedroom? Travis got hopeful and ran up the stairs.

He knocked on his own door. It was his room, too, but he knocked anyway. There was no answer so he went in. Jon wasn't there, but right off he noticed something was different. The big cardboard box was gone. Had Jon sold his swords and computer?

The bookshelf and all the books that had been on it were gone, too; many of those books belonged to Travis. And the blankets, pillows and sheets from Jon's bed were missing along with all the stuff from his dresser drawers and closet. Did he sell his clothes? He was getting pretty good at magic, but he still needed clothes. Was he planning to be the naked magician?

Travis searched the room and couldn't find Fang II anywhere. That got him worried. What if Jon had sold the rabbit, too? He hoped not. Travis was thirsty and went into the bathroom for a drink. As he gulped down a cup of water, something in the trashcan caught his eye. It was white and red and partly covered by toilet paper. He moved the paper out of the way and jumped back.

The only thing left of Fang II was a mess of bloody fur in the bottom of the trashcan.

Travis covered his mouth and backed out of the bathroom. He couldn't take his eyes off the trashcan. Suddenly, the hairs on the back of his neck tingled. *Ghost fingers!*

Travis spun quickly.

Jon stood there holding two overstuffed shopping bags. He set the bags on his bed and looked at Travis with narrowed, suspicious eyes. "What are you doing in my room?"

Travis was scared, but he was angry with Jon, too. He inched toward the door. "It's my room, too! Where's Angie?"

"She's running errands while I sleep."

"You're not asleep."

"I couldn't sleep. I have much work to do. I must work hard and fast."

Travis did his best not to cry, but it wasn't working. Finally, he blurted out, "You killed Fang II! Why'd you do that?"

"I was hungry."

Travis couldn't believe what he'd heard. "You *ate* Fang II? I hate you!" He screamed it at the top of his lungs. All Jon did was smile and take things out of the bags.

Travis ran down the hall certain that Jon would try to skin and eat *him* next. He couldn't hold back the tears any more as he wept for that poor rabbit. But he also wept for his brother, Jon Bishop. How had he changed so much? The old Jon wouldn't have hurt the rabbit at all, let alone eaten it! But this new Jon…he probably didn't even cook it first! Only a demon or a crazy person would do that. Travis stopped in his tracks. *Was Jon really possessed by a demon? Or was he just plain crazy?*

When Angie got home Travis told her about the rabbit. "Angie, Jon's gone crazy! He sold everything he owns and he ate Fang II!"

"He ate the rabbit? He cooked it and ate it?"

"He didn't cook it."

About that time Jon came into the room. Angie was on fire.

"Jon Bishop! I can't believe you killed that poor rabbit! Why would you do such a thing?"

"I was hungry," said Jon in a steady voice.

"That's what happens when you skip breakfast. Why the rabbit? He was Travis' pet!"

"I let Travis play with it. The rabbit was mine."

"Normal people don't go around eating their pets! And you sold your clothes! The swords, okay. They were yours. The computer, too. But your clothes? What do you plan to wear to school? And the bedding was mine, buddy boy! You didn't pay for any of it! You owe me money! Don't even think about leaving the house for the entire week. You're grounded!"

Jon seemed to ignore her as he fiddled with a magic card set he had bought. Without looking up he asked, "How much do I owe?"

"If I remember correctly the sheets, blankets and pillows were about a hundred dollars! How could you do such a thing?"

Jon looked at her. He put one hand out, palm up, to show that it was empty. Next he turned it down and waited a few seconds. When he turned it over again, he was holding a one-hundred-dollar bill. Angie gasped.

"We are even," he said, giving her the money.

"How'd you do that? Is this even real?"

"It is magic, and it is real. Soon I will be the greatest magician in the world."

"I didn't know you could do that. Is that what you spent the money on? Is all this for your show? Are these magic tricks?"

"Of course."

"Oh. Well, keep practicing. That was really pretty good. But you're still grounded and I'm still mad at you." When Angie left, she seemed completely dumbfounded. Travis hung his head as he followed her out. Angie wouldn't even think about poor Fang II again, not with Jon getting to be so good at magic. He could do almost anything he wanted and nobody would care as long as his magic worked.

Travis closed the door behind him and looked up at Angie. He could tell she was feeling better, but was confused about some things. She held the hundred-dollar bill in front of his face.

"Did you see that?" she asked. "Did you see what he just did?"

Travis nodded. "It's like the tennis ball."

"Yes it is. Let me tell you something, Travis. If this is something teenagers go through, well, fine. Is that the money he got selling his stuff?"

"I don't care about money. What about Fang II? Jon ate him!"

"I grounded him for a week for that, and I might go for two. I'm sorry, Travis, I'm new at being a parent. I'm not really sure what to do about a teenager who eats pet rabbits."

Chapter 18
SATURDAY MORNING MANNERS

GRANNY

Granny Price had worked at Mike's Pub for a week and was getting used to coming home after three in the morning, especially on the Friday night shift. She'd done bouncer work before, and Mike's place was typical. She'd broken up two fights and tossed out an obnoxious drunk who kept spilling his beer on people he didn't know. Basically it was another day at the office, only this weekend she got her first paycheck. She could finally give Angie and Chris rent money and not feel like a moocher. She was thankful to have the work, especially when her labor skills were somewhat limited. But a vague inner torment had churned in her gut since she'd started the job and tonight she finally figured out what the problem was. Because of her late-night hours she rarely saw her new family, and she *missed* them.

The revelation had come as a complete shock. Before Matilda had transformed into Granny, she'd looked out for herself and had done everything her own way in her own time. She'd spent most of her life as a confirmed bachelorette who'd gotten set in her ways and wouldn't tolerate intrusions from family or friends. When she eventually figured out how selfish she was being, the loneliness set in. Soon after that she suffered an emotional breakdown. It wasn't easy to admit she'd been a worthless mother. At that point Matilda knew something had to change in her life or she was going to die alone, her heart ruined by guilt.

That's when she decided to find her family and give them a try. Now that she knew them the family bug had bitten her. She really liked the kids and she wanted to connect more with Angie and Chris, too. But because of her work hours she'd hardly seen them since they met. It was kind of a slap in the face, really, because in a way, her life hadn't changed. Here she was living in the same house with the family she wanted to know, but their paths rarely crossed. She was asleep when they went to school or work, and they were asleep when she got off, except for Chris, who spent way too much time in the basement and not at work. He had to be running out of sick days. She wanted to speak with Angie about it, to find out if everything was okay between them, but she saw her daughter about as often as she saw the kids, which was practically never. The few times they did meet, especially recently, Angie had been upset and distant. Something had happened to Chris and Jon during some cave adventure, and Granny knew nothing about it. Kelly had told her it was a long story. Matilda decided to take the time to hear it out, every last word.

Matilda, when you wake up you're going to talk to everyone in this house until you're completely caught up with all the good stuff.

She had a plan and decided to set her alarm clock an hour earlier than the usual one P.M. It wasn't a big difference, but the kids weren't in school and Mike had closed the bar because of plumbing problems that couldn't be fixed until Monday. She had a rare Saturday night off, so there'd be plenty of time to become reacquainted with the family. First she needed a good night's sleep, because nobody wanted to be around Matilda Price when she hadn't slept enough. When she was tired, she could be downright dangerous.

Granny washed down a peanut butter sandwich with a glass of warm milk and dragged herself to bed. She was eager to see her family, but right now she was exhausted and nothing—absolutely nothing!—would get her out of bed before noon.

PARRISH

Dr. Parrish arrived at his old house a little after seven in the morning and began unloading tools and lumber right away. He noticed Angie's minivan was gone next door, which meant they'd probably left early for the chess tournament. Good, their place was empty. He would have liked to see Kelly play, especially after she trounced him three times in his classroom, but he didn't want to bother anybody with his noise.

Parrish carried a bulky miter saw with one hand and a stack of eight-foot-long trim under his other arm. He set everything on the porch and wondered if anybody had broken into the house while he'd been gone for the last two years. What if all the materials he'd left inside had been stolen? He hoped not, that would cost a fortune.

Returning to the truck he felt a twinge in his shoulder and glanced back at the porch. The mitre saw wasn't *that* heavy. He rubbed the sore spot, then realized he'd let himself go weak. That settled it. He could either get back to the gym soon and start working out again, or just admit he was getting old.

None of his friends knew it, but Parrish had been a terrific athlete in high school and college, playing football and throwing the shot put and discus in track. In his youth he'd had tremendous power and speed, but now, at age fifty-six, he had trouble recalling exactly how powerful and how fast he'd once been. He could still remember his forty-yard dash times and the distances of his throws, but the feeling of extreme fitness was pretty much gone.

Parrish leaned on the hood of his old red Toyota pickup truck and studied the run-down house. When he and Colleen had purchased the place they couldn't wait to fix it up and move in next to their friends, Angie and Chris. But when Colleen got sick, they forgot all about the house. And when she died, well—

This was the first time he'd seen the place since before the funeral. The memory brought back vivid images of his wife dressed in her blue jean coveralls and red baseball cap. Something about that outfit had really attracted him. He hung his head sadly. He'd never find another woman like Colleen.

In spite of his sadness, seeing the old place again brightened his spirits. He stood up straighter than he had for the last two years with a new look of determination on his face. If he remembered correctly the hardwood floors needed refinishing and tile still had to be laid in the kitchen and bathrooms. He also had to put underlayment in the kitchen and trim out the bedrooms. He shook his head as the jobs came back in a wave. He needed to make a list.

Twenty minutes later Parrish had made up his mind what to work on first. As soon as he got started memories of his late wife arrived in a flood. At one point he broke down and cried. But he gathered his emotions, wiped his eyes and forced himself to keep going. Soon enough the hard work made him forget about his grief, at least temporarily. His primary tools of the day were the loud, screeching miter saw, an air hammer, and a claw hammer. Parrish actually enjoyed the noise because to him, noise meant progress. He was amazed at how much progress one person could make when he had the right tools.

GRANNY

Granny rolled over in bed and squinted sleepily at the ceiling. What in the world woke her up? She normally slept like a dead person, so it must have been something really loud and unexpected, like a jet engine or an atomic bomb going off. She lay there a few minutes, pondering the possibilities and slowly drifted back to sleep.

Suddenly, a power saw screamed from the house next door. Granny nearly leaped out of bed. She squeezed her eyes shut and tried her best to ignore the irritating sounds. Moments later a mind-piercing, rhythmic hammering occurred, which was followed by another blast of that fingernail-on-a-chalkboard-screeching saw. She reluctantly opened one weary eye and glanced at the alarm clock. It was only half past eight.

"No way. Somebody needs a lesson in Saturday morning manners!"

Wearing only her tattered gray warm-ups, Granny left the house and walked barefoot across the dew-sodden lawn. She passed an old, red pick-up truck and marched up the front porch of the house next door. She knocked, perhaps a little too hard, as the force cracked one of the stained glass panel windows. Several pieces of glass tinkled across the floor inside. A moment later the door flew open.

A huge man towered over her, his face red and sweaty from work. She glared up at him fearlessly, daring him to say a thing about his stupid broken window. They stepped toe to toe, both ready for a fight.

"You broke my window!" he said angrily. "What's your problem, lady?"

"What's *my* problem? What's *your* problem? You're out here at this ungodly hour makin' all that racket! Some of us work late, you know! I need my sleep!"

In her anger and readiness for a fight, she hadn't really looked at him. All she knew was this big lout was keeping her awake. Either he remedied the situation, or there was going to be trouble. But when she met his gaze for the first time, determined and angry, something quite unexpected happened. Matilda's anger melted in a sudden, measureless moment. She covered her mouth with one hand, completely surprised by her new feelings, but also to stop herself from saying anything else that would upset this big, beautiful man. She didn't want to admit it, but she'd fallen in love with him at a single glance. If her heart hadn't turned to jelly, she would have been embarrassed.

Right off she knew she'd blown it. Here was a man—*her* man—the man of her dreams, and his first impression of her was a brutal, angry old bat with the compassion of a Nazi storm trooper. She knew he would curse her all the way to hell, and she would stand by and take it, helpless to stop him or even to want to. If he hit her in the head with a two-by-four, she wouldn't have minded. She almost wished he would, so they could restart their relationship on even ground. Then she noticed his expression had also changed. The anger was gone from his voice. His gaze softened.

"Uh…uh…perhaps I *was* being a bit thoughtless," said the man, groping for words. "I'd be happy to start later in the day. Maybe after lunch?"

"No," said Granny. "No, really, it's my fault. You have a lot of work to do here all alone. I'm being selfish. I apologize, it's the way I am. I'm trying to change."

"Mark Parrish," said the man, holding out his hand to shake.

"Matilda Price," said Granny. "I'm Angie's mother. I'm staying with her and Chris for a while." Out of habit she squeezed his hand as hard as she could. He didn't flinch. He even seemed to hold back so he wouldn't hurt her. He smiled and held her hand a bit longer than was required for a handshake. She was happy to let him.

"Matilda," he repeated. "Lovely name. Chris and Angie never mentioned you were staying with them. Uh, would you care to tour the house?"

"I'd love to, Mark."

They finally released each other's hand and walked into the foyer, careful to avoid any broken glass on the floor. As she tiptoed around the glass, Granny realized that nothing else in the world mattered. She could only ponder how they'd found each other in this huge, often unforgiving world, both lonely and perhaps a little angry at life. But now life seemed okay again. Parrish and Granny smiled at each other as he went on with the tour. Granny remembered how she was dressed and got embarrassed.

"Oh, my. I'm sorry, Mark. I have to go freshen up a bit. I haven't even brushed my teeth. Excuse me."

She walked off at a faster pace than normal, leaving Parrish staring after her as she crossed the chilled, soggy lawns again. A barrage of questions flew through her mind as she went. Was Mark Parrish fixing up the house because he owned it and was going to move in? Or did he work for somebody else who owned it? He'd gotten very polite all of a sudden. Did that mean he liked her, at least a little? Would he mind some help from a total stranger?

It appeared there was plenty of work to do on the house and Granny was just the person to help him finish up. All at once it became perfectly clear why she'd spent seven years of her life working construction in a man's world. She'd done it so that some day—today!—she could help Mark Parrish work on this house. Nobody was better suited for the job than Matilda Price. She knew how to swing a hammer.

PARRISH

Parrish finished placing the baseboard in the master bedroom and stood up to admire his work. At least he hadn't lost any skill while he'd been away. He could still trim out a house. He set his hammer in a tool bucket while he took a seat on a portable workbench. Colleen Parrish had chosen all of the trim and design points of the master bedroom. She'd had a decorator's eye combined with incredible good taste. Parrish studied the window seat they had built together and nodded approvingly. But he wasn't just thinking about the window seat.

He sighed heavily. "I'm sorry, Colleen," he said aloud. "But I think the time has come for me to move on. She seems nice, you know? It's what you wanted, remember? I don't know where she came from, but I think she likes me. I *know* I like her."

When he heard a light knock at the front door, Parrish rushed down the stairs. He opened the door and saw Matilda Price standing before him dressed in denim coveralls with a red plaid work shirt and a New York Yankees ball cap. She also wore work boots and a tool belt with a hammer dangling in the strap.

"Chris had some tools in the garage, looked like they'd never been used. I've come to work," she said, looking very pretty with makeup and her hair in a bun. She became a little shy. "That is, if you need the help."

"I can always use help," said Parrish emphatically. "Especially from such a lovely helper. Shall we continue the tour?"

"That'd be grouse."

Grouse? Parrish was a little confused. What the heck did that mean? "I'll take that as a yes."

As they went into the living room Parrish watched her. There was something special about a woman wearing work clothes. The accentuated curves and rugged beauty really caught his eye. Especially *this* woman.

Chapter 19

THE TOURNAMENT

KELLY

My feelings were hurt because Jon and Chris had both refused to come watch me play in the Halloween Classic Open Chess Tournament. I understood Chris, he'd gotten so weird lately he never left the basement. I'd tried several times again to read his thoughts and come up empty. How could that be? I'd never had any trouble doing it before the cave, though lately he blocked me the same way Jon did. Then I remembered I couldn't read the minds of crazy people. All at once it was clear. Chris may not be possessed by a demon, not at all. He'd gone crazy! Unfortunately, that meant whatever was on his mind these days would stay a secret.

But Jon was my brother. He'd always been proud of my game, even if he wasn't much of a chess player himself. With Jon it was always about family. Not this time. Not while he was having head problems. My first tournament ever and he'd stayed home to practice magic. At least Angie, Travis and Melissa were here to support me.

My first opponent had been a novice teenage girl who'd entered the tournament on a dare. I beat her fast. But my second challenger, an elderly woman with green-dyed hair and purple contacts in her eyes, was much tougher. I have a thorough understanding of the game and of course I like to read an opponent's thoughts to know what moves they might be planning. But that didn't work on this lady. This woman was insane, though nobody knew it yet except me and I couldn't read her mind at all. She was a good player, too—but not good enough. I put her away in twenty minutes.

In my next to last game, the semifinal, my opponent was a doctor from a local hospital, Dr. Winthrop. He was a handsome, white-haired man, and perfectly sane, but he'd played very little chess and it was amazing he'd gotten as far as he had. I beat him in four moves without reading his mind. Dr. Winthrop was shocked and embarrassed. Here he was, a medical doctor, a surgeon no less, blown away by a thirteen-year-old girl!

"No offense, young lady," said the doctor after our match. "But I'll never play this game again for as long as I live." He shook my hand and told me good luck, but he left the tournament clearly shaken. Word spread fast about that match and from then on and a lot of people were talking about me. I'll admit it made me feel a little cocky. But I also felt badly for him.

Now I was in the championship game against a gray-haired man with a medium-length beard. When I read his thoughts before the game, I knew that he'd lost only four times in his life, all to his father when he'd been young and still learning the game. After that he'd won every game he'd ever played and this wasn't his first tournament.

I forgot about being cocky and became really nervous because the guy, Dr. Morris Leach, planned everything he did at least four moves ahead. In addition to that he also kept a vast number of counter moves in his thoughts, and even had counter-counter moves for many of those. He was a genius with a fierce memory. I had a great memory, too, and I knew the game just as well as Dr. Leach. I also knew he'd beat me unless I understood his strategy, so I made a point to stay inside his head during the game.

In short, I cheated. Yeah, I know. It's like being able to see an opponent's letters in a game of Scrabble. Cheating bothered me on several levels, but that was how I'd always played. I was really good at two things in life: playing chess and reading the thoughts of others. And I wasn't able to do the chess thing without including the mind scans. It would have been like driving a car with my eyes closed.

Every now and then I sent a little message to Travis to let him know how things were going.

He's gonna move his bishop next, isn't he?

I'm opening up a huge trap. He'll never see it coming.

He's falling for it!

I tuned in to Melissa's thoughts once as she and Angie watched the final game on a big-screen television that gave the audience an overhead view of the pieces on the board. I was surprised to learn that deep down Melissa found chess a little baffling and boring. But she was pulling for me with all her heart.

All at once Melissa looked around suspiciously. She *knew!* I quickly backed off and stayed out of my friend's mind. Melissa may not have been telepathic, but she sure was sensitive to anybody who was.

Back at the game I made what I figured to be my third-to-the-last move. Two more moves and Dr. Leach would be toast. Sure enough, though he hesitated, Dr. Leach moved his rook in front of my pawn. A safe and smart tactic, but it would doom him in the end. I concentrated on him very hard. I let him know what a great move he'd just made.

Dr. Leach smiled slightly at the mysterious compliment that came from somewhere inside his head. But he remained tense and alert. I had to be very careful in the way I controlled him. He was much too intelligent to take lightly.

She's going to win it, thought somebody in the audience. I looked up in surprise. My mind had wandered since his last move. I didn't mean to pick up the personal thoughts of people around me, but sometimes it happened. Just for fun, I tuned in to some others.

She'll be the scholarship winner, for sure.

She could be the next Bobby Fisher!

I've never seen anyone play as well as that girl. I wonder where she came from?

I fought off a smile. It felt awesome to be admired. All I had to do was make the next move with my bishop (ironic huh? Bishop wins with her bishop. That'd be a good headline!) and Dr. Leach would realize he was beaten. There'd be nothing he could do at all. Then everyone would think I was the most amazing chess player in the world. Or at least in my part of the world.

Somebody compared me to Bobby Fisher! Oh, yeah, I'm cool!

And I was, too. Except for the guilt that had welled up inside me since I beat that very first kid. It was one thing to beat my friends and family once in a while, but it was something else entirely to win at this level, and keep on winning. I reached for the bishop, then pulled my hand back. All I had to do was make the move and fame and glory would be mine. But technically I'd cheated. These people didn't know I could read their thoughts, not that it would have mattered. They certainly couldn't read mine. That wasn't just *playing* the game, it was *fixing* the game.

I took up the bishop and held it ready. Dr. Leach's eyes got big as saucers when he realized what I was going to do to him. He knew he'd lost the match and there was nothing for it. But I did the unexpected. I put the bishop back where it had been, and slid my queen to one side. It was still a good move, if I'd been a novice.

"Check," I said calmly.

Dr. Leach nearly collapsed with relief. Whatever had made me change my mind had completely opened up his chance to win. He moved his own queen to the space directly beside his king, blocking my queen. But the move was more than that.

"Check*mate*," said Dr. Leach, breathing a huge sigh of relief.

I tried to look as if I hadn't seen it coming, but in fact, I'd set up that one, too. I'm not bragging, it's just a fact. When I smiled, it was genuine. I turned over my king in submission and shook Dr. Leach's hand. The audience was mostly disappointed, but they still applauded for both of us.

"Good game," I said.

"*Great* game!" he cried. "You're the toughest opponent I've ever had!"

"Thank you. You're really a great player."

I left the stage and met the family. Melissa and Angie hugged me.

"That was an amazing display of strategy," said Angie. "If you practice some more, I think you can beat that guy. He knows it, too."

Travis hugged me because I was his sister. But he didn't say anything out loud.

What went wrong?

Nothing, I replied. *Nothing went wrong.*

But you had that guy. I could tell.

I made a mistake, all right? I did my best.

"I don't think you did your best," said Travis irritably. "I don't understand. If you'da moved the bishop like you started to, you woulda beat 'im!" Travis stormed off without us.

"Beaten him," I corrected automatically. Of course he never heard me.

Melissa was bewildered. "For a little guy he's pretty intense about winning."

"Oh, yeah," I said, embarrassed. "He gets it from Jon." There was no way I could explain it to anyone but Travis, and I wasn't even sure he'd understand.

"I think you did just fine, sweetie," said Angie as she hugged me again. "I'm proud of you."

Chapter 20

SPIES

KELLY

Like everyone else in the house I'd grown sick and tired of the way Chris treated us whenever we went near his personal domain—the basement. All we had to do was start down the stairs and he'd yell and threaten to clobber us if we didn't get out fast.

"Stay away from my secret recipe!" he'd shout at the top of his lungs. I guess being demonically possessed or crazy, whichever, could turn people into jerks.

I didn't like the way he was acting, so I decided to find out what I could about his "secret recipe." I did it the easy way first, by reading his mind, but it was like trying to run through a stone wall. I was so frustrated I wanted to cry. My telepathy wasn't working with him, so I just gave up trying. If I was going to find out about that recipe, I'd have be very sneaky. That, plus Chris would have to stay out of the basement for a while, which he rarely did these days. I finally got my chance that Saturday after the chess tournament.

I tiptoed through the kitchen, avoiding places where the floorboards might creak. I opened the basement door and stood at the top of the stairs, listening. The house was deathly quiet. The only thing I heard was the wall clock ticking in the foyer. The basement was empty.

I lightly snapped my fingers. A second later Melissa popped out from behind the kitchen doorjamb. Her dark eyes were alert with the thrill of being a spy in action.

"Are you sure Chris isn't here?" she whispered, as we started down the stairs.

"Angie took him to the grocery store ten minutes ago. This might be our only chance to find out about his stupid recipe."

"Where's Travis? Doesn't he want in on the action?"

"He's in the den watching TV. We'd better leave him out of this in case we get caught. I don't want *him* to get into trouble since it's *our* idea."

When we got into the basement I couldn't believe how neat it was. Except for a small area around the workbench where Chris was developing his *product*, there was hardly anything else in the room. In a far corner he had left a pair of steel utility shelves against the wall that were loaded from floor to ceiling with buckets of paint. Adjacent to the workbench he'd arranged some smaller bookshelves and an old metal desk that was covered with papers and colorful spills from whatever he was trying to invent. Some test tubes, beakers, a mortar and pestle, and an alcohol Bunsen burner were also on the desktop. The rest of the room was empty.

"He's really cleaned this place. The last time I was down here junk was stacked to the ceiling!" Of course that meant my bedroom was the only messy room left in the house. I began to have guilt pangs about picking up my clothes.

"Come on," said Melissa. "Let's see what's cooking."

We went to the workbench and found measuring cups, spoons, a blender, more beakers and test tubes, and a dozen tall jars full of strange liquids. Some of the liquids were clear and some looked like muddy soup. But most contained bright colors, like red, orange, blue or green. I leaned over a container and sniffed the contents cautiously.

"That smells good! Kind of fruity. This one's good, too."

Melissa smelled one. She made a face and backed away. "Whew! That smells like rotten oranges!" She sniffed again. Another face. "That's even worse! There's fruit flies everywhere." Melissa pointed at a jar containing a clear, blue liquid that was full of almond-sized, brown objects with legs. "Are those cockroaches? Yuck!"

"This place is gross. What do you think he's making? Some kind of fruit drink?"

"If he is *I'm* not drinking it! Maybe we should get samples of everything? We could get them chemically analyzed."

"How much would that cost?"

Melissa shrugged. "Probably too much. Hey, is that a hairbrush? And it's full of hair, gross! What's that doing down here?"

"Who cares? Let's go, I've seen enough." At that moment I spotted a stack of legal pads at the end of the workbench. "This must be his recipe!" We each took up some of the pads and tried to read what was written on the sheets. But the markings were strange, like some foreign language with a weird looking alphabet. Even the numbers were difficult to read, though it was clear enough that they were numbers because of the way they were arranged.

"What language is this?" I asked, unable to decipher the mysterious scribbling. "Is it Greek?"

Melissa shook her head. "I know a few Greek letters. It's something else."

"We should take one of the pages and try to figure out what it says later. Maybe the letters are on the internet." I was about to tear off a page when Melissa grabbed my hand.

"You should take a sheet off one of the *bottom* pads," she suggested. "He might notice if something on top is missing."

"Good point." We moved all the pads out of the way except for the bottom one, where I tore off one of the sheets from the middle. "This is good." I folded the paper and stuffed it into my pocket. "It's got lots of different symbols on it." We re-stacked the pads and stepped back to make sure they looked okay. "Let's go."

"But we still don't know what he's making," said Melissa. "Let's take some samples. We can worry about how much it will cost to analyze them later."

"Well, okay." I checked the time on my cell phone. "What can we put them in? Test tubes?"

Melissa looked around. "There aren't any clean ones, but that beaker looks clean. Which jar should we sample?"

"I don't know, maybe the red one there. It's kind of pretty and...." I stopped mid-sentence and looked up at the ceiling. I felt the blood drain from my face.

"What's wrong?" asked Melissa.

"He's coming!"

We started for the stairs, but the back door rattled and began to open. I froze with Melissa at my shoulder. We gawked at the door, eyes wide with fear.

Hide! I shouted into Melissa's mind. But where?

The back door swung open. Luckily, Chris was loaded down with bags of groceries and kept his back to us as he tried to close the door with his foot. Melissa ducked under the old desk. I looked to join her, but there was only room for one. I was trapped in the open. My feet were stuck to the floor. I was so frightened I nearly screamed. I saw the tall metal shelves stacked with paint in the far corner of the basement. I slipped behind one shelf and pressed my body against the wall. A moment later Chris closed the door and set the shopping bags on Melissa's desk. I watched it all through a space between paint cans, afraid even to breathe.

Suddenly, Chris looked up. "Who's in here?"

I nearly swallowed my tongue. My heart pounded so loud I was sure half the neighborhood could it. Chris scanned the room suspiciously. Then he relaxed, apparently satisfied it was a false alarm. I watched him move the stuff out of the shopping bags and set everything on the work-bench. I saw boxes of cough drops, all different brands and flavors. And there were several quart-sized jars of cranberry juice and some cans of navy beans.

Chris began to mix the ingredients into a large pot. Next, he mashed it all into a runny, red paste. He scooped out a portion of the paste and dropped it into another pot, where he added three cherry cough drops and poured in a measured amount of tonic water. He constantly stirred the mixture with a wooden spoon, and taste-tested it every so often. Whenever he added something to the pot he wrote it down on the top legal pad.

Chris nodded to himself and looked around the workbench. He took up the hairbrush and started vigorously brushing his hair. I looked on, puzzled. I'd never seen him brush his hair so hard before and he seemed to be shedding because the brush filled up rapidly with thick, dark hair, which wasn't easy considering he was going bald.

Chris stopped and pulled enough hair out of the brush to make a toupee. He dropped the whole mess into the pot. I gagged and covered my mouth. Was he going to eat that?

Chris took the jar of fruity-smelling red juice and poured it into the mix. He stirred it some more before dumping the contents into the blender, which he ran for several seconds before shutting it off. Finally, he took off the lid and sipped the mixture.

I couldn't watch. I closed my eyes and turned away. Chris was drinking his own liquefied hair!

For the next few minutes Chris paced the room, deep in thought. Something wasn't quite right. I tried to scan his mind to see what he was thinking, but again I couldn't get a reading. It was so frustrating. He didn't look like a demon, and if he were possessed wouldn't he be floating above the floor or vomiting pea soup across the room? He *did* hit his head, he'd had that big lump on his forehead when we were in the cave with him. Would that make him crazy?

Chris paced in my direction. He turned and marched toward the stairs. A moment later he did an about-face and came toward me again. This time he kept walking. He went right up to the wall and paused next to my shelf. I couldn't move. I didn't dare. He was in front of me less than a meter away. If he glanced to his left we'd be face to face.

Abruptly, Chris turned to his right and hurried back to the blender. I let out a long, low sigh of relief. He went to the workbench and took down a rubber mallet from a hook on the wall. He reached into the blue mixture and removed several dead cockroaches. Setting the cockroaches on the workbench, he proceeded to smash them into tiny, mushy pieces with the mallet. He scraped up the roach guts and measured out a specific amount on the electronic scale. He dumped it all into the red mixture in the blender and turned it on high. When it was done, he tasted it.

Chris smacked his lips.

"Very good," he said, nodding to himself. "Yes, *very* good."

He unbuttoned the top of his shirt and took out a gold chain from around his neck. I'd never seen him wear anything like that before. Hanging from the chain, like a necklace, was a solid black cylinder, which looked a lot like a lipstick case. Chris removed the top, revealing the end of a thin silver tube. He held the tube over the mixture in the blender and touched the base. The tube lit up.

I had a good view of the blender and its contents as I strained to see what was going on. Clearly, the liquid wasn't disturbed at all by anything he did with the cylinder. Did something happen when it lit up? I couldn't tell, but the entire act seemed terribly important. Maybe Chris had some magic of his own.

Chris stirred the ingredients with a dirty spoon, then tasted it. He got very excited. He danced about the room and jumped up and down, clapping. He abruptly made himself stop.

"I have much work to do! I must work hard and fast!" His eyes were wild as he went about the room emptying all the other jars into one gigantic pot. He carried the heavy pot to the rear exit, where he struggled to find the doorknob. Finally, he opened the door and stepped outside.

"Kelly! Let's go!" Melissa came out from under the desk. We started for the stairs again. But Chris was only gone a moment. When he came back, we were in the middle of the basement. We barely had a second to duck behind Melissa's desk.

Chris hadn't seen us yet, but this time we weren't hidden. And he was coming our way. If he set the pot on the desk he'd notice us for sure. Somehow I had to stop him.

Chris! Go back outside! Hurry! It's your recipe!

My blast of mental commands had no effect on him whatsoever. He never even heard them. He continued to approach and I couldn't stop him.

TRAVIS

Travis turned off the TV and followed Angie into the kitchen to help her put away the groceries. Whenever she went to the store he liked to help put things away so he could keep his mental inventory up to date. He was about to hang a roll of paper towels on the rack by the sink when he got a distress call from Kelly.

Travis! Help us! We're in the basement! Hurry!

Travis looked up confused. It had to be Kelly, but what was she doing in the basement? She had definitely said, help *us*. So who was down there with her? And why were they there? She must have been crazy to go in the basement.

"Where's Chris?" he asked, as Angie left the room to get the rest of the groceries from the minivan.

"He went to the basement," she said back to him, disappearing out the front door.

Kelly needed a diversion. Somehow Travis had to distract Chris so she could escape. He had to do it fast. But what could he do?

Desperate, he took up a roll of paper towels and got the new cell phone out of his pocket. He flipped open the phone camera and got ready to take some pictures. Then he charged down the basement stairs, yelling like a maniac.

"Aaaaaaah!" Travis stomped his feet as loud as he could all the way down.

Chris was so startled he dropped the big pot he was holding. It clanged loudly and rolled across the concrete floor. He spun around and stood there, glaring. Travis snapped a picture of him.

"Get out of here!" said Chris angrily. "My recipe is a secret!"

"Your recipe is *stupid!*" said Travis. "And so are *you!*" He threw the roll of paper towels as hard as he could. To his surprise, it struck Chris right in the face. Travis snapped a photo when it hit him. Chris picked up the roll and crushed it with one hand. Travis snapped another photo.

For a moment they just stared at each other. Travis was scared and Chris was so furious his eyes flashed bright green. He didn't even look human. Travis took two more snapshots. Chris got madder and madder, but he still didn't do anything. Somehow, Travis had to get him out of the basement or Kelly might have to spend the night down there. Finally, he did the one thing that always seemed to tick off adults, even though it was totally stupid.

"Nanny-nanny boo-boo!" Travis danced in place and shook his butt at Chris. That did it. Chris' face grew scarlet. He tossed the paper towels at Travis.

"I'll get you!"

Travis ducked the towels and ran for his life up the stairs. He sprinted through the kitchen and blew past Angie as she set a final bag of groceries on the counter. Chris was right on his heels, but Angie caught Chris by the arm and jerked him to a halt.

"What's going on here?"

Chris shoved her away. "He was in the basement! He hit me in the face!"

"He hit you?"

"With this!" Chris picked up the crushed paper towels. "Wait till I get my hands on him!"

KELLY

Melissa and I were half way around the block when we met Travis going the other way.

"You got out!" said Travis, breathing hard.

"You did great, Travis!" I said. "He never even noticed us. We went out the back door as soon as he went after you."

"You're pretty fast, Travis," said Melissa, impressed.

"I took pictures of 'im when he got mad!" Travis grinned. "Look." He showed us the pictures he took of Chris on his cell phone. We laughed so hard.

"Oh my gosh!" said Melissa. "We need to put them on the internet! How come his eyes are green?"

"It's the flash, I guess," said Travis, not really knowing.

"But don't most people's eyes look red? It's called red-eye. I've got software that removes red-eye on my computer. I don't have anything for green-eye."

"Maybe it depends who you are?" I said it with a shrug.

"Thanks a lot for saving us, Travis," said Melissa. "How did you know we needed help?"

"Kelly told me," he said, grinning. "It's a good thing she can read minds, or you guys would be dead now."

As soon as he said it I gasped. Melissa looked at me, then at Travis. Travis covered his mouth, helpless. "Oops."

"You *are* telepathic!" said Melissa. "I knew it!"

"How did you know?" I asked, totally distressed.

"Because I've heard you thinking, though I was never sure if you were speaking with your mouth or your mind. That is, until back there in the basement when you told me to hide. I was looking right at you and you never opened your mouth."

Melissa, you're my best friend. Please don't tell anyone.

Melissa lit up excitedly. "You did it again! This is so cool! Kelly, don't worry." She stopped in midsentence. *I'll never tell a soul, unless you make me.*

I got the message loud and clear. I smiled. I knew Melissa was telling the truth. "I was going to tell you eventually. But nobody else on the planet knows except my big mouth brother here. Not even Jon knows, though, for some reason he can completely block me out of his head."

"Sorry, Kelly," said Travis really feeling bad. "I never slipped before. Melissa's like part of the family. I didn't even think about it."

I glared at Travis, then softened. "We'll let it slide, little bro'. Besides, we both owe you." *Be more careful next time!*

Travis nodded like he meant it. His expression became distressed. "Do you think Angie'll be mad at me?"

"I wouldn't worry about Angie. It's Chris who's ticked off. Maybe you should apologize to him right off, it might calm him down. Let's go home."

As we started back to the house, Melissa asked the same question that had been on my mind since I'd seen it. "So what's with that thing around Chris' neck? What do you think it does?"

"How did you see it?" I asked. "You were under the desk."

"There was a hole in the privacy wall. I saw everything he did."

"What thing?" asked Travis.

"I don't know," I replied. "Maybe it kills the germs in those pots. But it doesn't matter because I am *never* drinking any of that nasty stuff. *Never.*"

"We didn't do very good detective work," said Melissa. "We didn't get any samples at all."

"No," I agreed. "I guess his secret recipe is still a secret."

———

When we got home, Angie waited at the door, arms akimbo. "Travis Lane Bishop, just what did you think you were doing?" She glared down at him. "Why'd you throw paper towels at Chris?"

"Cuz I couldn't find a rock," said Travis angrily. "Chris is bein' a jerk! He won't come out of the basement and he yells at us for no reason if we even go near the stairs."

Melissa and I both nodded, but Angie ignored us.

"You can go to your room, young man! You're grounded for the next five days. And don't even think about seeing any of your friends next weekend!"

"I can't go to my room," said Travis. "Jon won't let me in."

"Then you can stay in the living room. You've been sleeping in there anyway. And no TV!"

"How come Jon gets to do what he wants? He ate my rabbit and kicked me out of my room and all you did was ground him."

"Jon is almost an adult. We have to deal with him differently. Besides, he never hit Chris in the face with a roll of paper towels."

Chris came up behind her with a look on his face like he wanted to tear Travis' head off. Travis gulped and moved behind Melissa and me like we were bodyguards, or something. We were scared, too, but we stood our ground. Angie was shocked by our reaction, but she was more shocked by Chris.

"You *will* stay out of the basement!" said Chris, pointing a threatening finger at Travis. "The basement is *mine*! I am making something very important. I must work hard and fast!" He turned and poked Angie hard in the shoulder with his finger. *"Keep them out!"*

Chapter 21

PAIN

MARIA

Only one pain is worse than being dumped by the person in the world you most truly love, and that's the pain of being trapped in pre-breakup purgatory. Maria Sanchez knew it well. She was caught in it now and she felt like a bug in a toilet where the swirling tide was gradually pulling her down. Whatever she'd said to make Jon unhappy, whatever she'd done to utterly displease him, why couldn't he just tell her? Why'd he insist on this roundabout way of torturing her soul when it could all be finished in a moment? Why? Knowing the answer, she sadly shook her head. Because he was a boy, that was why.

Maria knew that boys and girls handled breakups differently for different reasons. When a girl grew tired of a relationship, her decision was usually quick and unexpected. *It's over.* Girls didn't mess around with *who* felt guilty or *whose* fault it was that things didn't work out. They simply ended it and moved on, often leaving the former boyfriend hurt, dazed and confused. He never saw it coming.

But a boy who wants to break up will try other tactics in order to shift the blame away from himself. He'll treat his girlfriend as thoughtlessly as possible, even to the point of dishing out cruelty. He'll ignore her, stop calling her altogether, laugh at her, and sometimes even abuse her, all because he hopes she'll become fed up enough to dump *him* first. That's the plan, anyway. Maria would have laughed if she hadn't been hurting. The silly plan rarely worked, though, because girls can be very forgiving creatures when it comes to love, and they rarely take the bait.

But for some reason boys just didn't understand that basic concept. In the end after all his prolonged shenanigans, the boy still had to deliver one of the cruelest lines in the history of the world: *I just want to be friends.* Ironically, the boy is next bombarded by the very same anger and tears he'd hoped to avoid. No, boys just didn't get it.

Maria thought about all of this as she stuffed books into her backpack on Monday afternoon. She hated what was happening to her since Jon had changed, but most of all she hated what had happened to *them*. Their relationship had been deeply emotional and heartfelt and she knew the final pain of departure would be nearly unbearable. Right now there was no departure, only the deadened pain of pre-breakup purgatory. She was sick of it.

Why did Jon have to be so silently heartless? Why didn't he just tell her, face to face, that it was over between them? Her emotions were caught in the grip of numbness, which made everything inside her ache, almost as if she had the flu. One day she'd been the light of his life, the next he'd forgotten her name. He'd never called her—not even once—since he'd been rescued from Pandora's Cave. Now he didn't speak to her in school unless she spoke to him first. He clearly didn't feel the same way about her any more. In fact, he didn't seem to feel anything at all.

Angie had phoned her after the cave incident and told her what the doctor had said about Jon's possible amnesia. He had forgotten so much, the names of friends and family, how to drive his car, his class schedule, his lover. Maria couldn't take it. She didn't know how to deal with memory loss.

Her eyes stung. Tears fell on her backpack. She looked around, hoping nobody noticed. Luckily, she was alone in the hallway, so she wiped her eyes and slammed the locker shut. She slipped the pack over her shoulders and headed for the main entrance.

Thanksgiving was next week. Would Jon want to eat with her family? If he did, it'd be an awkward meal. Her parents were angry with Jon for a couple of reasons.

First of all, he hadn't been to work for weeks and he never said anything about quitting. Missing work was bad enough, but the big reason they were mad was because of the way he was treating their daughter. Maria was daddy's little girl and she knew it was eating away at her father to watch her suffer like this. Maybe it would be best if Jon skipped Thanksgiving this year. Especially if all he planned to do was break up with her.

Break up. The thought hit her in the gut like a sucker punch. She balked and nearly stumbled into the door. Her emotions rose inside her like too much steam in a pipe, building pressure that couldn't be held back. She was going to cry again and it was going to be a big one. She had to find her car before anyone noticed. She pushed open the door and went outside.

That's when she found Jon, sitting by himself on one of the benches in front of the school. Her heart nearly broke at the sight of him. She stiffened up. *Don't let him see your pain.* Somehow she recouped enough of her dwindling self-control to try to ignore him, but it didn't last long. A girl who's in love can't do that. A girl with her heart and soul hanging in limbo needs to know the truth.

Maria took a seat on the opposite end of the same bench. "Hi, Jon," she said in a small voice.

Jon looked up as if from a trance. "Hello, Maria," he said, detached. "I am waiting for Angie to take me home. I forgot how to drive."

Trying her best to disguise the fact she was on the verge of tears, Maria decided to cut to the chase. "Yes, I heard. Why haven't you called me, Jon? Are you mad at me?"

"I am not mad," said Jon without emotion. "I am becoming the greatest magician in the world, Maria. You will see. I will be the greatest."

"I hope you do become the greatest magician," she said honestly. "But can't you still love me? What happened? Ever since you went into that stupid cave you've been different."

"I am different. I am the greatest magician in the world."

By now several other students had gathered to watch them. Maria could be hot-tempered at times and she knew they were hoping she'd make a scene. They wanted to see a good fight, if it happened. Sorry to disappoint, but she wasn't in a fighting mood.

Maria glared at Jon through bleary eyes, finally shaking her head in defeat. "It's like you're mentally ill, or something. You don't even seem like yourself. You never do anything nice any more, not like you used to."

"Like what?"

"You gave me roses once, remember? That was so sweet and random, it wasn't even my birthday or Valentine's Day. Now I can't even get you to smile."

Jon smiled, but it didn't seem genuine. All at once he waved his hands around like some kind of Ninja wannabe. Maria didn't understand what he was doing. Was he trying to hit her? She leaned away from him, but he stopped flailing and stretched his arms out perfectly still, palms down. A second later he held a huge bouquet of red roses in his right hand. He was wearing a short-sleeved shirt and when the roses actually appeared, his hands hadn't moved at all. Maria gawked. So did everyone around them. Jon handed her the roses.

"These are for you," he said gallantly.

Maria took the flowers and smelled them. "Jon! How'd you do that?" Her eyes became bright and hopeful again. Did she dare believe he could still love her? "They're beautiful!" She hugged him and he hugged her back. But when she pressed against him and tried to get a kiss, he pushed her away.

"What?" she asked. "Why won't you kiss me?"

"I have much work to do. I must work hard and fast." That had definitely been the wrong thing to say. Everyone in school was sick of hearing it, especially Maria. She looked at him, totally confused by his indifference. She was torn between feelings of hope that came with the flowers and a renewed fear of rejection.

At that moment Brandon came out the door. He smiled when he saw them together. "Hey, nice flowers, Maria. Did our man here give 'em to you?"

Maria nodded. "He did magic and they just appeared."

"Magic?" Brandon looked at Jon. "You've been working on magic for awhile, man, but you never show me any tricks. What can you do besides flowers? How about bringing back my camcorder? That cost me two grand."

Jon looked at him. "Does anybody have a deck of cards?"

"A card trick?" asked Brandon. "I'd rather see my camcorder."

A boy nearby who had seen the flower trick rummaged through his backpack and pulled out some cards. "Here you go," said the kid. "They're a little used."

Jon took the cards and began shuffling them in remarkable ways. No matter how he shuffled, he never set them on any surface. Everything was done in the air. Maria gaped at his skill.

While he worked the cards, Jon said, "I'll need a pen."

Brandon supplied the pen when Jon stopped shuffling. "Pick a card and show it to somebody. But not to me." Brandon took a card and discreetly showed it to Maria and the other boy. It was the ace of hearts. "Now write your name on it."

"I saw this trick on TV," said another girl who was watching. By now over a dozen people were crowded around them as Brandon wrote his name on the card. Jon told him to put it back in the deck, and he did. Jon shuffled again.

"What's going to happen?"

"What's he doing?"

"He's gonna to make the card rise from the pile," said the girl.

Instead, Jon threw the cards on the ground. They landed face up, in a nearly perfect straight line. "Find your card."

While Brandon and the others searched, Maria looked on, confused at how Jon's display of love for her with the flowers had so easily been set aside by a card trick.

"It's not here." Brandon held up the deck. "So I guess you've got it?"

Jon slowly smiled. He pointed his chin at one of the parents who had just driven up in a minivan. "Check his shirt pocket."

Maria got involved in spite of her torn emotions. "No way."

Brandon and the others took off running toward the minivan. The kids surrounded the vehicle and the man behind the wheel was clearly nervous when he lowered the glass. "Yes?"

"I know this sounds kind of strange," said Brandon, "but can you look in your shirt pocket and see if something's there? It's a magic trick."

The man smiled uncomfortably. "Oh, of course. But I can tell you now there's nothing in my pocket." When he unzipped his jacket and reached into his shirt pocket, his expression changed. "What's this?" He removed a playing card and gave it to Brandon. Maria looked over his shoulder and saw the card. It was the ace of hearts with Brandon's name written under the center heart in his own handwriting. Brandon showed it to the man first, then to the kids.

"Oh my God!"

"That's incredible!"

"How'd he do that?"

Brandon looked at Jon and grinned big. "Man, you're ready for the big time! What else can you do?"

"Give me some room."

Everyone cleared a big circle around him. The man in the car got out to watch. Maria had to find a place where she could see him through the gathering crowd. Several more cars stopped as dozens of students and adults were there by now. Jon closed his eyes and tilted his head back slightly. He dropped his hands to his sides and started to wiggle his fingers rapidly, like he was playing an invisible piano. Then he rose off the ground. Everyone gasped. Jon rose nearly five feet in the air and held it there.

Maria looked up and saw nothing but clear, blue sky above them. She shook her head in disbelief. "That's not possible."

"He's levitating!" said the man who'd had the card in his pocket.

Jon slowly dropped down. He staggered when he touched ground, like he was disoriented. Everyone applauded, but some of the people got nervous and left. Others patted him on the back and congratulated him for the amazing feat.

Brandon laughed. He clapped Jon on the shoulder. "Is he hot, or what? Have you ever seen anyone do that?"

"There was a guy on TV once, but he only went like a foot above the ground."

Jon declared that he was tired and needed to go home. Maria noticed his foster mother, Angie McCormick, staring at him in shock. She must have seen him levitating, too. Maria went up to him and gave him the flowers back.

"Jon, here," she said, completely spooked by what she'd just witnessed. "I don't think we should see each other any more. There's something unholy about what you just did. It's not right."

Jon looked at her a moment, then held the flowers in front of him. In a flash, his hand was empty. The flowers vanished the same way they'd appeared.

"I agree, Maria," he said without expression. "I have much work to do. I must work hard and fast."

Chapter 22

ATTACK OF THE BULLY

KELLY

I never saw what popped me in the cheek while I ran full stride down the soccer field. Spinning through the air, I didn't see the ground, either—until I landed face-first. The force slammed my nose into the dirt and knocked the wind out of me. I lay there and gasped for air.

Whoa! Shooting stars! They were dancing just above the ground in front of me!

I'd never seen stars in the afternoon before, and certainly not close up. After a few seconds, though, the stars went away. When I got my breath back I noticed a sharp pain in the center of my face. My nose was bleeding.

I slowly pushed up to my hands and knees and blinked back the tears. Had I been hit by a car? I looked around. No, I was on the soccer field behind the school. What had I been doing? My memory gradually returned. We'd been playing soccer in P.E. class. I didn't consider myself to be much of an athlete, but up to this moment I'd been having a really good game. I'd played defense and stopped several attacks by the other team, including one when Michael Mall dribbled straight at me and I stole the ball from him. I remembered the startled look on his face as I passed it off to a teammate. Not many kids in gym class could do that to Michael. I would have smiled thinking about it, but my nose stung too much.

The last thing I remembered was running to intercept another pass to Michael. That's when everything went blank. I knew I'd gotten hit and now I was on the ground with a bloody nose. But again, what had happened?

I never saw the foot that smashed into my ribs and lifted me off the ground.

"Get up and fight!" A menacing figure stood over me in the bright sunlight.

The kick hurt, but not as bad as my nose. I rolled away from the attacker and sat on my knees. Dazed as I was, I had no problem recognizing the voice. Donnivee Fox.

That explained a lot. Donnivee must have blind-sided me with a punch to the head when I was running. I normally kept better track of her, but I'd been enjoying the game too much. The thought made me angry. Wasn't that the reason we were outside playing? Weren't we supposed to have fun and enjoy sports in P.E. class? Why should I even *have* to worry about a bully?

My first instinct was to find Coach Lewis. I quickly scanned the area and spotted him way across the field by the woods, discreetly talking on his cell phone. He did that every day, though it was against the rules. I had scanned his thoughts once, a few weeks ago, and found out he was calling his girlfriend. No use trying to get his attention. He wouldn't hear me, even if I screamed.

I tried to stand, but my legs were watery. I couldn't get up. Was it because I was afraid? Or was I still woozy from the landing? I wasn't certain, so I stayed on the ground and tried diplomacy.

"I'm not gonna fight you, Donnivee. You win, okay?"

"Fine. I win. I'm still gonna beat the crap out of you."

"Why?"

"Because it's Tuesday." Donnivee's response made no sense. But when she leaned down and punched me in the side of the face, things got clearer. I flopped back to the ground, my cheek stinging. If Donnivee needed an excuse to kick somebody's butt, then any excuse would do. In that respect, 'because it's Tuesday' made perfect sense.

I couldn't believe what was happening. How long was this going to continue? Why didn't somebody do something? When I sat up again, the class had formed a ring around us to watch, though nobody was outwardly encouraging the fight to go on. I mentally checked out each of the other kids to see what they were thinking. To my surprise, most of them wanted to see me rise up invincibly and clobber Donnivee. That gave me a little confidence, which I desperately needed right now. But the thoughts of Manson Stanfield, Donnivee's only known friend, stood out louder and clearer than the rest.

Beat her! thought Manson, as if willing her bully friend to act. *Beat her bad!*

Two other boys in the group thought the same thing, only they weren't feeling personal about it. They wanted to see Donnivee beat up somebody for the entertainment value. That infuriated me. How dare them want to watch a person inflict pain on another human being, just for *laughs*. I made a mental note to deal with those boys some day. Right now I had more serious issues.

I took a deep breath and tried to force some strength into my legs. I got to my feet, keeping a careful eye on Donnivee. But Donnivee had already planned her next move. She ran forward and swung a knockout punch at my face. This time I got a glimpse of it coming. I managed to duck. The blow glanced off my shoulder. Donnivee stumbled forward. But losing her balance didn't stop her from swinging. She began to throw punches like a wild woman.

I had no hope of keeping up with the blows or defending myself. One struck me in the head, another in the cheek. Donnivee was a fighting machine with one focus now: beat me to a pulp! I did the only thing I could think of. I turned and ran away.

The move gained me some time. Donnivee threw a grand slam right cross at my head just as I took off. She missed entirely and the force of the swing sent her tumbling to the ground. When she got up, she had dirt all over the side of her face. The other kids laughed at her. They apparently thought I'd made a clever defensive move. Yeah, right. I was running for my life. Laughter only made Donnivee more determined to pound me. I heard her thoughts loud and clear.

I'm gonna rip your head off!

I considered making a break for Coach Lewis, but Donnivee would probably outrun me. If that happened, my face would be turned into hamburger before he ever noticed anything was going on. Abruptly, a two-part plan popped into my head. Why hadn't I thought of it sooner? I stopped and faced my assailant. It was time to initiate Plan A.

"All right!" I screamed. "Come on! Let's do it!"

Donnivee stopped her maniac charge and became more cautious. She still kept moving forward.

Thank, God! I thought, catching my breath. Plan A had slowed Donnivee's attack. But Plan B was more involved and potentially dangerous. If Plan B didn't work, not only would Donnivee beat the snot out of me, but everyone in the class would know I was telepathic. It was a huge gamble, but what choice did I have? I needed an army and I needed it *now*.

I blasted mental orders to the kids around me. *Allen! Block her! Krista! Get in front of her! Michael! Stop her! Paul! Help Michael!*

Without knowing why, each of the kids reacted to my psychic commands. Allen jumped in front of Donnivee. Krista hurried up beside him and did the same thing. A moment later Michael and Montel also blocked the way. I was so shocked I nearly lost focus. I'd never telepathically ordered people around before, not really. Sure, I'd sent in suggestions to influence their thinking, like in chess matches, but a direct order? I'd always been too afraid they'd figure out what I was doing. If I had tried to get them to help by using my voice, they would have laughed at me and done nothing. Something about being inside their heads, though, made it different.

Steven! Becca! Antoinette! Stop her!

In the span of thirty seconds I had commanded nearly every kid in the class to help fend off Donnivee. None of the kids would have done anything on his/her own, but they seemed helpless to resist my orders for assistance. I became more calm and reassured. As long as I kept a tight grip on the thoughts of my *army*, Donnivee would have a tough time getting to me.

Donnivee tried to push past the crowd, but nobody gave way easily. "Let me get her!" she cried. She shoved at Zack Coleman. When he stumbled aside, Michael stepped into his place. He was much bigger and stronger than Donnivee, so she didn't try to go through him. But when she changed direction to go around him, Zack was blocking her again. I decided Donnivee wasn't going to give up against this sort of passive resistance. I changed tactics.

Donnivee, you're surrounded. We're all gonna beat you up!

The class encircled Donnivee. She was surprised, suddenly unsure of herself, but still full of bravado. "Come on! I can take every one of you!" She danced in place, fists ready for action. As the circle grew tighter, her eyes revealed the fear she really felt. The group wasn't afraid of her at all and they outnumbered her twenty to one. She looked over at me. I faced her just outside the circle, glaring. She knew I was doing this, but couldn't grasp how.

I concentrated on controlling the others. Donnivee began to shake her head in desperation. Tears formed in her eyes like she was afraid for her life. She quickly wiped them away, but for the first time she fully understood the situation. This new girl could beat her. I took in every doubtful thought as the circle closed to within arm's length of Donnivee. All at once the bully fell to her knees and began to sob.

"No!" she cried. "Don't hurt me any more!"

The words had a chilling effect on me. Don't hurt me *any more*? Nobody had hurt her at all, yet, so why would she say such a thing? Donnivee was confused. Maybe she'd had enough.

I released the others and told them to go have fun playing soccer. In a flash the kids all broke away and went after the ball again, including the two bloodthirsty boys who'd hoped to see a fight. The entire time Donnivee was surrounded, those boys had stood to one side watching. They never responded to my commands. At that point things became clear to me. Though my ability to control other people was the main reason they got involved, they only acted because they wanted to help to begin with. I hadn't entirely controlled them after all. Instead, I'd only directed them.

Donnivee knelt on the ground, helpless and pitiful. I looked hatefully at the girl who had given me a bloody nose and some aching ribs. I wanted to kick her teeth in and stomp her face into bloody mush. At that point, I probably could have. But those haunting words came back to me. *Don't hurt me any more!* I was angry at myself for having a heart.

"Don't you *ever, ever* try that again," I said, choosing my words carefully. "If you do, I'll take it to the next level."

Donnivee glared up at me helplessly. I scanned the beaten girl's thoughts and asked the question a lot of people wanted to know. *Why are you so mean?*

Only one thing came back out of Donnivee's head. *She beat me. And she never even threw a punch! I hate her so much!*

All this time Manson Stanfield had looked on in total disbelief. I detected her nearby and went hard and fast into the cruel girl's mind.

Why is Donnivee like that? What made her so mean?

Manson blinked in confusion. It never occurred to her to wonder why the question had been asked or where it came from. But she felt obliged to answer.

"She can't help it!" said Manson. "It's not her fault. Her father beats her all the time!" She covered her mouth in shock as she met Donnivee's cold, hurt gaze. At that point Manson was certain that her friend might now be her enemy. I listened to it all as Donnivee climbed to her feet.

"How could you, Manson?" said Donnivee. "You said you'd never tell!" Donnivee burst into tears and sprinted for the locker room.

"I don't know." Manson chased after her. "I thought you needed help!"

I looked angrily across the field at Coach Lewis. I'd had enough of his slackness and sent him a mental order. *Coach Lewis, do your job!*

In one fluid motion, Lewis put away the cell phone and looked up in time to see Manson chasing Donnivee. He ran over to me and saw the blood on my shirt and face.

"What's going on here?" asked Lewis. "Did Donnivee hit you?"

"No," I lied. "We ran into each other chasing the ball. It was an accident."

"Oh. Okay." Lewis looked like he didn't believe a word of it, but with me standing there and Donnivee on the run, what else could have happened?

Off and on for the rest of the day I considered what Manson had said about Donnivee's home life. If her father really did beat her, then maybe it *wasn't* her fault she was so mean. For the first time ever, I felt sorry for the class bully.

But something else was on my mind. I had controlled almost the entire class, *made* them do what I wanted! The feeling was incredible. My confidence soared like a hawk in the wind. I was *superior*. Nobody could ever hurt me again because *I* was in charge. And, yet, I hardly knew what I was doing. What if I got *really* good at controlling people? If that happened, I'd be untouchable! I nodded. Power had a sweetness I'd never experienced before. And I liked the flavor.

Chapter 23
MAJIK JUICE

KELLY

Travis got home from school that day, surprised to see Granny and me waving to him from beside the minivan.

"Over here," said Granny. "Give me your backpack."

Run! I said inside his head. Without thinking, Travis ran to us and gave his pack over to Granny.

Why'd you do that? he asked mentally, knowing that I'd made him run. He gave me a puzzled look.

Because I can.

He didn't like my reply, but he didn't worry about it. He could tell something big was happening or Granny would not be out here like this. "What's goin' on?"

She explained. "Chris has a real important meeting. He wants Angie and both of you along for the ride. It's my job to get you into the van. In you go, now."

Travis followed me into the captain's chairs, while I asked the questions that were on his mind, too.

"Who's he meeting? What's it all about?"

"Bottling company execs," said Granny. "He wants to sell his product."

I had trouble with that. Chris sell something? The old Chris was too shy and the new Chris was too mean. Either way his product had better be good. But I knew it wasn't. It was the stuff he made in the basement with roaches and hair in it. I made a face just thinking about it. Chris didn't have a ghost of a chance selling something made of roaches and hair.

Chris burst out onto the front porch. He wore a dark blue suit and a white shirt with a blue patterned necktie. His thin hair was slicked back and his shoes were so polished they might have been brand new. I had never seen him look so sharp. Chris carried a leather briefcase and a cardboard mailing tube over to the minivan.

"Angie move it!" He shouted like he was angry, but that wasn't unusual these days. He stood by the van and tapped his foot impatiently.

Travis and I looked at each other. "Maybe we should stay home," I suggested, my voice a little shaky.

"Yeah," said Travis. "I don't know nothin' about drinks, but I *do* know I don't wanna be with *him.*"

"You don't know *anything* about drinks," I said, trying to teach him better English. He rolled his eyes at me. He must have been practicing eye rolls lately because it was irritating.

Angie hurried out of the house searching through her purse along the way. "I'm coming, darling! Wait. The keys!" She turned and went back inside.

"Don't you *dare* make me late!" Chris' tone was menacing. It really ticked me off to hear him talk to Angie so mean like that.

Granny didn't like it either. "He's acting like he's chairman of the board. Maybe I'll have a quick chat with him before he goes." Granny walked up to Chris and stepped toe to toe, like she was picking a fight.

"I gotta see this!" Travis pressed his face against the window to get a good view. I was right beside him.

"You're rather demanding all of a sudden," said Granny, clenching her jaw.

She'd caught Chris unaware.

But the surprise on his face changed to cold, calm hatred. He half-smiled at her. "Don't worry, Matilda. Once I sell my product, I'll be out of your hair."

"Does that mean you'll be a nice boy again?"

"It means I can leave. Get out of my face."

Travis looked at me in surprise. *He can leave? What's that mean? I don't know.*

After a long, challenging glare, Granny finally stepped away. When she walked around the minivan and returned to us, she lowered her voice. "I don't know Chris all that well, but I never would have guessed he'd stand up to me."

"He probably wouldn't have before the cave," I said.

"The cave?"

"Granny, you've missed a lot."

"You and I will definitely have a chat about that later. Good luck with our nervous little boy."

"I'm not nervous," said Travis defensively.

"She means Chris," I explained.

"Huh?" Travis thought about it until he saw Chris pacing again. "Oh."

When Granny went into the house, she passed Angie coming out.

"Got 'em!" Angie held up the keys and hurried to the van. Travis looked at me, feeling very afraid. He didn't want to go with Chris anywhere for *any* reason. Chris' new *man-in-charge* personality was scary.

As Angie opened the driver's door I whispered how we felt. "Angie, we don't want to go with him. Chris acts like he's possessed by a demon." There, I said it. I didn't actually make an accusation, but I planted the seed.

Angie nodded. "I know what you mean. I think he's just nervous about his presentation. But he won't leave without us, all of us. He thinks having the family along will help his chances of impressing the bottling executives. Will you go? Please?"

My brother and I exchanged a quick glance. *Angie's scared, too,* I said inside his head. *She needs us.*

Travis shrugged. "Can we go to McDonald's on the way back?"

"Absolutely."

Travis looked for my approval and I nodded. "Okay," he said. "We'll go."

———

We arrived at the offices of the Summit Beverage Corporation at 4:47 PM. The place was a complex of multi-story buildings of different heights and shapes. The walls of each structure were made of silver, mirror-like material, bright and beautiful. It reflected trees, sky, cars, people—everything. It was like living, ever changing wallpaper on the outside of the building.

As soon as Angie parked the minivan, Chris got out. He used his reflection from the building to straighten his tie and adjust his suit, before charging in the front door with the suitcase and the mailing tube. We were just getting out of the van when he disappeared inside.

"I guess he doesn't want us along after all," said Angie, a little put out.

A second later Chris popped his head out the door. "Let's go! I'm late!"

"You still want us with you?" said Angie, surprised.

"Yes!"

"Oh. I didn't dress for this kind of thing."

"What kinda thing is it?" asked Travis. He and I both had on blue jeans and hoodies. We probably weren't dressed for it either. We jogged to catch up, but when we did, Chris walked even faster. We finally caught him at the information desk. A sturdy looking security guard met us.

"Can I help you?" asked the guard.

"Yes," said Chris in a bold, direct voice. "I'm Chris McCormick. I have an appointment with Mr. Nabors. I apologize for being late, but I assure you he *will* want to see what I've got here."

"Just a minute, sir." The guard took up a phone and spoke in a low voice. He looked serious as he listened, then hung up. "You have less than ten minutes, Mr. McCormick. Mr. Nabors leaves the building promptly at five. Go through that door and take the elevator on your left to the third floor. His secretary will meet you."

A tall, attractive woman with dark red hair met us on the third floor, just like the guard said she would. "Are you Mr. McCormick?" she asked. "I'm Coryn Lantz, Mr. Nabors' personal secretary. Do you realize how late you are?"

"Yes," said Chris. "I apologize. We got caught in beltway traffic."

"Don't we all?" Coryn said it coldly, as if everybody used that excuse. "You only have five minutes to show him your product. Mr. Nabors will not stay past five P.M."

"I only need five seconds of his time," said Chris. "Five seconds and he'll become one of the richest men in the country."

Lantz was impressed. So was I. That was a bold thing to say. I'd never heard Chris be assertive before, except when he was grouching about us being in his basement.

"Is this your family? Perhaps it would be better if they stayed with me? Mr. Nabors isn't terribly fond of children, I'm afraid."

"They come with me," said Chris. "I need them."

Angie smiled when he said it. It made her feel like maybe they still had something left of their marriage, which hadn't been the case since we came out of Pandora's Cave.

Lantz opened the door to a large meeting room with a tremendous, rectangular wood table in the center. I gaped at the room. The carpet was deep red and felt thick and squishy under our feet. The wooden furniture was highly polished. Three men sat at the far end of the table, which seemed miles away from where Chris stood. A lot of money had gone into this place. *Big* money.

Travis stayed close to Angie. *That lady was right*, he thought to me. *Those men don't like kids. They don't like us at all.*

Do you feel ghost fingers?

No, but they don't want us here. They wanna go home and Chris is slowin' 'em down. I looked at the clock, 4:58.

Chris signaled for us to stay where we were, then marched up to the men and set his suitcase on the table in front of them. He opened the suitcase and removed a tall, rolled up poster from the cardboard tube. He spread the poster across the table and used the men's personal coffee mugs to hold down three of the corners. The men exchanged hostile glances when Chris handled their mugs.

They want to throw him out! I thought to Travis.

The elderly man seated on the right had white hair, and not much of it. He was feeble looking and had to lean on a silver cane even while he sat in the chair. The expensive suit he wore didn't hide his shaking hands.

The guy on the left was Asian, with cold, hard eyes that never seemed to blink. He was younger and wore an equally expensive suit, perfectly tailored. He stood against the wall with his hands before him, fingertips touching. He looked like he could have been either a hit man or an undertaker in another life. Maybe both.

The important looking black man in the big chair at the end of the table sat up tall. He was distinguished with perfect gray hair. I thought he looked like a model, except that his eyes were intense, like a predator watching its dinner. He checked his Rolex watch. I looked up at the wall clock again. Chris only had one minute.

The poster on the table showed a professional ad for three different flavors of his new fruit drink called "Majik Juice". I couldn't believe Chris was capable of making such an impressive presentation.

"I'm Chris McCormick," said Chris bravely. He offered to shake hands with the men, but they never moved. He went on. "You must be Mr. Nabors?"

Nabors was the black man who sat in the middle. He made a point to glance at his watch again. "You are late, Mr. McCormick. We leave at five. You have thirty seconds."

Chris smiled and began with confidence and conviction. "Gentlemen, I give you the future best selling product in the history of the modern world. I call it Majik Juice. Why did I pick such a name? Because if you take but one sip of any of the three flavors I offer, I guarantee you'll want to finish the bottle. And after that you'll want to buy more, because it tastes so *damn* good!"

He took three bottles of Majik Juice out of his suitcase. The bottles had professionally designed labels and looked as good as anything in the stores. He popped the top off each bottle.

"I'm so sure you'll like this and want to market it, I'm willing to offer you a personal guarantee. I will work for your company, completely free, every day for the next year if you don't like Majik Juice. It's *that* good. Here you go, gentlemen. Enjoy."

Chris presented each of the men with a different flavor. Nabors took the cherry flavor and glared unsmiling at Chris. He sniffed the contents of the bottle.

"One sip," said Chris.

Nabors looked at his fellow executives and took a tentative sip. He swished the contents around in his mouth for a moment before swallowing it. He showed no interest or reaction at all. Suddenly, he smiled broadly and nodded at his fellows.

"Man, he's not kidding. That's the best stuff I've ever put in my mouth! Try this!" The men traded flavors and discovered they liked one flavor as much as another. Nabors got up and shook hands with Chris.

"This is an original recipe?"

"Oh, yes," said Angie from across the room. "He's been working on it for the last month in the basement. It's like he had this brainstorm."

In an instant Nabors went from hardcore executive to friendly rich guy who saw a way to get richer. He called his secretary on the intercom.

"Coryn." A moment later she entered the room.

"Yes, Mr. Nabors?"

"We'll be staying a little late today, Coryn. Get the new product contracts."

"Yes, sir." Coryn left the room a bit dazed. Travis wondered why. *The bosses never stayed late before*, I thought to him. *Never.* She returned with a large notebook and a laptop computer.

"It's not smart business for me to tell you this, Chris," said Nabors. "But you're right. That is the best drink I've ever tasted, and it's not even cold! I'll make you an offer right now for your recipe. How does one-hundred-thousand dollars up front sound? And that's just the beginning. Our standard contract guarantees that you'll make money on every single bottle we sell of your Majik Juice. Between profit on every bottle, profit sharing and stock options I think we can make you rich beyond your wildest dreams! How about it?"

"How about *one million* dollars up front," said Chris firmly. "Or I go down the street. I have a five-thirty appointment with Mr. Clark Creedon at Northern Virginia Bottlers."

Nabors looked flustered. "A million? That's a lot of money, Chris." He looked at his fellows with worried eyes.

He's faking it! I sent Travis the mental message and smiled. *He thinks Chris should have asked for ten times that much!*

Travis almost said something to Chris, but in the end lost his nerve. These men were way too important for him to interrupt.

Chris looked at Angie, then back at Nabors. He went through his suitcase and took out a legal sized notebook, professionally bound. He reached under his shirt and removed the small black cylinder he'd used in the basement. He gave Nabors the notebook and the cylinder.

"This contains the exact recipe for each product," said Chris, pointing to the notebook. "And this is the secret ingredient. Make sure you touch it only once for each bottle. I don't think it'll ever run out. And I can arrange for you to purchase all the ingredients at a significant discount. The Reverend Beth Ann Foster at the Peoples Way Church now grows everything you'll need. They're in southern California, you know."

Nabors smiled back at him. "I saw her in the news the other day. Her church is taking California by storm. You drive a hard bargain, Mr. McCormick. I'll have Coryn draw up a standard contract immediately." They shook hands. Nabors studied the bottle. "Majik Juice, that's a clever name, with the spelling and all. Where did you come up with a name like that for a fruit drink?"

"This is far more than just another fruit drink," said Chris. "I think you'll find it to be the answer to many prayers worldwide."

"Well it's certainly going to answer my prayers!" said Nabors, laughing. "Just the other night I was praying for more money. And here you are. You and your Majik Juice."

"*Your* Majik Juice," corrected Chris. "Show me where to sign."

Chapter 24

JON DISAPPEARS

KELLY

The McCormicks were overnight millionaires because Chris had invented a fruit drink that was made of, among other things, human hair and mashed up cockroaches. I wanted to mention it every time I heard Angie phone another friend to tell them about the family's new fortune, but I always held back. What if she thought I was out of line and decided to send me back to social services? Heck, even if she believed me, and that was a BIG if, it would only ruin her good mood. For the first time in days she was really happy. I shrugged. Sometimes you need to look beyond the cockroaches.

"Chris acted strange ever since he came out of that cave," said Angie to one of her friends. "But now I see why. He had this great idea and he knew it would work. He's amazing! It's a side of him I never knew about. We're going to remodel the entire house, and we're finally going to convert the basement into an apartment and rent it out. I can't wait to go shopping! I won't have to worry about credit limits because all the cards are paid off!"

Angie was thrilled about the money and being able to spend it. I was too, because part of the spending meant new clothes and more nice things for all of us. I might even make a serious effort to keep my room clean now. Chris had gotten a fair deal with Summit Bottling and pretty much set up our family with income for life. But since his "product making" hoopla was over, Chris didn't seem to care anymore. He stayed out of the basement and had completely given up teaching. He just sat in the den and watched soap operas and talk shows on TV all day.

Angie pretended not to notice the way he was, but I knew better. I'd gone into her mind and picked up enough lingering worries about Chris to know she cared very much about how he was acting now. On the other hand, they had so much money, and thinking of new ways to spend it made it difficult to stay in a worrying frame of mind. When Angie came up with a new project idea, she'd go into the den and ask Chris about it. His response was usually a nod or a grunt, but that was good enough for Angie. She'd run off and make a list, leaving Chris to flip channels until he found another show.

I heard it all while I sat on the living room sofa and tried to read a book for school. Though I had the ability to scan the minds of many people at once and now knew I could even control them, I still had difficulty focusing on a book when more exciting things were going on around me. I listened to Angie instead of staying involved with the chapter. Even more distracting, Travis came downstairs wearing his winter coat. He stood at the front door like he was looking for someone.

"What are you doing?" I asked.

"The Dunlops are pickin' me up. We're goin' to an ice hockey game at the arena."

"Good idea with the jacket. I hear it's freezing in there."

"Well, duh. Why do you think they call it *ice* hockey?"

I ignored his sudden attitude. "I thought you were grounded."

"Angie let me off."

I shrugged again and tried to read some more. Jon came downstairs, still wearing the same T-shirt he'd had on for days, but he'd changed into blue jeans. He cleared his throat to get everybody's attention. "I have an announcement to make and I would like all of you to hear it."

"What's it about?" asked Travis.

"I will explain when everyone is here."

It took a few minutes for me to find Angie, and Chris just growled and refused to leave the den, but soon the four of us were gathered at the front door. Jon smiled big and seemed very excited as his gaze went from Angie to me to Travis. I got hopeful just thinking about what he might have to say. Did he have a new magic trick to show off? His announcement came as a complete shock.

"I will not be here for Thanksgiving dinner. Tomorrow we have school for half a day and then I leave for New York City where I will become the greatest magician who ever lived."

"New York City?" said Travis. "Will you be back for Christmas?"

"I will not be coming back. I have much work to do. I must work hard and fast."

"Not comin' back? Ever?"

"Not ever."

I certainly didn't like the sound of that. Even if Jon was different since the cave, he was still Jon and he'd gotten a lot nicer lately. "You have to come back! What about us? You can't leave us *forever*! What about Brandon? You and Brandon are gonna make movies, remember? You're gonna be a stuntman! And what's Maria supposed to do? You two are in love. You can't just leave everybody!"

"*Everybody* is not my concern. I have much work to do. I must work hard and fast."

Angie looked at Jon, clearly amazed at his boldness. She shook her head. "When did you decide this, young man? Have you spoken with Chris about leaving? Are you just going to run off?"

"Chris knows. I am not going to run. I am going to walk."

"You're going to walk all the way to New York from here? And what are you going to do when you get there? Where will you sleep?"

"I have a place to sleep."

"Have you been talking to somebody on the internet? Do you realize how dangerous that is?"

"He sold his computer, Angie," I reminded.

"Oh. Well, the answer is still no. You're *not* going. Don't even ask again."

"I did not ask. I am going. I must work hard and fast."

"You're just like your father! Every other sentence out of your mouth is 'I must work hard and fast!' Don't you get tired of saying that?"

I cringed. Angie had called Chris Jon's *father*. I expected Jon might explode, but to my surprise, he didn't say a thing. Maybe he hadn't noticed.

Angie continued. "Jon Robert Bishop, you are not going any place over the break. We're having our first official Thanksgiving dinner together as a family. It's something I've wanted to be able to do to my whole life. If you try to go, I'll call the police and have you picked up as a runaway. How could you just leave Kelly and Travis like that? Besides, how are you going to walk to New York and get back here by Monday? Did you forget about school?"

"I am done with school. I will not be coming back. I will be the greatest magician in the world and I will start my tour in New York City."

"Your *tour*?" Angie was incredulous. "Who do you think you are? David Copperfield? He's the greatest magician in the world and it took him years and years to reach that level. You don't just go out and do shows!

"Listen to me, Jon. You're a high-school boy with big dreams, really good talent and no opportunities. You have no money and no contacts. If you really want to set up some shows, Chris and I can work it out. We have extra money now. But you have to start locally and you have to finish high school. I know you're good at magic, I saw you levitate at school the other day. But you have to take it one step at a time. And you are not quitting school for this. Nobody will pay to see just two or three tricks!"

"They will pay to see *me*. I am the greatest. And money is not a problem." Jon turned his palms down and turned them back. In each hand were two stacks of twenty-dollar bills, still in the wrappers. My eyes bulged. Angie jumped back.

"Did you steal that?" I asked. Jon half-smiled back at me, but remained secretive.

Jon gave Angie the cash. "Money is no object. I am leaving tomorrow after school. Do not try to stop me."

"I *will* stop you!"

Jon smiled and went into the den. Angie followed him. "I mean it, Jon! Wait till I tell your father about this!"

I held my breath, again waiting for Jon's response about the *father* comment. But he offered no reaction. Talk about focused. Jon was so intent on going to New York he didn't seem to care about anything else.

A moment later a car honked outside and Mathew Dunlop appeared at the front door. Travis let him in. "Come on in, Mathew."

Mathew was dressed impeccably as always, wearing khaki slacks with a green sweater. He seemed to be in a hurry. "Hey, Ms. Angie. Hey, Kelly. Come on, Travis, we have to go. Game time is in thirty minutes."

"Okay," said Travis. "I'll be right there. I gotta say goodbye to my brother. He's goin' to New York tomorrow to be the world's greatest magician." I would have corrected his grammar, but Travis was on the verge of tears. He didn't want to see Jon leave any more than I did.

"Really? That's cool. What kind of tricks can he do?"

"I'll tell you in the car." Travis went into the den to find Jon. I peeked around the corner to see what he was going to say to him. To my surprise, he hugged Jon and returned to the foyer.

"Thanks for taking him to the game, Mathew," said Angie. "We'll get you guys together to spend the night real soon, okay?"

"Okay, Ms. Angie. Thanks for letting him go!" Mathew and Travis sprinted out the door as Angie waved to the Dunlops. I hung my head. I understood why Jon had to go to New York. But when he said he wasn't coming back, well, that hurt. Was there any way to change his mind?

JON

On the half-day before Thanksgiving Jon placed all his books in his locker at school and walked through the hallways alone. The building was nearly empty, even most of the teachers had already gone home. As Jon rounded a corner, somebody slammed into him so hard it nearly knocked him down. He caught his balance and found himself flanked by Spider Dedmon and a wary Robbie Leach. Kurt Lazarus stood in front of him, still wearing a cast on his right hand. His nose had an odd-looking dent in it where Jon had broken it weeks before. Kurt leaned down into Jon's face.

"Well, if it isn't Jon Bishop." Kurt looked around to be sure no teachers were nearby. He put his cast hand on Jon's shoulder and leaned close like he had something important to say. He practically whispered into Jon's ear. "Let me tell you a little secret, Jon-boy. Your grandmother's not here to protect you this time. Do you know what that means?"

Jon shook his head curiously. All at once Kurt sucker-punched him hard in the gut. Jon doubled over. His eyes flashed yellow. Kurt started to laugh.

"Now you know! Ha-ha-ha! How'd that feel, wimp?" He laughed hard and pointed at Jon. "Ha-ha-ha-ha…." All at once he froze in place and became utterly silent. Jon straightened up and continued down the hall as if nothing had happened. Kurt remained stuck in the laughing position with a stupid look on his face.

Spider freaked out when he tried to move him. "Kurt? What's wrong, man? Why don't you move?"

"What'd he do to him?" Robbie waved his hand in front of Kurt's face. His eyes never blinked. "Kurt! Wake up, man!"

Jon arrived at the foyer and right away noticed two sturdy policemen waiting at the doors, alert and ready. Principal Dillon was there, too. He said something into his walkie-talkie and marched toward Jon. Jon knew Dillon preferred to handle confrontational matters personally. He'd been expecting this.

Dillon stopped before Jon, a serious expression on his face. "Jon, can we talk?"

Jon nodded. "Sure, Mr. Dillon. What do you want to talk about?"

"About your trip to New York. Young man, it simply isn't going to happen."

Two male physical-education teachers appeared at Jon's left. They blocked one of the hallways. To his right, three other male teachers blocked the way. One of them was Dr. Parrish, who looked at Jon with pleading eyes. Jon was surrounded.

"It must happen," said Jon calmly. "I have much work to do. I must work hard and fast."

"Jon, your foster mother is very worried about you. I get the impression she really loves you and your brother and sister. All she wants is to have Thanksgiving dinner with all of you together. Now what's so wrong with that?"

"Nothing is wrong with that. But I must go to New York. I am the greatest magician in the world."

"I understand. I heard about what you did the other day. The problem is nobody knows you're the greatest magician in the world yet. And why would you walk? If you don't get any rides, it could take you weeks to get there."

"I need to arrive at least six days before New Year's Eve. Then the world will see the greatest trick ever performed in public."

"You're not listening to me." Dillon crossed his arms and stood before Jon like he meant business. "Your foster parents have legal custody over you while you're in their care and still under the age of eighteen. Do you see those policemen by the door? Well, if you try to leave, they're gonna lock you up in juvie to make sure you don't go any place. Now I'm thinking you'd rather spend Thanksgiving with your family than with a bunch of strangers in jail. Jail's a rough place, Jon."

"I have much work to do. I must work hard and fast."

"Does that mean you're still going to New York?"

"Of course." Jon turned and started for the door. The cops moved toward him. The teachers all moved toward him. Suddenly, Maria and Brandon burst in. Maria ran to Jon. She pleaded with him.

"Jon, please don't go. For me, okay? Don't you remember what we had?"

"Yeah, Jon," said Brandon. "You can't leave now, man. I'm gonna buy another camcorder, okay? We're gonna make that movie, the one I wrote a script for, like what we talked about. Let me show you the script, it's in the car."

Jon paused ten feet from the door. The cops stopped, the teachers stopped, and Brandon stopped. Maria hugged him. She kissed him on the lips, but he was unresponsive.

"You don't love me anymore, do you Jon?" she asked in a low voice.

"Actually, Maria, I have *never* loved you." Jon's response was icy cold. Maria shook her head and backed away from him.

"I hate you," she said just above a whisper. Brandon fell in stride with her as she went away.

"He didn't mean it, Maria," Brandon said to her. He looked back at his friend. Jon half-smiled at him. "He'd have to be nuts to say something like that to *you*."

Maria rubbed some gathering tears from her eyes. "It doesn't matter, I've put him out of my heart." She stopped and looked back at Jon one last time. "And I'm not letting him back in. *Ever*." Having said that, they left.

One of the cops stepped up to Jon. "Jon Bishop, we need you to come with us. We're going to take you home, or we're going to take you to jail. The choice is yours."

Jon looked out the windows by the doors. Angie, Kelly and Travis were outside waiting for him. He returned his gaze to the cop.

"You just do not understand, do you?" he said, smiling. "I *am* the greatest magician in the world. I have a show to do and I need to start my journey. Watch for me on TV."

He smiled at them and calmly crossed his hands in front of his waist. Then he vanished.

KELLY

Travis and I watched the whole thing through the front window. For a moment I thought maybe some glare had interrupted my view of Jon. But Angie saw it too.

I looked at Travis, astonished. "Did you see that? Where'd he go?" Travis only shrugged.

"I don't know." Angie stared unblinking.

"Maybe he really *is* the world's greatest magician!" said Travis. Angie gave him a tragic look of confirmation and hurried inside the school.

Mr. Dillon, the cops and the teachers gawked at the empty space in front of them. Nobody moved except Parrish. He went to the spot where Jon had stood and looked up and down and all about. He got on his knees and felt around on the floor. He stood up shaking his head. "He's gone all right. And he sure didn't use any smoke and mirrors."

"So how'd he do it?" asked one of the cops. "Did he say he was a magician?"

"The *greatest* magician," said Dillon. "He thinks he's going to be on TV."

"If he can do stuff like that, he *will* be," said the other cop. "Do you still need us, Mr. Dillon?"

"No. Thank you, officers. We'll look around some more, but I doubt we're going to find him anywhere in this building." Dillon went to where Jon had been standing and stomped his foot on the floor. "Tile on top of solid concrete. Unless I'm mistaken, that was no trick. Somewhere along the way that boy has picked up some *real* magic!"

JON

Traffic on Route 50 was heavy and so was the pall of dark clouds that promised to bring rain or snow very soon. Jon Bishop walked along the road with a determined smile on his face, carrying nothing at all. Several cars had slowed and nearly pulled over, as if the drivers were considering offering him a ride. But instead, they sped up and took off. Few people in northern Virginia picked up hitchhikers and this guy wasn't even sticking his thumb out.

But one car did slow down. Sitting behind the wheel of his high-performance Chevy Nova, Robbie Leach slowed the car to match Jon's pace and pulled up along side of him. Kurt Lazarus was in the passenger seat, with Spider Dedmon in back. Kurt rolled down the window and leaned outside. He was furious.

"You made me look like a jackass, Bishop! I'm taking care of you *right*, this time!" Kurt withdrew a small caliber handgun from his pocket.

In the back seat, Spider panicked. "No, Kurt! Are you crazy? I don't wanna go to jail!"

Jon stopped walking. He smiled at Kurt. "What do you think you are going to do with that, Kurt? Take a cold shower?"

"I'm poppin' you good!" Kurt squeezed the trigger. Nothing happened. He looked down at the gun, which had somehow changed into a common bar of soap. Kurt was so shocked he dropped the soap. "Get outta here!" The car sped off. Jon continued his walk as it began to rain.

A few minutes later a pickup truck pulled off the road. The elderly man inside the truck leaned over the seat and opened the passenger door. "You need a ride, son?"

Jon nodded. "Yes, thanks. I have much work to do. I must work hard and fast."

"Well, I don't know how fast I can get you to work in holiday traffic, but it'll be faster than walking. And a whole lot dryer. Hop in."

Jon got in and closed the door. The truck drove off.

Chapter 25
CHRIS GOES INSANE

KELLY

When we got home, Chris was pacing through the house and mumbling to himself like something really bothered him. He walked right by us three times, nodding or shaking his head, but never seemed to notice we were there. It was like he was having this great internal debate, but I couldn't read his mind so I had no way to tell if anybody was winning the argument.

We followed him back into the den where I noticed right away the TV was turned off. Did that mean he'd gotten over his infatuation with soap operas? As weird as Chris had been lately I'd never seen him like this. When he walked by us for the fourth time, Angie caught his arm and made him stop. Chris stared straight down, as if all his problems were located on the floor.

Angie spoke to him in a soft voice. "Chris, honey? Did you lose something?"

Chris snapped his head up suddenly, the look in his eyes pure madness. He waved his arms dramatically. "I've done my work! I worked hard and fast! I don't know what to do now!"

I sent Travis a mental message. *I think I know why I haven't been able to read his mind since the cave. If he was possessed he'd be human and I'd still be able to read him, right? I mean, I can read anybody unless they're crazy, so he's got to be crazy! Should we call the police?*

Not yet, thought Travis. *I don't feel any ghost fingers. Angie's nervous, though.*

She ought to be. If he's crazy anything could happen!

Travis nodded in agreement, but never took his eyes off Chris.

Angie held Chris' hand and stroked his arm to calm him. "Chris, listen to me. Jon went to New York all by himself. I'm so worried about him. We all are."

"Yeah," said Travis for support. "He disappeared in fronta everybody! Bam! He was gone!"

Angie looked at her husband pleadingly. "If I hadn't seen it myself, I never would have believed it. Chris, what are we going to do?"

We all waited while his disturbed gaze darted back and forth between us. It was like he could no longer focus on any single thought or object.

Chris continued, still animated. "Jon *had* to go to New York. He has much work to do. But I don't. Now I got nothing!" He wandered off into the living room again, wringing his hands.

About then Granny came downstairs, clearly not in the mood for more weirdness from Chris. She watched him intently as she spoke.

"He's been like that for over an hour," she said. "I think he's lost it, Angie. Maybe we should call the hospital?"

"And tell them what exactly? Stay out of it, Matilda." Angie was defensive. I zoomed in on her thinking and found out she was on the verge of a breakdown herself. Her love for Chris was unconditional and she wasn't about to admit he was insane. Not yet, anyway. She didn't want her prodigal mother giving her advice.

"Sure," said Granny a little put out. "So where's Jon? Did the police take him?"

I quickly explained what had happened at school. Granny was amazed.

"He just disappeared, you say? Right in front of everybody?"

"Vanished!" said Angie. "The principal was standing barely five feet away from him. This day is turning into a nightmare. I need coffee."

"Better make that two," said Granny. "And make it strong."

"Three, please," I said.

Travis frowned. "I don't like coffee, but I need somethin', too."

Angie turned before she headed for the kitchen. "And one hot chocolate?"

Travis nodded vigorously. "Thanks, Angie."

When Angie was gone, Granny whispered to us. "Do you think Chris has gone loony?"

I nodded. "What should we do?"

"I don't know. Of course, it's not all bad. He did come up with that Majik Juice stuff and I'd say he's done right well for himself. Wish I could cook like that."

"If you don't mind cooking with cockroaches and human hair," I said. "Trust me, Granny, you don't *ever* want to drink it."

"Cockroaches, you say? He put 'em in the drink? I'll take your advice, then. Never liked bugs in my beverage all that much, unless I felt like a crunchy snack, of course." Under her breath I heard her mutter, "It's a good thing I showed up when I did. Something strange is going on around here."

———

Angie was absolutely determined to have her first Thanksgiving dinner with her family, even if part of the family was missing. She, Granny and I spent the rest of the evening cooking and preparing the big meal for the next day. Angie acted as supervisor and head chef, since neither Granny nor I had any idea how to cook. Travis helped, too, for a bit, because he knew where everything was that they needed to make the meal. But eventually we ran out of things for him to do, so he went into the den and watched TV. We worked until well after ten, at which point we came into the den and crashed on the couch beside Travis. I had no idea cooking was such hard work.

"I think we're done," said Angie, removing her shoes and propping her feet on the ottoman. "I'll get up early and put the turkey in the oven. Who likes sweet potatoes?"

Granny gave her the thumbs up, but Travis shook his head. "No, thank you!"

"Not really," I said. "They smell good, but they don't taste anything like they smell."

"I'll cook enough for three. They're Chris' favorite, you know."

Travis felt very comfortable wedged into the tight space on the couch with me and the new family. There was a sense of security being with Angie and Granny that he hadn't known for most of his life. I felt it too. We had a home now and we had most of our family together again. Nearly everything felt right.

All of a sudden Travis was bombarded with waves of warm, loving emotion. It startled him, which startled me. We sat up quickly, confused about who was having the feelings. He looked at me and I scanned the others. He studied Angie and Granny, narrowing down the source.

It came from Granny! He'd never detected anything like that from her before, and now I sensed she was thinking about something incredibly important to her.

A moment later she cleared her throat. "Uh, Angie, I have a small favor to ask. Would you mind if I invited a guest to dinner tomorrow?"

Angie's eyes burned when she heard the request. "After what's been happening around here lately I'm not in the mood to have one of your biker friends or some drunken bar fly show up for Thanksgiving dinner. I don't think I could handle it."

"He's a very nice man, really."

"I said no. You've only lived here a few weeks. The least you could do is think about the children."

"Actually, I am thinking about the children. It's Mark Parrish."

The shock that came over Angie almost knocked Travis off the couch. I felt it too, through him. She glared at her mother in complete surprise, unable to speak for several moments. "How do you know Mark?"

"I've been helping him on his place next door. He's a wonderful man, you know. Very good with his hands."

"We don't need to hear about that."

"I'm talking about woodworking. He's marvelous."

Travis tuned in to both Angie and Granny, greatly confused by their contrast of emotions. It didn't take him long to figure out how each of them felt. Angie was confused and a little angry. But Granny had other emotions working.

Granny's in love with Dr. Parrish! he mentally said to me. *Really in love!*

I tuned in to Matilda Price's more intimate thoughts. Her happy thoughts made me wide-eyed and happy. *You're right! Isn't it sweet?*

It's gross! Do you think they get all slobbery, like Jon and Maria?

I'm sure of it.

Bleah!

"Mark Parrish." Angie said it like the name held some sort of stability in her life. "I'm sorry, Matilda. I didn't realize you knew each other. Yes, certainly, Mark is always welcome here. Maybe he can bring Chris out of his funk and get him back to teaching."

"I hope so, too," said Granny. "Still no word from the police about Jon?"

Angie shook her head. "I'm not going to worry about Jon any more. If he can disappear in the middle of a crowded room with everyone watching he can certainly take care of himself. He always could, I guess. I say we let him do his magic and if it works he'll get famous. If not, he'll be home soon enough."

"But he said he was staying in New York until New Year's Eve," I reminded. "He has something big planned for that night."

"That's over five weeks from now," said Granny. "What's he gonna do in the meantime? What about Christmas? Surely he'll come home for Christmas. At least for a visit."

"What if we never see 'im again?" said Travis. "What if he disappears doin' one of his tricks and *nobody* ever sees 'im?" Travis hung his head despondently. I could tell being reminded about Jon's departure put a real dent in his happy moment. His family was separated all over again, but this time Jon had left them because he wanted to, not because social services said he had to live in a different place. The whole thing was both mind-boggling and numbing at the same time. Travis got up and wandered into the foyer. I stayed discreetly inside his thoughts to make sure he was okay. He gazed out the storm door as if he thought Jon might appear at any moment with a big smile on his face and tell them he'd been kidding about going to New York. What would he do without his big brother?

TRAVIS

Travis looked out the door, but of course Jon never showed up. Instead Chris' reflection appeared in the storm-door glass. Chris was right behind him. Travis turned and looked fearfully into the man's crazed eyes.

"Move out of the way," said Chris gruffly. "I need to go home."

"You are home," said Travis, stepping to the side.

"My *real* home."

His real home?

Chris went outside to the edge of the driveway and stood along the curb. Travis decided to follow him, watching every move he made. He thought Chris might try to follow Jon to New York, but instead he just stayed in one place and kept an eye on the far end of the street. So what'd he have in mind?

Moments later, a yellow taxicab arrived and rolled to a stop in front of the house. Chris clapped his hands excitedly when the driver opened the window and leaned out.

"Where ya headin', buddy?" asked the driver.

"Crystal Creek Park," said Chris. He reached into his pocket and took out some hundred-dollar bills. He passed the bills to the driver.

"Crystal Creek Park?" repeated the driver. "Isn't that where that cave is? What's it called?" He thought for a moment, then snapped his fingers. "Pandora's Cave! Is that the place?"

"Yes," said Chris. "I'm going home."

KELLY

Travis burst into the house and yelled at the top of his lungs. "Chris is goin' to Pandora's Cave!"

Granny and I ran into the foyer. Angie stumbled in behind us, pulling on her shoes as she went.

"How do you know that?" asked Granny.

"I heard 'im tell the cab driver where to go!"

"He took a cab?" said Angie. "We've got to stop him!"

We quickly piled into the minivan and flew down the road. Angie had never driven so fast in her life. Even Granny clung to her seat with both hands. "You kids have your seatbelts on, right?"

I looked at Travis. We were strapped in the back, wide-eyed and scared. The minivan wove in and out of traffic. "You'd better believe it!"

"She's gonna get us killed!" said Travis in a low voice.

"Either that or get arrested! She's only got one thing on her mind. Chris!"

"Why would he wanna go back to the cave?"

"I don't know, but one thing's for sure. Chris is all out *nuts*."

Somehow we arrived safely at Crystal Creek Park just after eleven. Sure enough, the taxi drove off when we pulled into the parking lot. But the park was closed and the lights around the cave had been turned off. It was too dark to see Chris or anything else for that matter.

"Kelly!" said Angie. "Get the ranger! Get those lights turned on!"

I ran to the ranger station without question. The office was lit up and the TV was on as a figure moved around inside. I got to the door and burst in without knocking. Ranger Ned Taylor sat before the TV with a sandwich and a cup of steaming coffee. I startled him so badly he spilled the coffee on his leg.

"Ow!" he yelped, setting the mug on the desk. "I thought I locked the door."

"Sorry!" I said. I pointed to the cave. "You gotta turn on the lights, fast!"

"You're Kelly Bishop, right?" he said, surprised. "What are *you* doing here?"

"I'll tell you! Just turn on the lights!"

"Hell, I didn't notice they were off! That's the third time this week."

While I explained what was going on, I followed Ned outside where he opened the breaker box and flipped on the floodlights. The area around Pandora's Cave lit up brightly enough to look like mid afternoon. But the cave itself was pitch black, as always. I kept a wary eye on it, expecting a host of demons to rush out and grab us at any time. I didn't like being here, and if Chris had already gone inside the cave, I sure wasn't going in after him.

A figure charged out of the shadows, running toward the cave. Chris! I pointed, but Ned was confused. We were too far away to do anything. Angie and Travis were getting a flashlight out of the car. Travis also pointed. Nobody was going to stop him in time.

From out of nowhere a stocky figure sprinted across the lawn. Granny! Before Chris realized she was coming, she closed the gap and tackled him. Chris landed hard as they slid across the grass. He tried to wrestle himself free.

"Let me go!" he cried. "You can't do this! Let me go!"

He nearly got away. But Granny put him in some kind of cradle hold. She wrapped him up and squeezed tight. Chris wasn't going anywhere.

"Wow, Granny!" said Travis, running up beside them. "You can fly!"

"Not exactly," said Granny. Chris wiggled madly. Granny tightened her hold.

"Ahhh!" Chris yelped. "You're breaking my back!"

"Then stop moving!" said Granny.

"No! Let me go!" Chris was furious. His eyes flashed yellow. He gnashed his teeth at Granny, but she had him good. He couldn't bite her and he couldn't break free.

Ned arrived and took out some handcuffs. He and Granny rolled Chris onto his stomach. They cuffed his hands behind his back.

Granny whispered into Chris' ear. "Now you know what I can do to you, right? So listen to me well. If you don't stop upsetting my daughter, I'm gonna to upset *you*." Chris hissed at her like a wildcat. Granny released him and stood up, breathing hard.

Angie ran up with me. "Chris, darling! Why would you want to go back in *there*?"

"My work is done! Let me go! My work is done!"

"You're not leaving my only daughter so you can go live in a cave," said Granny. "Even if you are crazy."

"What do you want me to do about him?" asked Ned.

"We can't leave him here," said Angie, looking hopelessly at Ned. "You were right, Matilda, he needs help, I see that now. Is there some place we can keep him safe? Can we lock him up?"

"I could arrest him for trespassing," said Ned. "It's only a misdemeanor so they won't keep him long. But the magistrate will be off tomorrow for the holiday. If we put him in jail, you can get him back out Friday."

"Jail?" Angie paled. "I hate to do that to him, especially on Thanksgiving. Isn't there anything else we can do?"

"He needs psychiatric help," said Ned. "I know because my aunt's going through same thing. My cousin's been acting weird ever since he came outta that cave. He just keeps talking about having work to do, and all that."

"I did my work!" said Chris. "I have nothing else to do! I want to go back!" He struggled to his feet and tried to run toward the cave. Again, Granny tripped him up, but this time she sat on him. I sat on him, too, and so did Travis.

"I say put him in jail," said Granny. "At least you won't have to worry about him for a night or two. We can find a good shrink on Friday."

Everyone looked at Angie, who gazed pitifully at her husband. She slowly nodded. The ranger and Granny hauled Chris back to the station. Ned locked him in a storage room and called the local police. "They'll be here in a few minutes," he said.

"Where's Ripper?" I asked, noticing that we hadn't heard any barking since we got there.

"At the vet," said Ned. "He choked on a squirrel bone and had to have surgery. I'll pick him up in a few days and bring him back. I'll tell you, this place is scary when he's here, but when he's not, well, I don't like working this shift so much anymore. I can't believe I didn't lock the door."

"Don't blame you," said Granny. "But why were the lights turned off?"

"I don't know." Ned scratched his head. "Those lights have been cutting on and off randomly since before the night of the rescue. I'm gonna have to put some kind of alarm on the box, I guess, to warn me."

Angie leaned closer to Ned and placed a hand on his shoulder. "So, Mr. Taylor, what happened to your cousin? Is he...crazy, like my husband?" Ned lowered his voice, as if he were afraid somebody else might be listening. "I don't know what happened exactly. It was like he'd gotten knocked in the head and was suddenly smarter. I'm not talking about a couple of IQ points, here. I mean *way* smarter! He wasn't stupid before, you know, but he wasn't any rocket scientist. He had his associate's degree from the community college, but he was just a regular guy, you know? The biggest dream he ever had was to own a house, have a family and race his Corvette on weekends. That's it! Now you wouldn't believe it."

"Try us," I said. "We've got our own stories to tell."

Ned looked us over and apparently decided he could trust us. "He came out of that cave saying he had to work hard and fast. He must have said it fifty times that night, I got tired of hearing it. I finally asked him what he had to do that was so important. He said he needed me to drive him to the university in the morning because he forgot how to drive. I figured he just wanted to take some classes, you know? But it wasn't like that at all.

"We got to the science department and he walked up to this professor and said he wanted a degree. The professor asked, what kind of degree? And Eric told him he wanted a doctorate in genetics. When the professor found out he didn't even have a bachelor's he laughed and told Eric to enroll in some classes. Then Eric spouted off some advanced biotechnology stuff and the professor got all interested. I didn't understand a word of it, but they went into an office and talked for hours! That week Eric was tested by a whole bunch of professors. The test took days and when they were done, they gave him a Ph.D. in genetics. Go figure!"

"He got his doctorate in a week?" Granny was astounded. "But how?"

"Apparently those professors grilled him about everything under the sun and he knew all the answers. But he started telling them things they didn't even know. They all decided he must have done some original research, so they figured he deserved the degree. One of them is a consultant for *2x-Helix*, a technology company, and he suggested that Eric apply for a job there. The next thing I know my ordinary cousin is working for one of the top biotech companies in the world making six figures! My cousin! All because he went into a cave."

We were stunned. The next few minutes we told Ned all about Chris and Jon. Ned was much impressed by Jon's magic skill. He was surprised to learn about Chris' invention.

"Majik Juice!" Ned rubbed his chin. "I saw something about that in today's paper. That drink got FDA approval in record time."

"*Don't* drink it," I said. "Unless you like cockroaches and hair. I saw him make it in our basement and those were two main ingredients."

Ned made a face. "That's gross! You know, it looks to me like we've got similar problems here. Maybe we ought to keep in touch, you think?"

"That's a good idea," said Granny. "Got something to write with?"

Ned and Granny wrote out their contact information on Post-it notes and exchanged it.

"Mr. Taylor," said Angie. "Do you have any idea what really happened to the people who went in that cave?"

"No, ma'am, I don't. It just doesn't make any sense. But if you find out anything interesting, please give me a ring. I'll do the same. By the way, Ms. Price, that was a helluva tackle."

Granny grinned. "Thanks, Ned. I played a little rugby in the day." She looked up as a squad car pulled into the parking lot. "Police are here."

After filling out a police report we left the park. Travis asked Angie to drive slower going home since there was no emergency, and she just laughed. "Travis, did I scare you with my driving?"

"A little."

"A little?" Granny rolled her eyes. "You scared the heck out of me, and I don't scare easy. But, Angie, you did the job. You may have saved your husband's life."

Angie didn't smile, she was clearly just too tired. As it was we didn't get home until after one in the morning. Travis had fallen asleep in the car and I woke him up and led him to his bedroom. I plopped him into bed with his clothes still on. Before I got my pajamas on, I heard Angie crying from the room next door. Apparently, Granny was with her, trying to console her. I had a bad feeling about tomorrow. With Jon in New York and Chris in jail, it probably wasn't going to be such a great Thanksgiving.

———

The next day the intoxicating smells of Thanksgiving food filled the air at the McCormick house. I didn't remember anything in my life *ever* smelling so good. Apparently, Dr. Parrish had similar feelings when he showed up early and began snacking right away on the vegetable trays. The man wasn't very fat, but he was big and I figured he needed a lot of fuel to keep his large body going. But Parrish hadn't come over just for snacks and turkey. Parrish was in love with Granny just as much as she was in love with him. Travis told me he felt it as soon as the two adults were in the same room together. They rarely strayed far from each other except when Granny was in the kitchen helping Angie with the meal.

As great as everything smelled, and it smelled utterly wonderful, actually *eating* the meal almost made me cry. It tasted *so* good, better than any food I'd ever eaten. I didn't remember much about the holidays when I was little, except that I really liked Halloween and Christmas. Poor Travis had only been three and he remembered virtually nothing about any holidays. Whenever Jon told him stories about Thanksgiving dinner with our parents, Travis took his word for it. He couldn't recall a thing about it except the parades on TV with those giant balloon creatures floating over the street. Sadly, none of the other foster families I'd stayed with had ever bothered to make it a special day. When I asked one family why, I was told they couldn't afford it, that the only reason they kept me was for the money. Ouch! That was one question I never asked again. But Angie made it very special. It was just too bad Jon and Chris weren't there to spend it with us.

In spite of Angie's fantastic meal, she stayed depressed the whole day. Word about Chris being in jail had spread pretty fast and by midafternoon most of her friends knew about it. Some people called to cheer her up, though maybe they just wanted to learn the gossipy details about what had happened. Angie decided to call Dr. Sanderlyn the next morning, though she was concerned what he might think about her having two nut cases in the same house. Granny suggested they arrange for Chris to be taken to the clinic straight from jail, if possible. Angie reluctantly agreed.

After dinner, we all went into the den to watch football games. We had to drag Angie with us because she really didn't like sports that much. Angie, Granny, Travis and I all crammed together on the couch and though there really was no more room, somehow Dr. Parrish squeezed in beside Granny. Travis thought it was fun and I could tell Angie needed the laughs and physical contact. But I didn't think Parrish was very comfortable.

Angie's afraid Chris won't ever come back to her, I thought to Travis. *She's afraid of being alone.*

So is he comin' back?

I shrugged. I gave Angie a huge hug and wouldn't let go. "I'm sorry Chris isn't here. And Jon, too."

Angie tried to smile. "At least I know where Chris is. I know he's safe. I'm worried about Jon. Let's just try to have the best day we can, okay?"

"Okay. Angie?"

"Yes?"

"I love you."

Angie broke down crying. She buried her face into my shoulder. "I... love...you, too. Both of you!" Travis turned it into a group hug session while Granny patted her daughter on the shoulder. Parrish shifted his seat to the arm of the couch and looked like he wanted to be some place else.

———

The day after Thanksgiving Angie called Dr. Sanderlyn and arranged for authorities to move Chris out of jail and into Sunnyside. He told Angie she needed to stop by and sign papers that would admit Chris into the treatment program. I went too, since chances were good that Angie would have an emotional meltdown before it was over. After all, how could anyone put their beloved spouse into a mental hospital and not be affected? I wanted to be there for Angie.

That same morning Granny used the Mustang to take Travis over to Mathew Dunlop's house to play for the day. Angie told me Travis was terribly bored because none of his friends at school lived close by, so she promised to call Mathew's mother. I was the one who suggested that Granny should drive him. I didn't want Travis to be anywhere near Angie when she was so upset. The whole emotional effect on him might be more than he could handle.

When we got to the clinic Angie insisted that I stay in the car while she went in alone. I breathed a secret sigh of relief. Supporting Angie was one thing, but I did *not* want to go into any psycho ward, *especially* Sunnyside, which really didn't seem all that sunny. The stark brick building had no windows, no shrubbery, and no flowers. The front door had heavy iron bars built-in, and I don't know if there was a back door or not, but I had a feeling it would be a difficult place to leave if you didn't have a key. Nonetheless, I watched the whole check-in process as it happened through Angie's eyes.

Dr. Sanderlyn was a tall man, bald, overweight and probably in his sixties. I thought he seemed nice enough at first, but his thoughts confused me. Did he really want to help Chris? Or was he more interested in the money? I couldn't tell.

Almost immediately after Angie signed the papers, she became absolutely certain she'd done the wrong thing. She tried to convince the doctor to let her bring Chris home again, to give him one more try. But Nurse Agnes, the nurse in charge, physically guided Angie out of the lobby. Nurse Agnes was a mean-looking woman with cold, dark eyes and a small, turned down mouth. I got the feeling *nobody* argued with her.

"The doctors know how to treat your husband," said Nurse Agnes, directing Angie to the exit. "Perhaps you can see him again by Christmas. Don't call us. We'll call you."

Somehow Angie made it back inside the van before she fell apart. She cried like a baby and started bumping her forehead against the steering wheel until I stopped her. She hit it pretty hard, too. If the wheel hadn't been padded she might have knocked herself out.

I totally understood her pain. The idea of putting Chris into that place for who knows how long was suffocating. The worst part for Angie was she felt like a traitor. Apparently, this was one of those times when action *didn't* beat fear.

After a good long cry, Angie shuddered and straightened up. Her eyes were puffy and red as she squinted at herself in the rearview mirror. I sensed it was time to talk. Putting Chris away for a while was devastating, but it wasn't the end of the world. Sunnyside was supposed to help him get well.

"You know you had to do it," I said. "You *had* to. Chris would've gone right back to Pandora's Cave when they let him out of jail."

"I know, but you don't understand. Chris looked homicidal! There was no love in his eyes at all."

She was right. Chris *had* looked like he wanted to kill someone. It's a good thing he'd been shackled and guarded by two chunky deputies when they brought him in.

Angie rubbed her eyes and took a deep breath. "The guilt is eating me up, Kelly. Chris is my husband—I love him! I wanted to hug him one last time to let him know that, but Dr. Sanderlyn stopped me. He said Chris blames *me* for everything. I don't know what to think."

"Think about Chris being cured. I mean, that's why you brought him here."

Angie nodded. "You're right, I need to trust the doctor. He certainly knows a lot more about mental health than I do." Angie chuckled lightly. "Poor Chris. We got married in a church full of people he hardly knew. His hands shook so badly when he tried to put the wedding band on my finger, he missed it three times. His voice quivered and he looked like he was going to faint, but he got through it. That's the way he is, you know. Timid, sometimes all out scared, but when Chris puts his mind to something he'll do it no matter what the consequences. If he *wants* to be cured, he *will* be."

Good, I thought. *Angie seemed to be coming out of her funk.* But then I sensed that something else was going on. I looked deep into my foster mother's mind and saw what it was.

What if they can't cure him? What if Dr. Sanderlyn recommends that Chris be committed to a state institution? What if I never see my husband again? The tears were returning, I sensed it.

Luckily Angie's cell phone rang. She dug it out of her purse and looked at the caller ID.

"It's Mrs. Dunlop. She probably wonders if we'll ever pick up Travis. Hello? Yes, Mrs. Dunlop, we're on our way. He's not bothering you, is he? That's good."

Angie listened for a while, nodding her head now and then. "Really? A weekend with the President at Camp David? It must be exciting being a senator's wife."

Camp David. I'd heard of it but wasn't really sure what it was or why Angie was so impressed. I couldn't hear Mrs. Dunlop's voice over the phone, so I listened in through Angie.

"Where's Mathew going to stay?" asked Angie. "Were children invited to Camp David, too?"

"Oh, no," said Mrs. Dunlop. "The President isn't all that fond of children. He's no baby kisser, that's for sure. We won't be home until after five on Sunday so we're sending Mathew to my sister-in-law's."

"It'd be perfectly fine if Mathew stayed with us the entire weekend," said Angie firmly. "The boys will get a double dose of each other. If they still like each other after that, they'll be friends for life."

"Are you sure? I don't want to impose."

"Having Mathew over would never be an imposition. He's a wonderful boy. I'm cooking hamburgers and hotdogs on the grill around five. This time I swear there won't be a fire." Angie laughed uneasily. I guess she mentioned the fire in case Travis had said something to Mathew about it.

Mrs. Dunlop also laughed. "You're so funny! Mathew loves hotdogs. Thank you so much, Mrs. McCormick. Five it is! Uh, Mrs. McCormick, I don't know if you're always so formal, but I'd really like it if you'd call me Vanessa."

"I'm sorry, please call me Angie. It's just that your husband's a senator, and all."

"Believe me, there's nothing special about us. We're just regular people."

"Glad to know that. We should be at your place within the hour."

"Angie, when you get here, you'll need your ID. Jacob's meeting with some government people and security is kind of tight. I'll tell them you're coming."

"Thanks, Vanessa." Angie got off the phone. "Mathew is staying with us all next weekend because his parents will be with the President of the United States. And *I'm* on a first name basis with a senator's wife. Can you believe it?"

"That's so cool!" I said excitedly. "I can't wait to see their house. Travis says they have a lot of money."

Angie put the car in gear and drove out of the Sunnyside parking lot. I relaxed in the seat. It's a good thing Mrs. Dunlop called. That was just the distraction Angie needed to stop thinking about Chris for a while.

"Kelly?" said Angie. "Thanks for coming with me today. I know you're only thirteen, but often you seem almost grown up, you know?"

I grinned. If Angie knew I could read minds she'd certainly think more of me than just being *almost grown up*. I considered the idea of being a senator's wife, and that sounded cool. But actually being a senator sounded even cooler, so I made plans to look into politics sometime. After all, with my telepathic skills, I could become anything I wanted, maybe even president. And *nobody* could stop me! Nobody.

Chapter 26
RETURN OF THE SALESMAN

KELLY

On the way to pick up Travis it was my first time to ride through Mathew Dunlop's neighborhood. That was *some* neighborhood, too. Every house we passed was bigger and more impressive than the one before it. Each home was built on a huge manicured lot with at least one *crazy* expensive car in the driveway.

"*Wow!*" I said. "Everybody's rich! No wonder Travis likes it here."

"It's one of the most exclusive areas in the country to live," said Angie. "Look at that one."

On the right, way back off the road, was a huge three-story colonial with a row of white columns across the front. As far as I was concerned any house that had columns was automatically a mansion and that place absolutely qualified.

"Who *are* these people?" I asked, gawking at the wealth. "What do they do for a living?"

"You'd better ask the Dunlops about that. I can only imagine."

As we rounded a corner Angie swerved wide to avoid hitting a couple of old men who were rummaging through recycling bins on the side of the road.

"It's Doug One!" I said. Doug One was easy to spot because of his white hair, tan leathery face and thick glasses. The baskets on his

3-wheeled bike were loaded down with crushed aluminum cans. "Who's the other guy? Is he a Doug?"

"Doug Four," said Angie. "He collects trash of some kind. They're a long way from home to be on bicycles."

Doug Four was old, too, like Doug One. But he was built like a tank with broad shoulders and thick muscular arms. Though it was cold outside he wore a sleeveless plaid shirt and green work pants. His thick, silver-gray hair was combed straight back.

Macho man, I thought when I saw him, until I noticed Doug Four rode a silver and pink girl's bike with white wicker baskets on the front and back.

So much for macho man. I couldn't wait to see what the other five Dougs looked like.

Angie parked in front of the largest house of all, a stone three-story with eight towering columns across the front porch.

Definite mansion, I thought.

As if the size of the house wasn't enough, there were nine cars in the driveway—six black sedans, a sleek black limousine and a pair of matching silver Mercedes parked close to the garage. A brick wall as tall as a man was connected to the house on both sides and closed in the entire back yard.

"I knew the Dunlops had money," I said, "but that house is amazing. Their front yard looks like a soccer field! How many cars do they have?"

"The two Mercedes belong to the Dunlops. The others look like government vehicles. Mrs. Dunlop said her husband was having a meeting."

"Vanessa," I corrected. "First-name basis with a senator's wife."

Angie laughed. "I'd better remember that."

I scanned her mind to see how she was doing. At the moment there were no real thoughts of Chris being at Sunnyside. She'd probably break down and have a long cry when we got home, but for now things were under control.

When we got out of the van I waved to the Dougs down the street. Both Dougs waved back and returned to work. We detoured around the carpet-like grass and walked up the driveway. The instant we set foot on the Dunlop's property two important looking men in dark suits and overcoats stepped out of a black sedan and blocked our way. They looked official and a little bit scary to me. The taller agent on the left held up his hand, palm out, to tell us to stop.

"I'm sorry, Ma'am," he said. "Nobody goes past this point. Official government business."

The man who spoke was slim and blond, while the other guy was shorter, stocky and mostly bald. Both wore dark sunglasses, though it was cloudy and getting late in the day. They flashed important looking badges.

"ASA, Ma'am," said the shorter man. "We need to see your ID."

"ASA?" Angie had a blank look on her face.

"American Security Administration. We're under Homeland."

"Oh. I haven't heard of you."

"No, Ma'am."

The way he said it was like *nobody* was supposed to have heard of them. Were they top secret, or something? I made a quick scan of their thoughts and didn't really like what I got. The men were smug and proud about belonging to an agency within the government that very few people even knew existed. I asked them both who was at the meeting, but I did it telepathically. The men blurted out their response in unison.

"Mr. Mogen Deel and Senators Hathaway and Rodriguez are meeting with Senator Dunlop." The agents were aghast. They looked at each other, stunned and embarrassed. Neither man could believe he'd released important information like that to complete strangers. I tried not to laugh.

"Thank you," said Angie, passing over her driver's license. "But I didn't ask."

The short man blushed, checked her ID quickly and gave it back. "You're expected, Mrs. McCormick. Have a good day."

Angie thanked them and led the way to the front door.

I thought about the names of the people meeting with Mr. Dunlop. "Who's Mogen Deel?" I asked as Angie rang the bell.

"Never heard of him," said Angie. "But I've seen Senators Hathaway and Rodriguez on CSPAN."

At that moment the front door burst open. Travis and Mathew came barreling out, followed by a large yellow Labrador retriever.

"Hey, Angie!" Travis waved at us and tossed a soccer ball into the front yard. "Get the ball, Robo!" The dog chased after the ball, using its nose to push it over the grass.

"Hey, Ms. Angie!" said Mathew Dunlop, as he ran after the others.

Angie barely had time to respond. "Hi, boys!"

A moment later a petite and stunningly attractive black woman appeared at the door. Vanessa Dunlop had a warm smile and wide-set happy eyes. She wore a simple blue skirt, white sweater and knee-high blue leather boots. I liked her immediately, even without scanning her mind to see what kind of person she was.

Vanessa called out to the boys. "Stay out of the flower beds, okay?" She smiled at Angie. "Hi, Angie. Sorry about all the confusion around here. Between meetings and rowdy boys this place really rocks. Would you like to come in?"

"Can I take a rain check on that, Vanessa?" asked Angie. "I'd love to see your house, but we've got to get home so I can start dinner."

"Absolutely," said Vanessa. "I really want to thank you for keeping Mathew next weekend. When I told the boys he was staying two nights at your place they went crazy. They're so excited."

"I'm excited, too," said Angie. "It'll be fun."

We said goodbye to Mrs. Dunlop and Travis caught up with us on the way back to the minivan.

"See you, Mathew!" he cried, waving to his friend.

"See you, Travis!" said Mathew, waving back.

Mathew was about the same size as Travis, but he always dressed like he just stepped out of a fine clothing store. Even now, though he'd been running and playing all day with Travis and the dog, Robo, his afro-style hair was perfect and his button-down shirt was still buttoned and tucked neatly into his slacks. The only flaw I noticed were grass stains on his knees. I thought Mathew was just about the cutest little guy in the world, along with Travis, of course. Where Mathew was always neat and perfectly dressed, Travis was a typical mess. His face was flushed, his shirttail hung out of his pants and his hair stuck up worse than usual. But that was part of what made him so cute, too!

"I just love Mathew," I said.

"Why do you always say that?" Travis playfully shoved me.

"Because he's cute. I can't help it."

"Did you meet any senators, Travis?" asked Angie.

"Naw, they had a meetin' in the basement the whole time. Ms. Vanessa said we had to play outside or be real quiet inside, so we played in Mathew's treefort. It's so cool! An' we played soccer and football and army with his toy soldiers and had a big battle with zombies and aliens!"

"Zombies?" said Angie. She shuddered. "Don't ever mention that to Chris. He has a dire fear of zombies."

"But zombies aren't real," I said. "They're just in movies."

"Chris thinks they're real. He had…an experience when he first started teaching. He won't talk about it with anyone."

"He ran into zombies?"

"I don't know."

That threw me. Why in the world would a grown man believe in zombies? Did he also believe in fairies, vampires and werewolves? Then I remembered how nobody believed us when we told them about the demons. It made me wonder about what had happened to Chris.

The front door opened behind us as the people who were meeting with Mr. Dunlop emerged. Curious, I glanced back to see what a senator looked like. But when the first man came out I froze in my tracks.

"Travis!" I choked out the words. "It's *him*!"

Travis looked back and instantly became a few shades paler, if that were possible. It was the Salesman from Pandora's Cave!

"Thank you for a lovely afternoon, Vanessa. Your hospitality is top notch, as always. Please remind Jacob I'll call him tomorrow." There was no mistaking that baritone, man-in-charge voice. Travis looked at me fearfully.

"Whutta we do?" he asked.

I'll read his mind, I returned. *I'll find out what his plan is.*

You better be careful.

Why? He'll never know. I'm the only one who can read minds, remember?

Yeah, but he hangs out with demons.

Travis had a point. I'd better be discreet.

Angie noticed us staring at the Salesman. "Kids, do you know that man?"

"We've seen him before," I said quickly.

"In the cave!" added Travis. "He was talkin' to the demons!" I almost wished Travis hadn't mentioned it, but maybe now was the time.

Angie was baffled. "I don't understand. Do you mean Pandora's Cave?"

Travis nodded. "Yeah, an' he gave a speech to a bunch of demons."

"Demons? Really? In the cave." Angie sounded incredulous. Of course she did. Who'd believe a wild tale like that?

Travis went on. "They're gonna try to take over the world and make us live in caves!"

"Why wasn't I told about this?"

I made a quick scan. Angie didn't believe a word of it.

"Chris was still trapped in the cave and we didn't want to upset you worse than you already were," I explained. "If you'd known he was down there surrounded by demons—well, we were afraid you'd lose it."

"You were *real* upset," added Travis.

Angie studied us carefully. "You're serious, aren't you? You're not making this up." She unlocked the minivan and opened the sliding side doors. As we were about to climb in I looked back. I scanned the man lightly and picked up his name. So *that's* Mr. Mogen Deel. At least he wasn't a senator. I decided to ask him a couple of questions.

What's your plan with the demons? Why do you want to make people live in caves?

Demons are idiots, just like humans. They're all part of the greater strategy.

I was thinking about my next question when it suddenly struck me. People always spoke out loud when they responded to my telepathic questions. But the Salesman—Mr. Deel—had replied *inside* my head like it was the natural thing to do.

I looked up suddenly. Mr. Deel glared at me like he wanted to rip out my heart. I inched backwards to the van.

You little brat! How do you know? Tell me, NOW!

The words were inside my head as clearly as if he'd shouted them. No doubt about it, Mr. Deel was also a telepath. That meant trouble.

Suddenly, a terrible stabbing pain erupted in both sides of my head. I pressed my hands against my temples and bent at the waist.

"Oh...." I staggered against the van as everything around me went pale. The grass, the trees, even the cars in the driveway became bright white from burning pain. I looked up through clouded convulsing eyes and saw Mr. Deel. He seemed to glow, like something made him light up. He glared at me, clearly directing the head-splitting pain. My brain was going to explode and there was nothing I could do.

Travis jumped between the Salesman and me. He must have sensed what was going on and wanted to protect me. I tried to tell him no, but I began to lose consciousness.

In an instant the pain stopped. Normal colors returned and Mr. Deel didn't glow any more. For some reason he'd backed off from killing me. Was it mercy? I followed Mr. Deel's aggravated gaze, from side to side. At his left near the end of the driveway was Doug One, standing with his three-wheeler. On Deel's right was Doug Four, in front of our mini-van. Both Dougs stared at Mr. Deel the way he'd been staring at me. Something was going on between the three of them, but I was numb from the pain. I couldn't pick up any thoughts.

All at once the Salesman scowled and let out a low curse. He climbed into the limo. A square-jawed, uniformed chauffer closed the car door and got behind the wheel. The limo backed out quickly, then spun the tires and raced away.

Travis helped me collapse into the minivan seat. My heart pounded, my face was cold and damp. Angie moved quickly to the seat beside me.

"What happened, sweetie? Are you dizzy?"

"Dizzy…yeah." I tried to focus on Angie's face, but everything around her was spinning out of control.

"Why was that man staring at you?"

"We told you!" said Travis, aggravated. "He's the guy in the cave."

"Oh, come on, Travis, why would somebody like *him* be in a cave?"

"He was sayin' stuff to the demons. They liked it, too."

Angie shook her head. "Kids, whatever the problem is, I can't help you unless you tell me the truth. I'm not talking about demons, okay? There's no such thing as demons and monsters. Besides, you called that man a salesman. What could he possibly sell to anybody way down in a cave?"

"He was selling victory over humans," I said in a low voice. "He said if the demons did what they were supposed to do they'd win the surface of the earth in five years."

"And *we'd* all haveta live in caves," added Travis.

"*If* we survived." I finished it and took a deep breath. At last I could see clearly again. What had Mr. Deel done to me? Why had he stopped? "You don't have to believe us, Angie. But we're not lying."

Travis nodded. "Yeah, we've got a video of the whole thing, but the camcorder's still in the cave, but *I'm* not going in after it."

"We'll talk more about this when we get home," said Angie.

I understood. Angie needed proof, like Dr. Parrish, and the proof was in the cave. Good luck convincing her that any part of our story was true.

We didn't say much on the ride back. But Travis kept looking at me like he expected me to collapse at any second.

"I'm all right," I said.

"What'd he do to you?"

"I have no idea. But it *really* hurt inside, you know?"

Travis nodded. "He wanted to kill you, I could feel it. He was gonna, too. Until the Dougs stopped him. I think they know him."

"Thanks for trying to help me, Travis. But you should've stayed out of it. He might've hurt you, too."

Travis whispered. "Is Mr. Deel telepathic, like you?"

I nodded emphatically. "He's *way* ahead of me. I didn't know you could hurt somebody like that with just your mind." A nasty, bile taste rose into my throat, like I might throw up. I gagged, but fought it off.

"I'm so stupid, Travis. I thought I was the only one who could read minds and nobody could stop me. Well, Mr. Deel can stop me. Now that *he* knows *we* know about his plans, well, I don't think we're safe anymore."

"Yeah, we're just kids," said Travis, hanging his head. "But somehow we gotta find *somebody* who can do *somethin'* about Mr. Deel and those demons!"

Chapter 27

A VERY NASTY PLAN

KELLY

"My mom said I can spend the night Friday," said Melissa Godwin as she studied her reflection in the restroom mirror. I stood beside my friend and watched her make minor adjustments to her long-sleeved, charcoal blouse and black jeans. Melissa was slender and pale and I thought she was *so* pretty. Some days when she had on just the right outfit she looked like a catalog model. This was one of those days. Melissa's gaze caught me in the mirror. "What?"

I grinned big. "You'll be the first friend I've ever had stay over."

"Well, duh, you've only been with the McCormicks a few months. They kinda had to get to know you."

"No, I mean *ever*. None of my foster families would let me have a sleepover. They said there were too many kids in the house as it was."

"You've never had a sleepover? Not even for one person?"

I shook my head. "Never been to one, either. Well, that's not exactly true. My real parents took me to an overnight birthday party when I was like six. Three or four girls were there and my mom stayed to help. Does that count?'

"I think it better."

"Oh, Angie said don't eat supper before you come. She's cooking burgers and dogs around five. She made potato salad, too."

"I *love* potato salad. Wait, didn't she almost burn the house down last time she used the grill?"

"That wasn't exactly her fault," I said, laughing. "Well, maybe it was."

"Hey, do you think we can sleep in the basement? It'd be a good place to play with my Ouija board. Or do you think a Ouija board's too scary for Travis?"

"Travis is having Mathew Dunlop over for the whole weekend. With both of them they'll be fine. I'm sure Angie won't care if we're in the basement. She'll think it's cool. So, Melissa, have you ever used a Ouija board before? Do you know what to do?"

"No, but I'm sure there's something on the internet about it."

At that moment a toilet flushed in one of the stalls. I washed and dried my hands as Manson Stanfield emerged from the stall and smiled at herself in the mirror. I listened to her thoughts. Manson was nervous about being there with us and she had no intention of speaking. She pretended to be calm and unaffected, but I knew she was really afraid.

When Melissa saw Manson, her friendly demeanor changed abruptly. In fact, she became all out weird. "Hi, Manson," she whispered harshly into Manson's ear. "Seen any good fights lately?"

I was taken aback. I'd never seen Melissa act like that before. It was so convincing I wondered if it really was an act. Melissa had a look of pure madness in her eyes and a lurking menace in her voice.

Manson stepped back warily and looked at me. "Get away from me! *Both* of you!"

Melissa blinked and tilted her head to the side, the way dogs do when hearing a strange sound for the first time. Then she displayed an idiot's grin. "Come on, Manson. What's wrong? Have ya seen any good fights lately?"

"I'm late for class! You should be committed!" Manson ran out of the restroom in a hurry. In an instant Melissa returned to her usual self.

After the door closed I covered my mouth to stifle a laugh. "Oh my gosh! I can't believe you did that. If I didn't know you so well I'd swear you really *were* nuts! Manson sure thinks you are!"

"They both do," said Melissa proudly. "It's the only reason Donnivee hasn't come after me, too. Like I told you, she's afraid of crazy people."

When we gathered our backpacks and left the restroom I was happier than I'd been since we'd first gotten to the McCormick's house. For the most part it seemed like things were finally going my way. If only Chris and Jon would come home and be themselves again my life would be perfect.

MANSON

"Guess who's having a sleepover on Friday with her sick little friend in black." Manson kept her voice low in English class as she sat with Donnivee. The tardy bell hadn't rung yet and the teacher was setting up the data projector.

"Bishop?" said Donnivee. When Manson smiled Donnivee began chewing on her lower lip. "I know where she lives. My boyfriend took me by her place last weekend. There's only two houses on her street and the other house is empty. Lots of woods around and plenty of places to hide."

Manson's eyes lit up hungrily. "What're you gonna do?"

"I don't know, but it's gotta be good. I mean *real* good. I wanna scare 'em so bad they pee in their pants."

"They're going to be alone in the basement playing with a Ouija board. I think the only other person in the house will be the foster mom, and maybe her little brother and his friend."

"Ouija board, huh? Maybe we can use that to scare 'em. And I wanna beat the snot out of Bishop again, but this time I'll do it right."

Manson shuddered when she thought about the way Melissa had acted in the restroom. "What about Melissa? She's crazier than we thought."

"We'll distract her, you know? Kinda get her out of the way for a while." Donnivee punched her palm hard. Manson drew back fearfully. "Kurt doesn't like 'em either. He got in a fight with their older brother once."

"Who won?"

"You're kiddin', right? Kurt said he kicked that guy's butt so bad they put him in the hospital. That's why Kurt wore a cast for a while. He smashed their brother's face in and broke his hand."

"I wish I coulda seen that. I can't believe your dad lets you go out with Kurt. I mean he's nineteen! You're so lucky."

"If my dad knew I was datin' *anybody*, he'd beat me worse than usual. Hey, do you still have those masks we used last Halloween? The really gross ones with all the extra eyeballs?"

"The demon masks? Yeah, you want 'em? Do you want the demon hands, too?"

"Yeah. If they see some demons while they're messin' with a Ouija board they'll freak. It'll be better if they don't know who we are. But I wanna do a lot more than just scare her and beat her up. I wanna take something from her. Something she really wants. But what?"

They thought about it for a while as their English teacher closed the door and began taking roll. Manson got an idea.

"Maybe her dead parents gave her something she really likes, you know? If you could steal something like that she'd probably die."

"Yeah, that's good. Scare her, beat her up, and steal her memories. You're a genius, Manson. We'll plan the attack tonight."

TRAVIS

Travis got off the school bus more excited than he'd been since Chris had first told them they were going to Pandora's Cave. He hastily took the cell phone out of his backpack to see what time it was. Four-fifty-two. Sometime in the next twenty-four hours Mathew Dunlop would come over and they were going to have a blast. He waved to his friends on the bus as it pulled away, then looked at Dr. Parrish's house. A pale green van with the words *Mac's Heating and Air Conditioning* printed on the side was just backing out of the driveway. Travis put his phone away and watched the van follow the school bus up the road. *That truck's been there all week,* he thought to himself. *Did they finish?* He decided to go next door and find out before going home.

Dr. Parrish's front door was unlocked so Travis knocked and went inside. The first thing he noticed was how warm it was. Usually when he came in he shivered because it seemed colder in the house than it did outdoors. The second thing he noticed was the odor of fresh paint. Travis sniffed deeply. He loved that smell. He scanned the living area and saw that the walls and trim had been painted. In fact, except for the unfinished floors the downstairs looked ready to move into. Parrish and Granny had gotten a lot of work done in the last weeks.

Granny's voice called out from upstairs. "That you, Travis?"

"Yep! Can I come in?"

"Sounds like you *are* in."

"Come on up," said Parrish.

Travis put his backpack down and ran up the stairs. At the top of the stairs he passed another stairway that led to the third story bedroom in the tower. He was about to go that way when a miter saw screamed from a second floor bedroom. The noisy saw shut off as Travis peeked into the room and discovered Parrish and Granny putting down baseboard trim.

"Hey, Granny. Hey, Dr. Parrish," he said. "The place looks great!"

Granny gave him a hug and rubbed his hair. Parrish smiled proudly. "Why thank you, young man," he said. "We've come a long way and now we have heat!"

"I can feel it!"

"That's right," said Granny. "Mark's gonna spend the night here tomorrow."

Travis looked around. "Cool! But where you gonna sleep? There's no bed, or nothin'."

"I'll bring an air mattress," said Parrish. "So how'd you like to spend the night here, too?"

Travis got even more excited than he was before. "Can I sleep in the tower?"

Parrish nodded. "You bet you can. It's got the best view of the neighbors' house, that's for sure."

"The neighbors?" Travis laughed. "You mean us."

"We could roast marshmallows in the fireplace," said Granny. She winked at Parrish, who nodded vigorously.

"That's what I'm talkin' about!" Then Travis remembered Mathew. "Wait! Mathew Dunlop's gonna spend the whole weekend with us. Can he come too?"

"Sure," said Parrish. "The more the merrier. Of course, I may have to put you both to work if you stay here."

"Really? What can we do?"

"I don't know. What *can* you do?" Parrish looked down thoughtfully at Travis, who shrugged. The big man backhanded the problem away. "Don't worry about it, we'll find something. But tomorrow I want to stay here to make sure the heat works properly, and hopefully, I can lay the ceramic tile in the downstairs bathroom."

"Aren't you gonna be afraid in here by yourself?"

"Nah. Matilda will join me when she gets off work."

"Cool!" said Travis. He gave Parrish and Granny high fives and ran upstairs to look out the tower bedroom window. Below he could see the garage side of the McCormick's house and most of the yard. Way up here he stood nearly as tall as the big oak tree in Angie's front yard. Parrish was right. This room did have the best view of the neighbors' house.

———

As far as Travis was concerned the sleepover was going great in spite of the fact Kelly also had someone over to spend the night. He was glad it was Melissa because she seemed to fit in like she was part of the family. She was funny and crazy and just as sneaky as the boys when it came to spying. Plus with her around it gave Kelly someone else to hang out with. Before dinner Melissa convinced everyone to go down to the basement to tell ghost stories and she was really good at telling them. She told stories about demon dogs, zombies, vampires and murderous skeletons. After what happened in Pandora's Cave, Travis wasn't interested in hearing any scary stories. He was glad when Angie finally called them upstairs to eat.

When they sat down at the dining-room table it became obvious how much trouble Angie had had with the grill. She'd only used a charcoal grill once before and she'd ruined quite a few hamburgers and hotdogs before she got the hang of it. But in the end dinner turned out to be pretty good. Luckily, Mathew preferred badly charred hotdogs and Melissa ate mostly potato salad because she was thinking about becoming a vegetarian.

After supper the boys went to Dr. Parrish's house to see if they could help build something. Right after they got there Granny showed up because she got off early from her job at Mike's Pub. Dr. Parrish was so engrossed with laying ceramic tile in the downstairs bathroom he'd forgotten all about the boys. But it was obvious he was glad to see them when they came in. Travis noticed he was especially glad to see Granny, too.

"Since you've got heat now, you're done with the hot air blower, right?" said Granny, getting right to work. "Do you want me to move it out to the garage?"

"Better leave it in the corner with the kerosene," said Parrish. When I finish up the ceramic in the bathroom, I'm going to tape the kitchen ceiling. It's kind of cold tonight, and I want the drywall compound to dry."

"Don't you think your brand-new furnace will keep the place warm enough?"

"I'm a big believer in Murphy's Law and I like to have a backup plan."

"What's Murphy's Law?" asked Travis.

"I know what that is," said Mathew. "If something *can* go wrong, it *will* go wrong. That's close anyway."

"Very good, Mathew," said Parrish. "And that's why I'm keeping the heater and the kerosene around, just in case."

"So whutta you want us to do?" asked Travis.

Parrish gazed down at them and thought about it. "I've got just the thing. Come with me." He led them to the dining room where some tools and supplies were stored. He sorted through the pile and pulled out a pair of cordless drills and a large box of screws.

"How'd you guys like to do some *real* work?" he said, handing each boy a drill.

"We get to use drills?" said Mathew hopefully.

"As long as you're careful," said Parrish. He led them into the kitchen where the floor was covered with thick sheets of plywood, but the boards moved a little under their feet. "I've already cut the plywood and laid it down, but it's not attached. I need you to screw down all these sheets of plywood tonight so I can put ceramic on it tomorrow." He showed them how to work the drills and how to put in screws, then watched them do it. Travis was always interested in tearing things apart, but he was extra thrilled to be building something. He exchanged an excited glance with Mathew as they went to work. Parrish was clearly amazed at how quickly both Mathew and Travis grasped the concept and the coordination that went with drilling screws into wood.

"I think you boys have it down nicely," he said after several screws had been put in to his liking. "Let me know if you have any questions. I'll be in the bathroom working."

"How many screws do we put in?" asked Travis.

"Do you see all those dots on the floor?" said Parrish. The boys scanned the huge kitchen floor. There were hundreds of marks. "Well, I pre-measured and marked where I wanted the screws put in. I need one screw in every dot. If you finish that job, and do it correctly, I'll find more work for you."

"That's what I'm talkin' about!" said Travis.

"Yeah!" Mathew agreed. Both boys nodded eagerly and set off with their drills.

Travis noticed that Parrish watched them discreetly for a while, then quietly went back to his tile job. Travis spoke to Mathew as they worked.

"I'm sorry I don't have a tree fort to camp out in," he said. "That would have been cooler."

"Are you kidding?" said Mathew. "This is way more fun than the tree fort. I've never worked a drill before. Besides, it's kind of cold tonight, my treefort does better in the summer."

Travis worked like it was the dream job of a lifetime. When they had finished over half of the room, Mathew stood up and took out his cell phone. "Hey, Travis, can you take a video of me working? I want to show my parents what we're doing."

"Sure." Travis took the phone and aimed the lens at Mathew. Mathew drilled a couple of screws into the floor and looked up.

"Hey, mom and dad! We're helping Dr. Parrish fix his house! See?" He drilled another screw in, then took the phone from Travis and got some video of him doing the same thing.

Travis was a little embarrassed to be recorded as he worked. He looked up shyly and waved. "It's easy!"

"That's good," said Mathew approvingly. "Hey, let's finish this and go to the tower. Maybe we can take some video shots from up there."

"Yeah!" said Travis, as they both went back to work.

Chapter 28
OUIJA BOARDS AND SMORES

KELLY

Nothing could ever ruin the perfect night I was having with Melissa. So far we'd had dinner and watched two scary movies. Now it was nearly midnight and we were setting up the Ouija board in the basement where Angie had agreed to let us sleep. There wasn't much stuff in the basement any more, just a few boxes, tables and the other equipment Chris had used to invent Majik Juice. We dragged the desk across the room to a spot under one of the windows, hoping to add a little privacy to our sleeping area.

When Angie came downstairs to see if we needed anything, I noticed her eyes were a little puffy and red, like she'd been crying. I scanned Angie's thoughts and found out why. Chris, of course.

"A Ouija board?" said Angie. "Those things scare me."

"That's the idea," I said. "We want to be scared. At least a little."

"Yes, well, when I was your age my grandfather told me a tale about some kids that played with a Ouija board and one of them became possessed by a demon. He started acting weird and did strange things."

"What kinda strange things?" asked Melissa.

Angie thought for a moment. "He must have been killing small animals because they found a grocery bag full of animal bones in his bedroom. And he covered the walls in his room with tiny handwriting about how darkness and demons would some day prevail and the world would end. It took three Catholic priests to exorcise the demon out of him."

We gawked at Angie. "Is that, you know, true?" I asked.

"Not sure," said Angie. "But it kept me from playing with the Ouija board. Of course, you're not afraid, so maybe we need to fix the mood in here. You should have candles burning instead of an overhead light. I'll see if I can find some." She left the basement and came back a few minutes later with four tall, thick red candles and some matches. She set three of the candles around us and put the fourth close to the Ouija board, then turned off the light.

An intense eeriness filled the room as the candle flames danced. Shadows moved all around us. I held my breath. All of a sudden the basement was kind of spooky. If I were going to talk to some dead guy with a Ouija I'd rather do it in a brightly lit room.

"Candles are certainly easier to light than that stupid grill," said Angie, laughing. "Isn't this better?"

I gulped.

Melissa smiled. *"Perfect."*

"Before you start communing with the dead," said Angie, "have you ever had smores?"

I shook my head. "What's a smore?"

"Oooh, I love smores," said Melissa. "You cook marshmallows over a fire and sandwich them between two Grahm crackers and a piece of Hersey chocolate. They're *so* awesome."

I thought they might be really good. "Do we have any Grahm crackers?"

"I'll check," said Angie, as she went upstairs again. When she returned she shook her head. "We're out. The boys were going to roast marshmallows in the fireplace next door, and we're out of those, too."

"That's okay," I said, trying not to sound disappointed. "We can eat something else."

"No," said Angie. "I'm going to the store. You girls stay here. I'll be back in half an hour, okay? If you scare yourselves too badly go next door where Dr. Parrish and the boys are. Matilda might be there later. Is there anything else we need?"

"I forgot my toothbrush," said Melissa. "I can give you money if you need some."

Angie smiled broadly. "Sweetheart, money is the one thing we've got plenty of these days. Our bank account grows every time I look at it."

"Are there any stores open this late?" I asked.

"Oh sure, I'll be right back." Angie left the basement and went upstairs. Melissa held the candle under her face and tried to make her eyes look wide and ghoulish.

"It's time for the Ouija board," she said in her most sinister voice.

I thought about it and got both excited and nervous. "Are you sure? I mean, after what Angie just told us?"

Melissa reached into her purse and took out a folded sheet of paper. "I've got instructions right here. Got 'em off Ouija board.com."

"There's a website called ouijaboard.com?"

"Kelly, don't you know there's a website for everything?"

Chapter 29
MONSTERS IN THE NIGHT

LIPSLUDGE

Lipsludge was small for a demon, barely taller than the average eight-year-old human child. But he had something going for him that kept him from being pushed around by most of the much larger demons. He was fiercely aggressive and possessed superior leadership skills. The Boss had complimented him on numerous occasions, which made him the envy of his fellow demons no matter what color they were or how many eyes or arms they had.

At supper, while feasting on a hot bowl of delicious human and cave fungus soup, the Boss announced he needed a demon death squad to go on a mission of the utmost importance. As soon as Lipsludge heard about the mission he volunteered to go because it offered a chance for him to see the outer world at night, something he'd wanted to do since he'd been budded. But there was one thing that truly bothered Lipsludge about the mission. The entire idea had been suggested by the traitor-human Mr. Deel.

Lipsludge didn't trust Mr. Deel and he couldn't fathom why the Boss seemed to fancy him. Mr. Deel popped in and out of the deep caves whenever he pleased, and if he wanted some task accomplished that required a demon, the Boss ordered it done on the spot with little or no discussion. It almost made Mr. Deel seem like the boss! Of course, Mr. Deel *had* promised all demons that they'd rule the surface of the world soon, but how could anyone trust the word of a human—especially a traitor-human who wanted to destroy his own kind? Somebody needed to keep a close eye on Mr. Deel. But Lipsludge knew he'd have to do it on his own and he'd better be sneaky. If the Boss found out...well, *demon* soup was also a popular dish in the caves.

The spindly little demon emerged from the drainage pipe in the cul-de-sac at the end of Oak Avenue. He paused in the pitch-blackness of the tunnel, knowing he was entirely invisible to any humans that might be outside in the night air. He turned to his five companions.

"Da way's clear," he hissed in his softest demon whisper. Numerous sets of glowing eyes blinked open before him. Some were bright red, some deep yellow, and one set of three in a triangle shape was translucent pink. The other demons listened intently. "We're a demon death squad and ya knows da plan so don't screws up. Finds a good shadow and stays outta sight till I gives da signal."

"What's the signal?" asked the demon with pink eyes.

"Dammit, Klawfinger!" barked Lipsludge. "We wents over dis before we lefts da caves!"

One of the other demons nudged Klawfinger and whispered to him. "The signal is when Lipsludge says 'Get 'em boys!'"

"Get 'em boys?" Klawfinger scratched his head with a giant lobster claw-like hand. "Okay, got it."

"When we gets in da house, finds da right place and stays outta sight. Klawfinger, you hides by da big oak tree out front. Dere's plenty of shadow dere, even for you. No matter what, you keeps 'em in da house so we can deals wit' em'."

"Oak tree, got it. Hey, Lipsludge, if there's an oak tree do you think that's why they call it Oak Avenue?"

Lipsludge shook his head. "Yer as hopeless as a human."

About then the porch light came on at the front of the house. A moment later an adult woman emerged and walked to one of the cars. The demons shrank back into the shadows until the car had driven off.

"Das better," said Lipsludge. "Won'ts be as many of 'em now. Remembers, all of you. We'res Demon Nation! Let's go!"

Each of the demons whispered the words under their breath. "Demon Nation."

As the demons moved silently and quickly from shadow to shadow in the moonlit night, Lipsludge kept an eye on both his crew and the houses. The massive demon, Klawfinger, disappeared behind the great oak tree like he was supposed to and Lipsludge gave him the thumb's up. As Lipsludge went to the front porch of the McCormicks' house to test the door, a man-sized demon with four arms moved up behind him.

"Lipsludge," said the four-armed demon. "The house next door's supposed to be empty. They got lights in there."

"Don't worries about da house next door," said Lipsludge. "We does our job right, they won'ts even knows we wasez here. It'lls be a piece o' cake." He turned the knob easily and the door swung open. He looked back at Four-arms and grinned horribly. "Now ain'ts they courteous to leaves da door unlocked? Like I says, a piece o' cake!"

Chapter 30
BREAKING AND ENTERING

MANSON

Manson Stanfield ran along the roadway carefully watching every step. Her frog-demon mask was loose fitting with a tendency to block her vision and she didn't want to turn her ankle in the loose gravel. She followed Donnivee and Kurt Lazarus, who also wore horrible demon masks and grotesque rubbery hands. Kurt stopped running and ducked into a dense thicket at the edge of the cul-de-sac.

"There it is," he said, pointing at the McCormicks' house. They took off their masks. Kurt's was a horrible-looking oversized head with nearly a dozen fake eyes mounted in a bloody skull. He wiped sweat on his shirtsleeve. "That stupid mask is hot. I can't see for crap."

"We have to wear 'em or they'll know who we are," said Donnivee. Her mask was a cross between a vampire and some kind of grisly wolf-like creature. "I can't get caught. My dad would kill me."

"We won't get caught," said Kurt flatly. "I *never* get caught." He bent down and kissed Donnivee on the mouth. Right away she threw an arm around his neck and they started making out in front of Manson.

"This is real cool, guys," said Manson, a little peeved and plenty nervous. "Can't you wait till we're done?"

Kurt broke the kiss and laughed at Manson. "You're just mad cuz Robbie didn't show up."

"Wrong," said Manson worriedly. "I don't want to get caught cuz you two'd rather mess around than get to work. Look at that house next door, it's all lit up. You said it was empty."

"It was empty last weekend," said Donnivee. "Now it's not. So what?"

"So what? They could see us!"

"Not if you stay outta the light," said Kurt. "When you're in a house with the lights on at night, you can't see squat outside the windows. Come on."

Manson pulled on her mask and followed as the brilliant half moon cast shadows over the street and yard. A slow moving, curdling fog moved through the trees and was just beginning to settle above the ground. They knelt beside the Mustang, which was parked by the curb, and kept their heads down. Manson suddenly remembered something.

"Where's the minivan?" she asked. "They have two cars. I've seen the minivan."

"Who cares?" said Kurt. "It's not here. That means nobody's here but those girls."

"How do you know they're still here?" asked Manson.

Kurt pointed to one of the basement windows. Manson strained to see what was there, but all she could make out were several candles inside. A moment later a shadow moved by the window and she got a brief look at Kelly as she glided in and out of view.

"It's her!" said Donnivee. Manson could tell her friend was so angry that she could hardly keep from diving through the window after Kelly.

"Come on," said Kurt. "Back door." He led them around the garage while Manson nervously watched the house next door. She saw people in there working and moving about, but apparently Kurt was right. From inside the brightly lit house, they couldn't see anything outdoors, even if it moved.

At last they made it to the shadows behind the house and Kurt studied the situation.

"Stay here." He leaped up on the deck and silently crossed the rough wooden planks until he came to the sliding glass door. He tried the door.

Manson could just see him in the filtered moonlight as he pulled hard and the door slid open. "Can you believe these fools? They don't even lock up! Let's go!"

Manson followed Donnivee to the door, but her heart was pounding. There was no way she wanted to go into that house, though she was afraid Donnivee and Kurt might hurt her if she didn't. She looked around, her hands shaking as she stopped at the doorway.

"Wait," she said, trying to hide the obvious fear in her voice. "What if the foster mom comes back? If she pulls into the driveway we won't see her. We'll get trapped in here, or worse."

Donnivee gave her a dangerous look and Manson thought she might get punched. But Kurt nodded. "Good thinking, Manson. You stay here and keep guard. If somebody comes, scream. We'll get outta here fast. Anybody else who hears you will be so startled they'll probably wet their pants and hide. Come on, Donnivee."

"Don't be long, okay?"

"We'll be in and out like the wind," said Kurt.

Donnivee looked back at her best friend. "Yeah," she repeated. "Like the wind."

Manson waited reluctantly by the sliding glass door as Kurt and Donnivee moved through the kitchen and disappeared around a corner, Manson heard them talking.

"Manson was too scared to come in," said Donnivee angrily.

"So?" said Kurt. "We don't want her with us when we're messing around."

Manson was steaming hot inside the mask, but she was cold everywhere else. Maybe she was scared, she didn't know. But whether it was fear or just the brisk night air, she did not want to be here waiting for that stupid Kurt. They were going to get caught, she could feel it.

She stepped off the deck and went to the corner of the house by the garage. She heard the whirring of electric drills from the house next door and looked that way. Every now and then somebody would move past a window and cast a shadow across the narrow yard between the houses.

This whole thing was too stupid. If it were just her and Donnivee, everything would be fine. But Kurt was an idiot, even if he was nineteen. That settled it. Manson had had enough of breaking and entering.

She went back to the deck and glanced into the semi-dark house to see if her friends were coming out. All she saw was a glow of light from the hallway. They turned on a light? Kurt was so stupid! Manson Stanfield cursed under her breath and ran around the side of the house, right past the basement windows on ground level. She stumbled over something in the dark and pulled off her mask. Then she ran as fast as she could to the woods across the road and all the way home.

KELLY

"Okay, we got the candles lit, it's night and there's at least two of us," said Melissa, scanning the directions she'd gotten off the internet about using a Ouija board. "I'll be the medium because I know more about ghosts and stuff, okay? Remember, I'm the only one who can ask the questions. But if you have a specific question you want to ask just think it to me and I'll ask it."

I nodded, still uneasy about playing with the Ouija board. "Shouldn't we wait for Angie to get back?"

"We'll be fine. Now, sit close enough to me so our knees touch. Good. This thing here is called the planchette. We both have to put our fingers on it to make it work when we ask questions."

"Who are we asking questions to?"

"Spirits. Ghosts, you know."

"We're gonna ask dead people a bunch of questions?"

"Yep. But here it says we need to begin with some simple yes and no questions. I'll start. Spirits, are you with us?"

I looked at the planchette and held my breath. For a moment nothing happened. Then I felt it start to move. "You're doing that, right?" As soon as I spoke the planchette stopped moving.

Melissa shushed me. "I'm the medium! Don't talk or you'll scare them away. Let's try again. Spirits, are you with us?"

This time the planchette moved slowly toward the word *yes* on the board. I immediately went into Melissa's thoughts and listened to find out if she'd moved the device or not.

"They're here," said Melissa firmly. "I can feel their presence." All at once a shadow moved quickly past the window behind me. Melissa freaked. "A ghost!"

I nearly choked with fear until I picked up the thoughts of the person outside. "It's Manson Stanfield! She's afraid of something. She's running home!" I scanned some more. "Kurt Lazarus and Donnivee are in the house right now!"

Melissa pushed the planchette out of the way. "Come on, Kelly. We need some weapons!"

I searched the basement for something to use as a weapon and remembered seeing Chris a few weeks ago with a metal pipe and a baseball bat that he'd found under the stairs. We looked there and found both items. Melissa took the pipe, which was nearly as long as the bat, and met me at the base of the steps.

"Let's go," she said, as her eyes got a little crazy.

"Wait!" I said. "Are we gonna *hit* them with these? We could *kill* them!"

"Hit 'em in the knees. They won't run away."

I nodded and slowly followed Melissa up the basement stairs. As we passed silently through the kitchen we heard the ceiling creak above us. I looked up.

"They're in my room! They're looking for something of mine to *steal*!"

"Of course," said Melissa. "Why else would Donnivee come here?" We hurried to the stairway by the front door.

"Maybe we should call the police," I whispered, reaching into my pants pocket for my cell phone. "Wait, my cell phone's on the charger in my room."

"Mine's in my purse," said Melissa in a hushed voice. "In the basement. We can call later. I've got an idea. You go in the den on that side of the stairs, and I'll hide in the living room. When they come down, we'll clobber them from both sides!"

I was uncertain and tense, but I liked the plan. Donnivee and Kurt would never see us coming. How dare them come into my house and try to steal something! It made me hot with anger to think that they'd broken in just to hurt me and my family in some way. Maybe we could keep them trapped upstairs until Angie got home. Then they'd be in big trouble.

But as mad as I was, I wondered, could I *really* hurt one of them? What if they were crippled for life? Part of me said, *Good! Clobber 'em!* But my stupid compassionate side made me fearful that I might not swing the bat all that hard when it came down to it. I became angry at my own softness. They had come into my house for one purpose: to steal from me. They might even try to beat me up, too! I worked up my anger again and swung the bat at the air. I had a pretty good swing. The bat felt right in my hands.

I heard something from the top of the stairs. They were coming. I gripped the bat tightly and moved into position by the doorway. Across the foyer Melissa stood ready. We exchanged a brief nod and waited.

Suddenly everything went black. I blinked, straining to see. Except for whiskers of moonlight passing through the blinds on the front windows, the house was as dark as a cave. It must have been part of Kurt's escape plan. But how had he done it? He and Donnivee were upstairs and the breaker box was in the garage. Who turned off the power? Was it Manson? Did she come back? Did she even know how to do something like that? I mentally searched the garage. Nothing. Nobody was there.

I heard a metallic sound behind me in the den. It was like the blade of a knife being scraped across some jagged edge. I spun around. Somebody— or something—was there, the noise had been deliberate. Whoever it was *wanted* to be noticed. I made another scan in search of nearby thoughts. Nothing. But the feeling of being watched was strong.

I saw a pair of rheumy green eyes staring back at me from across the room. The eyes seemed to have no pupils and they put out a strange glow, like dim flashlights in need of new batteries. I froze. Every muscle in my body turned to mush. My heart pounded like a jackhammer. Those eyes looked familiar. As if to confirm my thoughts, the thing with the eyes spoke in a whispering, raspy voice.

"Pretty girl...."

Chapter 31
A PLACE TO HIDE

KURT

Kurt Lazarus was having the time of his life. For Kurt, nothing was cooler than breaking into someone's house and having his way with pretty much everything in there. And this time he had a girl with him. If things went according to plan he'd tear up the place, steal something valuable and maybe talk Donnivee out of her clothes. He already got the feeling she'd do anything to please him, and he had a pretty good idea what that meant. This bedroom was as good a place as any for it to happen.

He set his mask on the bed and took hers off. Then he pulled Donnivee close and kissed her hard on the mouth. She pressed against him, which got him aroused almost more than he could stand. Kurt didn't care if she was only thirteen. Age didn't matter as long as he got what he wanted. But she saw something behind him and pushed him away.

"Look at that picture," she said, crossing the room to the desk. "I'll bet that's her real family, you know? Her dead parents. I'll bet it's the only photo she's got, too."

"So?" Kurt was peeved. He wanted some sex action and he'd better get it soon. He should have known not to hang out with a stupid eighth grader. She had the attention span of a slug and didn't really know what she was doing when it came to love. He preferred girls who had experience. Of course, he didn't mind breaking 'em in, either.

"So it's the *only* picture she's got with her parents in it. I'm gonna burn it and mail the ashes to her later."

Her cruel ingenuity surprised him. Kurt nodded his approval. "I like the way you think."

She took the photograph from the wall and pulled the backing off the frame. She tossed the frame on the bed but kept the photo as she scanned the room. Kurt knew she was looking for something else to destroy or steal. He wrapped his arms around her from the back and pulled her close.

"How 'bout you an' me doin' it right here?" he whispered into her ear. "Right now."

Donnivee looked back at him and kissed him. "No." She broke away again and started going through Kelly's dresser drawers. She took out a pair of panties and held them up. "Oh, man look at these boring panties."

Kurt looked. Whenever he saw a girl's panties he found nothing boring about them. He shrugged, trying to act like they didn't have an effect on him. "What's wrong with 'em?"

"I wear thongs," said Donnivee. "This stuff's for little kids. Come on, I got what I came for." She tossed the panties aside, put on her mask and left the room.

When Kurt heard her say thong he had to wipe the drool off his chin. Maybe this chick was more experienced than he'd first thought. He grabbed his mask and went with her. At the top of the stairs he made Donnivee wait while he listened. The house was quiet and seemed empty, but with the lights on they still needed to be careful. It wasn't like they had the cover of darkness to hide in. He was about to start down the stairs when suddenly he froze.

Something didn't feel right. Kurt tilted his head toward what might have been a tiny sound. What was it? He held his breath and listened.

Tick. Tock. Tick. Tock.

Kurt let out a huge sigh of relief. A damn clock ticking in some other room! He almost broke out laughing. He glanced at Donnivee and saw her wide-eyed fear. He smiled and shook his head.

"It's nothin'," he said, starting down the stairs.

Suddenly the lights went out. The entire house was pitch black. Donnivee gripped Kurt's arm just above the elbow. Her grip was so strong it shut off the blood to his hand. He yanked his arm free but she grabbed him again. He waited and listened. He still heard nothing but the clock ticking, which appeared to be downstairs some place. So who turned off the lights?

Somebody in the house must have seen them. Now they were playing a game. Dammit, if he got caught again he'd do time in jail, and it wouldn't be juvie this time. But if he escaped and Donnivee got caught she'd turn him in to save her own butt. Even if she didn't want to turn him in, the cops would talk her into it. Cops could make you say all kinds of stuff whether you wanted to or not.

Kurt returned to the hallway and looked for a place to hide. He opened the first door on the right, somebody's bedroom. In the moonlight he could just make out a jacket hanging over a chair. There were words on the jacket, like a logo, or something. He inched into the room with Donnivee still holding onto his arm. He took a tiny penlight from his pocket and clicked it on. Normally he didn't like using flashlights in dark houses. They were like beacons if somebody was outside looking in. But he needed to know whose room this was before he tried to hide in it. He aimed the beam at the jacket.

"Satan's Sidekicks." He read it in a whisper. "That's a motorcycle gang. Hell, this is the old lady's room. We don't wanna be in here." Donnivee shook her head in agreement and followed him back into the hall.

The next door was narrower than the others, more like a closet than a bedroom. Kurt opened it slowly in case it squeaked. But the door was utterly silent. *These dopes must oil their hinges*, thought Kurt. *Good for me.* He shined the light inside the closet.

The closet was tiny with four shelves, starting about hip-high and rising nearly to the ceiling. The shelves held stacks of clean linen along with bath towels and washrags. Kurt nearly dismissed any possibility of hiding in there until he noticed the mound of dirty clothes on the floor. It was a laundry closet. He estimated the amount of space in there and looked at Donnivee. It would be a tight squeeze for sure. But nobody searching for intruders would make more than a glance into a space that small.

"Get in," he said, pulling off her mask again and giving her a nudge. He pointed the beam of light at the floor of the closet.

Donnivee looked confused. "In there? No! I'm not leaving you!"

"I'm not leaving you either. Get under the clothes on the floor. I'll be right behind you."

"Can we fit?" As she spoke she crawled into the closet and sat in the laundry pile. After some scrunching and adjusting she managed to move the clothes around her until she had a small space to hide. She looked up at Kurt. Kurt tossed some of the clothes over her head and made certain she was completely hidden. He reluctantly squeezed his much taller frame into the tiny area beside her. It took some doing, and he had to sit with his knees in his chin as he ducked under the lowest shelf, but he finally made himself fit. He covered himself with clothes and sat pressed against her shoulder.

"Don't move and don't make a sound," said Kurt in a whisper. He smiled at Donnivee to keep her calm until he realized she couldn't see him in the dark under the clothes. "Nobody'll find us in this little closet. Nobody'll even look in here. Nobody."

Chapter 32
DEMONS EVERYWHERE

KELLY

I nearly fainted dead away. I'd heard those words before and the voice was familiar enough to be somebody from my own family. But this wasn't family. Not even close.

I screamed, or thought I did. But nothing came out. My mouth hadn't even opened. I tried to run for the front door, only a few feet away. But my legs didn't move. My entire body was leaden and stiff, as if I were paralyzed. It was like one of those nightmares I used to have as a young child. The monsters chased me and I couldn't run. Only this was no dream. This was real. The monsters were coming and I was frozen like a corpse.

Something grabbed my arm. I jumped. I didn't want to see what it was, but I looked anyway. A hand gripped me firmly. It looked human.

"Let's get out of here!" Without waiting for an answer Melissa yanked me out of the den and opened the front door. Before we went outside we looked over our shoulders. The sickly glowing eyes moved toward us, slowly, confidently. The horrible voice spoke again.

"Pretty girl!"

Somehow I found my legs. I also found some courage, though this didn't seem like the time to stand and fight. I willingly followed Melissa out the door to the front porch. Just being in the moonlight made it feel somewhat safer. But the feeling was short-lived. As soon as we hit the porch a massive shadow passed over us and blocked the light. From behind the great oak tree something huge and hideous stepped out of the gloom. We stopped cold.

"What the...?" This time it was Melissa who froze in terror. She gawked at the creature, clearly unable to comprehend what was happening.

I saw two massive legs beside the tree. My gaze followed the line of the creature's body ever upward from the ground to the treetop. Whatever blocked our way was big—*real* big—close to seven meters tall! It stood over us menacingly with huge lobster claws snapping. I thought I saw a reddish tint to it in the moonlight. But how could anything that large have been so impossibly hidden behind the tree? Where had it come from? What was it?

Suddenly the evil words came back to me as clearly as if I'd heard them only minutes ago.

We know where you live, Kelly and Travis. We'll grab you in the dark, when the night comes. The dark belongs to usss!

"Pandora's Cave," I said with a shudder. "Demons! Go back inside!"

"What about the one in there!" Melissa was freaking out.

"It's smaller. Go!"

Melissa obeyed and rushed into the house again. I followed closely, one hand on my friend's shoulder, the other holding the bat. The outside demon let us go as if it wanted us to return to the house. I made a mental note of that as we entered the foyer and slammed the door.

Melissa turned the bolt lock, breathing hard. "If that thing really wants in, the door isn't gonna stop it!"

"Nope. I have a feeling we're right where they want us to be."

As soon as I spoke the smaller demon came at us, teeth bared. Its knife-like claws were long and sharp. I saw it first. I reared back and swung the bat, high to low. On the way down the bat struck the small chandelier. Pieces of glass flew everywhere. The glass bounced off the walls and scattered across the floor and stairs. But I never stopped the swing. The bat smashed into the head of the small demon, splitting open its skull. I felt a warm, greasy fluid splash over my face and arms. I couldn't see it, but I knew it was demon blood. The demon collapsed to the floor, unconscious or dead. Either way it stayed down and kept quiet.

"Come on!" I led the way upstairs, crunching over broken glass. When we reached the top of the stairs, Melissa turned and thrust her steel pipe in the direction of anything that might have followed us. The stairs were empty. I ran into my bedroom to look for my cell phone, but it wasn't there. Where was it? I heard Melissa challenge the demons in the hallway.

"Come on! I dare you! Come up the stairs!"

I ran from my room and joined Melissa in the hallway. It took a moment for me to realize I'd left my cell phone in my locker at school. I stood desperately beside Melissa, who kept the pipe directed at the stairs. The house wasn't as dark on the second floor because the window at the top of the stairs had no blinds. As a precaution I reached around Melissa and raised the sash.

"What's that for?" asked Melissa.

"Just in case. Do you see 'em?"

"No. Maybe that's all there were."

"Maybe." *But that would be lousy strategy*, I thought to Melissa. *You can't just send two demons after us. Are demons really that stupid?* I glanced to our right down the hall. Still nothing.

"I guess we shouldn't have messed with the Ouija board," said Melissa reluctantly. "Angie was right. That thing's dangerous."

"This has nothing to do with the Ouija board," I said. "This is *personal.*"

A set of sickly, yellow eyes blinked open a few feet in front of us. Some kind of distorted creature hung invisibly in a coal-black shadow on the stairway ceiling. I gasped when I saw it. The creature had been hanging directly over us when we came up the stairs.

"Oh...!" Melissa saw it too. We watched the demon calmly lower itself from the ceiling with two strong arms, as two more arms hung freely from its thick shoulders. The four-armed demon dropped to its feet on the stairs and stood before us, eyes glowing grotesquely. When it grinned, its nasty long teeth showed white as ivory, as if they glowed in the dark like its eyes.

I spotted motion in the hall. This time something *was* there. The demon creeping toward me was also man-sized, but it had a dozen tentacles instead of arms. Its head was triangularly shaped, almost like a crocodile, with long, wicked teeth and catfish-like barbels protruding all around its mouth.

I nudged Melissa. She turned and saw the other demon.

What do we do? I asked inside Melissa's head.

Get crazy, said Melissa. *Everyone's afraid of crazy people, even Donnivee.*

What if it doesn't work?

If it doesn't work we're gonna miss out on the smores.

The demon with tentacles had a foul, fishy smell that permeated the hallway. It narrowed its cruel, green eyes and pointed at me with one of the longer tentacles. "What's yer name, human? Be quick about it!"

"Why?" I asked in a shaky voice. I stood sideways to the demon, holding the bat out of sight behind my legs. I couldn't believe what was happening. Here I stood in my own home having a conversation with a demon from Pandora's Cave. There were other demons in the house as well. The evil creatures had come all this way just to find *me*, and probably Travis, too. Apparently demons didn't like witnesses to their existence, which meant Melissa was now in danger as well.

Use someone else's name! I was surprised to hear Melissa inside my head when I hadn't even been tuned into her. The idea was a good one.

"My name is Donnivee Fox."

"Donnivee?" The demon shook its ugly head. "Bahh! Whut about you?" It pointed at Melissa. Slime droplets slid off the pointing tentacle and landed on the rug. I screwed up my face at the repugnant smell.

"Manson Stanfield," said Melissa, never taking her eyes off Four-arms, who glared at her from the stairs.

"They ain't right!" cried Tentacles. "Whud'we do with 'em, Grund?"

The four-armed demon, apparently named Grund, was still on the stairs with Melissa's pipe aimed in its face. Grund smiled with an odd glint in all three of his yellow eyes. "We can't believe a thing these lying human scum say."

"Yeh," agreed Tentacles. "But whut'da'we do with 'em?"

"I say get 'em! We can sort out who's who when Lipsludge wakes up."

"Yeh. Lipsludge'll know whut ta do."

I considered what they were saying. Lipsludge must be the smaller demon I bonked on the head with the bat. So I hadn't killed him after all, just knocked him out. He must be the leader of this group. I was about to ask what they wanted when suddenly three slimy tentacles darted toward me.

Apparently the creature didn't realize I planned to fight back. I swung the bat at its head. *Crack!* The grotesque green demon staggered back and fell against the wall. It screeched loudly, like a car hitting the brakes on dry pavement. I covered my ears at the piercing, irritating sound.

At the same time Grund grabbed one end of the pipe that Melissa was holding. The four-armed demon must have expected her to pull back on it, but she surprised him. Instead of pulling it, she jammed it forward into the demon's startled face. Grund lost his balance and toppled over backwards. He rolled down the stairs and slammed hard into the front door.

Tentacles was stunned, but he wasn't as dumb as he was smelly. In what must have been a standard defense reaction, he extended all his tentacles straight up and out, like the fur on a cat when it's about to fight. It made him look huge and terrifying. I gasped. Then I slammed the bat down onto one of his feet. Tentacles released his irritating scream again and hobbled away from me down the hallway.

I started after him, but Melissa caught my arm. "What do we do?"

"Maybe we should hide?"

"I don't know. Those things can hide a lot better than us."

At that moment headlights flashed across the front of the house, which could only mean one thing. I looked at Melissa.

"Angie's home!"

With Angie home I felt a wave of hope. Maybe it was childish of me to believe that the mere presence of an adult would make the monsters go away, but right now it was all the hope I had. I was about to rush down the stairs until I looked below. From where we stood the foyer was pitch black.

I checked my pace and began the slow terrifying descent toward the front door. I took it one wary step at a time, keeping the bat cocked and ready. Melissa followed, allowing enough distance between us to be able to swing our weapons.

"It fell against the door," said Melissa, pointing with the pipe. "Right there."

I nodded. "It's too dark. I can't see the floor." When I reached the bottom step I heard the crunch of broken glass under my shoes. I poked cautiously at the shadowy area in front of the door. All I touched was hardwood floor. "It's gone." As an extra precaution I tapped the floor at the den entrance searching for the smaller demon the others had called Lipsludge. More hardwood. "They're both gone."

"I guess demons don't stay hurt for long."

"I guess."

"I don't like the way those things can move in the dark. It's not natural."

"*Nothing* about them is natural. Watch our backs. Don't let 'em out-flank us."

As Melissa kept a wary eye on both the den and living room, I released the bolt lock and slowly opened the door. Once again moonlight flooded through the storm door into the foyer. Surprisingly, we were just in time to see Angie come up the steps carrying a bag of groceries and a box of drinks.

Angie smiled when she saw the door open. "Thanks, Kelly. Why are the lights off? Are you two getting braver with the Ouija board?"

I paid no attention to her. I was looking for the giant demon. I scanned the big oak tree as well as the rest of the front yard. Nothing.

Angie noticed the weapons. "What's wrong?"

"The power went off." I blocked Angie from getting inside.

"Really?" Angie looked at the house next door. Dr. Parrish's house was brightly lit up. "It's not a neighborhood problem so it must be a circuit breaker. I'll check on it. Can one of you take the drinks? My fingers are about to fall off."

Melissa took the twelve-pack of canned drinks and set them on the floor inside the door. I leaned forward and whispered to Angie. "They're in the house. We need to get out of here as fast as we can. Get your keys ready."

Angie also lowered her voice. "What's going on?"

"We'll tell you in the car," I said it firmly, guiding Angie back off the porch.

"We should go next door," said Angie. "Mark and Matilda are there. Did someone break in?"

"Oh, yeah," said Melissa. "They're in there all right."

Angie fiddled with her key chain and held up a tiny can of pepper spray. "Come on." My confidence grew a little as we followed Angie off the porch. Pepper spray had been added to our meager arsenal of weapons. And now we had an adult with us.

As soon as we reached the sidewalk that confidence was shut away by an overwhelming sense of dread. Somehow I understood what the giant creature behind the tree would do. I couldn't see it anywhere, but apparently its job was to keep us in the house for the other demons to deal with. Certainly, it would try to do its job. In my mind I counted down. *Three-two-one....*

A broad shadow obstructed the light almost like a switch had turned off the moon. I raised the bat. The creature was right on time. Demons could be predictable—something worth remembering. The freaky part was I'd been alert to its presence, even to the exact moment it would show up. Yet I still hadn't gotten a glimpse of it before it was suddenly in front of us. How could something so huge appear out of nowhere?

It moved around the tree and blocked our way to both the minivan and to Dr. Parrish's house. Angie froze up when she saw it, swept by terror. She had never experienced anything like this before and wasn't able to process it. At first she thought it must be some kind of wild animal. But when it became visible in the moonlight and stood up to its full height, she recognized its humanlike form—except for the hands. A palpable dread flooded Angie's mind. I heard every confused and terrified thought.

"Stay calm," I said, not feeling calm at all. I would have screamed, but my vocal cords were twisted into knots of fear. I could barely speak. "We'd better go back in the house."

Angie and Melissa nodded. They returned to the front door with me. But this time the huge demon seemed to have a different agenda. It lumbered forward, great claws snapping. I saw it first.

Duck! I sent the order directly into the minds of Melissa and Angie. The massive claw swept over us. At that instant we all dropped to our faces on the porch. But the creature was faster than it looked. It missed grabbing Angie by mere inches. The claw smashed through one of the front windows. Glass showered over us. Blinds and drapes were ripped from inside the house and dropped on the lawn. I crawled as fast as I could toward the storm door. I reached for the handle.

"Look out!"

Melissa had yelled it. I looked back. The other claw rushed at me like a small car. I rolled away from the entrance just as the claw smashed through the storm door. The beast tore the storm door off the house and tossed it aside like a toy. It focused on me. The demon's eyes lit up with excitement. I thought I saw it smile.

"It's coming back!" Melissa scrambled for the doorknob.

Angie cried out. "Oh my God!"

I rose quickly, making for the door. But I stepped on shards of glass and slipped. I landed hard behind the wooden post that held up the porch roof. The demon had me trapped.

"Yer mine!" Its voice was husky, deep. I thought it sounded hungry. The claw came in fast. I closed my eyes. I hoped it wouldn't hurt too much to be crushed and eaten alive.

TRAVIS

Travis sat on his bedroll by the wall making sure everything was just right in case he and Mathew ever decided to go to sleep. Mathew's bedroll was next to his with enough space between them for flashlights, food and drinks. They had plenty of everything, including extra batteries, a box of gram crackers, a bucket of popcorn, some twinkies, and a two-liter bottle of soda. He nodded with satisfaction at what might be the perfect set up.

"What'dya think, Mathew?" said Travis. "Should we move everything under the window, or leave it here?"

"This is good," said Mathew. "I'm not gonna to sleep anyway. I'm gonna stay up all night."

"That's what I'm talkin' about! Me too." Travis shuddered with excitement. This was so cool! Here he was sleeping over with his best friend in Dr. Parrish's house. The house didn't have carpet or anything so it was kind of like indoor camping. Mathew was right, they weren't ready for sleep yet. Heck no, Travis couldn't sleep if he tried, he was way too excited. All kinds of things could happen.

Crash! The sound of shattering glass tore through the night. Travis jumped to his feet, eyes wide with surprise. He and Mathew exchanged looks of alarm. Did Dr. Parrish or Granny break something downstairs? It happened again, only this time it was much more than just glass. *Smash! Crunch! Boom!* A moment later a desperate scream pierced the air.

"Kelly!" cried Travis. "That came from *my* house!" Both boys ran to the window. To Travis it sounded like his whole house was being torn down. That scream was definitely Kelly. He pressed his face against the glass, but there was too much glare from the ceiling light in the room to see anything. Mathew ran to the door and turned off the light. Instantly the view outside was clear. Mathew returned to the window.

"What is it?" said Mathew. "What happened?"

"I dunno." Travis scanned the area and saw the damage. "Omigosh!" His mouth dropped wide open when he realized what had happened to his home. The roof of the front porch was totally caved in and debris had been scattered all across the yard. It looked like a bomb had gone off near the house. Something moved beyond the porch behind the great oak tree. He pointed. "What's that?"

An obscure figure rose suddenly from the darkest shadows around the tree. It stood up on two legs, manlike, and was easily as tall as the second story windows. It appeared to have great lobster claws instead of hands.

"It's some kinda animal!" said Mathew. "It's big!"

"What's going on up there?" said Granny from downstairs. "Are you boys okay?"

Travis heard the heavy, fast moving footsteps of Granny and Dr. Parrish on the stairs. A moment later they burst into the room.

"What happened?" said Parrish. "What broke?"

"Next door!" said Travis, looking back at Granny. "There's a big animal in the yard."

"Woh!" Mathew spun his head suddenly, his expression full of disbelief. "It moved around the side of the garage. Then it *disappeared*!" Sure enough, when Travis looked outside again nothing was there. His throat tightened with panic. Where were Kelly, Melissa and Angie?

Parrish and Granny came up behind them. Granny spoke. "Show me."

"Right there." Mathew pointed. "It went into those shadows. I can't see it any more, but it was *huge!*"

"What happened to the roof?" said Granny. "What's that on the ground by the tree? Is that a door?"

"It's the storm door," said Parrish. "There's curtains and some torn up window blinds. Is that the porch rail over by the road? We'd better get down there. Travis, you and Mathew stay in the house and call the police. Give 'em my name if you have to, but get somebody here as fast as you can."

"Got it!" Mathew took out his cell phone and made the call to the police. Travis listened to Granny and Parrish talk on their way downstairs.

"Where's the ten pound sledgehammer?" said Granny.

"In the dining room by the ladder," said Parrish. "What are you going to do? Bash somebody's head in?"

"Krikey, Mark, I can't shoot 'em. I don't have my gun."

Travis heard the rattle of Parrish's tools from the first floor. The aluminum extension ladder flopped onto the hardwood with a metallic clang. He heard more footsteps until finally the front door slammed shut. The house became eerily silent.

Mathew ended the call. "The police are on the way!"

Travis kept his gaze glued to the house next door. Whatever was going on there sounded bad.

Mathew stood with him, holding the phone up to the glass. "If we see that thing again, I'll get a video of it."

Travis stared at his home in total disbelief. How could this be happening? Why would somebody tear their house apart? What was that thing they saw in the front yard?

Like a slap in the face it all came back to him. Travis remembered that horrible day in the cave when those creatures had chased them. He grabbed Mathew by the shoulder.

"It's not an animal! It's demons! They've come to get us just like they said they would!"

Chapter 33
WE WANTS THE KELLY BISHOP

KELLY

I was trapped on the porch. The giant claw came at me too fast to get away. I closed my eyes and screamed.

Suddenly, *thunk!* I heard the noise, but what? No pain? I opened my eyes. The creature's claw was caught on a wooden column that held up the porch roof. This was my only chance to escape.

"Kelly!"

I snapped my head to the right. Melissa reached for me from the doorway. She and Angie had gotten inside the house! I stretched one hand toward Melissa. Then something made me take a quick look back. The lobster demon seemed confused by what had happened. But it squeezed its claw shut. The post broke like a dry twig. Out of anger and frustration the demon tore away the post and much of the rail. It tossed everything across the yard. Then it pounded both claws on the porch roof. I looked up as the roof came crashing down.

At that instant Melissa grabbed my outstretched hand. She dragged me into the foyer on my belly. With everyone inside, Angie slammed the front door and locked it. A split second later the porch roof collapsed with a clamor that shook the entire house. The terrible demon abruptly stopped its rampage. The house became still. Moonlight flooded in through broken windows and shredded blinds.

Melissa collapsed on the stairs in front of me, exhausted by terror. But Angie was too wound up and afraid to keep still. She repeatedly glanced toward the door as if she expected it to be ripped off its hinges at any moment.

"Action beats fear," she muttered to herself. "Action beats fear." She grabbed Melissa's hand and pulled her to her feet. "We gotta get outta here!"

Melissa was nearly out of breath. "It...won't come after us...in the house." She shifted the pipe to her other hand. "It didn't the first time."

"*What* won't come after us in the house?" cried Angie. "What *was* that thing?" An unstable wildness gleamed in her eyes. She was scared half to death.

I lay on the floor amidst fragments of glass from the broken chandelier. I was too upset to speak. I wanted to explain to Angie as much as I knew, but everything outside had happened so fast it still seemed like a blur. I could hardly believe I was alive. It took massive concentration for me to rise to my feet.

Thanks, Melissa, I thought to my friend. Melissa looked me in the eye and nodded ever so slightly. Sadly, there was no reason to celebrate. We weren't free of the demon menace. As far as I could tell the house was still crawling with the evil, hideous creatures. I scanned the dimness, searching for their glow-in-the-dark eyes. So far nothing.

"Well?" Angie's voice shook badly. She was on the verge of tears. "I want the truth this time."

"It's the same thing we told you before," I said. "That thing outside is a demon from Pandora's Cave. If you don't believe me now then there's no hope for you."

I watched as Angie groped for a means to understand what was happening. But instead of understanding, she returned to logic, which for her was a good thing.

She rushed to the phone table in the foyer and picked up the receiver. "It's dead. My cell phone's in the van. Look, girls, we need to call the police before that *beast* rips my house apart. Who's got a cell phone?"

"Mine's in the basement," said Melissa. "I'm not going back down there."

"Mine's at school," I said. "Sorry. Listen, Angie, there's more demons in the house and they can hide in places you wouldn't believe."

"*In* the house?" Angie jumped. She spun all about. "Like where?"

At first I couldn't answer her. Melissa pointed to an area of darkness in the den. "Like there."

I looked. Sure enough three yellow eyes stared back at us. I recognized the four-armed demon, Grund.

"Give up, you worthless human trash!" said Grund. "We're the demon death squad! You can't win, so give us the Kelly Bishop!"

"Yeah!" Another demon approached from the kitchen. With its seven red and gooey eyes this creature was different from the ones I'd already seen. I couldn't make out many extra details in the dark, but I could tell it was man-sized and covered with long fur. "We want the Kelly Bishop!"

My blood ran cold. The demons only wanted one thing—me!

I had suspected it all along, but hearing it from their own mouths made it official. My fear became overpowering. I tried to swallow but couldn't. My legs were so heavy I doubted I'd be able to run, even if it meant my life.

In spite of my own situation I became intensely worried for Travis. Did they realize he was staying next door? Had they already taken him away? My spirits fell. The demons had us surrounded. The situation was hopeless. Reluctantly, I knew what I needed to do. I had to surrender and go with them. If I didn't, they'd kill Angie and Melissa and anyone else who got in the way.

I was about to give up, when Angie winked at me. If I'd scanned Angie's thoughts and known what she had planned, I would have stopped her immediately. But the wink caught me off guard. It brought back a brief and pleasant memory of my father winking at me, and me unable to wink back because I couldn't close just one eye. I nearly said that aloud when Angie stepped up to Grund, face to face.

"If you want the Kelly Bishop, you've come to the right place. *I'm* Kelly Bishop." Angie pretended to be brave, though her voice shook.

Grund smiled, his cold, white teeth glowing in the night. "Of course you are."

I was shocked. Angie was willing to sacrifice herself for a foster daughter she'd only known a few months? How dare her! "What are you doing? They came here for *me*!" I faced Grund in a panic. "She's lying. *I'm* Kelly Bishop!"

Grund's yellow gaze darted back and forth between us. A look of confusion washed over his demon face. "Yer both lying scum! An' *you've* changed yer name!" He pointed at me.

"You're right!" said Melissa, catching on. "They *are* lying scum. *My* name is Kelly Bishop!"

Are you crazy? I shouted it inside Melissa's mind. *You're my best friend but this is my problem!*

It's our problem now, thought Melissa right back at me.

I looked at Melissa and Angie. Were they insane? Didn't they understand? These creatures weren't playing games. The yellow demon already said it, they were a demon death squad! They intended to take us, or me, to the caves. They were going to *eat* us!

Out of the corner of my eye I saw something move in the living room. I scanned the filtered darkness, searching. There, by the coffee table! It had two arms and two legs. That was good. Then I saw four red eyes. Not good. Whatever it was had two distinctly different faces, one on either side of its head and each face had two eyes. It stood so tall it had to hunker down to keep from bumping into the nine-foot ceiling. Good God! How many of those nasty things had come here?

All at once I felt incredibly foolish. I had very nearly given up and turned myself over to the demons. Was I insane? Since when had the word *failure* become part of my vocabulary? Jon would have a few things to say about that, if he were here. He would never consider surrender. No, the only thing Jon would worry about was how many demons he could destroy before they got away. Where was he right now?

My feelings of hopelessness scattered like smoke in a breeze. There had to be another way out of this. There simply *had* to be! There was *always* an alternative.

My gaze went to the top of the stairs, which was the only path of escape the demons had allowed us. So why was that? What was their plan once they herded the *humans* upstairs?

I felt my shoe bump against something on the floor. I looked down and saw the box of canned sodas. I got an idea.

"Which girl is it, eh?" The bulky demon in the living room spoke with a ridiculously high-pitched voice. "How do we know who ta grab?"

"Les takem all," said Grund, rubbing his scaly chin with one of his four hands.

"We got strict orders," said the demon with seven red eyes. "We only take the Kelly Bishop."

"But they already seen us! They'll tell!"

"Who'd believe 'em?" said Seven-eyes. "And who cares? We're Demon Nation!"

"Demon Nation," said the others in unison.

They spoke among themselves, discussing which of us to take to the caves. I reached down and opened the box of sodas. I removed two cans and passed them over to Angie and Melissa. I got one more for myself and left the box on the floor.

"Follow my lead." I whispered just loud enough for Melissa and Angie to hear. I suddenly laughed out loud. Melissa laughed along with me, but Angie could only force a smile.

"Demons are so *dumb*!" I said, pointing directly at Grund. Grund frowned back. I heard his teeth grinding in anger. "I can't believe they fell for our plan, but here they are, *trapped* in our house. Good plan, *Kelly*."

I said it to Melissa, who responded appropriately. "Thank you, *Kelly*. I told you they'd fall for it. Like you said, demons are *dumb*!"

I spoke to Angie next. "Now that you brought us the secret weapons, *Kelly*, I think it's time to use them. Don't you?"

"Uh, well, of course," said Angie, trying to catch on. "I mean you told me the demons would come here tonight, so of course I got the secret weapons."

Melissa chimed in. "You demons thought you surprised us, didn't you? Ha! We've been waiting for you. We've got you right where we want you."

"Yep," said Angie. She had the basic idea now. "Right where we want you."

Grund's look of confidence slowly faded as he considered what we were saying. I couldn't read his mind but his face was like an open book. Could the humans be telling the truth this time? Could it really be a trap?

I vigorously shook my can of soda. Melissa and Angie did the same. "Demon repellent!" I said. "It gets in your eyes and eats away your eyeballs!" I smiled confidently as if my story were absolutely true.

Grund exchanged a worried glance with Seven-eyes. The demon in the living room scratched its head. I nodded to the others and pulled the tab on my can.

"Now!" I aimed the soda can straight at the faces of the big demon in the living room. Melissa and Angie did the same with Grund and Seven-Eyes. The spray from the cans showered all three demons as they covered their eyes and screamed horribly.

We tossed the cans and raced up the stairs. As expected, it was a trap. Lipsludge and Tentacles were in the second floor hallway waiting for us. Angie shrieked when she saw them. But I had my own plan. I pointed to the window.

"Go!"

Melissa didn't argue. She rolled over the windowsill and out onto the roof. A moment later Angie practically dove through the window. I remained behind. I raised the bat, ready for a fight.

Lipsludge spat orders to his cohorts downstairs. "Gets up here, you foul slime!"

The demons below screamed and ran about the house. They crashed into walls and knocked over furniture. Another window smashed.

"She blinded us! With demon repellent!" It was Grund.

Lipsludge threw up his hands. "Morons! Der ain'ts no such thing as demon repellent!"

"There ain't?" The demons stopped wailing. They came to the foot of the stairs and blinked up at me. In an instant their expressions changed from fearful to homicidal. They charged straight for me.

I ducked through the window and took up a position beside Melissa. We were both ready for battle. We had no choice. Angie stood beside us. She aimed the pepper spray.

Tentacles tried to climb after us first, but Melissa cracked him in the head with the steel pipe. Tentacles screeched and fell back inside the house. Next came Lipsludge. Angie blasted him in the face with the pepper spray. Lipsludge froze partly in the window. He screamed and rubbed his eyes.

"It burns!"

Grund shoved the smaller demon aside and crawled onto the roof. I swung the bat hard. Whoosh! Grund ducked. I missed by a mile. His quickness surprised me. I swung again. Whoosh! Nothing but air! I kept swinging, again and again. Grund dodged to the side. He leaned back. He retreated to the peak of the roof. The more I tried to hit him the more he got out of the way. Then, unexpectedly, he stumbled and fell over backwards. Before he could find a handhold, he dropped off the roof into the back yard. *Thump!*

I grinned at Melissa and Angie and leaned on the bat, out of breath.

Melissa got excited. "Who's next?" She waved the pipe like a madwoman. I'd seen that insane expression the day we encountered Manson Stanfield in the school restroom. "Come on! You're not afraid of a *human*, are ya?"

The answer to her question came quickly. Seven-Eyes crashed through the window like a wrecking ball. Melissa jumped back. Just before it landed she took a wild swing. The pipe struck the furry beast in the shoulder. Seven-Eyes lost his balance and landed like a ton of bricks on the concrete driveway below. But Melissa lost her grip on the pipe. It flew out of her hands and disappeared in the night.

"Yes!" I said. I exchanged a high-five with Melissa before we noticed the three other demons had gotten onto the roof. The creatures stood confidently just a few feet away, victory grins plastered across their hideous faces.

"We wants da Kelly Bishop," said Lipsludge, waving his fist. "We gets her an' we goes. Gives us the Kelly Bishop!"

"Go to hell!" Angie used her most defiant voice.

"Beens there, dones that," said Lipsludge matter-of-factly. He let out a shrill whistle. "Klawfinger! Now!"

Suddenly the giant lobster demon rose from behind us on the side of the house. It grabbed Angie with one giant claw and raised her high into the air.

"Got 'er!" said the huge demon proudly.

"No!" shouted Lipsludge. "Not her! Gets the little ones! We wants da little ones!"

Klawfinger dropped Angie like a rag doll. I watched in horror as my foster mother bounced off the edge of the roof and disappeared over the side.

"Angie!" I had no time to grieve. Tentacles and the Two-Faced demon came at us from the front. Klawfinger's great claws swept in from behind. We were trapped.

There's always another way! I tossed the baseball bat at Tentacles and took Melissa's hand.

"Come with me!" We both ran down the slope and leaped off the roof.

Chapter 34
SOMEONE ELSE'S NAME

KURT

Kurt Lazarus squirmed out from under the dirty laundry pile, desperate to stretch his legs again. But when he stood inside the cramped hall closet, a shelf jabbed him in the back. He stumbled against the door and accidentally stepped on Donnivee's hand.

"Ow!" she cried.

"Be quiet!"

"Help me up, Kurt."

"Stay where you are. I'll check the hall."

"But, Kurt...."

"Shhh! Don't move!" Kurt pressed his ear against the closet door and listened. It was quiet now, but just a few minutes ago, man! Did he pick the wrong house to break into, or what? This place was crazy! Somebody hated these people even more than Donnivee, if that was possible. For the last half hour it sounded like he was in the middle of a war zone, but the battle had moved outside. He pulled the grotesque monster mask over his head and slowly opened the closet door. The mask made him sweat, but there was no use giving anyone who might still be around a free peek at his real face—not without a fight, anyway. He cautiously stepped into the empty hallway.

The first thing he noticed was the window at the top of the stairs—it wasn't there any more. Just a big open hole with broken glass and scraps of wood all over the place. That explained one of the many crashes they'd heard, but not the *big* one. The big one had felt more like an explosion or an earthquake. The whole house had shook.

Kurt knew they had to move fast. If the fighting came back inside he'd be right in the middle of it. And if the cops showed up and caught him he'd be dead. No more juvie for Kurt Lazarus. Nope, he'd be hanging with the big boys in the state pen. Nobody his age wanted to be locked in a cage with those guys. He'd be fresh meat. Kurt shuddered. He'd rather die than go to prison. If he could just get out of here alive he might consider ending his life of crime.

When he turned to go back to get Donnivee she was standing right behind him. He bumped into her before he saw her. He jumped in surprise.

"Ahh! Dammit, Donnivee! I told you to stay in the closet."

"I'm stayin' with *you*. Did you hear what Kelly told those guys? She told them she was *me*!" She spoke in a low voice, but not low enough for Kurt.

"Get your mask and be quiet! We're not outta here yet."

He watched as Donnivee returned to the closet and retrieved her mask. They both still wore the latex monster hands, but Kurt was used to them by now and hardly realized he had them on.

"You heard her, Kurt." Donnivee went on as if she really had his attention. "She tried to get me in trouble just to save her own scrawny butt! What'd I ever do to her?"

Kurt turned in surprise. Was she kidding? Did she want him to make a list? He decided not to go there. Instead he clamped a hand over her mouth and gave her a threatening look. "Shut up." That time she listened.

Kurt led them downstairs and was shocked at what he saw. Windows and blinds broken, curtains shredded, holes in the walls, pieces of glass and destroyed furniture everywhere. At the bottom of the stairs he stepped in some kind of black goo on the floor and slipped. He caught himself on the stair rail.

"Whoa! Nice catch." He never bothered to inspect the goo to see what it was, he was too intent on getting out of there. "Come on." He practically sprinted to the back. Kurt slid open the glass door and stepped onto the deck. He took in a deep breath of the cool night air. Man, did it feel good to be outside again. Donnivee closed the door behind them.

"Manson ran out on us!" she said, a little too loud. "I'm gonna kick *her* tail, too!"

"It's a *good* thing she ran," said Kurt. "She'd be extra baggage. She did the smart thing just like we're gonna do. But first we gotta find out what's happenin' out front." They left the deck and followed along the rear of the house. The back was very dark, except for a flickering, orange glow on the trees at the perimeter of the yard. It was so dark, in fact, Kurt couldn't see Donnivee right beside him.

All at once a piercing shriek filled the air. Kurt dropped to the ground and crawled under large shrub. A glacial chill touched his spine. He'd never heard such a terrible sound in his life. What the hell was it? Donnivee moved in beside him under the bush.

"What was that?" she asked, as shaken as he was. "It wasn't human!"

"Keep your mouth shut, all right? You're gonna get us caught."

They heard cries and shouts from the front of the house, but none of it made any sense. Kurt was worried. They weren't safe hiding under a bush and one thing was for sure…the fight wasn't over.

He got back to his feet and crept to the end of the house. Donnivee stayed right with him. "There's a fire in the front yard," he said in a low voice, peeking by the corner. "I can't see what's burnin' unless I go around."

Donnivee nodded and pressed close to him. All at once a chorus of shrill, frantic howls pierced the night. It was a mournful sound, like a host of tortured souls screaming in agony. Kurt swallowed hard. For the first time in his life he believed in monsters. He looked down at Donnivee, unable to hide his fear. Then he remembered she couldn't see his face behind the mask. Good thing.

If he ran now he'd be home in an hour and nobody would realize he'd ever been there. Every instinct in every bone in his body told him to take off. But he also knew if he ran, Donnivee couldn't keep up with him, and if she got caught the cops would eventually nail him, too. They'd offer her some kind of deal because of her age and he'd get screwed. No, somehow they *both* had to get out of there and it'd be a whole lot easier if nobody saw them. He leaned around the corner to get another look.

The landscaping on that side of the house included some tall, thick boxwoods. Beyond those he could see flames and moving shadows. But he still couldn't see where the fighting was because of the bushes and a decorative flagpole centered in the flowerbed. The pole was about his height and the flag blocked much of his view. He wanted to rip it out of the ground and toss it into the fire.

Suddenly, Kurt got the feeling they weren't alone. He looked behind them but saw nothing in the darkness. "Put your mask on," he said to Donnivee. "In case somebody sees us."

Unlike before Donnivee didn't ask questions, she just did what he told her and pulled on the mask. At this point Kurt could almost smell her fear. He took her arm and gave her a gentle squeeze. "Nobody's gonna know we were here except you, me and Manson."

Her tension eased a little. He could tell because she hugged him from behind.

He only felt safe for a moment. He got the sensation again, only this time it was more like he was being watched. He turned quickly. Nothing. But the feeling festered inside him like spoiled mayonnaise. Somebody was close. *Real* close. He could almost feel their warm breath. He scanned the area again, but darkness was darkness.

Then a few feet away, a set of sickly yellow eyes blinked open. *Three* of them. Except for the color and the number they seemed to be real. The other weird thing about them was the way they glowed in the dark. Kurt was impressed. Whoever it was had on a helluva costume! But why would anybody other than a thief be wearing a costume tonight?

"Who are you?" came the gruff order from the stranger in the dark.

Donnivee let out a tiny cry. Kurt leaned over to her. He whispered softly, "Use someone else's name."

Right away her eyes lit up under the mask. She had an idea.

"I'm Spider Dedmon," said Kurt as bravely as he could. Good thing he had on the mask. If the guy could see his face he'd know he was lying.

Donnivee spoke boldly to the stranger. "I'm Kelly Bishop. I live here." The guy didn't seem to care about Spider Dedmon's name, but when he heard Donnivee speak he got very excited.

"Yer the Kelly Bishop?" He must have been a foreigner. His husky voice had some kind of accent.

"That's me."

"But you're demon kind."

"What?" Donnivee was clearly confused by what he meant.

Kurt thought he understood. He whispered to her again. "It's your mask. He's got one on, too. He must be one of those fantasy role-playing freaks. Play along."

Donnivee nodded at the stranger. "Yeah, sure, I'm demon kind. Aren't we all? Look, I'm Kelly Bishop, okay? I'm the real deal. You can tell everybody I broke the windows in this house and I tore up the furniture, too. I hate my foster parents and most of all I hate Melissa Godwin."

Kurt knew she was enjoying this. Donnivee would have fun doing anything that got Kelly in trouble.

The guy clapped his hands in the dark. It sounded like more than one person clapping. "Good fer me!" All at once he leaned forward and scooped up Donnivee with one hand. He tossed her over his shoulder and strutted off. Kurt looked on in disbelief.

"Hey, buddy! She's mine!"

"I found her. Beat it! Or th' Boss 'll put you in th' soup!" The stranger shoved Kurt into the wall and went on his way. Kurt lost his balance, but caught himself on a bush. What'd he say? Boss? Soup? What the hell was that fruitcake even talking about?

"Stop!" cried Donnivee. "Kurt! Stop him!" The figure clamped a hand over her mouth. Her cries were muffled as they disappeared around the corner.

Kurt's anger overcame his sense of self-preservation. He'd had enough. He wasn't going let some clown just walk up and take his girl like that. Hell, she was only thirteen. What was this guy anyway? A pedophile?

Kurt followed them around the house, pulling up the flagpole along the way. Maybe he'd just crack the guy in the skull with the flagpole and kick in his ribs while he's down. Or better yet, he could spear him in the back. That would teach him for sure. A swarm of vengeful possibilities flashed through Kurt's mind as he came up behind the stranger.

At the front of the house he could see the guy clearly in the firelight. What he saw stopped him in his tracks. The guy held Donnivee over his shoulder with two well-muscled arms. A third arm kept its hand clamped firmly over her mouth. And the fourth arm swung freely as he moved. Kurt stared in disbelief. Four arms? Helluva costume!

"Four arms or not," said Kurt aloud. "Nobody steals *my* girl until I'm done with her!" With that he raised the flagpole like a javelin and charged after them.

Chapter 35
LADDER TROUBLE

TRAVIS

The towering lobster demon took hold of Angie with one claw and raised her high into the air. Travis looked on from the third-story window in Parrish's house, wide-eyed and helpless. Though his heart jumped, the rest of him remained paralyzed with a terrible awe. That creature was going to crush Angie in half. It would crush her and probably eat her. All Travis could do was stand there and watch it happen.

"No! Not Angie. Not my mom!" Travis' eyes bulged in all-out panic. He turned to Mathew, who promptly shut off the cell phone video recorder. Travis knew Mathew had made a video of everything they'd seen from the window so far. But he wouldn't record something as gruesome as that.

Travis looked back at Angie. At that very moment the demon released her. She dropped fast, landing face-first on the roof. The force of the impact bounced her over the edge.

"Angie!"

Travis lost sight of her somewhere between the demon's massive body and the house.

He was on the verge of tears, when Mathew pointed. "There she is!"

The lobster demon moved with purpose to the front of the house. It left Angie behind, clinging helplessly to the edge of the roof. Twenty feet below her was the concrete sidewalk. It looked like she was losing her grip.

Travis freaked. "Come on!"

"What're we gonna do?"

"I dunno!"

Travis sprinted downstairs with Mathew right on his heels. When he got to the living room he saw the extension ladder on the floor. "Ladder!"

Travis grabbed one end and Mathew took the other. Without any discussion Travis led them out the front door and off the porch.

As they hustled across the grass toward the McCormicks' house, Dr. Parrish blew past them going the other way. His face was all scrunched up and his eyes were crazy with fear. The big man stomped across the porch and made it into the house without saying a word.

Travis and Mathew got to Angie and laid the ladder on the ground. "Hang on, Angie!" shouted Travis. "We got a ladder!"

Angie dangled by her fingertips with her head bowed. It seemed like she might be in a lot of pain. She tried to answer, but her voice was just above a whisper. She spoke in short spasms.

"Can't...hold...."

Travis placed his end of the ladder on the ground and ran to help Mathew.

"Other end!" cried Mathew, pointing. Travis looked. He was right. The ladder was upside down! They hastily reversed ends and struggled to lift the ladder against the wall.

"It's heavy," said Mathew straining against the weight.

"It's cuz we're little," said Travis back to him. He gritted his teeth as he wrestled with the heavy object. "We can do this!"

"We have to!" said Mathew.

Travis fought with every ounce of strength he could muster. His foot slipped. The ladder dropped a little. He regained his foothold and kept pushing. Beside him Mathew yelled a fierce cry of power. The ladder went up. At last the top end fell against the house.

"It's right beside you!" said Travis excitedly. "Can you get on it?"

"Be careful," said Mathew.

Travis watched breathlessly. Angie swung a leg onto the nearest ladder rung. Slowly she shifted the full weight of her body from the roof to the ladder. It took many long seconds for her to complete the move. When she finally stood on the ladder Travis felt a huge surge of relief. She made it! But then something happened to her. He wasn't sure what, but he immediately sensed it when her emotions just stopped flowing. Had she lost consciousness? All at once her hands let go and her feet slipped. She fell quickly.

Her legs dropped between rungs as she flipped over backwards, falling headfirst. Her knees hooked on a rung and jerked her to a halt. The ladder shuddered violently. Angie hung upside down, arms dangling. The uneven force of her weight shift caused the ladder to slowly tilt to the left. The whole thing started to slide down the wall.

Travis gawked. Somebody had to do something and it had to be *now*!

He leaped onto the ladder and climbed up several rungs as fast as he could. He leaned his full body weight away from the direction of the fall. The ladder slowed, but continued its descent. Travis looked down in desperation. He needed more weight.

Below him Mathew must have seen the problem. He immediately scrambled up the ladder just under Travis and held on to a lower rung. Both boys stretched their bodies outward away from the ladder's center of gravity. The ladder teetered dangerously on one leg. If it moved another inch they'd all crash onto the sidewalk. Angie moaned from her upside down position.

"Go up!" said Mathew with white-knuckled effort.

Travis understood. It was sort of like a seesaw. He went up another step. Then another. The ladder shifted. It slid across the wall and straightened up. When both legs were back on the ground, Mathew jumped off and did his best to hold it firmly in place. Travis moved to the center of the ladder and held on tight. He glanced down at his friend.

"Thanks," said Travis, trembling with fear.

"No problem," said Mathew back to him. "Better hurry. What can I do?"

"I don't even know what *I* can do."

"See if she's okay."

Travis nodded and crept up to Angie very slowly. She seemed completely gone, until he spoke to her, almost in her face. Her eyes blinked open.

"Travis? Why are you...upside down?"

"It's you, not me," he said, lifting her head to show her what had happened. "Can you pull yourself up? Like doin' a situp?"

"Sure." She tried. Her effort lasted barely a second. She shrieked. "Ohhh...my ribs!"

Travis had to think fast. They couldn't stay on the ladder all night. "I'll lift you." He ducked his head under her back and climbed up another rung. With her back supported by his shoulder all she needed now was a light shove. Travis pushed her up. Angie groaned in agony when she reached out and pulled herself into a sitting position on the same step that had caught her legs. It took her a while to untangle, but a few minutes later she was safely on the ground.

"Thanks for saving my life, boys," she said, collapsing on the sidewalk beside the house. She grimaced every time she breathed. "I'd hug you both, but it hurts too much."

"It's okay, Ms. Angie," said Mathew. "And don't worry, we called the police. They'll be here any minute."

"Where's Kelly and Melissa? Are they all right?"

Travis looked up suddenly. During their efforts to help Angie he'd forgotten all about Kelly. He didn't know where she was. Melissa either. He wasn't even sure if they were still alive until he heard their screams from the front yard.

Chapter 36

KLAWFINGER

KELLY

I took Melissa's hand and ran down the roof. Together we leaped from the house, arms and legs flailing for balance. I held my breath against the flutters in my stomach.

Thump-thump!

We landed on top of the minivan, one behind the other. The van rocked. The metal roof sagged. I collapsed in a heap on top of the van. Melissa fell off the side. Luckily she caught the luggage rack as she rolled. Somehow it twisted her around. She landed in the driveway on her feet.

She blinked up at me, eyes wild. "Oh-my-gosh! That was so cool!"

I stood up on the van. "You're crazy! We need a plan!"

"What kinda plan?"

Before I could respond something rattled overhead. I looked up. Lipsludge stood in the gutter on the roof just a few feet above me. He waved his gnarly hands.

"There! Gets the little ones!" He pointed directly at me.

I choked as everything happened at once.

"Run, Kelly!" It was Granny.

Granny and Parrish raced toward us from the house next door. Granny lugged a heavy sledgehammer. Parrish carried a much smaller hammer, like the kind used with ordinary nails. They both looked ready for a fight.

Suddenly, Parrish froze midstride. His gaze locked on something over his head beside the garage. A moment later the lobster demon lumbered from that direction into the front yard. Granny dove out of its way to avoid getting stepped on. The demon spied Melissa and me. Its eyes lit up with excitement, smiling again.

My mouth went dry. Should we get inside the van? Should we split up and run in different directions? I tried to form a plan—but my mind froze.

"Run!" Granny practically screamed it.

Forget the plan! I jumped off the van. I landed and took off in a full sprint. There was only one plan. We *had* to make it to the far end of the house. It was our only hope. If we could just get around the corner somehow we could...we could...we could do what? I had no idea what came next. All I could do was run.

Melissa stayed with me, step for step. We'd nearly made it when I glanced back.

Apparently the lobster demon never noticed the minivan. It caught one foot on it and kicked it so hard the windows exploded. A glassy spray flew out in all directions. The van flipped over on its side. The demon fell forward and struck the ground with tremendous force. It slid on its belly across the dry grass. But it landed very close to us. In a single, quick move it reached out and snagged us both, one in each claw.

"Gotcha!" Its voice made a heavy, diesel sound.

I struggled against the force of the rock-hard claw. I struck it with both fists in an effort to break loose. All I got were sore knuckles. I wasn't getting away. This was it. I'd be killed by a demon from Pandora's Cave. Sadly, my best friend would die with me. I wanted to apologize to Melissa for getting her involved in this mess. I also wanted to thank Granny just for being our granny when no one else wanted the job. Most of all I wanted to scream in terror. But to do that any of that I needed air and the demon's grip was very snug.

Snug, yes, I realized. But it didn't cut me in two like the post on the front porch. In fact it didn't really hurt. If killing us was the plan then we should have been torn to pieces by now. No. For some reason the demons wanted us alive.

The lobster demon rose to its full height. It celebrated by lifting us high in the air and pumping us up and down. "Yes!" It was very excited. My mind rocked with confusion. On the one point I wanted to get free. But at the same time I was afraid the demon might drop us.

Granny stopped before the great creature, clearly unsure what to do about it. But Parrish was quicker. He looked from his tiny hammer to the gigantic demon and back at the hammer. I heard his next thought clearly.

Size does matter! Parrish tossed the hammer and sprinted full speed back to his own house. Granny never noticed he was gone until he'd already disappeared inside.

"Mark?" Granny spun about searching for Dr. Parrish. She raised her voice. "Mark, no! They need us!" Granny took a deep breath and drew the heavy sledgehammer over her head. "Krikey. I never did have sense enough to back out of a fight. Put down my granddaughter!"

Granny slammed the sledgehammer as hard as she could onto the lobster demon's foot. The business end of the hammer crushed through the flesh. The demon's eyes bulged. It reared back its ugly head and let loose a wicked, ailing howl. My flesh went cold. I'd never heard anything so tortured and frightening in my life.

The demon staggered in pain. It stumbled against the house and smashed an elbow through the second story window in Travis' bedroom.

"Ya gots 'em, Klawfinger!" said Lipsludge. "Good work! Now gets to the tunnel!" The small demon squirmed over the edge of the roof and slid down the downspout. He dropped onto the pile of rubble that used to be the front porch.

Tunnel? What tunnel? I looked to the end of the cul-de-sac. The only thing that resembled a tunnel was a drainage pipe that went under the road. It certainly didn't have enough headroom for a twenty-foot tall lobster demon to pass through. Did they have another tunnel?

The lobster demon didn't head for any tunnel. Instead of following orders Klawfinger went after Granny. The big demon wanted revenge. Granny ran for her life.

Klawfinger raised its right claw, the one that held Melissa. The roller coaster look on Melissa's face told it all—she was frightened half to death. The claw swept across the lawn straight at Granny. Granny hit the ground, face-first. The claw whisked by her, just missing.

But the demon was quick. Before Granny could get up it brought the lethal claw straight down at her. Granny barely saw it coming. She dropped the sledgehammer and rolled out of the way.

WHUMP!

The blow missed Granny by inches. The claw pounded a shallow hole in the front lawn.

"Ooof!" It was Melissa. I looked up in alarm. The fear was gone from Melissa's face. In fact she appeared to be unconscious, or worse. Her eyelids were slack. Her body flopped limply in Klawfinger's grip.

"Don't move, Matilda!"

I heard the familiar voice and looked up. Parrish. He'd come back! I saw him running across the lawn with a five-gallon can on one shoulder. What was in the can?

"Kerosene!" cried Parrish, as if he'd heard my thoughts. He caught up with the tall demon and began pouring kerosene all over its feet and legs as high as he could reach. The demon didn't appear to even notice him at first.

"I...don't know what's going...to happen...girls," said Parrish, about to drop from exhaustion. "But be...ready!"

Soon enough he'd soaked the demon and much of the ground around it. He tossed the can in the direction of the cul-de-sac to get it clear of the house. I saw a ribbon of fuel leak out of the can as it bounced across the yard. Next Parrish took out a book of matches. He lit a match and dropped it onto one of Klawfinger's soaked feet. Flames shot up in an instant. A trail of fire swept across the yard. It raced toward the empty kerosene can.

Parrish ducked when he saw it. A second later the can exploded in a fireball. The giant demon stopped trying to squash Granny and looked down. Its legs and the ground around it were completely enveloped in flames.

Tentacles and the two-faced demon leaped out of a broken window and met Lipsludge near the front door. The demon with seven eyes appeared from a dark shadow and joined them. The demons all stared at the fire like it was something they'd never seen before.

Scorching flames raced up the lobster demon's legs above the knees. Dr. Parrish jumped back and shook his fist at the demon.

"Ha!" he said triumphantly.

Granny joined him, again holding the sledgehammer. She smiled at the sight. "Be ready to run, girls!" she said.

"It's fire!" cried Lipsludge, mesmerized.

"Yeah," said Klawfinger in his deep voice without emotion. "I'm burning."

My eyes were wide as saucers as the flames rose toward us. Maybe this wasn't such a great idea. What would happen next? Would the huge demon use me and Melissa to beat out the fire? Or would we simply burn up while trapped in its claws?

All at once the demons began to howl. It sounded like a tainted mix of hungry wolves, colicky babies, and long fingernails dragged over a chalkboard. The hair stood up on the back of my neck. A moment later Klawfinger tossed both of us aside like potato sacks. Melissa plopped onto the large boxwood at the end of the house.

She moaned and looked up in a daze. "What happened?"

"Tell you later!" Parrish quickly lifted her into his arms and hauled her away.

I landed on my hands and knees in the grass at the edge of the fire. I was so surprised to be free I couldn't believe it. I started to get to my feet when Granny tucked me under one arm like a football and followed Parrish to the garage end of the house. We ducked around the corner and nearly bumped into Angie and the boys.

"Do you believe in demons now, Dr. Parrish?" asked Travis.

"Travis, you've got my full attention," said Parrish, as he set Melissa down. "I never should have doubted you and Kelly. I never will again."

Granny kept a close eye on what was happening out front. "I guess demons don't like fire," she said. Her expression abruptly changed. "Well, I'll be stonkered! Look!"

"What?" We crowded behind her at the corner. Everyone wanted to see.

That stupid Klawfinger had sat down in the middle of the flames. He rubbed burning kerosene over himself with those great claw hands. Patches of fire burned all over his body. Instead of suffering and burning, according to plan, he giggled at the feel of the scorching heat. The other demons dove headfirst into the flames. It quickly became a regular demon pool party, but with fire instead of water.

The four-armed demon, Grund, rounded the far corner of the house in a panic. He carried what looked like a much smaller, wriggling demon over his shoulder. His excitement showed when he saw the fire, until sirens sounded in the distance.

"Police!" cried Travis. "Now we'll get 'em!"

When Grund heard the sirens he seemed to sober up on the spot. He pointed in the direction of the sound with his free hand. "Don'tcha see who's comin'? We gotta move out!"

It took a while for Lipsludge to regain his composure. Apparently, the fire felt just *too* good. He looked up slowly. "Yeah! Gets movin' you blokes! Moves it, moves it, moves it! Klawfinger, ya droppsd the girls!"

Klawfinger looked around for Melissa and me but didn't see either of us. The giant demon shrugged, looking embarrassed.

"Don't worry about 'em!" said Grund. "I got the real Kelly Bishop right here! She confessed...after I tortured her of course!"

The hairy demon gave Grund a high five. "I like torturing humans. I like to stick pins through 'em an watch 'em wriggle, ya know?"

"Shuddsup, ya morons!" said Lipsludge. "Runs fer the tunnel!"

The demons set off at a fantastic pace. From behind the house another demon appeared, one I hadn't seen yet. It had a thin, human looking body with a huge head and long, skinny fingers. The skinny demon waved a pole with a flag on it as it chased after the others.

"Come back here!" cried the skinny demon. "Bring her back! She's mine!"

By the time two police squad cars skidded to a halt in front of the house, the demons had vanished into darkness beyond the cul-de-sac. The cops searched the entire area, but all they found were footprints and splotches of oily black goo. They never found any other trace of the demons or the mystery tunnel, either. I wasn't surprised. After all, the night belonged to *them*.

Chapter 37

DEMON PROOFING

KELLY

"Demon infestation? We get that sort of thing all the time in the mountain states. Not so much in your part of the country, though." The male voice that came through the speaker on Angie's cell phone had a pleasant Midwest twang and sounded sincere.

I was dumbfounded. No way! The insurance company actually had a name for it? I tried to read the man's thoughts to be sure he wasn't kidding, but my telepathy didn't work over the phone.

"Are you serious?" said Angie to the man. I scanned her mind. Angie wasn't as concerned about getting repair money for the house, as she was timidly hopeful that somebody else in the world had encountered demons, too. It was important for her to know that we weren't alone. "You've heard about this kind of thing before?"

The agent's friendly attitude instantly changed. "Lady, do you think I'm an idiot? I mean you're trying to make a claim based on demonic destruction! That's the lamest *scam* I've ever heard. Even if it were true we don't cover demon damage. Read your policy! You're lucky I don't report you to the police." He hung up.

Angie put away her cell phone. "Jerk. Guess I should have lied and said it was vandals."

It was the morning after the attack. Angie and I were on our way back home after spending what was left of the previous night at the Thrifty-Nifty Motel. We'd gone to the motel because I'd absolutely refused to stay anywhere near the house, even after police had arrived. My reasoning was simple—what if the demons came back?

"I won't argue with that kind of logic," said Angie with an understanding nod. "We'll pack a few things and take Melissa home on the way." Angie had insisted that everyone go with them, especially Travis and Mathew. But the boys had begged her to let them finish out the night with Parrish and Granny at Dr. Parrish's house. They weren't afraid at all!

What's wrong with them? I wondered. *Don't they realize what everyone has just gone through?*

"You said it yourself, Angie," said Travis convincingly. "The demons weren't lookin' for boys."

"That's right," said Mathew, backing him up. "They only wanted Kelly."

"But if anything happened to you," said Angie. "Well, I just think you should come with us. Mom?"

I gasped. It was the only time I'd ever heard Angie use the M-word with Granny. But Granny didn't view danger the way most people did and she completely missed or ignored Angie's subtle hint for support.

"The cops'll be here all night," said Granny matter-of-factly. "You go ahead and get some sleep. We'll keep the lads safe."

With what had just happened nobody could doubt Granny's courage and devotion to "keeping the lads safe." Not after she'd single-handedly taken on a giant lobster demon with a sledgehammer. So Angie let them stay. She'd packed an overnight bag for two, then rushed off in the Mustang with us before another demon attack could occur. I breathed a sigh of relief in the back seat with Melissa. For a change it was good to be away from home.

Before searching for a motel, we dropped Melissa off at her house. Angie told her parents we'd lost power, which was certainly true enough, and it was a good enough reason to bring her home. They didn't suspect anything unusual had happened and we didn't drop any hints.

By the time we left the motel the next morning, Angie had already been on the phone with contractors, cleanup crews and home security companies. Some of them were supposed to meet us at the house. Calling the insurance company had been a long shot.

"I'm so sorry," I said, hanging my head. The wave of guilt that flowed through my bones made me feel just terrible. "If I hadn't come to live with you nothing would have happened to your house."

"If you *hadn't* come to live with us those creatures would have followed you some place else. Another family couldn't have protected you as well as we did. None of this is your fault, young lady. Those *demons* did it all on their own."

"But how can you pay to get everything fixed? There's so much damage."

"Did you forget how much money we got when Chris sold the Majik Juice recipe? Kelly, that stuff is already selling like crazy and we get paid for every single bottle. There's enough money in the bank right now to fix the house ten times over and more comes in every day. The only reason I haven't spent much of it is because Chris and I always discuss big expenditures like this before we do anything. But he's in the hospital and Dr. Sanderlyn won't let me see him and our house is full of holes, so I'm getting it all fixed. But this time I'm going to do it right. This time it's going to be demon proof!"

"Demon proof? Is there such thing?"

"We'll find out. Of course, demons are probably like cockroaches. They can always find a way in. But we're going to make it really hard for them."

"Even the big one? The lobster demon? I had nightmares about that one last night."

"Let me put it this way. Chris and I put a lot of time and a lot of love into this house. It's *our* house and no frickin' demons are going to make me leave! If they come back they're going to be in for a big surprise. We'll be ready."

I couldn't imagine what Angie had in mind, so I peeked and saw all sorts of ideas in her head, some wilder than others. Everything from imaginary demon traps to video surveillance at every corner to machineguns mounted in the hallways to an armored panic room in the basement. Man, she wasn't kidding! Angie was fired up for a fight, almost like Granny.

"Don't forget you promised to go by the emergency room today," I said firmly. "How do your ribs feel?"

"I kept ice on them all night. They're a little better and I doubt they're broken. I just hate to waste my time in the ER, Kelly. They take forever unless you're half dead. But a promise is a promise."

When we arrived at the cul-de-sac there was a small fleet of vehicles parked in front of our house. Some belonged to the contractors that Angie had called and the rest were with the police. Yellow crime scene tape was strung up all around the property, even down into the woods near the drainage pipe. The damage to the house looked worse in the daylight.

"Crime scene tape," said Angie, as if she were thinking aloud. "Is it too much to hope that the police might believe our story?"

A young female uniformed officer immediately approached us. "I'm sorry, ma'am, but we're in the middle of an investigation here. Oh, Mrs. McCormick! I didn't recognize you. You can park in the driveway. But please park *beside* the van, not behind it. We've got a tow truck coming to clear it out of here."

"You should know my insurance company won't cover any of this, including the van," said Angie. "They won't pay for the tow either, but I can write you a check."

"There's no charge for the tow. The van is evidence."

"Evidence? So you believe us?"

The officer shrugged noncommittally. "Mrs. McCormick, I realize you need to go into your house and deal with the contractors, but you'll need to wait until our crime-scene investigators are done. Perhaps you could show the outside of the house first?"

"We can do that."

The officer nodded politely and moved a squad car out of the way. Angie parked and we got out. Glass from the minivan windows crunched under our shoes.

"Your poor van," I said. "Do you think it's totaled?"

"Oh *yeah*," said Angie. "Listen, when they finally let us inside, go to your room and gather up about a week's worth of clothes and whatever you'll need for school. We'll be staying at the motel until the house is ready. In the mean time I need to speak with the contractors about fixing this mess."

"Okay."

I looked on as Angie walked up to the mostly male group and introduced herself. She shook hands all around.

"I'll explain what I want done while I show you the damage," said Angie. "We can't go inside until the police leave, but there's plenty on the outside we can talk about first. Just so you'll know, I want more done to this house than the obvious repair work. *Lots* more. Money is no object."

One contractor, a tall, bearded man wearing a *Blandford Construction* hoodie, stepped up to her. "Pardon me for asking," he said politely. "But did you get hit by a tornado?"

"No, Mr. Blandford," said Angie. "We got hit by demons, which is why police investigators are all over the place. But it's a very long story. Now if you'll follow me you can see where the window over the garage is completely missing. We need to replace it. In fact we need to replace all the windows and doors. But I want them stronger than before. In fact I want them *indestructible*."

———

While I waited for the police to let us in the house I studied the dozen or so crime-scene technicians who were on site. An FBI forensics team was working with the local police. FBI! Who brought *them* in? I tuned in to some of the thoughts and conversations around me, starting with two women working in the foyer.

"It's blood," said a large woman taking samples off the floor. "I'm sure of it."

Another woman on the stairs leaned over her. "Black blood? What causes that?"

"I don't know. Could be something genetic."

"If that's the case it'll be unique DNA. These guys could be easy to track down."

Easy to track down? I thought to myself. *She was tripping unless she knew something I didn't.*

Across the yard I noticed two more technicians exploring the area in the woods around the drainage pipe that went under the road. They took photographs and made measurements and wrote stuff down in a notebook.

"There's no way that thing came through this pipe," said one of the techs. "It was just too damn big."

"I'm with you. But the footprints lead right here and we've searched this area thoroughly. There's not another print anywhere beyond this pipe entrance. Evidence shows the creature went inside."

"It would've had to slither like a snake to fit in there. Even then...I don't know. Let's take comparative measurements off the video when we get back. I want to know exactly how big that thing was."

Did he say video? I probed inside his mind. *What video?*

The guy clearly thought his coworker had said it. "You know what video, the one the senator's kid made with his cell phone. I saw it. Man, it was freaky."

"You talkin' to me?" said the other tech, looking up surprised. "I saw it too, remember?"

"Well, you asked like you didn't know what I was talking about."

"I didn't ask. I didn't say anything at all."

While the men argued over who had spoken and who hadn't, I got excited. Mathew had recorded what happened last night! Without trying to get any more information from the police I sprinted over to Dr. Parrish's house and knocked on the front door.

About a minute passed before I heard footsteps inside. When Granny opened the door I rushed in and gave her a huge hug.

"Granny!"

"Hey, sweetie." Granny hugged me back.

Dr. Parrish came up behind Granny and patted my head. "Sorry I nearly burned you and your little friend up last night," he said, laughing. "Who would have guessed demons liked fire so much?"

I also hugged Parrish, which clearly surprised him. "Of course they like fire," I said. "I mean they're demons. Hey, is it true? Did Mathew make a video?"

Granny and Parrish looked at each other. "That's supposed to be top secret," said Parrish sheepishly. "Who told you?"

"I heard the police talking about it. What did it show?"

"Well, it showed the damage on the house," said Parrish as he went over what he remembered. "And it showed you, Angie and Melissa on the garage roof fighting those monsters. I think the FBI Agent in Charge was impressed with the way you guys held your own, at least until they outflanked you. The last thing on the video showed Angie getting picked up by your buddy with the claws."

"The big one's name was Klawfinger. That's what the others called him." I clapped my hands excitedly. "This is great! We have proof! Now we can get the police to go back in the cave and get the camcorder! It's got everything on it, even that salesman guy, Mr. Deel. He needs to be in jail, you know. He's up to something."

"Yeah, maybe," said Granny. "But you know how cops are."

I blinked up at her. I had no idea how cops were. I knew nothing about them.

Granny tried to explain. "Well, er, they can be a little difficult to convince sometimes. Don't expect them to go running down into the cave just because of a video."

"Let's face it," said Parrish. "They didn't believe a word we said until Mathew took out his cell phone and showed them what he recorded.

Smart kid, just like his daddy. That's when the cops got serious. Once they figured out Mathew was Senator Dunlop's son, they got *real* serious. Mathew gave the whole thing credibility."

"Mathew called his parents and told them everything," said Granny. "Fifteen minutes later the FBI showed up and took over the investigation. About three hours ago the Dunlops came here all the way from Camp David and took Mathew and Travis home with 'em. It was still dark and the boys couldn't hold their eyes open. We figured they'd sleep most of the day at the Dunlop's house and at least they'd be in a bed. I don't know where they'd sleep around here."

"So who's got the video? Do you? I want to see it!"

Granny laughed. "You'll never see that video, little girl, not since the FBI took Mathew's phone. It'll probably become top secret, like Area 51 and Bigfoot."

About then Angie showed up. She met both Granny and Parrish with a hug. "One of the contractors told me he could have us back in the house in two weeks, maybe less. That'll give us time to get ready for Christmas. You won't believe the security we're going to have! The house will be like Fort Knox when they're completely done. I just wish I could talk to Chris about the money we have to spend."

"What's stopping you?" said Parrish.

"Well, Dr. Sanderlyn and that mean nurse, of course. They told me not to call them, that they'd call me when it was time to see Chris."

"It's been, what, a week since Chris went in there?" said Granny. "There must be some improvement. You should call anyway."

"I can't," said Angie, shaking her head. "Mom, they're professionals! Besides, his nurse is kind of, well, she's kind of scary."

"I could fix the nurse for ya," said Granny.

"I don't want you beating up his staff."

"Angie, this is utter bulldust! You just stood up to a whole host of demons to protect the ones you love. It's on the video! If you ask me you need to give ol' Doc Sanderlyn a call right now. Treat *him* like a demon—he'll get the message. After all, you're the one paying the bill. Tell him you need to see Chris immediately, no matter what condition he's in. If you can stand up to demons, you can sure handle one old doctor."

The pep talk gave Angie some confidence. She raised her chin and pounded her fist into her palm. "You're right, mom!" she said with firmness in her voice. "It's time to find out about my husband!"

Chapter 38

PADDED CELL

DR. SANDERLYN

Dr. Sanderlyn entered the padded cell in Ward A with more caution than usual. This was the cell where they kept Chris McCormick. Sanderlyn skimmed the background notes he had taken on McCormick when the police first brought him to Sunnyside. *McCormick had survived an earthquake while inside a cave. He came out of the cave, utterly changed, according to his wife. He stopped going to work and stopped calling in sick.* Dr. Sanderlyn thought the possibility was strong that Chris suffered from post traumatic stress syndrome. He read further. *A few weeks later he invented Majik Juice. Then he had a breakdown and tried to go back into the cave.* Sanderlyn shook his head. The entire scenario was a collection of strange and seemingly disconnected events. What kind of therapy could help that man?

Admittedly McCormick's case was unusual, but certainly not unprecedented. After some thorough research into this type of abrupt personality change Dr. Sanderlyn discovered a number of similar cases that had occurred over the last ninety years. A few of the earliest cases suggested demonic possession as a possible cause, but only after vague references to some "most unusual and unexplainable events." Sanderlyn chalked those interpretations up to psychology still being a "fledgling" science at the time. The study of human behavior using true scientific investigative techniques was only just getting started way back then.

No, thought Dr. Sanderlyn, *demonic possession was an excuse put forth by religious zealots and crackpots. Most likely Chris McCormick's problem was a type of sudden onset paranoid schizophrenia, where the behavior just sort of kicked in. But why had it kicked in at all? What had happened in that cave that would make a man change so completely?*

Chris McCormick had no personal or family history of mental illness. It seemed to have come out of nowhere, almost as soon as he'd finished inventing that fruit drink. Even though he still had a full-time job as an English teacher at Chantilly High School, McCormick firmly believed he'd finished his work and needed to go live in a cave. Not just any cave, either. Pandora's Cave, the one where he'd been trapped for many hours after the quake. Dr. Sanderlyn scanned the latest notes he'd taken and took up a metal stool that was always left outside the door. He put the stool in the center of the room and sat down.

If McCormick really struggled and stretched his restraints to the max, he might be able to make it to within a few feet of the stool, but no closer. Just in case, Sanderlyn signaled to the powerfully built male orderly who'd come in behind him to take up a position not far away. No use chancing it with McCormick. They'd had problems with him already. The guy could be downright dangerous when he got upset.

Sanderlyn studied his patient with experienced eyes. Chris lay on the padded floor curled into a ball. His upper body was tightly wrapped in a straight jacket, with light, metal chains to restrict his movement. Sanderlyn had treated hundreds of patients over the years and as a result he pretty well knew what to expect. Sure enough, Chris pretended to ignore him, like he always did. Some behavior patterns never changed. But Chris knew he was there, Sanderlyn was sure of it. He'd seen him twitch when the door opened.

"Hello, Chris," said Dr. Sanderlyn in his most professional, but tender voice. "How are you feeling today?"

Chris kept his back to him while he responded. "I'm feeling like I need to go outside. I'd like to go to Crystal Creek Park for a visit."

"Crystal Creek Park again. Of course, this has nothing to do with going back into Pandora's Cave, I presume."

Chris jerked around. He drew back his lips and snarled. "Of course it does! It has everything to do with going back into the cave! My work is done! The Boss wants me back! Let me go, you stupid human slug!"

Dr. Sanderlyn drew back instinctively, but he tried not to show any fear or surprise. The orderly took a step forward, but the doctor waved him off. Chris was playing his control game again. Some patients were stronger than others and could hold out like this for weeks, even months. But science had ways of re-teaching normal behavior, even in such dangerous and deteriorated individuals as Chris. Sanderlyn offered his "carrot."

"What if I were to let you go back there? Just for a visit, mind you. Would you like that?"

Chris looked at him wildly. "Of course! Take me now or I'll rip off your arms and put them in my soup!"

"Oh, it won't be now. Not today anyway. There are papers to fill out and arrangements to make. But it's not entirely out of the question, though I'll need something from you first. It's not much, really. If you help me a little, I'll try to help you. What do you say?"

Chris eyed him suspiciously, but nodded slightly. "Listening."

"I need you to answer some questions, that's all. Honestly. A moment ago you called me human, as if you think of yourself as something other than human. Are you a god?"

Chris flinched. "You're such a fool! Let me go!"

"You know I can't do that unless you give me what I want."

"What do you want, you pathetic piece of walking, talking man-flesh?"

Dr. Sanderlyn was taken aback. He had never been called that before, not even by Chris. "I want you to tell me why you just called me human. And I want to know specifically why you want to return to the cave. What's there for you? How do you plan to live? Work with me, Chris, and I'll arrange a trip to the park very soon."

Chris scowled at him. "You lie!" He rolled over and faced the wall again.

Dr. Sanderlyn was about to try a new tactic when his cell phone vibrated. He usually ignored it when he was working with a patient, but this seemed like a good moment to take a break. He answered.

"Yes?"

"Dr. Sanderlyn, I have Mrs. McCormick on line two. She's asking to see her husband again."

"Tell her he's not ready to see anyone, especially her. I'll try to arrange a visit around New Year's, if she can be patient."

"Sir, this woman was easy to deal with a week ago. You'd better talk to her this time, she means business."

Dr. Sanderlyn considered the situation. Nurse Agnes was an absolute tyrant on the phone. She could frighten or manipulate almost anyone. Mrs. McCormick had been amiable and easily directed. Something must have happened that steeled her up. He punched a button on his cell phone and cleared his throat.

"Hello, Mrs. McCormick. This is Dr. Sanderlyn. How can I help you today?"

Chapter 39
DO YOU BELIEVE IN MONSTERS?

MARIA

Maria Sanchez wasn't in the mood for religion right now. She wanted to be left alone. As she sat before the mirror in her bedroom and brushed her long, shining black hair, she wondered why her parents couldn't understand how she felt, even after she'd made it so perfectly clear to them. They were about to attend Mass as they did every Sunday, and she was expected to go. *The Sanchezes go to mass as a family! It's what God wants!* How many times had she heard her father say that? It was practically the family motto. He should carve it on a sign and hang it over the hearth in the den.

She slammed her hairbrush on the vanity and ground her teeth. Was it so much to ask to be left alone for once in her life? Didn't they care how she felt? How could they not sense the terrible internal anguish that consumed her like quicksand?

Maria needed to be alone to think, to clear her mind of all the rubbish that had been trapped in there for weeks. But thinking caused problems because eventually all thoughts returned to Jon Bishop. She hated him. It was hard to believe she'd ever loved him, though didn't someone once say you can only hate the ones you truly love? In her case that made good sense. Love and hate were powerful emotions that could rule a young woman's life, take control in ways nobody really understood. Her dad said it was hormones. Maria saw differently. For Maria it was all about the heart.

Why did she continue to care? If none of her feelings for Jon mattered any more, then why was her pain still so jagged and relentless? He'd gone off to New York to become the "greatest magician in the world". He might pull it off, too, she realized fearfully. But the magic he was doing, well, it was inhuman. And the way he'd acted after the cave trip—he'd become a total stranger to her. All because of that damn cave. She hated Pandora's Cave and everything about it. If only she could somehow destroy it with a mere thought.

But perhaps now there was a different kind of hope. Kurt Lazarus had called her last night. Normally she would have hung up on him, or never answered his call if she'd recognized his number. But he seemed different this time. He apologized to her right off for the way he'd acted in the past. That was new. Kurt never apologized for anything, he'd inherited too much of his father's foolish pride to do that. Kurt said other things, too.

"Why have you called me?" she asked, angry to hear his voice. Angry at his gall to think she would ever listen to what he had to say. Angry at *everything*.

"I want to go out with you, Maria."

"I know how you treat the girls you go out with. Drop dead, Kurt."

"No, I've changed, believe me. I've seen things…things you couldn't imagine."

"What sort of things?"

"Maria…do you believe in…monsters?"

He'd actually said it, choked out the words. *Do you believe in monsters?* Nobody could have expected that one coming from Kurt Lazarus. She shuddered. Kurt had called to ask her out, but first he wanted to confess to her about seeing monsters. She'd thought he was either crazy, high, or both, until he swore to her he would never commit a crime again. He even promised to be nice to her and everybody else. "Polite" was the word he'd used. He must have found that one in a thesaurus, it wasn't part of his own vocabulary.

He said other things that made her wonder. He offered to take her any place she wanted to go for dinner, any time, and then to any movie or show she wanted to see, it didn't matter to him. Even a chick flick! To her amazement she hadn't tossed the phone across the room when she'd finally hung up. It had been the first time since she'd known Kurt that she hadn't gotten mad at him. They'd actually said goodbye to each other instead of go-to-hell, or something much, much worse.

Kurt seemed almost likable. Because he believed in monsters.

She thought about him replacing Jon in her heart. Was it even possible? Her mom would say she was vulnerable, on the rebound from a broken relationship. She should wait. But Maria wasn't so sure. Kurt was a nice looking guy, and rich. If his cruel streak was truly over he'd be worth giving a second chance. Not only that, but Mr. Lazarus owned the strip mall where her parents' restaurant was located and Kurt had guaranteed Maria that if she went out with him on a regular basis he could get his dad to lower the rent. That would help her parents out a lot. Was seeing Kurt a possibility? Could a relationship with a guy like that work out after all?

When she stood up from the vanity a tiny strip of white at the edge of the mirror caught her eye. It looked like a piece of paper had been wedged between the mirror and the wood frame. She used her fingernails to dig out a small rectangle of paper. She gasped when she saw what it was. A wallet-sized photograph of Jon.

Maria was surprised. She thought she'd thrown all his pictures away. How had it gotten there? Then she remembered hiding it when she and Jon had first started dating. Jon hadn't met her parents yet, and she'd been certain they wouldn't go for her dating some orphaned guy with no real home or family. As it turned out, her dad and Jon had gotten along great. Jon often spoke about how he needed to support his younger brother and sister, like he was their father or something. He had strong feelings of family, even though he didn't have parents any more. And his willingness to accept responsibility had reminded Mr. Sanchez of himself. Her dad had always spoken fondly of Jon. He saw him like a son.

"You told me you loved me, Jon Bishop," said Maria, staring at the picture. "You told me we were going to spend the rest of our lives together. How could you say all of that if you didn't mean it? After all the time that was ours, how could you say you *never* loved me? You make me sick!"

She tore the photo into tiny pieces and threw them all into a small trash can in the corner of her room. "I hate you! You'll never have my heart again!"

Maria straightened her dress and checked herself over one last time in the mirror. She was dressed well enough for church. If God didn't like the way she looked he could just.... She didn't know how to finish the thought. What could she say that would upset God?

All at once she glanced back at the trashcan. She hurried over to it, glaring into the bottom of the can. Tears welled up in her eyes and fell over the pieces of torn photograph like rain on a funeral.

"Why did you leave me, Jon? Where have you gone?"

JON

Jon Bishop walked along the busy highway with his thumb out and his T-shirt blowing in the cold, stiff breeze. His eyes were fixed on the city skyline across the river ahead of him. New York City: the greatest city in the world. It was the only place he could go to become the greatest magician in the world. He could almost feel its energy.

Dozens upon dozens of cars flew past him, the occupants never paying him any mind. But it didn't matter to Jon. He really didn't care if they picked him up or not. The important thing was to keep moving. Even if he had to walk the rest of the way he'd get to New York eventually. Jon had learned by watching other travelers that if he stuck out his thumb while he walked, sometimes people would give him a ride. Getting rides brought him closer to his goal much faster than walking. It was certainly worth the effort to hold up his thumb.

Sure enough it happened again. A silver minivan pulled over in front of him and stopped. Jon had also learned to *run* to the vehicle so the driver wouldn't get impatient and leave him behind. This time he sprinted and arrived at the passenger side door at the same time the window opened. An elderly man and woman smiled at him. The woman drove, the man sat in the passenger seat.

"You going to the city, young fella?" asked the man, whose white mustache curled up stiffly to a point on both sides of his mouth.

"Yes, I am going to the city," said Jon with a smile. "I am going to New York City. I can see it just over there."

"That's right," said the man. "We can only take you as far as Times Square, but if that works for you, hop on in."

The passenger side door slid open by itself. For a moment Jon thought that the man and woman might have magic of their own until he remembered the doors on Angie's minivan did the same thing. He climbed inside and sat back in the warm car. The door closed.

"Let me guess," said the woman, whose white hair had been stacked in plate-sized rings on top of her head. "You're going to New York to be an actor. Or a singer. No, you look athletic. You're a dancer. Right?"

"I am going to New York City to become the greatest magician in the world."

"Magician?" said the man. "That's different. Marge and me, well, we're the greatest hotdog vendors in the world. That's our supplies behind you."

Jon glanced behind him because he sensed the man wanted him to. Other than the fact they were giving him a ride he had no interest in what these people did for a living.

"Aren't you cold?" asked the woman named Marge. "It's barely forty degrees out there and you don't even have a coat."

"No, I am not cold."

"Are you from England? You sound like you're from some place like that. I had a buddy from London. He was a newspaper reporter."

"I am not from England," said Jon, bored. "I am from Virginia."

"I see. So what kind of magic do you do?"

"Can you pull a rabbit out of a hat?" asked Marge.

"Yes. But everybody does that. I can do anything."

"Anything?" asked the man jokingly. "How'd you like to magic me about five grand right now? I could use the money." He laughed at the thought as he looked back at Jon and winked.

Jon considered for a moment. He turned one hand over, palm down, then turned it back up again. In his hand was a stack of one hundred-dollar bills, still in the wrapper. The old man's eyes lit up.

"Wow! Damn, boy, you *are* good!" He got even more excited when Jon handed him the cash. "I can't take your money, son. You're going to need it for your shows."

"I do not need it," said Jon. "You can have it. I got it for you."

"Is it real?" asked his wife. The old man tapped her on the arm and shook his head.

"That's not *even* polite, Marge." Then he looked at Jon. "Is it?"

"It is real. Money is easy to magic, as you say."

"Easy?" The old man and his wife exchanged glances. He took out a business card and gave it to Jon. "If you need a place to stay while you're in the city you just call the number on that card. That's my cell. We'll make sure you have a real nice place, okay?"

Jon took the card and put it in his pocket. "Okay." He sat back and gazed at the approaching New York City skyline. His time was near. Soon he would be the greatest magician in the world.

Chapter 40
DEMON FIGHT

DONNIVEE

Donnivee Fox sat on the stone floor guarded by a dozen slobbering, toothy demons who watched her with eyes that never blinked. They talked about her, too, she could tell. They spoke in low voices so she couldn't hear them and they said *bad* things about her. *Unspeakable* things. Things that would make everyone laugh at her and put her down and try to hurt her. Donnivee had scores of issues that really set her off, but when she heard people talking about her...dammit! That was at the top of her list! It made her want to kick in their teeth and break their arms and punch their faces into hamburger! She stood up suddenly. Her mind was a haze of scathing hatred. Her fists were clenched. She'd fight every one of them! Only...these things around her weren't people. They weren't even close.

She glanced over her shoulder and understood why she was so popular. They were cooking something—or getting ready to—inside a massive, black pot that was bigger than her bedroom at home. The acrid smell of a coal fire burned all around it, causing heavy steam to rise from inside the pot. Two lanky, horned demons stood on a rock scaffold built beside the fire and stirred the brew with long wooden poles. She'd already seen several buckets of body parts tossed into the mix, including a human hand.

In spite of the unholy warmth inside the cave Donnivee shivered. It wasn't easy to face up to the fact that most likely she was going to be lunch.

More than anything right now she wanted to run. She might have tried, except for the shackles on her ankles that were chained to a thick iron ring embedded in the floor. The shackles were rough and tight and had already rubbed her legs raw. Run? She almost laughed. Even if she got away where could she possibly go? She looked at the long stone trail that wound upward through the enormous cavern. If she could make it to the mouth of the cave she could get home. She knew the way from there because when the demons had brought her in she'd seen the sign, *Pandora's Cave*. She'd seen the ranger station too. She knew where she was. But getting that far would be a problem.

It'd be an uphill run for a good quarter-mile, maybe further. And if she made it to the top she'd have to deal with the winding, pitch-black tunnels that these creatures knew so well. She'd never find her way through the tunnels without a light. Apparently demons didn't need light, they could see in total darkness.

Donnivee had to face the facts. She'd probably never get out of this cave alive. This must be how a bird feels when it's caught in the jaws of a cat just before the chewing starts.

She licked her dry, cracked lips, salty from the tears and sweat that had poured out of her under the latex mask. That stupid mask. She wanted to remove it, to let her face cool off and her hair hang down, but the demons didn't realize it was a mask. They thought it was her real face. They'd even tied a gag around the mouth of the mask to keep her quiet, never realizing the rubbery teeth inside the rubbery lips were all fake. The silly mask might be the only thing keeping her alive at this point.

"What do we do with 'er?" said the four-armed demon, Grund, the one who had brought her all the way here on his shoulder. "Why'd the Boss want us to get 'er?"

"The traitor human wants 'er," said the little one, the one the others called Lipsludge.

"If ya ask me the Boss listens to that filthy human slime way too much," said Grund with a mutinous look in his three yellow eyes.

"Don't lets him hears you says that. Or you'll bees in da soup instead of the Kelly Bishop."

There. They said it. They were going to throw her in the soup and eat her. All because they thought she was Kelly. Donnivee began to shake. The mind-numbing fear of certain death grew within her and spread like cancer to every part of her body. A noxious pain slithered through her stomach. Suddenly, she gagged. It was a big one, as if she'd stuck her finger down her throat and jiggled it side to side. The gag turned into a wave of uncontrollable dry heaves. She dropped to her hands and knees, doubled over in spastic contractions. She heaved repeatedly. Her face was flushed behind the mask, her belly ached from the strain. Somehow she got it under control and held back the vomit. Good thing, too. Throwing up inside a mask would be just plain nasty. Especially when she couldn't take it off. When she was done she looked up. The demons gawked at her with baffled expressions. Guess they'd never seen another demon almost toss her cookies.

A tall gray demon with arms and fingers like long, skinny tree branches appeared through an arched doorway. The doorway led into an even larger cave where a strange reddish glow lit up both caverns. Donnivee saw movement in the other room, but not enough to know who or what was moving or what they were doing. Often she heard what sounded like the crack of a whip. A moment later she'd hear an agonized scream. Once she heard an entire chorus of grisly screams that made her skin crawl. They sounded human. Donnivee decided not to think about the other cave.

"Where'd Klawfinger go?" asked the gray demon.

"He went to get da Boss," said another.

Lipsludge stood up and ambled over to Donnivee. He stood nearly eye-to-eye with her, though she was still kneeling.

"I been wonderins, human," said Lipsludge, tilting his head as he studied her face. "What's da traitor human wants with da likes of you? You looks more like one of us, than one of dem. How comes he wants ya?"

Donnivee's fear had reached the boiling point. Hell, she was already on the menu. What'd she have to lose by fighting back now? She clamped her jaw firmly and threw a well-aimed right cross at the little demon. The blow caught Lipsludge squarely in the side of the head. It was so strong it lifted him off the floor and sent him rolling into the feet of a large, hairy demon with seven red eyes.

Donnivee scowled under the mask. She forgot she even had it on. Her eyes were on fire. The demons around her tensed up. She expected them to retaliate. Sure they would. The entire group would attack her to avenge their little buddy. And she'd fight them to the death. Then they could eat her if that's what they wanted, but at least she'd be dead first, not cooked alive in the soup.

The demons looked from Donnivee to Lipsludge and back to Donnivee. They all started laughing. Lipsludge stood up groggily and staggered a few steps. It took him a second to refocus. When he did, he bared his teeth and claws. He was going to attack. Donnivee willingly braced herself for the fight.

At that moment the towering lobster demon stomped back into the room from the other cavern. Donnivee gasped when she saw it. Somehow it seemed even bigger in the cavern. But the lobster demon's head barely reached the shoulder of the gigantic creature that followed it.

An enormous red demon ducked under the arch and strutted in from the other cave. It was thick and massive, with powerfully muscled legs and arms, and a large head with a single horn growing from the center of its forehead. As it moved it seemed to be chatting with someone—or something—that was much smaller.

Donnivee nodded slowly. So *this* was the creature they were waiting for. This was the one that would kill her and toss her lifeless body into the soup. Oddly, being ripped to shreds by such a terrible creature seemed better than boiling alive.

Then she saw the man. He was tall, dark and handsome with a touch of gray at the temples, just like in the movies. He looked important, too, all dressed up in a dark three-piece suit and tie, with highly polished shoes and a briefcase that perfectly matched what he wore. Donnivee's hopes rose when he looked her way. She smiled at him, hoping to get his attention. But again she forgot about the mask.

The four-armed demon, Grund, got very excited and ran up to the big red one. He pointed right at Donnivee. "I got her, Boss! The others were playing in fire, but *I* did my job!"

Right away Lipsludge forgot about Donnivee's right cross. He scowled at Grund. "Yer gots lucky, Grund! I'll makes ya sorry ya saids that!"

"Shut up," said the Boss in a deep bass voice that seemed to vibrate right through the stone floor. "You all did your jobs."

The demons that had participated in "the Kelly Bishop" raid stood up tall and proud. But the man in the suit didn't seem impressed.

"This is the girl you brought us?" said the man with a tiny hint of doubt. His rich baritone voice had an almost magical quality to it. "*This* is Kelly Bishop?" He went over beside Donnivee and studied her. Her heart pounded harder than it had before. What was he doing? Why did they want Kelly? She noticed the man's skin was pale, but all his outstanding features were dark, almost black. The hair, the neatly trimmed beard and mustache, the color of his eyes. Even his unbreakable gaze had a certain darkness about it. But who was he? Why was he here? It didn't matter as long as he'd come to rescue her.

"I told you they were crack troops," said the Boss with pride.

But the man clearly wasn't satisfied. He looked at Donnivee hard, like he knew all the lies she kept hidden deep inside her heart.

"I'm sure your troops are as good as you say, your Lordship. But this is *not* the girl."

Grund disagreed. "But she said she was da Kelly Bishop! She said it!"

"Dey all saids it," said Lipsludge. "Dey was protectins 'er."

The man looked at Lipsludge, almost impressed. "Very astute, young demon. There may be hope for your kind yet. Yes, this one did tell you she was Kelly Bishop. But the only person she was protecting was herself."

He reached down and pulled off the mask.

Donnivee blinked in relief. Cooler air rushed across her cheeks. She wiped her face on both sleeves in an effort to clean up.

The demons all let out a simultaneous gasp. Some changed their position to get a better look at her.

"He pulled her head off!" said Grund.

"But she's got 'nother head inside!" said Tentacles.

"I never seen a human that could change heads!" said another.

Now that he'd exposed her, she understood he wasn't there to help her escape. But how could he have known? Only one way. He had read her mind. She became nervous and upset.

"Wrong human girl?" said the Boss with a shrug. "So what's da problem, Mr. Deel? You got magic. You can take the real girl any old time you want."

"I'm afraid my best chance to get her was ruined by your *crack* troops." Mr. Deel's words dripped with heavy sarcasm. The Boss growled at the slight. Deel went on. "You see, your Lordship, there are other powers in this game. Unfortunately the real Kelly Bishop has made a ripple. She's been noticed. At this point I'm forced to remain subtle. If she happens to die, my name cannot be associated with her at all. Do you understand?"

The Boss nodded. "So if *we* take her for the soup, *you* get blamed?"

"Exactly, your Lordship. That was my one chance to utilize your skills and personnel to acquire her. But since your death squad failed I'll need to think of something else."

"What do we do with this one?"

The man looked at Donnivee like she was nothing more than a lowly cockroach. She felt it, too. He brushed her off with a wave of his hand. "Do what you want."

The Boss grinned horribly. "Grund. Put her in the soup!"

Before Donnivee realized it, the four-armed demon lifted her over his shoulder and held her so tight she could hardly breathe. Lipsludge came over and unlocked her shackles. The small demon grinned at her from below.

"I gets her eyes!" said Lipsludge, drooling with excitement. "Her eyes is mine!" Grund started up the stone steps to the top of the scaffold.

"I can get her for you!" cried Donnivee desperately. "I can get Kelly Bishop!"

Grund lifted her over his head. He was about to drop her into the boiling soup when the Boss stopped him with a glance.

"You need me!" she said again. "I can bring Kelly Bishop to you! I know her! We're friends!"

"No, you're not friends," said Mr. Deel, knowing her thoughts. Grund stood over the pot like a statue, waiting for his next order.

Donnivee looked down. A sickly green liquid bubbled below her in the pot. The smell of vomit and decay rose in the steam. Every so often a human body part would rise to the top while the demon *chefs* stirred. First a head, then a hand, then part of a man's thigh still wrapped in a pantleg. After that she saw a body part from some other creature, possibly a demon. Donnivee gulped, terrorized. No, she didn't want to die like this. She didn't want to die at all.

"Ah," continued the man as if he were still scanning her thoughts. "But you do have an intense hatred of the Bishop girl. It's completely irrational, but you despise her worse than anyone else on the planet, except for yourself, of course. You may be useful to us yet. Your Lordship, perhaps you should hold off on the soup idea. She's young and healthy. I suggest you put her to work in the mines. Let her have a glimpse of the future of mankind."

The Boss laughed. It sounded like a diesel locomotive struggling to get moving. "I like the way you think, Mr. Deel. Evil, like me. Grund, take her to the mines!"

Donivee practically fainted with relief. The handsome man who dealt bravely and cleverly with demons had saved her life. Grund dropped her to his shoulder and lugged her back down the scaffold steps. Donnivee saw Lipsludge running along beside her like a small boy full of excitement.

"Guess you won't get my eyes now, will you?" said Donnivee boldly.

"No, I don'ts," said Lipsludge back at her. But she could tell he wasn't disappointed. "I gets somethin' better. I gets ta tortures ya every day for the rest of yer life!" He clapped his hands and danced along as Grund took Donnivee through the archway into the other cave, into the red place—the place where people screamed.

Chapter 41
SLEEPLESSNESS

KELLY

"Nobody beats sleep." I spoke to an empty room, to no one there. "Nobody. When you're sleepy, sleep can knock you out with one quick punch in-the-you-know-what!"

I laughed at myself. What did that even mean? I sat at a table in the motel room surrounded by homework, struggling to stay awake. Somehow I'd fought off sleep for three days now, but I couldn't stay awake much longer.

"This no-sleep thing's makin' me weird." I spoke to my reflection in the mirror. Of course it was. My eyelids were so heavy I couldn't see the words on the page of my English book. More than anything in the world I wanted to close my eyes and drift away for a nice, long nap. I would have, too.

But since the demon attack, sleep had been hard to manage. Whenever I tried it I had terrible nightmares, and they were getting worse every time. I'd gotten to the point where I was downright *afraid* to sleep. All at once I had an idea.

What if I dozed off for just a few minutes *before* the nightmares set in? If it worked I could repeat the process dozens of times until it all added up and I'd gotten enough rest. Or maybe I'd get lucky this time and there wouldn't be any nightmares. Perhaps I'd fall into a deep, *dreamless* sleep with no demons to harass me. Thinking about it really didn't matter because I was totally exhausted. Dreamless or not, I plopped my head on the table and fell asleep in an instant.

It felt wonderful to have my eyes blissfully shut. Everything around me seemed peaceful and calm.

I heard a scratching sound. I sat up quickly. What was that? Was somebody at the door? All at once the power went off. The room was instantly dark. I rose in a deep panic. With demons looking for me, darkness was the *worst* place to be. I noticed small bands of light filtering through the closed blinds. The motel's exterior lights! I had to get outside. It was my only hope.

I rushed to the door and opened it.

"Demon Nation!" The creature's words were hoarse and deep. At the same instant a huge, scaly hand reached in. Its long claws caught me by the throat. I screamed as loud as I could and never made a sound.

I woke up at the table, gasping for air. I searched the lighted room, wide-eyed and fearful. I felt awake, but was I *really*? It was getting more and more difficult to tell. I checked the time on my phone and saw it was just after six. Angie and Travis should get back soon with the groceries and some supper.

A car door slammed outside. It startled me so bad I nearly jumped out of the chair. I got up and peeked through the blinds. Just some ordinary people moving their things into the room next door. No demons. How do you spell RELIEF?!

I was definitely awake. Wide awake...again. But for how long this time?

Okay, I needed the rest, no doubt about it. That was one reason I'd asked to stay in the motel while Angie and Travis went to the store. But the other reason I'd stayed—the *real* reason—was because I needed to know if I could even *be* alone any more. For the last three days all I could think about were those terrible monsters coming after me. Now I was all by myself. This was the first test. Would I pass?

Still trembling from the bad dream I spoke aloud: "Maybe I'll surprise Angie and put my clothes away. That'll keep me awake for a while."

I had literally been living out of my suitcase since we got to the motel and by now the piles of dirty and clean clothes were all mixed up. Angie had asked me to put the clean clothes in the drawers and the dirty ones someplace else if I wanted them washed. I hadn't done it yet because the job seemed too much like work, but in the end it took me only a few minutes to get the suitcase emptied.

That was easy enough. Now for the backpack.

I set my old pink Barbie backpack on the bed and unzipped the largest section. Seeing the backpack reminded me of Pandora's Cave. It also reminded me of the promise Dr. Parrish had made a couple days ago. He told me he would call FBI Special Agent in Charge Smith and ask him to go back into the cave and look for Brandon's camcorder. It was a logical and good idea because the tape in Brandon's camcorder held plenty of evidence that the demons existed, even more than Mathew's cell phone video. I hoped it showed that Mr. Deel guy too. The camcorder was the answer to my problems. It was the only thing that would get *somebody* to do *something.*

The question was, had Parrish made the call yet? What if he forgot? Would it be rude to remind him?

Something else nagged at me, too. When Travis and I escaped from the cave that day, the hideous creatures had threatened us both.

We know where you live, Kelly and Travis. We'll grab you in the dark, when the night comes. The dark belongs to usss!

But they hadn't threatened Parrish at all. Why not? He'd been in the cave, too, and he heard what they said. So why didn't they want him? And how come they didn't try to get Travis the other night? I was certainly glad they didn't, but the threat was to get us *both.* Were demons so dumb they could only capture one kid at a time? Or did it all mean something else? I didn't like being singled out.

One other thing bothered me, too, something that probably had a lot to do with the nightmares. The demons had come all the way from Pandora's Cave that night just for *the Kelly Bishop.* But they left *without* me. Didn't that mean they'd be back?

I removed the last of the clothes from the backpack and put them in the drawer. That was when I noticed something bulging in both side pockets. I opened the first side zipper and was amazed at what I saw.

A moldy, green and white peanut butter and jelly sandwich.

"Yuck!" I tossed the sandwich in the trashcan. Angie had made the sandwich weeks ago when we'd gone into the cave. I screwed up my face as I unzipped the other side pocket. No telling what slimy thing was in there.

Whatever it was had been tightly wrapped inside a black trash bag. I had no recollection of putting it there. Maybe Travis had found some rocks he wanted to keep.

I unwrapped the trash bag and dropped the item on the bed. My eyes got wide as saucers when I saw what it was. My heart began to pound. Brandon's camcorder! It had been in my old Barbie backpack the whole time!

"Oh-my-gosh!" I said aloud. "Jon must have put it in there!" This was incredible. The FBI didn't have to send anybody into the cave after all. They just needed to look at the tape.

I took up the camcorder and switched it on. Nothing happened at all, and I soon saw why. The lens was cracked and so was the chamber that housed the tape. I pushed the eject button several times, but again nothing happened. Either the camcorder was broken or the battery was dead. It didn't matter. I'd found it and the tape was still inside. I was absolutely certain Agent Smith would want to see it. And when he did *somebody* would do *something* about those demons!

I looked up at my reflection in the mirror. "Oh, no. What if Dr. Parrish already told Agent Smith about the camcorder? What if they're going to the cave right now? I gotta stop them!"

I dialed Parrish's number on my cell phone. He answered. "Dr. Parrish?" I almost shouted.

"Kelly," said Parrish a little surprised. "How are you? Listen, I know why you're calling and I'll be honest with you, I haven't contacted Agent Smith yet, no excuses. But I promise I'll do it tonight, okay?"

"No! *Don't* call him! Not yet, anyway! I found the camcorder, Dr. Parrish. It was in my old backpack all the time!"

"And the tape?"

"Still inside! But the camcorder's broken. We gotta find somebody who can fix it or at least get the tape out."

"It's a mini-DV camcorder, right? I can get the tape out. I can also record the entire video on my computer and put it on a DVD or flash drive so anybody can watch it. It might take time if the tape is damaged, but I've got some great software for that kind of thing."

"How soon can you do it?"

"Let me speak to Angie and we'll figure it out."

"She's not here. She's shopping."

"Okay, when she gets back, tell her to call me. We'll find out once and for all what's on the tape!"

"Yes! Thank you!"

As I hung up I suddenly realized there could be only one reason the demons had come after *me* and nobody else. Besides Travis, only one person connected *me* to the demon world. *Mr. Deel.* He knew I was telepathic, just like him. He'd been inside my mind like I'd been in his. When he wasn't driving around in his limo he was giving speeches to demons. It had to be Deel!

But why would Mr. Deel want me to be demon food? Was it just because I was telepathic? Or was it something much darker? I lay back on the bed, holding the camcorder close against me. Now more than ever I needed to know what was on that tape. Everyone in the world needed to know.

While I waited for Angie and Travis to return I got drowsy again. But this time it didn't matter. I knew when the police saw the tape they'd probably send a whole army down into the cave to deal with the demons. I'd be safe and my family would be safe. Finally I wasn't afraid any more. At last somebody would do something and I could close my eyes again at night.

Then for the first time in three days I fell into a wonderful, deep sleep that lasted nearly twelve hours. Holding the camcorder close, like a Teddy-cam, I dreamed nice dreams about *somebody* doing *something* about the demon conspiracy.

The End? Not even close...

The Demon Conspiracy Series continues with Book #2:
The Doomsday Shroud

Chapter 1

DEMONS DON'T DIE

KELLY

When the demon alarm went off in our house at three in the morning (on a school night no less!) it felt like spikes were being pounded into my eardrums. It was *so* loud! I *hated* that thing! But there wasn't time to worry about the noise. I had to be quick or I'd be demon fast food before dawn. Let's face it, there's only one reason for the demon alarm to go off. *Demons!* They were after me again. I put on shoes, grabbed a metal baseball bat and got ready to rumble.

In the hallway I met Travis, who was loading up a slingshot with an egg-sized steel marble. His snow-white hair stuck up worse than usual and he was barefoot, but he was ready for battle. I was scared, but he looked like he wanted a good fight. I don't think he realized what kind of danger we were in.

I gotchur back, said Travis inside my head. *Go to the panic room.*

Not yet, I thought back to him. *I want to see the demon.*

You sure?

I nodded. Our mental connection was loud and clear in spite of the blaring alarm.

All at once Granny flew out of her bedroom still dressed in work clothes. She had on blue jeans, a white blouse and her black leather jacket with the logo and name of her motorcycle club printed on the back. *Satan's Sidekicks*. Granny shouted over the irritating alarm.

"Where's Angie?" She hefted a ten-pound sledgehammer, though in my opinion she really didn't need a weapon. That woman is *strong*. She's fearless, too. She'd risk her life to protect Travis and me. She already had.

A moment later Angie burst from her room carrying an i-Pad and a container of Mace the size of a large bug spray can.

"One demon!" she shouted. "Behind the Christmas tree! This one's got *two* heads." She held up the i-Pad, which contained an App that ran our security system. On the screen I saw a digital thermal image of a two-headed *something* waiting for us in the den downstairs.

Granny squared her broad shoulders. "Krikey, how'd it get in?"

"We'll figure that out later."

"Should we wait for the police?" I only asked because some demons can be tough to fight. Plus the alarm system was hooked into the local police department, so a squad car would be at the house any moment.

Angie shook her head and pointed to the stairs. "It took them twenty minutes to get here last time. I'll take lead."

Granny raised her hammer. "I got rear." It actually sounded more like *I got reah*. I loved her Australian accent.

This was the third time in a month demons had tried to grab me in the night. The first time had been right after Thanksgiving, when my family saved us, but not before the demons made a wreck of our house.

It took two weeks to get the place fixed the way Angie wanted. The same night we moved back in another demon came after me. It was like they'd been watching, waiting for their next chance to get me. But that time we were ready.

Motion detectors had caught the creature's image and security lights lit up the outside like a football field. The demon had run off. Video surveillance cameras got some great shots of it, so we knew it wasn't a deer or some other large animal that set off the alarm. That particular demon had bright yellow skin, four arms and his name was Grund. We'd met before.

But unlike Grund, the two-headed demon downstairs had somehow gotten past the security system and *inside* the house.

So why were demons after *me*, little ol' Kelly Bishop? It could be because I knew about their secret plan to take over the surface of the earth in the next five years. Or maybe it was my telepathy, though I couldn't read a demon's mind at all, so technically I wasn't a threat to them. But demons have human friends and one of them had a *serious* problem with me being telepathic.

Until a few weeks ago I figured I was the only telepath in the world, and I'll admit I got a little cocky. But then I ran into a man named Mogen Deel, who's got the same ability, only he's *way* stronger and dangerous, too. He nearly killed me with his mind! It's like Granny once said, it doesn't matter how good you are at something, there's always going to be someone else who's better. When it came to demons, Mr. Deel called the shots and they did mostly what he said. For some reason he wanted me on the demon menu.

I wish Jon and Chris were here, I thought to Travis. *We could use the manpower.*

Travis nodded. Jon Bishop, our sixteen-year-old brother, was pretty much an expert with swords and martial arts in general. But Jon couldn't help us now; he'd gone off to New York City to become the greatest magician in the world, though, honestly, we almost felt safer that he wasn't around. I think he might be demonically possessed.

Chris McCormick was our foster dad who'd invented a fruit drink a few months ago that made the family rich. He went crazy and they locked him away in a psycho ward. He's probably possessed too.

Travis and I followed Angie down the stairway. The foyer was shadowy, but the den was so black I couldn't even see the sofa in front of us. Angie slowly reached into the room for the light switch. We tensed, ready for action. She flipped the switch.

Nothing happened. Demons had cut off the power again! So now we had to enter a pitch-black room to fight a two-headed monster that could see in the dark. And the monster wanted to kill *me*. *Nice.*

Angie touched the screen on the monitor and the annoying alarm stopped. OMG! The silence surprised me so much I stumbled into Travis.

"Computer, backup lights!" Angie shouted it, probably because her ears were still ringing from the alarm. Her voice triggered the security computer system to use a different power source and just like that auxiliary lights came on.

I saw the husky demon crouched in the corner of the den behind the Christmas tree. Sure enough, it had two ugly heads, both covered with scab-like discolored skin with four green eyes on the front each head. Most of the demons I'd seen before were brightly colored, but this one was drab olive green with thin, orange tiger stripes all down its body. The demon's eight eyes bulged in surprise when it realized we could see it. It quickly gathered its wits.

"You-ah!" It pointed right at me with a meaty arm. "Da Kelly Bishop-ah. Yer *mine*-ah!"

One thing about demons is they all have a different way of speaking. Some pronounce words perfectly, while others use accents from all over the world. A few talk kind of weird, like this one. All the ones I'd heard so far spoke English.

The demon blinked its eight glow-in-the-dark eyes, then swatted our Christmas tree out of the way with webbed hands. Glass shattered as lights and decorations flew everywhere. The creature lumbered straight at me, crushing presents on the floor in its haste.

Since I was the one-and-only person in the house that demons ever came for, my job was to get to the panic room that Angie had built in the basement. The rest of my family would do the fighting. Sounds kind of wimpy, but I'm definitely not one of those super girls who beats up all the bad guys. I gripped the bat firmly and started toward the kitchen.

The demon charged. Angie stepped in its way. She sprayed a long blast of Mace straight into the eyes on its left head. The demon yelped and covered the burning eyes with one hand. But it could still see just fine with the four eyes on its right head. It stiff-armed Angie. She flipped over the recliner chair and fell out of sight. A second later her head popped over the chair.

"Mom!"

"Got it, Angie!" Granny took the sledgehammer and popped the demon under its right chin. The demon straightened up with the blow. It back-peddled a few steps. Granny popped it again. And again. Each time the hammer struck, the demon stumbled in reverse. But this beast was tough, and strong, too. It yanked the sledgehammer out of Granny's hands and let it fly across the room. I heard it crash into something. So what else in our house had been destroyed?

While Granny wrestled with the creature, she yelled. "Kelly, go!" A moment later the monster tossed her out of the way and came after me again.

I sprinted through the kitchen to the basement steps. Travis and the demon were on my heels. In the distance I heard police sirens making record time, but again probably too late. Travis turned and fired off the steel marble. *Thwuck!* The demon roared in pain and crashed into the kitchen table. It thrashed and floundered, then sent the table and all the chairs clattering across the floor. Travis ducked out of its way. The demon kept coming.

"Run Kelly!" I heard Travis fire off another steel marble. *Thwuck!* The demon roared.

As I flew down the stairs I glanced over my shoulder. The demon was a few feet behind. Two of its nasty green eyes were focused on me. Four more were swollen shut from the mace and the last two had big steel marbles stuck in them. Could I beat it to the panic room? I leaped off the steps and landed in a full sprint.

Just as I got to the door of the concrete and steel reinforced room, a gnarled, slimy hand caught my arm and jerked me into the center of the basement.

"Gotcha now-ah! Come wid me-ah! I take you to-ah the Demon Nation!"

Demon Nation. I was starting to hate those words. I broke free and answered with the bat. I struck the demon in the shoulder. *Thump!* I hit it again on top of its left head—my left, that is. *Crack!* The last shot I took was on one of its twelve-toed feet. *Whack!* The demon danced a brief jig of pain. I can fight when I have to.

But demons recover quickly. It knocked the bat out of my hands, which bounced across the concrete floor. The monster slapped a lock-steel grip on my wrist and pulled me toward the back door. I fought it all the way. I dragged my feet and grabbed for the stairs, but I couldn't stop it. That sucker was too strong. Just as the demon grabbed the doorknob to go outside, I heard a booming voice.

"Kelly! Hit the deck!" I went limp as a rag and dropped to the floor. The demon growled at me.

"Get up-ah!"

Gunfire erupted. *POW! POW! POW! POW!*

Gooey black blood sprayed all over me. The demon released my arm and fell like a lump to the floor.

———

I was so shook up I could hardly move. When I looked, I expected to see a policeman standing there, but instead it was Granny holding a hand-gun. She slid the gun into a shoulder holster under her jacket and helped me up.

"Are you okay, sweetie?" We hugged each other, breathing hard. I pressed my face into her jacket and took in the ruggedly sweet odor of old leather. I love that smell.

I nodded. Angie and Travis hurried downstairs. Angie had fire in her eyes.

"Matilda, I told you when you moved in, absolutely *no* guns in this house. You've had that ever since you got here, haven't you?"

Granny nodded. "Kind of a good thing, too, don't you think?"

Angie was furious. "I can't believe it! You know how I feel about firearms and you deliberately went against my wishes." She went to a steel cabinet and produced some heavy chain and a large padlock. "Hurry, tie it up. Make it tight. We'll put it in the panic room until the police leave."

"Tie it up?" Granny was confused. "I shot it four times point blank with a .357 magnum, straight through the heart."

"We don't even know if it *has* a heart."

"Good point. What'd'ya plan to do with the body?"

Angie shook her head. "Maybe we should call the press, let them take pictures."

"I don't know. We might end up in one of those tabloids lookin' like freaks. Do you think Mark would want it? You know, to dissect or something in the name of science?"

I changed the subject. "This demon came here all by itself. That's twice it's happened. The first time they brought a small army and now they're working alone. Why?"

"Maybe our security system scares the others away," suggested Granny. Somebody pounded on the front door upstairs. Granny looked up. "Police. Angie, you'd better go chat with 'em. The kids and I will move our two-headed friend to a more out-of-the-way place."

"It took 'em twelve minutes and twenty-two seconds this time," said Travis, checking his watch. "Eight minutes faster than before."

"But they're still too late." I wasn't cutting anyone any slack about this. Especially the police.

"The only way they could possibly show up in time to help would be to move in with us." Angie shook her head and went upstairs. Travis and I helped Granny move the dead demon into the panic room.

"Is this why we have a panic room?" asked Travis, tugging on one of the creature's scaly feet. "To hide dead demons in? I thought it was a hidin' place for Kelly."

Granny laughed. "I guess a panic room's a lot like a garage. You have every intention of using it for one thing, but soon you find yourself using it for completely different purposes."

Her logic made me smile.

"We did better this time," she continued. "The alarm gave us plenty of warning, though it's way too loud, if you ask me."

"I agree," I said.

"Me, too," said Travis. "My ears are still ringin'!"

"But it did the job." Granny looked my way. "We stopped another demon from getting you. We've got problems, though, like how to fight the nasty things. But we're a whole lot safer now than we were a couple weeks ago."

She's right, I thought. The first demon attack had taken us completely by surprise. But after that Angie went all out to have the house redone and she'd spared no expense to have the best security systems installed on the property. We had plenty of money now, because of Majik Juice sales. Chris' amazing fruit juice was the hottest selling bottled drink on the market. Angie used the money to install thirty-two security cameras inside and outside the house. Most were hidden but some were in plain view to scare away bad guys and maybe demons, too, if they understood what a camera was for. And we had all kinds of detectors that turned on security lights and set off the alarms. Motion detectors, audio pickup systems, thermal systems, CO_2 detectors that identified a person's breath, and even pressure receptors around the yard in case another giant lobster demon was outside looking into a second story window.

In addition all the windows were bulletproof and the doors were solid steel with huge bolt locks. The only way to open the doors from the outside was with an electronic touchpad that had a secret personal identity number, or PIN, and we were the only ones who knew the number. The entire house was hardwired to the main power supply, with solar and battery backup, just in case.

Also, the outside of the house was now brick. Angie figured it wouldn't be too hard for demons to break through vinyl siding, so she had the contractors remove the vinyl and replace it with red brick. I was impressed the contractors had been able to do so much work in such a short time, but Angie found out if you pay people enough money they'll work around the clock to get a job done. And they did, too. There had been at least a dozen companies working all through the night *every* night.

Granny closed the panic room door and we started upstairs. Then we heard a desperate, muffled voice.

"Lemme go-ah! Ya can't hold me here-ah. I won't hurt nobody, I swear-ah!" The demon had come back to life.

———

We gawked at each other at the top of the stairs. The demon had only been dead for twenty minutes and now it was back again! What kind of death was that?

About then Angie returned to the kitchen. "I complimented the officers on getting here so fast, but I told them it was a false alarm. I don't know, maybe next time we should show them a demon's body. I don't want them to think we're crying wolf, you know?" Angie stopped in her tracks as soon as she saw us. "What?"

"You know that demon we killed?" said Travis. "Well, it just said somethin'."

We rushed back into the basement and opened the panic room door. Sure enough, though the demon was still wrapped in chains, it certainly wasn't dead any more. Both heads looked at us pleadingly, fear in its two good eyes. The bullet holes in its chest were gone.

"I've got to get a bigger gun," murmured Granny.

Angie flashed her a look, then spoke to the demon. "Why did you come here?"

The demon stifled an obvious chuckle. "To get the Kelly Bishop-ah for the Demon Nation, of course-ah. The Boss put a bounty-ah on her head and whoever brings her back-ah gets all the soup-ah he wants forever-ah!"

"Why did you come alone?" I asked, being careful to stand behind Granny.

"Cuz the bounty-ah only counts as one-ah. If I had help-ah, I'd have to share my soup-ah. Slopgreez don't want to share-ah. Slopgreez wants all the soup for himself-ah. I got two mouths to feed-ah."

"You name is Slopgreez?" asked Angie.

The demon nodded. "But I don't wants her any more-ah. Let me go-ah back to the Demon Nation, I'll never return-ah. I promise-ah."

"Like we can believe anything a *demon* says." Angie crossed her arms. "If you want to see your cave again you'll have to tell us what we want to know first."

Its two functional milky green eyes narrowed. "Like what-ah?"

"First, why should we believe anything you say?"

"Demons can't lie-ah. We ain't like humans-ah, it ain't part of our nature to lie-ah."

I could read people's minds easily enough, but so far I hadn't been able to pick up on any thoughts from a demon. Too bad. I definitely didn't trust this one.

"Why does the Boss want the Kelly Bishop?"

"Don't know that-ah. Only know he wants her-ah bad."

"He's doing what he's told," I said boldly. "The man, Mr. Deel, is the one who *really* wants me. And *he* tells the Boss what to do."

Slopgreez became belligerent. "No-ah! Nobody in the Demon Nation tells the Boss nothin'-ah! He'll put you in his soup-ah for sayin' that!"

"Not if he keeps sending in slackers like *you* to get her," said Granny with a chuckle. "Beside, we're not part of the Demon Nation, are we?" The demon scowled darkly.

Travis had his own questions. "So how come you were dead and came back to life? Were you fakin' it?"

"Slopgreez don't know what fakin' it-ah means. Demons die and come back-ah. You can't kill us forever-ah. We're immortal-ah."

"Immortal?" spat Granny. "I'll bet I could find a way to keep you dead."

Slopgreez glared at her. "Many have tried-ah. No such thing-ah. There, I told you what you wanted-ah. Can I go now-ah? I swear I won't come back-ah."

Angie shrugged. "I suppose it wouldn't hurt to let it go. I mean, if demons really can't lie and all. It did cooperate."

"I don't know, Angie. I don't trust it." Granny subconsciously touched the holster under her jacket. "Maybe we should try to kill it again, you know? Chop it into lots of little pieces and set them in the sun."

The demon's dark eyes flashed fear. "Slopgreez been good to you-ah! Please-ah, let me go!"

I scanned Angie's thoughts and realized she'd already made up her mind to release Slopgreez, as long as he didn't try anything stupid. Angie made her offer. "You've got to promise you'll never come back here, and that you won't try to harm any of us ever again. Especially the Kelly Bishop."

Slopgreez nodded both heads vigorously. "Oh, I do promises-ah. I-ah will never come back-ah or try to harm the Kelly Bishop-ah again. Never-ah!"

The Kelly Bishop. It was kind of weird hearing everybody talk about me in the third person like I wasn't even in the room. I guess that's the nature of demon-speak.

Slopgreez looked and seemed sincere, but who could tell? I mean both of its heads spoke at the same time and sounded like they really meant it. But I had to remember, it was a demon. I didn't know much about them but it seemed that words like truthfulness and trustworthy probably weren't in their vocabulary. I was very uneasy about letting this one go. But if you couldn't kill them, what *could* you do with them?

Granny reloaded her magnum as Angie unlocked the padlocks. We all unwrapped the chains. Granny caught the ugly creature by one of its throats and lifted it off the floor.

"You ever come back this way I'll make sure you regret it."

"I'll never come back-ah, I swear-ah on the Boss' left foot!" She released the demon and drew her handgun.

"Travis, open the back door."

I moved as far from the demon as I could get, but stood ready with my bat. Travis opened the door. A red security light came on over the door and he punched in the code. The light changed to green. He took out his slingshot, loaded another steel marble and took aim.

The demon's eyes grew large with anticipation. It looked to Angie for approval before it went anywhere. She nodded at the door. The demon took off running, but not before it hissed at me on the way out. Then it started laughing like a crazy person. We followed it outside.

"What's so funny, Demon?" called Granny.

"Somethin' I said-ah," replied the demon as it trotted across the yard. Security lights came on and lit up the area. "I said demons couldn't lie-ah. But that was a lie-ah!" The demon broke down laughing so hard it stopped moving. Travis fired. The marble struck it in back of its right head. *Thwack!* At the same time Granny shot it in the leg. It took off running again with a slight limp.

"Ow!" it cried. "I'll be back for the Kelly Bishop-ah! You can count on it-ah!"

Granny shot it again, but the creature escaped into darkness.

"We shoulda killed it," said Travis, looking at me upset. I knew exactly how he felt.

"We *did* kill it," said Granny. "Krikey, there's got to be a way to keep those things dead. Something a bit more permanent anyway, you know?"

I shivered in the December night air. We'd see that demon again, I was sure of it. The question was when would it come and how ready would we be?

"Damn those things," said Angie. "You know, I should have asked it how it got in the house. I'll call the contractors in the morning and let them know the house isn't entirely demon proof."

"You're gonna tell 'em 'demon proof'?" asked Travis.

"No. But I paid a lot of money to make sure things like this couldn't happen. By the way, mom, I finally figured out what you can get me for Christmas."

"You're cutting it close," said Granny. "Only a few shopping days left and all. What is it?"

"I want you to teach me how to shoot a gun. And maybe you can help me buy one later, too."

"But you hate guns," I said.

"Yes, ordinarily. But these demons are tearing up my house and trying to steal my foster daughter. As far as I'm concerned, this is *war*. Guns are pretty handy in a war."

If you'd like updates, free giveaways, or information on how to get your copy of Book #2, THE DOOMSDAY SHROUD, go to my website at www.rlgemmill.com

Thanks for joining Kelly, Jon and Travis in this adventure. Enjoy the story? Here's what you can do next:

If you loved the book and have a moment to spare, I would be **really** thankful for a short review on the website where you bought the book. Your help in spreading the word is gratefully appreciated.

Available in eBook and print formats.

ABOUT THE AUTHOR

When R. L. Gemmill was 20, he hitchhiked from Virginia to California to visit relatives. Along the way he climbed Handy's Peak in southern Colorado, had all of his food stolen by ground squirrels in the Grand Canyon, and most importantly, began to read books while snowed in on the campus of Michigan Tech University. He had been writing books since the age of 12, but actually *reading* books changed everything. Gemmill has taught biology and anatomy in Virginia for 32 years and is now retired.

R. L. Gemmill's favorite quote (which saved him from depression and worse): "If your life bores you, risk it." James Dickey, author of *Deliverance*.

Made in the USA
Lexington, KY
26 July 2015